the life she *wants*

ROBYN CARR

the life she wants

MIRA

Recycling programs
for this product may
not exist in your area.

ISBN-13: 978-0-7783-1967-2

The Life She Wants

Copyright © 2016 by Robyn Carr

www.MIRABooks.com

Printed in U.S.A.

First printing: October 2016
10 9 8 7 6 5 4 3 2 1

the life she wants

This is for Therese Plummer,
beloved narrator, gifted actress and the voice of my heart.

prologue

When the truth became brutally evident she wondered how it had escaped her for so long.

Emma Shay Compton knew that her marriage to Richard looked like a fairy tale to many and though she had loved Richard, she had always felt something was lacking. She couldn't put her finger on it, it was so vague. Richard was good to her, generous, though he was an extremely busy man, and soon after their wedding he became remote. Distant. She told herself mega-rich brokers don't sit around the house coddling their young wives; they work sixteen-hour days. They're never far from their phones. They seem to command multitudes. And if a person, even his wife, wanted to get on his calendar, she had to plan ahead. So, whenever she felt that something was wrong with her marriage, she'd blame herself.

When Richard's lawyers began to meet with him to discuss problems with the SEC, she barely noticed. When she asked him about media reports that his company was being investigated for securities fraud, he calmly said, "Slow news day."

Then he lectured her. "Pay attention to the financial pages—it happens every day. Several multibillion-dollar banking and investment corporations are currently being investigated. The SEC has to justify its existence somehow. I resent the time suck, but it won't last long."

She didn't worry about it, though she did pay attention as he suggested. Of course he was right—there were many investigations, steep fines, reorganizations, buyouts, companies shutting down. The banking and investment world was under very close scrutiny.

Then he said they had to appear in court, he and his legal team. He wanted her by his side and asked if she could get it on her schedule and she laughed. "I'm not the one with a full schedule, Richard."

He smiled his perfect, confident, calm smile. He touched her cheek. "You won't have to do or say anything."

The morning they were to appear in court he had noticed the suit she laid over the chair and said, "Perfect." Then he went into his bathroom. Sitting at her dressing table, she was smoothing lotion on her legs. She heard the water running in his sink. And then she heard, "Son of a bitch!"

He'd cut himself shaving and swore—not unusual for him. But she met her own eyes in the mirror. Suddenly she knew. She'd been living a lie and everything said about him was true.

Her husband was a cold, calculating liar and thief. And she couldn't pretend anymore.

chapter *one*

It's the little things that will break you. Emma Shay had been thinking about that a lot lately. She stood strong while everything was taken from her, while she was virtually imprisoned at a little motel near the Jersey shore, while her husband was buried, while the media spun a sordid tale of deceit and thievery that implied she'd been aware, if not complicit, in her late husband's crimes. Stood. Strong. But, when the heel broke on her best sling-back pumps and she tumbled down the courthouse steps, she collapsed in tears. The photo was printed everywhere, even *People* magazine. When she was asked to please stop coming to her yoga studio, she thought she would die of shame and cried herself to sleep. No one had ever explained to her that the last straw weighed almost nothing.

Everything in her Manhattan apartment and vacation home had been auctioned off. She packed up some practical items to take with her and donated some of her casual clothing to women's shelters. Of course anything of value—the art, crystal, china, silver and jewelry had been seized quickly, even items she could prove had nothing to do with Richard's business, including wedding gifts from friends. They took her designer clothing. Her Vera Wang wedding gown was gone. She was allowed to keep a couple sets of good sheets, towels, one set of kitchenware, some glasses, a few place mats, napkins and so on. She had a box of photos, most from before Richard. She stuffed it all in her Prius. The Jag was gone, of course.

She had been offered a financial settlement, since they couldn't establish that she had anything to do with Richard's Ponzi scheme; couldn't prove it since she was innocent. She hadn't testified against him—not out of loyalty or because it was her legal prerogative, but rather because she had nothing to say, nothing upon which to leverage some kind of deal. She hadn't been in court every day out of support for Richard but because it was the best way for her to learn about the crimes he was accused of. She had come into the marriage with nine thousand dollars in savings; she left as a widow, keeping nine thousand in a checking account. It would be her emergency fund. She started a trip across the country, leaving New York behind and heading for Sonoma County, where she grew up.

She'd given it all a great deal of thought. She'd been thinking about it for months before Richard's death. She could've kept the entire settlement and retired to the Caribbean. Or maybe Europe. She'd been fond of Switzerland. She could change her name, color her hair, lie about her past... But eventually people would figure her out and then what? Run again?

Instead, she surrendered the settlement, gave up everything she could have kept. She didn't want Richard's ill-gotten gains. Even though she hadn't swindled anyone, she couldn't, in good conscience, touch any of it.

There were people she knew back in the Santa Rosa area, a few she'd stayed in touch with. The area was familiar to her. There wasn't much family anymore—her stepmother, Rosemary, had moved to Palm Springs with her third husband. As far as she knew, Emma's stepsister, Anna, and half sister, Lauren, still lived in the house they'd all grown up in. They'd all washed their hands of Emma when Richard was indicted. In fact, the last time she'd talked to her stepmother was right before Richard's death, when all the walls were tumbling down. Emma was literally in hiding from the angry victims of Richard's fraud—victims who believed Emma had gotten away with some of their money. Rosemary had said, "Well, your greed has certainly cost you this time."

"Rosemary, I didn't do anything," Emma reminded her.

And then Rosemary said what everyone thought. "So you *say.*"

Well, Rosemary had always thought the worst of her. But Emma hoped the people she knew in Sonoma County wouldn't. She'd grown up there, gone to Catholic school and public high school there. And she thought it was extremely unlikely any clients, now victims, of Richard's New York–based investment company hailed from the little towns in Sonoma County.

Her closest friend, possibly her only friend at this point, Lyle Dressler, found her a little furnished bungalow in Sebastopol. Lyle and his partner lived in the town, so she had some moral support there.

Emma was thirty-four and had married Richard Compton nine years ago. He was a sharp, handsome, successful forty-five when they married. At twenty-five she'd been completely under his spell. He might have been twenty years older than her, but forty-five was hardly considered old. He was fit, handsome, brilliant, rich and powerful. In fact, he was considered one of the most desired bachelors in New York City.

Rosemary and Emma's sisters had certainly liked him *then*. They were eager to travel to New York to attend any social event Richard would grudgingly include them in. But they hadn't offered one ounce of support to Emma during the takedown.

The few years of marriage before the investigation and indictment hadn't been heaven on earth, but they weren't bad. Her complaints seemed to be standard among people she knew—he was busy, preoccupied, they didn't spend enough time together even when they were traveling. The first friends she'd made through work in New York had gradually drifted away once she settled into her multimillion-dollar marriage. She'd never quite fit in with the elite crowd, so she'd been a little lonely. It seemed like she was always around people, doing her part with committee work, exercising, decorating, entertaining, feeling that she must be indispensable to Richard. However, he was all she really had. It was a dark and terrible day when she realized he was a complete stranger.

Before her fifth anniversary, the investigation had begun. Before the seventh, indictments had been handed down and assets frozen. She spent her eighth anniversary in court. Richard's defense attorneys had managed many a delay but eventually there was a trial—a circus of a trial—and she appeared to be the trusting, good wife, head held high. Richard's mother and sister had not come to the trial and refused interviews. She'd always assumed they didn't think she was good enough for Richard, but after the trial she changed her opinion. They must have known all about him. He was dark and empty inside.

He never talked to her about it, at least not until the ugly, bitter end. When she asked about the investigation he just said they were out to get him, that business was tough but he was tougher, that they'd never prove anything. At the end there had been a few brief, nasty but revealing discourses. *How could you? How could I not? How could you justify the greed? My greed? How about their greed? Do they have to justify it? They wanted me to do anything to make them money! They wanted me to spin straw into gold even if I had to lie, cheat and steal! Each one of them just wanted their payday before it all broke!*

The feds proved everything with ease. Employees cut deals and testified against him. Truckloads of documentation proved securities fraud, theft, mail fraud, wire fraud, money laundering... The list was long. When the end was near, when he'd attempted a getaway and been unceremoniously returned by US Marshals, when his offshore accounts had been located and identified, when he faced a long jail sentence with no nest egg left hidden away, Richard shot himself.

Of course no one believed Emma had no idea. Apparently people thought he came home from the office and bared his soul over a drink. He had not.

The Richard she knew was obviously a con man, a chameleon. He could be so charming, so devoted. But he always had a plan and always wanted something more. *Why wouldn't I marry you? You were an outstanding investment. Perfect for the role! It's a well-known fact—people trust married men more than single men.* He was a narcissist, a manipulator, a liar and cheat. He was so damn good at it, a person could feel almost honored to be manipulated and lied to by him. He had the looks of Richard Gere, the brilliance of Steve Jobs, the ethics of Bernie Madoff. Thank God he wasn't as successful as Bernie. Richard had only managed to steal about a hundred million.

What *did* she know? She knew he was private; he didn't talk about work, which she thought was normal behavior for a powerful man. He was an amazing communicator socially and in business, but once he stopped courting her, he stopped telling her stories about his family, his youth, college, about his early years on Wall Street. She knew he didn't have many old friends, just a lot of business contacts. She never met college pals or colleagues from his early professional days. He did routinely ask her about her day, however. He'd ask her about her schedule, her projects, what she did, who she talked to, what was happening in her world. When he was home, that is—he was often working late or traveling. The thing that set Richard apart from other, mediocre con men—he knew how to *listen*. People, herself included, thought they'd learned something about him when he hadn't said a word about himself. But he listened to them. Raptly. They were thrilled by this attention.

One nine-year marriage, a few years of which had been weirdly adequate, five years of which had been a nightmare. Now she wondered when the nightmare would end.

Emma drove directly to Lyle's flower shop, Hello, Gorgeous, named for Barbra Streisand, of course. Lyle had been wonderful to her through this whole ordeal. He hadn't been able to be in New York with her very often. Not only was it a great, costly distance but there was also the small complication that his partner, Ethan, had never been particularly fond of Emma, though he didn't really know her. Lyle had made a couple of trips, however, and called almost daily during the rough patches. She understood about Ethan. But Lyle and Emma had been friends long before Ethan came into his life. For reasons unknown, Ethan had never warmed to her. Emma suspected good old-fashioned jealousy, as if Emma might bring out Lyle's straight side or something. So Emma and Ethan had always had a rather cool regard for each other.

But since Richard's debacle, Ethan's regard had gone from cool to frigid.

But—and this was an important but—if Ethan went on about his dislike and disapproval of Emma too much, he was going to lose Lyle, and he might be bitchy but he wasn't stupid.

Emma stood outside the shop and took a deep breath before walking through the door. And of course, who should be behind the counter but Ethan. "Well, Emma, I see you made it," he said as though it took effort to be kind.

"Yes, thank you," she answered carefully.

"Rough journey?" Ethan surprised her by asking.

"In every way," she said.

"Well, there you are," Lyle said as he came from the back and rushed over to embrace her. "Would you like a cup of coffee or something before we head over to Penny's house?"

She shook her head. "I parked down the block in the only available space. I'd like to get going—I have a lot to do."

"Sure," he said. He turned to Ethan. "I'm going to give Em a hand, visit with Penny a little. I'll probably grab something to eat with them. I won't be late."

Ethan lifted his chin and sniffed, but his reply was perfectly appropriate. "I think I'll drop in on Nora and Ed. Sounds like a good night to get a little uncle time."

"Excellent. Give them my love."

Then, hand on her elbow, Lyle escorted her out of the shop. "I'm parked right here. I'll drive you down to your car," he said.

"Oh, please, no," she said, laughing. "My butt hurts so bad, I hate to even get back in the car. I'm going to walk—it's only a block. And I have a cooler with some drinks for us. Listen, I don't want to…" She tilted her head toward the store. "I don't want to cause any friction. If you'll just get me to the house and introduce me to your friend, I can manage from there."

"No worries, Emma. I explained to Ethan days ago that I was going to lend a hand when you got here." He chuckled. "He was very adult about it. It's time for him to pay his sister a visit anyway. They live a mile away and Ethan doesn't visit as often as he should. I think I visit more than he does—we have a gorgeous niece. He can go over there and complain about me and my stubborn ways. Besides, I want to make sure you're all right."

She smiled at him with gratitude. "I might never be all right again," she said. "All I want right now is a little quiet and anonymity."

"Have you heard from Rosemary?" he asked.

"I did her the courtesy of emailing her that I'd be moving to a small bungalow in Sebastopol and told her I could be reached through you. I don't even trust her enough to give her my new cell number—I bet she'd sell it to the press. I take it you haven't heard from her?" He shook his head and this came as no surprise. Rosemary had been in touch when she thought Richard was rich and powerful; after his fall from grace, she behaved as if she didn't know him. "We haven't made amends. She wasn't exactly supportive."

"Your sisters should be helping you now," he said.

They had never done anything to help her. "We've never been that kind of family," she said. Indeed, they weren't family at all.

"I can relate," Lyle said.

Emma knew Lyle had always had a hard time with his father, but at least his mother adored him. She gave his upper arm a squeeze. "Well, you've saved my life here. I'd be lost without this little place you found."

"It found me. Penny is elderly, but don't use that word

around her. She's what we'd call spry. Almost eighty and still walking three miles a day, gardening and playing the occasional game of tennis. But the problem with living forever, the money thins out eventually."

"And she knows everything?" Emma asked.

He nodded. "As you wished. She said, 'We've all hooked up with the wrong person here and there, poor girl.' This little bungalow is a sort of guesthouse, a casita, though her house, the main house, isn't that much bigger. Prepare yourself, it's all quite small. She doesn't need a keeper. No care involved. But a little bit of rent will probably help you both." He shook his head. "I don't know that you've ever lived in anything this simple, Em. It's old, musty, small and tacky."

"You have no idea how much I'm looking forward to it."

The guesthouse was actually a remodeled freestanding garage with a wall and large picture window where the doors once were. The window looked out onto a pleasant tree-lined street. It was a tiny, two-room bungalow with a small bathroom and galley kitchen. A patio separated the guesthouse from Penelope Pennington's two-bedroom house. "And of course you're welcome to use the patio at any time," Penny assured her. "And if you ever have any serious cooking to do, feel free to borrow my kitchen."

It was an attractive little arrangement. Penny had the driveway removed years before and now there was a carport and storage unit. In front of both little houses and on either side of the driveway and carport were two small patches of grass, shrubs, trees and flowers. From the patio one could reach Emma's little abode on the right or Penny's on the left. A tall, white fence with a gate bordered the property.

It took less than half an hour to unload Emma's small car. There wasn't much furniture in the bungalow—a bed and bureau, a small table and two chairs, a couple of lamps, a small sofa and two armchairs. She had her own bedding and kitchenware. She found the guesthouse quaint and cozy. Her boxes and suitcases had yet to be unpacked, but she didn't care. Lyle went off to a nearby market to get dinner, bringing Penny and Emma a huge Greek salad, some hummus, flatbread and a bottle of wine. They had their dinner at Penny's, sitting around her little dining table, and Emma loved her at once.

Then at last it was just Emma and Lyle, sitting in her cozy living room with a final glass of wine. She sat in a musty old overstuffed chair upholstered with a floral pattern, her feet up on an ottoman that didn't quite match. Lyle relaxed on the sofa, his feet up on the coffee table.

"This place really needs a fluff and buff," he said.

"I love it," she said. "I think this will be my reading chair."

"How can you read with the flowers in that gaudy print screaming at you?"

She laughed at him.

"Have you given any thought to what kind of job you're going to get?" he asked.

"Well," she said, taking a thoughtful sip. "I was considering being a life coach. What do you think?"

"You can certainly provide plenty of experience with what *not* to do," he said.

"I can honestly say I haven't felt this relaxed in years," she said.

Lyle was quiet for a moment. "Emmie, I don't know what it's going to be like for you around here. It's a quiet town, but not without its resident gossips and petty meanness. Know what I mean?"

"I grew up around here, remember?" she said. "No matter where I go, it's going to follow me. But I was never indicted for any crime. And believe me, they looked hard and long."

"I just want you to be ready. In case."

"In case people are nasty to me or snigger when I walk by? That's why I came here rather than trying to find some new place where I could be a stranger with a new identity—everyone figures it out eventually. Lies don't last—Richard was proof of that. Let's just get it over with. I was married to the late Richard Compton, the infamous broker and thief. There's no way to undo it. And I didn't have to think about it long—the stress of trying to keep it secret is something I'm just not up to. I could change my name, color my hair, even get a nose job if I had any money, but eventually everyone is going to know it's me. It's hopeless, Lyle—Google me and see for yourself."

"Under Emma Shay?"

"And Emma Shay Compton, Emma Compton, Emma Catherine Shay."

"Dear God," he groaned. "I hope it dwindles away quickly," he said.

"It's all on the record. Anyone who's curious is welcome to read all about it. There are even a couple of books, though they're not very accurate."

"How'd he do it, Em?"

She knew exactly what he was talking about. Richard's suicide. She took a breath. She was surprised he hadn't just looked it up—it was splattered, like Richard's brains, across all the papers and internet news sites.

"After he'd attempted to run via a colleague's private jet with a fake passport, he was returned to jail and held without bond. The lawyers managed to negotiate house arrest with an ankle bracelet. After the guilty verdict was returned he tried to negotiate sentencing by giving up offshore account numbers, hoping to reduce his sentence. But no matter what, he was going to jail for a long time. He opened the hidden safe behind the bookcase in his home office, pulled out his loaded Glock and shot himself. In the head."

Lyle shook his head. "He didn't want to go to prison…"

"I'm sure it was more than that," she said. "Oh, there was no doubt prison would be horrendous, but that's not why he did it. There was no material wealth left. There were no more offshore or Swiss accounts. It was really over. He was going to go to prison for fifty years and even if he was paroled early or could escape, there was nothing to allow him to retire quietly in Aruba, or some other remote island. With his stash." She sighed. "It was the most important thing to him. The wealth."

"I'm surprised the police didn't know about the safe or the gun," he said. "Didn't you say they searched the apartment?"

She shrugged. "I don't know if they ever saw it—they weren't looking for it. They confiscated his computers and lots of files from home and his office, all his electronics, but their warrant wasn't for things like guns or drugs. I didn't know about the gun."

"Did he do anything at all to try to protect you?" Lyle asked.

She just shook her head.

"And after he was buried?"

"It was a couple of weeks yet until everything was gone and the paperwork on the auction and the sale of the apartment was final. I closed his office door and slept on a cot in the kitchen. It was the safest place for me. Marshals were watching the apartment and there was a doorman." She made a face. "It was so horrible."

"I'm only going to say this one more time, Emmie, then we're moving on. I'm just so, so sorry."

"Thank you," she said softly. "Listen, you go home. And tell Ethan that I appreciate how decent he's been and assure him I'm not going to be pestering the two of you. I found I do very well on my own. It's lovely to be near you, but you don't have to worry that this out-of-place girlfriend is going to be the needy type and make you feel invaded. I'm not going to be your third wheel."

"We have some very nice friends, a lot of them gay men, and there are more than enough third wheels in our crowd. Don't worry about it. Call us whenever you feel like it."

"You've been wonderful. You've always been a better friend to me than I've been to you," she said.

"Not true. There've been very kind gestures here and there..."

"Shhhh," she warned. Before the trouble began, she had a household budget that was ridiculously large and she economized, leaving her a nice balance. It was her money and she used some to help fund the start-up of Hello, Gorgeous. Best if no one ever knew. Lyle had been interviewed about their relationship, possibly even investigated, but had never been any kind of suspect. In fact, they didn't speak of it. Emma was fairly sure Ethan didn't even know the details.

"Suffice it to say, I'm glad you're here," Lyle said. "I've missed you. And now there are a couple of things I should tell you. People have asked about you, which of course they would. But a couple of old friends have asked a few times recently. Asked what you would do now. Riley came into the shop and asked if you were all right. She knows we've always been in touch, just as you know I keep up with her, but where you two are concerned I made it a policy to never carry tales between you. She wanted to know if there was anything you needed."

"Guilty conscience," Emma said.

"Easy, Emma. She might be one of the few people who can actually understand what you're going through," he said. "I know you're not sympathetic, but she had to rebuild her life after you left. And Jock called. Divorced and living in Santa Rosa. He wanted to know if there was any chance you'd be coming back this way when it was all over. He said to tell you that if you need anything…"

"Seriously?" she asked.

"Very sincerely. I'm not his biggest fan, but he did offer support."

She said nothing. Of course she knew they were both here, Riley and Jock. Back when they were all so young, her best friend and her boyfriend. She'd returned for brief visits a few times after leaving so long ago and had not spoken to them, but she always knew they were still around. When she decided to come back here for good she knew it was possible she'd run into one or both of them eventually.

"Might be time to move on from that haunt, Emma," Lyle said.

"I have moved on," she answered. "I've moved on from a lot of things. And I'm not going back one step."

chapter *two*

When Emma Catherine Shay was nine years old, a fourth grader at St. Pascal's elementary school in Santa Rosa, a couple of new kids came to school. Riley and Adam Kerrigan. Riley was in Emma's class and the teacher asked her to be responsible for helping Riley get acquainted and adjusted.

Emma, known for being friendly and a child who wished to please, was annoyed. First of all, she already had two best friends—Susanna and Paula—and Riley's hanging around was interfering with her routine. Second, Riley apparently couldn't talk. She followed along or sat at the lunch table all quiet and nervous. When she did speak, she could barely be heard. Third, and Emma knew this was wrong, but the girl was a rag doll. She wore old clothes that didn't even fit her right.

Riley's older brother, Adam, so somber and quiet, waited after school to walk home together so at least Emma didn't have that chore. And all of it—spending time with Riley—was monotonous. But, so Sister Judith would be proud of her, Emma did the best she could with the odd little creature with the unhappy personality. At the end of the second day Riley surprised Emma when she spoke softly. "I know where to go and what to do now. You can go be with your friends."

Emma felt like a turd. "We'll just *all* hang out together," she said, hating her overzealous conscience.

Then, over the next few days, Emma learned that Riley, Adam and their mother came to Santa Rosa to live with Riley's grandparents in their tiny house because Riley's dad had gotten very sick and died. So now Riley wasn't just shy and poor, she was also bereaved. Emma was stuck with her.

But Emma couldn't deny that she was completely sympathetic—she'd lost her own mother, though she had been too young to remember her. Her father had remarried when she was just a toddler, probably largely to have help with his child. He had married Rosemary, an efficient and hardworking widow with a three-year-old daughter, Anna. Three years later they had a baby together, another girl. Baby Lauren. The only mother she had ever known was her stepmother, and of the three children, Rosemary liked Emma least. Emma understood by the time she was ten that it had been a marriage of convenience.

Emma was plotting her escape from Riley when a few things shifted as Riley got more comfortable with her new surroundings. First off, she was hilarious and once they got laughing, they could hardly stop. When she wasn't feeling scared and lonely, Riley's voice was strong and confident. She was very good in school and rose to the head of the class quickly. She could help Emma and not the other way around. And Riley's mother, June, turned out to be the most wonderful, loving, fun and positive woman in the entire world, embracing Emma and making her feel so cherished. Riley's grandparents acted like it was their lucky day the Kerrigans moved in even though they were stuffed into the little house.

They were crowded and money was tight but there was more laughter there than there had ever been in Emma's house. Riley and Adam wore hand-me-down clothes, their grandparents were elderly, and June Kerrigan cleaned houses and waitressed to make ends meet, but Emma was always welcome, made to feel like a member of the family.

Emma's home life wasn't nearly so happy. Rosemary wasn't abusive in any obvious way but she was emotionally flat where Emma was concerned.

Rosemary complained about how hard she had to work at the DMV, how much stress she had in her life, how messy and lazy Emma's father was, her weight, her friends and a variety of issues. Aside from Anna and Lauren, there didn't seem to be much she enjoyed. Although Rosemary always referred to Emma and Lauren as her daughters, there was little doubt that Anna was her favorite. It wasn't long before Emma was happier at Riley's house than at her own. And hardly surprisingly, Rosemary didn't mind her absence at home much.

We were going to be each other's maid of honor. We were going to have children at the same time so they could be best friends, too.

From the day Sister Judith forced them together until high school graduation, Emma and Riley were inseparable. Riley's grandpa called them conjoined twins. They stuck together through thick and thin, through the sudden death of Emma's father when she was sixteen, Rosemary's third marriage to Vince Kingston, and every issue that plagued teenagedom. Their friendship was cast in iron and they had very few tiffs. Until they fell out over a boy. One Jock Curry. Yes, it was his given name. He was named for a grandfather.

They'd both crushed on him in high school. They thought he was smart, sexy, athletic, funny. Every girl wanted him and he apparently wanted every girl, but once he settled on Emma during their senior year, that was it for him. He said his roaming days were over. Of course, he was all of seventeen at the time. He tried to talk Emma into going to the same community college he'd chosen or at least staying close to home, but she had a scholarship and was going to Seattle Pacific University, known for its interior-design program. Of the two girls, she was the least likely to get a scholarship, but even with one, Riley's family couldn't afford any part of the expense of living away from home or attending an out-of-state university. Emma could manage with working part-time, taking out loans, and Rosemary was able to send a little money—fifty here, fifty there. And she had big dreams; she was going to design the interiors of five-star hotels and luxurious mansions!

Riley enrolled in the same community college as Jock, lived at home and began cleaning houses just like her mom always had.

Jock had no specific plans except to get the minimum education, work part time, play a little baseball and enjoy himself.

Emma didn't suspect anything was going on in her absence until right before Christmas break. Riley was acting strangely. Jock and Riley were hanging out together a lot, but shouldn't that be expected? Her guy and her best friend, going to school together and everything? She trusted them, after all. Then she had this nagging feeling it wasn't all right, that it was a betrayal. Riley was different toward her; Jock was a little too much himself—jovial and confident and relaxed. He'd gone from ragging on her about taking more time to talk to him on the phone to not noticing how long it had been since they'd had one of those long, whispery, late-night conversations.

She suspected her best friend was too close to her boyfriend. When Emma confronted her, Riley burst into tears, admitted it, swore it wasn't entirely her fault, that Jock had taken advantage of the fact that she'd always liked him a lot, that she had been so lonely without her best friend.

Jock had said, "Hey, grow up. It didn't really mean anything. Besides, what did you expect? You didn't have time for either one of us."

Emma never really did understand how something like that *just happens*, especially when both Riley and Jock insisted they hadn't meant it to, that it was all a terrible mistake. Then they both turned it back on her, as if it was her fault for going away to school. All she knew was that she was devastated and had lost the two most important people in her life. She could never trust either one of them again and the feeling was so painful it doubled her over. She went back to Seattle after Christmas break completely decimated by the hurt. She tried to date and that didn't go well. Riley wrote her a couple of letters, left her a few messages, but Emma was too hurt to respond. And she didn't go back to Santa Rosa until summer break. Even then, she hadn't wanted to—there was nothing there for her anymore. Her father was dead, her stepmother was a cold fish who clearly hated her, her stepmother's new husband was an old lecher, her sisters didn't care about her...

She didn't stay in Santa Rosa long. She learned what no one wanted to tell her. Oh, but Emma's stepsister Anna couldn't *wait* to tell her—Riley was pregnant. While Emma was at school, those two had been knocking boots like mad and now they were having a baby. Emma bid a tearful goodbye to Lyle, cleared everything out of her father's house, the house she grew up in, and headed back to Seattle as fast as she could. She got herself a job, joined a sorority, visited Santa Rosa very rarely and very briefly. When she did go, she stayed with Lyle.

Even Seattle wasn't far enough away. Upon her graduation, she secured a job in New York and moved to the other coast. Within three years she was a buyer for one of the largest independent department stores in the US and traveled all over the world for her household wares. She was a specialist in interiors and had fantasies about starting her own design firm.

But then she met Richard...

If there was one thing Emma had learned from the experience it was that she could hold a grudge. The fact that Riley's relationship with Jock hadn't lasted, proving that he wasn't exactly a good catch, didn't lessen her feelings of being betrayed. The undeniable truth that she'd dodged a bullet when her relationship with Jock fell apart didn't give her much comfort. The further fact that she'd gone on to marry a handsome, rich, successful man also hadn't induced her to forgive and forget.

But then what she went through with Richard—his fraud, deceit, demise—taught her something else. There were bigger things to worry about than a fifteen-year-old feud with a childhood friend.

There was no going back, Emma reminded herself. She was moving forward.

Emma hadn't worked outside her home and marriage for nine years but boy, had she worked in it. She visited several employment agencies with her résumé, her degree, even details of her experience volunteering at the Metropolitan Museum of Art, working on gigantic fund-raisers, massive decorating projects and entertaining on an enormous scale, but that simply wouldn't do it after the interview. She felt it was in her best interest to be honest, then immediately doubted her wisdom in that. If they didn't want to take her on as a client because they feared trusting her, then they didn't want her because of the potential negative press attention it might draw to them. Clients might leave businesses that employed her because of her notoriety. Of course, they didn't say that. They said they were sorry, there didn't seem to be anything available, but if she'd leave a number...

She had to throw her net wider. She had a list of businesses to apply to that ranged from galleries and stores to convention centers, wineries and even political parties. She stopped explaining that her late husband had been *the* Richard Compton and instead said that after a bad marriage, she was reentering the workforce. After two weeks with zero success, she went to several smaller employment agencies, not the ones that specialized in decorating, customer service, event planning and those things that were ideal for her. After all, she could always type and file. She could operate a computer. She thought the reception she received was positive...until they looked into her background, which was a simple matter nowadays with a computer search. Even though she wasn't up-front about her history, they obviously Googled her and she was politely informed there was nothing available that might suit her.

After four weeks, she was inconsolable.

"Isn't this some kind of discrimination?" she asked Lyle.

"It definitely is," Lyle said. "But I'm not sure what kind."

Just when she thought things couldn't possibly get bleaker, she took a job in a fast food restaurant. She thought of it as a placeholder until she found a real job. Her boss was nineteen years old. She did everything she was told to do, putting great effort into it. They'd given her an evening shift because she was mature and the restaurant was overrun with high school and college kids. But she had trouble keeping up. She took home a paycheck for five days of shift work at about five hours a day in the amount of $91.75—they deducted FICA, Social Security, state and federal taxes, uniform costs. Her net pay was $3.67 per hour. Her feet and back were killing her.

She wondered if she'd have to succumb to a disguise and create a new identity.

★ ★ ★

Emma answered her cell phone knowing it would be Lyle, but praying it would be someone with an offer of a better job. It was Lyle.

"Do you know a man by the name of Aaron Justice?"

She laughed. "Unforgettable. A friend of my father's. An attorney. He must be a hundred years old by now."

"More like seventy-five. Apparently one of your sisters said you could be reached through me and he'd love to hear from you. He said maybe you could meet for a coffee or something. He's been concerned about you. He would like to see you, to assure himself you're okay."

"Now, isn't that sweet," she said. "It's not a trap, is it? He's not representing someone Richard screwed, is he?"

"Does that actually happen?" Lyle asked.

"It hasn't happened yet, but I'm ready for it."

"I have his number," Lyle said. "Call him, ask him what he wants before you make a date to see him. But really, he's just a little old man."

"Oh, you have no idea," she said with a laugh. "Aaron is only a little old man on the outside. I think in his day he was a very prominent attorney."

It took her a few minutes to work up her courage because it would simply break her heart if Aaron Justice were foe, not friend. Her father, a CPA with a small but busy business, was close to Aaron, and Emma had known him all her life. Not only had they seen him and his family socially, Aaron was the lawyer who took care of John Shay's will and a few other legal matters, too.

"I want only to see you, my dear girl," Aaron said. "I've followed your ordeal in the news and have been concerned. Come and have a cup of coffee with me."

The very next afternoon that she didn't have to work they

met in a coffee shop in Santa Rosa, and when she saw him, it brought her to tears. He seemed to have gotten smaller, but his embrace was still strong and she might have held on too tight. He was a very dapper, classy gentleman and of course just seeing him again after eighteen years made her miss her father.

They sat in a small booth, ordered coffee and held hands across the table as they caught up on the more personal news. His wife had passed away a few years earlier, his grandsons were teenagers and he'd taken them on a few exciting trips. He was relieved to see her looking so well, as beautiful as ever and he was glad she was back. Finally, after about twenty minutes, he asked her if she could talk about it.

She tried to give him the bullet points; how shocked she was by the facts, stunned to learn she was married to a stranger, how the walls came tumbling down and Richard bailed out. "Once they were satisfied that I had nothing to do with the scheme, I was offered a settlement. My conscience wouldn't let me take it, of course."

"Your father would have been proud of that," Aaron said.

"If my father had witnessed that horrific takedown, he would have been mortified."

"He was a staunch and conservative man," Aaron said. "It sounds as if he would have approved of the way you chose to handle it. I hope your father's trust helped out a bit."

She laughed. "What trust, Aaron? Rosemary said there wasn't much."

"I seem to remember it being a tidy sum for his family."

"Eighteen years ago, maybe," Emma said.

He frowned. "I realize you were only a girl and John hadn't wanted the balances to be reported to anyone—it might've filled the three of you girls with fanciful notions, sent you out car shopping or something. But it was divided—your share and those of your sisters could only be used for health and welfare. Rosemary would have needed it to sustain the family, and there was tuition to pay, of course…"

Emma was shaking her head. "I borrowed and had a partial scholarship. She might've used it for education for Lauren and Anna."

"Didn't Rosemary give you money for college?"

"She sent me spending money from time to time. Maybe she was afraid to touch the money, saving it for her old age. She ended up marrying a real jerk. They moved to Palm Springs."

"Rosemary changed lawyers immediately," Aaron said. "I have no idea what's happened in the last eighteen years, but you were due to inherit from your father's estate—half at the age of thirty and half at thirty-five. It was important to John that you learn to make your own way and earn a living before you came into any money or you'd have blown it on shoes or something."

She smiled. "That sounds like him," she said. "He was so cautious."

"It was an irrevocable trust, Emma. As trustee, Rosemary could only use your portion on your needs, not on Anna's or Lauren's. Have you ever had an accounting done?" Aaron asked.

"Of what?"

"Of your father's estate. The terms of his will."

"Aaron, I was married to one of the richest men in New York. Why would I worry about my father's will? He had a small office in a small town and lectured me if I threw a pen out before it was writing in invisible ink! I wouldn't call him a tightwad, but he didn't let go of a dime before he'd squeezed all the juice out of it."

Aaron laughed. "It's true. And he married a woman who liked nice things…"

"Well, she didn't waste any money on me. After my first

year of college I admitted defeat with Rosemary and hardly ever came home to visit. And you know what happened when I struck out on my own. I fell in love with and married a thief."

"May I make a suggestion? You should ask for an accounting of your father's estate. There's still the house. It's a substantial house."

"She said the mortgage alone was killing her," Emma pointed out.

"Emma, the house was insured against your father's death. There was no mortgage. I still have a small practice, mostly just for old clients and friends. If I were your attorney, I could look into this."

She started to laugh. "Oh, Aaron, you are so sweet. I can't afford an attorney! I'm working at a fast food restaurant! Besides, if there turned out to be something left of his estate after all these years, would I have to fight for it? Because I can't even consider going to court. Not ever again."

"Here's what would happen. I would see her lawyer or accountant, petition for an accounting of the proceeds of the estate on your behalf, and if there turned out to be something left for you, you'd have to sue. It usually doesn't go that far unless there are millions at stake. If it's a small amount, the trustee is usually happy to settle to save money. And if there is anything, I won't charge a fee of any kind until you can afford it. It wouldn't be a contingency or percentage, just my usual fee. Which," he said, laughing at himself, "is a steal."

"Well, I won't be suing anyone, that's for sure. I won't even ask for anything from her—she hates me and at this point the feeling is mutual. I'm starting over. But you are kind and I appreciate your generosity."

"Let's find out, Emma. There was once some money involved. And your father's house. That was a rich house, wasn't it? Everyone envied it."

"He built it with my mother," she said. "He never said but I think they hoped to have a few children." She shook her head. "Even the idea of money makes me sick. I live in two rooms. I pinch my pennies in a way that would make John Shay so proud. And I can't bear the idea of owing you money for services that you're really doing as a favor."

"If it turns out there's nothing there or if you choose not to pursue the recovery of it, my fee will be zero."

Her eyes got a little round. "Why, Aaron, I think you wouldn't mind catching Rosemary with her hand in the cookie jar!"

"You found me out," he said. "John was such a gentle man. She seemed to suck the life out of him."

"I think he married Rosemary to have help with me," she said. "It must have been so hard for him. And everyone who knew my mother loved her. I don't think people even like Rosemary. She's a hard woman."

He was quiet for a moment. "John was a good friend. He was careful with his will. It would take months to get an answer, Emma. Months before you have to decide how to proceed. For your peace of mind, I'd be happy to look into this for you."

She shrugged. "Why not? What can it hurt? I won't get my hopes up. If Rosemary was involved, I'm sure she's had a real party spending it. She quit working the week my dad died."

"Then I have something important to do and it makes me so happy to do it for you." He squeezed her hand. "I'm glad you came home, Emma."

Lyle was finishing up for the day, standing at the counter while he looked at the orders for Saturday delivery. In August

sales started picking up again after summer. In summer there
weren't any floral holidays and people had their own blooms.
Summer in Sonoma County was pure heaven.

The door to the shop opened and he smiled to see Riley
Kerrigan come in. Took her long enough, he thought. He
hadn't seen her in at least a couple of months. She looked fantastic, as usual. You'd never guess by looking at her that she
owned a domestic and industrial cleaning service. She looked
more like a bank executive or high-powered attorney. After
all her years of secondhand clothes followed by scrimping to
get by and build her business, Riley was making up for lost
time in the wardrobe category.

"Hi," she said. "I thought I might catch you before you
left for the day. How's it going?"

"It's all good. How's everything at Happy Housekeeping?" he asked, knowing full well that was not the name of
her business.

"Happy, happy, happy. So. Is she back?"

He nodded. "Over a month now," he said. "Tell me something—did it take willpower to wait this long to ask?"

"I didn't expect her to call, if that's what you're getting at.
How is she?" Riley asked.

"Doing very well, in spite of everything."

Riley's smile was very small. "Emma has a way of bounc-
ing back."

"If she can bounce back from this, she's a superhero. She
stayed in that apartment alone, slept on a cot, even though
her husband's blood was all over his study. Because no one offered her a guest room, not even the legal team who were so
well paid. And she wasn't safe in a hotel—too many victims
of Richard's fraud threatened her. I offered to go out there
but she wouldn't have it—she didn't want me in jeopardy. She
made the drive to California by herself—she said she needed

the time alone and away. Her husband has been dead a few months. It took her a month here to find a bad job. She says she's holding up very well. I'm amazed she's even standing."

"I'm sorry she's going through this, but she wouldn't want my sympathy or my help. If you think of anything I can do without, you know, getting involved, let me know."

"Sure," he said. "She says she's over it, by the way. Your feud."

"Me, too," Riley said. "But still…"

"She said that, too."

Riley smiled at her dear friend. They'd been the three musketeers in high school—Emma, Lyle and Riley. She gave a quiet laugh and shook her head. "Can I buy the man in the middle a drink?" she asked.

"By all means," Lyle said. "I think she's forgiven you by now."

"Good to know. I still hate her, but I'm not mad at her anymore."

"Oh, great." He started turning off lights. "Let's go drink."

Riley stopped by the grocery after a glass of wine with Lyle. They'd been friends for a long time. Usually threesomes don't work very well, but in this case, Lyle being a guy and all, there was no issue. At least not until Emma and Riley had their epic breakup. Then Lyle was stuck in the middle, trying not to take sides. He'd managed to remain loyal to both women for sixteen years.

She was lost in thought, her hand absently palming a honeydew melon.

"I'm not sure if you're going to bowl with that or put it in your cart," a male voice said.

She looked up and smiled. She'd seen this guy before. Starbucks, maybe. "Sorry," she said, taking the melon, though she didn't really want it.

"They look good today, don't they?" he asked. "Hey, do you know where I can find roasted peppers? Fire roasted," he said, consulting a list.

She shook herself for a second, coming back to grocery land and leaving thoughts of poor Lyle and their triangle far behind. "Um, over there with the olives are some prepared in the jar. That's all I know about."

"Artichoke hearts?"

"Same place in the jar, or some in the frozen section."

"Parmesan?"

She smiled at him. He was very good-looking. "You're making artichoke dip, aren't you? Let me see that," she said. She glanced over the recipe. "There aren't any roasted peppers in this recipe."

"I know—it's for something else. I'm just picking them up for a...a neighbor."

"Thank goodness. Okay, be sure the artichokes are packed in water, add a half cup of mozzarella, a sprinkle of chili powder and a cup of chopped spinach and some lucky woman will propose."

"Dynamite. Thank you," he said, turning to go. Then he turned back and said, "Chili powder?"

"With the spices. Not too much, now." She blessed him with a sweet smile. Then she resumed her vegetable shopping. *Hmm*, she thought. *A straight guy in the grocery store. If he were gay, he'd know how to make artichoke dip.*

Her thoughts fled instantly back to Emma and Lyle. Well, they were going to have to share Lyle. He was the best friend she had.

chapter *three*

Emma faced an entirely new set of priorities. She was able to pick up extra hours at Burger Purgatory and in her spare time she looked for a better or second job. They kept her hours just under full-time to save costs on benefits, but she had to buy health insurance anyway—it was now the law. Terrified to touch that emergency money she had stowed away, she was stretching her money as far as it would go—rent for Penny took the top position because she was certain the elderly darling needed it. Plus, she needed a place to live while she starved to death. Utilities for her little bungalow was second and she conserved dramatically, even shortening the length of her hot showers, which was a huge sacrifice as she now smelled like French fries all the time. Car insurance and gas came next and only then did she buy food. She did manage to eat at the burger joint sometimes, though that was problematic. First of all, it wasn't part of the deal, but she noticed that all employees partook. There seemed to be an unwritten policy—they'll never miss a few fries, but let's not be obvious about it. And *never* in front of customers. Also, it was not healthy! It was calorie intense, carb heavy and salted to the max. After a few weeks, her pants felt uncomfortably tight and her ankles seemed chronically swollen.

September arrived and with the start of school, the teenage employees vacated the day hours, so at least she worked that shift. She was sure there had to be a better job for her somewhere and equally sure it wouldn't be easy to find it. Emma never thought of herself as having it easy while growing up—she held part-time jobs during high school and college, went to college on loans and scholarships, but she was given an old car to use to get to school and work. Still, she'd had it a lot easier than Riley had.

Her first couple of years in New York had been a real eye-opener—urban living was incredibly expensive. But she was a beautiful, single young woman in a city full of them and in no time she had roommates. She took the subway, learned all the cheap haunts for entertainment and had dates—quite a few of them. The thing about New York City—she never felt alone.

And here, in her two rooms in Sebastopol there was an interesting transformation—the girl who had wanted to design and decorate the interiors of mansions and five-star hotels found living simply to be a welcome pleasure. There was no flab in her life, no unnecessary junk to carry.

She had one dinner with Lyle and Ethan and it had been passably friendly on Ethan's part. She visited with Penny when Penny was enjoying the patio, but fall was approaching, the weather was getting cooler, so Penny wasn't outside as much. Penny's car was often gone; she was a very active senior and had many friends.

Emma walked through Sebastopol on her days off, anonymous and reluctant to look for work there for fear she'd alert them that the notorious widow was among them. She answered every ad for work in Sonoma County that paid more than minimum wage.

Sebastopol was lovely; old buildings and storefronts were brightly painted, many with their wares and fresh fruits and vegetables on sidewalk display. Ethan liked to put out big pots of fresh blooms, and Emma stopped there often, complimenting him lavishly, fully intending to win him over to her side. She loved buying two apples, two tomatoes and one banana at a time. She even occasionally splurged on a small bunch of flowers and when she did, she noticed Ethan gave her a discount and Lyle smiled slyly.

And, after eight weeks, when the leaves were just beginning to turn, she went home from Burger Brain-Bleed, hungry and swollen, smelling like grease and body odor, and lay down on her bed and cried. If this was what her life was going to look like from now on, she wasn't sure she had the stamina for it. And she was damned afraid if she started dipping into her precious nine thousand dollars, she could end up homeless.

Spoiled, the devil on her shoulder chided her. *You said walking away from the money was the least of your concerns, but did you really mean it? Because here you are, working for a living like the rest of the world and you can't take it!*

She was immediately ashamed. So she got in the shower to cry, trying to hide from her conscience. Then she got out and dried her hair and heard that voice again. *If you think it's hard busting your ass for minimum wage, think about how you'd feel when you learn your life savings is gone. That it was spent on a second home in Aruba and a private jet.*

"I can't do this," she said aloud. "Please, it wasn't my fault. Please."

★ ★ ★

The next afternoon, while she was wiping down tables in the burger joint, she saw a familiar face. Actually, she saw the familiar back of a head. She knew it was him; she'd know that thick, willful brown hair anywhere. Adam Kerrigan, Riley's brother. He was with a teenage girl who had to be Maddie, Riley's daughter. She took a couple of steps, smile on her face, then stopped herself suddenly. What if he hated her? Adam had kept in touch for a while after Emma's falling out with Riley, but when she married Richard she didn't hear from him anymore.

But why should he hate her? Because of what Richard had done? Would he, like so many others, assume she knew what was going on? Or that she had some stash just waiting for the heat to fade? *Let's just find out*, she thought. *Let's find out right now.*

"Adam?" she asked.

He looked up, his mouth full of burger. His eyes were round and surprised. He chewed and swallowed quickly and the girl covered her mouth as she laughed at him. He wiped his lips with a napkin. "Emmie Cat?" he asked in disbelief, falling back on an old pet name he'd given her when they were kids. It was short for Emma Catherine.

The nickname reassured her and made her smile. "It's me. How are you?" He started to get up. "No, no," she said with a laugh. "Don't get up." And she slid onto the plastic bench at the table across the aisle from him, hanging on to her cleaning rag.

"You work here?" he asked.

"I do," she said. "And believe me, I do work. No wonder this place runs on teenagers. They're the only ones with the energy to keep up. How are you?"

"I'm well, thanks. Emma, this is Maddie. Maddie, meet Emma Shay. We went to school together."

"Although he's much older," Emma teased. He was, in fact, three years older.

"How long have you been back?" he asked. And he asked with a distinct absence of hostility.

"A couple of months. Remember Lyle? He found me a little place I could rent and it seemed like the logical thing to do."

"Of course I remember Lyle. I see him all the time. How is it? Being back after all this time?"

She shrugged. "Tough," she said. "But tell me all about you. I confess, I haven't been in touch so I have no idea—"

"Excuse me," Maddie said. "I'm going to take a quick run to the ladies' room while you two visit." She grinned impishly. "I'll try to stretch it out." And with that, she slid out of the booth and left them alone but for the half dozen customers at the counter.

Emma smiled. "She's so beautiful, Adam. And so sweet."

"She is," he agreed.

"And how about you? Did you marry?"

She thought his expression was sweet and maybe a little sad. "I came close a couple of times, but it wasn't in the cards. Uncle duty keeps me busy enough."

"Isn't Jock around?"

"Sure, he's around now and then. He was briefly married when Maddie was very young and…well, no one knows better than you how hard it can be if the chemistry isn't right with the stepmother…"

Only too well, she thought. And suddenly she fought tears. Not because she was faced with the child of her best friend and boyfriend. *Ex*-friend and *ex*-boyfriend. Conceived while she was away at college. "Wow," she said, her eyes having gone a little liquid. He would probably think she wept from some long-ago broken heart, but that had nothing to do with it.

Adam surprised her by reaching out, putting a big hand on her shoulder. "You shouldn't have stayed so out of touch, Emmie Cat. Fifteen years is too long for old friends."

"Uncle Adam," she said uncomfortably, looking down and giving her eyes a wipe.

"Well, it turns out it really does take a village," he said with a laugh. "Riley, me, my mom, Jock—it was a community effort. Worked out pretty well," he added. "Maddie is an awesome kid."

"I bet you're an awesome uncle."

"I do my best. I teach high school so I'm kind of an expert on her species. And Jock works at an electronics store so we have all the phones and toys and laptops we need."

"The same store he worked at way back when?" she asked.

"Same one, but he's a manager now."

"And you're still teaching?" Emma asked. "I guess you chose the right profession if you're still at it."

"I think that's a yes. Listen, I'm sorry about everything you went through. Condolences, Emmie."

"Thank you."

"There were a hundred times I thought about getting in touch, not knowing how you were holding up. When I did finally get to it, your number had changed so I just checked with Lyle now and then. Everyone knows you had nothing to do with anything…illegal."

"Thank you, again."

"We were just talking about you a few weeks ago, wondering if you had made it back home. We were remembering the old days."

"We?" she asked before she could stop herself.

"Me. Mom. Riley. This is a coincidence, running into you here, like this."

A tall, skinny kid came over to the table. "Taking a break, Ms. Shay?" he asked.

"Just answering a couple of questions for a customer, Justin."

"Can I help?" Justin asked, turning to Adam.

"I don't believe so," Adam said authoritatively. "I'll just take a moment of Emma's time. If you'll excuse us."

Justin looked taken aback, but then he turned and left them.

"He's a despot," she quietly informed Adam. "But jobs are in short supply, it seems."

"Could you use a letter of recommendation?" he asked.

She stood. "I could use a do-over," she said. "But thanks for asking. Do you teach around here?"

He shook his head. "Napa. High school science. I'm playing a little hooky with Maddie today. We were at the DMV so she could take her test for her learner's permit. Riley wanted to do it but the truth is, Riley and Maddie don't do well in the car together so Maddie prefers driving with me or with Jock, and he's working this afternoon. Of course Maddie couldn't wait. When do you get off work?"

"Not until nine, why?"

"We should have a cup of coffee or glass of wine, talk about how you'd like me to word that letter of recommendation."

Maddie was back, sliding into their booth.

"Oh…ah… Listen, you don't know what you're suggesting…"

"I don't? Why not? We're still friends, right?"

"It's not that… Well, it's partly that since, you know…" She took a breath. She wasn't going to say in front of this sweet fifteen-year-old, *That's my boyfriend's baby and probably the major reason I went off the rails in the first place.* She leaned closer to Adam. "Take a whiff of this place. This is what I smell like after work."

He threw back his head with a hearty laugh. "See you later," he said.

She meandered back behind the counter, kind of dazed. Half of her wanted to run and hide—being around Adam would only serve to remind her of the past and all she'd lost. But the other half was elated. Could she and Adam be friends? They'd talked a few times after Maddie was born, but their conversations had been so superficial, both of them afraid to let the standoff she had with Riley taint the relationship she had with Adam, who she had always so admired. Truth was, she'd always wondered if Adam had kept in touch out of guilt over what his sister had done.

She'd done all right in the friends department during college and her first years as a single woman in New York, but she'd always kept people at a safe distance, afraid to trust again.

That was perhaps the deepest wound of all.

Emma's earliest memory of Adam was him standing by the fence outside the school playground to make sure Riley got home all right. Even before she realized she liked Riley, she wished she had a big brother like Adam. When she left Burger or Bust that night, he was across the parking lot, leaning against the hood of his SUV, arms crossed over his chest. Waiting. He looked like an older version of that twelve-year-old boy. Except he looked a lot happier now, like maybe the chip on his shoulder was gone.

Yeah, that's what it had been—that serious, stubborn, perhaps fearful boy in his scuffed shoes and torn jacket, left to take care of the family after his father had died. Emma had worried about this faux date all afternoon until she saw him and then realized she was always thinking about herself, her troubles. She was always afraid of being found out, exposed, blamed. But Adam had been only a kid when he lost a parent, but a kid old enough to understand and remember his loss. And he'd been so brave, always looking out for his mother and sister. He was right there at St. Pascal's until high school, but even when he was older and went to a different school, he was so often on hand to watch over Riley. And Emma, as well.

"I can't believe you're really here," she said. "You have a date with someone who smells like burgers and fries."

"I think we'll get through it. How do you feel about a glass of wine or a drink?"

"I'd love a glass of wine."

"Great. Where do you hang your hat these days?"

"A little spot in Sebastopol. Not too far from Lyle's."

"Perfect. I know just the place, right on the way to your place. Follow me?"

"I'm parked right over there. The Prius."

"Let's do it," he said.

She followed him along some of the back roads toward her little town, but he turned down an alley and she got a little confused. Concerned. But then he parked behind what she thought, by the twinkle lights strung between the boughs of trees, must be the patio of a restaurant. The Cellar, the sign on the back gate said. He got out of his car, she got out of hers and he opened the gate to a patio. There were a half dozen tables; a couple of women sat at one, wine and fruit before them, but it was otherwise deserted. "They're going to close soon, but we're friends. I'll get us some wine, something to snack on and they'll say good-night before they leave."

"Huh?"

Adam chuckled. "Would you like to see a wine list?"

"No," she said. "I usually just have a sauvignon blanc."

A woman wearing an apron came out of the back door. "Just in time, as usual," she said. "How are you, Adam?"

Adam leaned toward her to kiss her cheek. "Excellent. Kate, meet my friend, Emma."

"Nice to meet you. What can I get you?"

"Get us a bottle of Napa Cellars sauvignon blanc, a half wheel of Brie with some crackers and fruit, two waters. And thanks."

"Just give me two minutes," she said.

He held out a chair for Emma. "What kind of place is this?" she asked.

"Just a small wine bar. I've known the owners for a long time. For friends and relatives, they say good-night when they lock up, we take the bottle if there's anything left, leave the glasses on the table and slide the dishes and leftover food right through that little serving slot so the birds don't invade. They'll close in about..." He looked at his watch. "I'm sure they're cleaning up now and will be out of here in fifteen minutes."

Sure enough, Kate was back instantly with the wine, glasses, a tray of food. Right behind her a young man followed with a bucket of ice on a stand, placing it beside the table. Kate opened the wine and Adam indicated that Emma should taste. And she presented a bill. Adam signed off on everything and thanked her. Before Kate escaped into the bar the women bid her good-night and went out the back gate.

"Why couldn't I have found a job in a place like this instead of Burger Buster?" Emma said.

"This particular place is run by a family and I think you have to marry in, but it's perfect, isn't it?"

"I think I have to broaden my search, now that I have restaurant experience, if you use the term loosely."

"Listen, I want to hear all about it—your return, your job-hunting, anything you feel like talking about, but we have to get one thing out of the way first. Maddie. She doesn't know that you were Jock's girlfriend or that you and Riley were best friends and…that whole complicated mess. She's innocent of that."

Emma considered this for a second. "Jock and Riley never told her the details?"

"Emmie, I don't think *I* even know all the details, when you put it that way. I didn't have any trouble guessing. Riley and Jock never married. They weren't even together when Maddie was born."

Her mouth fell open. All these years she had this mental image of Riley and Jock, young and in love. Of course she knew they hadn't stayed together, that he'd gone on to marry and divorce another woman, but she thought that for at least a while they were a couple. "You're kidding!"

He shook his head.

"Doesn't that just figure?"

"What are you saying?" he asked her.

"Well, my half sister and stepsister, Drizella and Anastasia, couldn't wait to bring me the news that my best friend was pregnant and planning to marry my boyfriend, but they never mentioned the happy couple didn't stay together. I found out later, of course, but not while I was hurting over it. Because, hey, that might've made me actually feel less…" She stopped herself. "In fact, those few times we talked, you didn't mention they weren't a couple."

"I tried not to mention Riley and Jock at all," he said. "They were on and off for a little while. Maybe that's not accurate, either—they weren't together. They tried to create an amicable relationship for Maddie's sake, but they never even lived together. In fact, I think I'd need a chart and a graph to understand where Maddie came from because Riley and Jock were like oil and water. But I don't want Maddie to think badly of either of them. Well, let me be honest, I wouldn't be devastated to learn she thinks a little badly of Jock. He pissed me off. He got my sister pregnant and didn't exactly step up to the plate. He was pretty useless back then, but he was just a kid. And he is her father. I'd rather we all get along. And I don't want Maddie blindsided by a lot of nasty gossip."

"I won't be saying anything, Adam. I'd prefer to forget it ever happened," Emma said. "At the time, it was awful."

"I think it's safe to say a lot of people were hurt."

"You're in luck. If anyone remembers me they will have much juicier stuff than my best friend and boyfriend getting together while I was away at school sixteen years ago. All the same, Riley and Jock should explain it to her before anyone else does."

"Of course. The minute she's capable of understanding at least a little bit. I'm kind of an expert on teenagers. Girls Maddie's age are filled with a kind of tragic drama and fatalism that can easily cast them in a dark place. I've watched it. We've had our challenges as a family and it hasn't always been easy, but one thing we did manage. We managed to make sure Maddie never felt like a mistake. She always felt loved and wanted. I think."

"It never came up?" Emma asked. "Didn't anyone ask how Riley ended up having Jock's baby when he was supposed to be my boyfriend?"

"I only recall once or twice. Riley said you and Jock had broken up when you went away to school, which was at least partially true. It's been a long time—I just want to be sure Maddie always feels secure."

How lucky, Emma thought. Since she was just a kid she had known two things about the Kerrigan family. They had very obvious struggles; life for them had never been easy. But they had enough familial loyalty and love to glue them together. Emma had always envied that because she'd never had it.

Emma's problems began long before she lost her boyfriend to her best friend.

Emma was a bit too young to understand her placement in the family when her father married Rosemary Caliban, but it didn't take her long to instinctively know she was only loved by her father, and her father was a lonely, unhappy, broken man.

His wife gone, John Shay married someone who appeared, on the surface, to be a good match. A woman who was willing to help raise Emma. But Rosemary was a stern woman with a mean side and a streak of jealousy a mile wide. She brought a daughter to the marriage, produced a second and clearly preferred both of them to Emma. Once Emma was an adult and could look back on it she supposed it didn't help that people often remarked on how pretty she was. And her daddy couldn't stop himself from commenting on how much she resembled her late mother, with her chestnut hair and large dark eyes. Rosemary undoubtedly despised hearing that, and who wouldn't?

Emma remembered Rosemary doing subtle things to show her favoritism. She'd fold Anna's and Lauren's clothes and toss Emma's on the bed, took her two girls shopping and to lunch while Emma was with Riley, never inviting her. Emma even suspected the gifts she got at Christmas were of lesser value and almost never fit. Rosemary would help her daughters with the kitchen cleanup when it was their turn but Emma was left on her own. When John Shay stepped in to help Emma, she knew he had noticed and that made her feel worse, not better. When her father died it was the Kerrigan family that comforted her more than her own. It was obvious Rosemary didn't miss John much.

It wasn't long before a man moved in—her new stepfather, Vince Kingston. Vince wasn't gentle and sweet like her father had been. He was a crass idiot who made crude and suggestive remarks to his new stepdaughters, but Rosemary just ignored him. Emma gave him a wide berth, as did Anna and Lauren. Emma wasn't quite sure where she belonged. Or if she belonged anywhere at all.

That was always an issue with her, that she had no real family. This seemed especially important during her high school years, and when her father died…it seemed hopeless. She felt so self-conscious, as if everyone at school knew she was basically an orphan. And who was there for her through the confusion and sadness? Riley, Adam, their mother, June, and Riley's grandparents. They were the family she always longed for.

It was like Adam was always watching over them all.

On her second glass of wine, fortified with a little cheese and fruit, she asked him about his grandparents. She knew they had passed away, but hadn't heard until they'd been gone awhile.

"Well, Grandpa died when I was twenty-two. He wasn't sick long. Cancer took him quickly. Gram just went along, died in her sleep a year later. I was twenty-three and had just finished my teaching degree. My grandparents left the house to Mom, of course. It took me five more years to move out, get my own place. Riley and Maddie took a little longer and for the life of me I'm not sure why they even bothered—they're at Mom's all the time." He laughed. "But then, so am I. I check on her a lot. I do the guy chores around the house and try to take her out to dinner regularly. I hate her always cooking for all of us, even though she loves to cook. She volunteers with a bunch of church ladies, taking meals to the elderly and infirm."

Emma looked down. "I missed your family. Your mother most of all. I think she was more family to me than Rosemary ever was."

"And she misses you. You know, it wouldn't look like you're giving in to stop by the house and say hello. There's no commitment involved. It might be time to rethink this feud."

She laughed uncomfortably. "You don't understand. I'm not angry anymore. It's just... We can't be friends again, Adam."

"Who? Me and you?"

"Oh, I like the idea of being your friend," she said with a little laugh. "Especially since you know these nifty little hideaways where you can have wine under the stars. But I can't have you trying to work things out between me and Riley. We're done."

He gave her a steady, half-amused look. "Really, Emmie Cat? After all you've gone through in the past few years, you're worried about friendship with Riley?"

"We wouldn't trust each other anyway..."

He laughed. "It's been over fifteen years. You don't have to trust her. Who cares if you trust her? You don't even have to like her. But when you think about things, you'll figure out she was never your enemy."

"She wasn't exactly my friend!"

"If she'd been a better friend, maybe you could've married Jock. I'm sure that would've been great."

"Compared to who I did marry? Might've been, yeah! At least it wouldn't have been Richard. But determined to have a better life than the one I left behind, I—" She paused for a moment. "All right, all right," she said. "Don't think I haven't looked at it from that angle. But please, don't get ideas about reuniting us."

He put up his hands, palms toward her. "Heaven help me." He took a sip of his wine. "The truth? I wish the two of you could make amends. You were always stronger together than apart. I refuse to believe you still mourn the loss of Jock. It just seems that now, after everything, staying mad at my sister wouldn't be very high on your list of priorities."

After what she'd been through with Richard, there was a part of her that wished she'd married Jock, let *him* ruin her life, that she'd never left California, never met Richard. She shook her head. "That's certainly true—my priorities are completely different now. And I don't really think of our situation as a feud. I'm sure if we ran into each other we'd be perfectly cordial. Even friendly. But the days of slumber parties are over. I have to get on my feet. I didn't think I'd start off with a great job, but I thought I'd get a decent job, even after not working for nine years. I have a degree. With my experience, I could make a damn good concierge or event planner. Turns out that even though I didn't do anything wrong, I also have a shady past by association. Even though I wasn't arrested, people don't trust me. They're afraid I was his partner in crime. After all, he had several employees who rolled over on him, took deals to testify. People suspect me, think I didn't testify because I was protecting him. I didn't testify because I had nothing relevant to say. Let that be a lesson to you, Adam. Don't hang around with felons. Sitting in the courtroom while they're being tried might help them, but it won't do much for you."

"Why'd you come back, Emmie?" he asked. "I thought you'd disappear and we'd never see you again."

"I had nowhere to go," she said. "Oh, I thought about going somewhere I could be unknown but you know what?

Someone's going to figure me out eventually and then it'll only be worse. I will have added deception to suspicion. Besides, my credentials are in my name! And I couldn't stay back there. I was a leper. Not only couldn't I even get a job with McBurger back east, there were also hostile people who wanted revenge on me just for being associated with Richard. I was in hiding for months. Around here I've found some resistance, but I did manage to get a job. A small job, but a job. Maybe when people see I'm a hard worker, it'll ease up. I'm a little afraid to think about how long that might take." She took a sip of her wine. "I have to admit, I didn't think it would be this hard. Have you ever tried to make it on minimum wage?"

He just gave her a wan smile. Of course he had. When they'd moved to town, June had worked two jobs—cleaning houses and waitressing. She worked all the time. Emma remembered when June soaked her feet at the end of a long day, so sore, so weary. And that after just losing her husband.

"How'd you end up with Richard Compton?" he asked.

"Oh, the usual way. I met him when I was out with friends. In a restaurant. I was in the bar with my girlfriends and he was having dinner with clients. We had a nice conversation. He was clearly interested, which was flattering. He asked for my number and I wouldn't give it to him. I took his business card but he intimidated me, so I didn't plan to call him. A few weeks later he showed up in the store where I worked—he'd been back at that restaurant and one of my friends told him where I worked. I made him work really hard for a date, but honestly? I was completely smitten. Richard was very handsome, very classy. So charming. You don't weasel people out of a hundred million dollars by being an asshole. He could charm the pants off anyone.

"I didn't know how rich my husband was when I married

him. I mean, I knew he was successful and lived well, but I didn't know much more than that. I certainly didn't know he was getting rich illegally. Had I known, do you think I could have stayed with him? But it's not like I ever saw a tax return. I didn't have a key to a safe-deposit box or anything. I didn't know there was a safe in his study. I guess because there was another larger and visible safe, the police never expected it, either. It was hidden behind a bookcase. Richard was not what you'd call transparent."

Adam frowned. "Didn't you sign the tax return?"

She shook her head. "We filed separate returns—Richard took care of it. There was a prenup, a generous prenup that would settle me with more money than I'd ever know what to do with. Of course I came to understand about his wealth, that he could afford almost anything. He never questioned what I needed."

In vitro, Emma? What the hell. Knock yourself out.

But, Richard, you'll have to have a few tests...

No problem. I'll schedule us with the best doctor in the city.

"This is a whole new world," she said. "No one is going to pity me, learning how to live on two hundred a week after nine years with a Manhattan apartment and a vacation home in the islands. But... Well. Once I get a second job or a decent first job, things should be easier."

Adam smiled at her. "I'll keep my eyes open," he promised. "If you find something around here and need a strong letter of recommendation..."

"You're going to say you're pretty sure I'm not a bad person?" she asked.

"I'll say I've known you almost my whole life and have always known you to be strong, smart, honest and reliable." He pulled his wallet out of his back pocket and withdrew a card. He wrote something on the back and handed it to her.

"My cell number. I don't very often find myself at the Burger Bomb in south Santa Rosa. Call anytime."

She turned it over and saw it was a business card. Kerrigan Cleaning Services. Industrial, business, residential. Riley Kerrigan, President and CEO.

Emma looked up into his eyes with a question.

"The work is hard but she pays over minimum wage and promotes from within the company. She's a good leader." He shrugged. "If desperation for rent and food ever take precedence over bad feelings about the past."

"Never gonna happen, Adam," she said, handing back the card.

He closed his hand around hers, refusing to take it. "The first thing you're going to have to learn about scrabbling to get back on your feet—never turn your nose up at an opportunity. Especially for pride's sake."

"You're reading me all wrong," she said. "I don't have any pride left. But I do have to protect myself in the clinches."

"As you should. And know this—my sister has done a lot for women, women like you who are trying to get on their feet, start over, build a functional life and their self-esteem, usually out of the ruins of divorce or being widowed."

"You're proud of her," she said.

"Oh, yes. Riley amazes me. Keep the card. It has my number on the back."

She slid it into her purse, thinking it would be a cold day in hell before she'd ask Riley Kerrigan for help.

The very next day the mean little tyrant at Burger Belch fired her.

chapter *four*

Riley Kerrigan ran a tight ship and an efficient workplace. She kept her office in Santa Rosa, for easy access to Marin County, San Francisco, Davis, Napa Valley. It had been her goal from the start to service companies and individuals who could afford the best. The fact that this demographic was also the most difficult to please, the greatest challenge, was irrelevant to her. She was confident she had the best service providers.

There were only two full-time office staff: Riley, and her secretary, Jeanette Sutton. She had had five rooms—a spacious office for herself, a front reception area for Jeanette, an office for Brazil Johnson, the CFO and numbers woman, a conference room for meetings and a small lunchroom and restroom. Brazil was rarely in the office; she worked from home whenever she could. Riley's director of operations, Nick Cabrini, worked in the field, but there was space for him in the office if he needed it, either in Brazil's office or the conference room. Makenna Rice was the head housekeeper and trainer; she used the conference room occasionally.

Riley kept an office because customers responded to it, particularly business clients, although some home owners also liked to see her base of operations. It gave her credibility. Nick drove one of the company cars; he dressed sharp, carried a computer in his expensive briefcase and when he gave estimates or checked on cleaning crews he looked professional. She had two hundred employees, most of them part-time by choice. Some of her full-time employees took care of the same properties on a regular basis. She had night crews who cleaned office buildings, day crews in residences and crews on call for emergencies like fire or flood damage—regular hazmat duty. Her liability was high and well managed, her income was in the mid hundred-thousand range, her business net worth was now extremely high, her mother's house was paid off, her retirement savings gaining strength, Maddie's college fund nearly maxed and her state of mind—excellent.

It had been a long time coming. Many years of eighty-hour weeks.

When Riley was eighteen and a new high school graduate, she took a few classes at the community college that very summer and helped her mother with her housecleaning jobs. Back then they worked for cash, under the table, and too often they were treated like they belonged under the table, out of sight. Customers would take last-minute trips or vacations and forgo housecleaning service for a couple of weeks, not paying them. Clients complained about the cost; they added duties without making preparations in advance, without asking or offering to pay extra. "Oh, June, I have to run a couple of errands. You don't mind keeping an eye on little Eric, do you?" or "June, I'm way behind on the laundry, can you pitch in?" and "Junie, darling, looks like it's time for a good window washing." And as far as Riley knew, her mother hadn't had a raise in at least ten years.

"We have to fix this business," Riley had said. "Even some of your oldest customers take complete advantage of your good nature."

"I think of some of these people as my friends. I just like to help when I can," June always said.

"Well, they don't think of you as a friend. They treat their friends with far more respect, so don't be fooled. And none of them are worried about your retirement. We're going to find a better way to get it done and earn a decent living. And maybe a little security."

Riley set up a business plan at the age of eighteen, recruited a couple of college girls who were going to school part-time just as she was, got a business license for two hundred dollars and went looking for more clients. She called her company Kerrigan's Kleaning and had business cards printed. At first, she didn't have any overhead except the personal time it cost to do paperwork because Riley was paying taxes, social security, salaries and issuing 1099 statements to employees. Within months Kerrigan's Kleaning was humming along and even growing.

Then she got pregnant.

What a dark, terrifying time that was. Emma abandoned her, which came as no surprise, and Jock was suddenly MIA. He offered to give her money for an abortion, then he offered to marry her, but he had a black eye in the suspicious shape of Adam's fist. She turned down both offers. She did threaten to sue him for support, however, because in all areas she had a mind for business. She remained at home with her mother, brother and grandparents, where she had loving support.

She continued to work with her cleaning service. The bigger she got, the more she thought she'd better make this idea work because there was certainly no man waiting in the wings to take care of her. In fact, not only were Jock's support payments spotty at best, he didn't even show up at the hospital when she went into labor. Adam and her mother were with her, her grandparents waiting in the hall.

Jock came much later, after her family was gone, and though she tried to forget it, the image of him crying as he held the baby was forever burned into her mind. But she wasn't falling for his malarkey again.

The whole pregnancy was emotionally difficult and Riley felt she'd ruined her life with one terrible choice. But when she saw Maddie's perfect little face, everything changed. She might've had regrets, but now she also had purpose. And she worked like a demon because she had a daughter, and her daughter was going to have a devoted family, a good home and opportunities.

Jock started coming around after Maddie was a few months old, and the hurt and anger were almost too much for Riley. How dare he pretend to act like a father now! Every encounter was a strain; they fought and sniped at each other and not to be left out, Adam got into it, threatening Jock. Maddie was about nine months old when they had a blistering fight because Jock wanted to take her to his mother's house so his family could meet her, and Riley said she'd be damned if he was taking her anywhere.

"Stop!" June said. She took the baby from Riley, passed her to Grandma and sat the three of them at the table. "Don't anyone say a word if you value your life. That child is a happy baby who will live to be ninety if I have my way. But if all she hears from her parents and her uncle is fighting, what do you think that will do for her self-esteem?"

"We don't have any joint custody thing going on here," Riley snapped.

"You have money for a lawyer?" June asked Riley. She turned to Jock. "Do you?"

"If he wasn't responsible enough to take care of the mother, what makes you think he's responsible enough to take care of a baby?" Adam nearly shouted.

"Do you want this little girl to grow up wondering who her daddy is?" she asked Adam. "Or wondering why her mother and uncle kept him from her? This stops here and now. We don't raise voices around her, and Jock deserves a chance to grow into a good father. Part of that is spending time with his daughter. And if you two keep bullying him the only one who will suffer will be Maddie."

"I just want to do the right thing," Jock said.

"Too late!" Riley and Adam said. And then they both said, "Sorry," as they saw June's black scowl.

"Of course you can take the baby to your mother," June said. "First you have to learn the car seat, and I'd make you show me you know how to change a diaper but since your mother will be there, I think we're safe. I'll make you up a bottle and I want you to have her back in three hours. After today there has to be notice, Jock. Riley's a good mama and she is not the least bit flexible. Planning will be the key. We will all be cooperative and the number one priority will always be Maddie."

"If he'd planned before, Maddie wouldn't be here," Riley hurled.

"Was that a thank-you?" Jock asked.

"I'm warning you…" June said.

After that confrontation, things went a bit more smoothly with Jock but it was at least a couple of years before Riley's resentment of him calmed into a tense acceptance. This was not the life she had planned—a baby with a reluctant father who had no real love for her. And the fact that she had loved him, however briefly, only made her shame burn brighter.

Her mother had said one more thing to Riley. Privately. Knowing her daughter so well. "That pride will be the end of you," June said. "Try to put your focus on Maddie, not your injured pride. Please."

She built herself up one emotional brick at a time, becoming a tough, professional businesswoman. Her residential service grew. When she scored her first office building cleaning contract, she celebrated. She also provided what they called a mover's special—the cleaning of empty houses to get them ready for new occupants. That was a tough job that paid well and sometimes she, her mom and Adam would put in twelve- or fifteen-hour days to get it done. Sometimes Jock would babysit…at June's house.

Then she started researching industrial cleaning services, instinctively knowing the real money was there—mold, water damage, fire damage, sewage and odor removal. The only things she left alone were harmful chemicals and crime scene cleanup. She contracted one team, giving them the lion's share of her profits. But then she had them train a second team of industrial cleaners and they became *hers*. She ran her business from her mother's dining room table while spooning strained peas into Maddie's mouth and later, while helping Maddie with her spelling words and math exercises.

As a family, they had a bit of a setback when her grandparents passed, but she found that as long as she stayed ahead of the personnel and contracts, the company functioned very well. June worked part-time for Riley's company, a few jobs a week. The rest of the time she helped raise Maddie. When Maddie was ten, just five years ago, Riley changed the name of her company to Kerrigan Cleaning Services, rented office space and *cleaned up*.

From that home pregnancy test to here was a long and difficult passage. But she had people she knew who, barring death, would never desert her, would always forgive her, love her as unconditionally as she loved them. Maddie, her mother, Adam. Since Jock, she had not been in a romantic relationship.

Nor had she had another best friend.

Today was a fairly typical day. She started with a meeting with Brazil and Jeanette, going over office matters. She approved billing, answered emails, took a meeting with a man who was looking for a full-time domestic for a 14,000 square foot house. He'd already been given an estimate and offered a contract by Nick but was seeing the owner, Riley, because he balked at the idea that it would require a contracted team who would be paid by the hour when additional out of contract duties came along, chores such as, "Clean up after this wedding reception held in our house and courtyard." He could spend ten million on a house but wanted upkeep cheap. She stood firm. She let him go. He would be back.

She visited three teams on-site, found two to be managing well and one to be having some internal difficulties. It was a team of three housekeepers, two of whom had created a bond of friendship, probably behaving meanly to the third, an older woman she'd known a long time, who had been a team trainer and team leader. She'd been down this road so many times—the team leader was undeniably trustworthy with extremely high standards. The younger women wanted to get their eight hours done in six, probably cutting corners. They could take advantage of the trainer's skills, letting her take the detail work, but apparently they were shortsighted. She could have a meeting with them, counsel them, give them pointers on working together effectively. Instead, she said, "I'll create a new team for you, but for the rest of this week work together with no friction."

Then she turned it over to Nick Cabrini, her director of operations, with instructions to redistribute them. All three of them. Those two snotty women who abused the older cleaner weren't getting away with this.

The women loved Nick; her few male employees respected him. In fact, *she* loved Nick. He was young and personable but very rigid about their policies. He was never too harsh, that she knew of, but he was always firm. He was also bilingual. He had a good education and hoped to start a company of his own in another specialty—he wanted to get into transportation, limo and car service. But his best quality? His mother taught him to clean like a wizard. He could spot a smear or speck of dust at fifty yards.

His counterpart was Louis Spinoza, a retired firefighter who headed up their industrial restoration division. Louis had tons of hazmat experience, had worked construction on and off and, as many firefighters did, had worked a second job for years—in cleanup.

Riley grabbed a chicken salad on her way back to the office and ate it at her desk. Just when she was starting to feel that afternoon lull, who should show up but Adam. He gave a couple of raps on her door and stuck his head in.

"Is madam busy?" he asked.

She pushed her salad aside. "I'm always busy, but you're so welcome to come in. Out of school early today?"

"Nah, I just don't have any other duties."

"Good, I'm dying to hear about Maddie's driving test from an objective person. She says it took her fifteen minutes and she aced it."

He grinned. "Twenty minutes and she missed one, but she challenged it and even showed them the page on which her answer was located. I'd have given it to her."

"You'd give her a kidney," she said, laughing at him.

"Well, true," he said, sitting in the chair in front of her desk. He balanced an ankle on the opposite knee. "There is something we should talk about. I ran into Emma yesterday after the driving test. I met her later for a drink."

Riley frowned. "Oh?" she said. "Ran into—"

"We stopped for a hamburger on the way home from the test and guess who was working there? Little paper cap, apron and all."

"Maddie didn't say anything…"

"She teased me a little bit on the way home. I just told her Emma was an old friend we went to school with." He took a deep breath. "You're going to have to tell her, Riley. You're going to have to explain about Emma and Jock. And you."

"Why?" she asked quickly. Defensively.

"Because it was a thing around here. I don't know everything that went on, all I know is Jock was going steady with Emma when suddenly you were pregnant with Jock's baby. And had a huge blowout with your best friend. A couple of families were thrown into a tailspin, all kinds of agony and grudges resulting. Riley, Maddie has a best friend. A couple of them. She needs to know what happened to you."

"That has nothing to do with Maddie," she said. "Maddie was born into a loving family, she knows the facts about who her father is, she spends plenty of time with him, especially when sports are involved. Maddie is secure."

"Secure with the sanitized version of this story? First of all, someone is going to tell her someday that there was a whole lot of cheating and hard feelings going on. Probably when people who have known us almost our whole lives notice that Emma is back in town—that might bring the whole drama to mind. It'll get so much more interesting to add that Emma left California permanently, probably at least partly because of that, and ended up married to an internationally famous con man. And second, we've never been that kind of family—the kind that short-sheets the truth."

"What does it matter?" she asked in a voice that verged on desperation. "It might not have been tidy but it wasn't complicated. Emma was gone, we were left behind, spent a lot of time together. Do I regret it? Not when I look at Maddie. But I wish Jock had been someone else's boyfriend!"

He leaned toward her. He was patient. His handsome eyebrows tented with concern. "Riley, what you don't want is for the question to come up. You want to make the circumstances clear to Maddie. Because of this—there were a series of unfortunate misunderstandings and events that caused some anguish, but I'd like to think things always work out in the end. I hope things can work out for Emma—she's been through hell. I think things worked out for you. At the end of the day, things worked for me—I have a beautiful, brilliant niece. I hope Maddie has the life she wants even though she has this mixed-up family of a lot of single parents. There's a sweet spot somewhere, Riley—that place where the good outweighs the bad. Know what I mean? That tender truth. The honest truth."

"You don't know what you're suggesting…"

"You've become a very successful woman, Riley. You have everything to be proud of. There isn't a single one of us who doesn't have to own a questionable decision or two but very damn few can show how they took that one misstep and turned it into pure gold."

"And if Maddie loses all respect for me?"

He shook his head. "Not possible. Maddie admires you more than anyone. Except maybe me," he said, grinning. "I think I'm your biggest fan."

She softened her expression. Adam was all goodness. All goodness wrapped up in the most beautiful package.

"What was she doing working at a fast-food restaurant?" Riley asked.

"As she tells it, it was the only job she could get. She wasn't sure if it was the fact that she hadn't had a job in ten years, outside of being married to a millionaire, or if it was because she was married to a notorious thief. She suspects the latter and I'm inclined to agree. People won't take a chance on her."

"Why would she tell anyone? She should have changed her name!"

"She goes by Emma Shay, but she's not disguised. Employers are pretty savvy nowadays. They look up their applicants. They check Facebook and Twitter, just like you do. And she looks exactly as she did fifteen years ago."

"Sixteen," Riley said uncomfortably. Her fingers ran through her short, shaggy blond hair at her temples, smoothing it over her ears.

"Aw, Riley, you've always worn this thing like a hair shirt. We should've talked about this years ago but you were busy self-flagellating. Emma belonged to me and Mom, too, you know. She immediately knew who Maddie must be. Listen, even though you didn't confide everything in me, I know the whole thing wasn't entirely your fault. Last night I told her you and Jock weren't even together when Maddie was born and she was surprised. Surprised and disappointed in Jock. This should've come out years ago, not last night. That's how little communication she's had with this place."

Riley felt tears threaten to rise. "I tried to tell her—she wouldn't speak to me. Lyle could've told her, but he was determined to stay out of it. Besides, she was busy, Adam. Flying all over the world in that private jet…"

"I have no doubt she'd have walked away from that had she known what was really going on there. I thought you'd be sympathetic. She was lied to. Everyone abandoned her."

"And so now she's been struck down again? Poor Emma, she just keeps picking the wrong guys."

"Was that sarcasm?" he asked.

"I apologize. I'm feeling a little like a cornered animal. Oh, God, why am I apologizing to you? Emma doesn't know I was flippant about her troubles!"

"I gave her your business card. I told her you paid more than minimum wage."

"You can't be serious," she said, astonished. "She couldn't make in a year what her fresh-flower budget was."

"*Was* being the operative word. You might hear from her. She's having a hard time getting by."

"Lyle hasn't said anything," she said.

"Lyle has always been Switzerland where you two were concerned, which is why Emma knew so little about you and Jock. But get ready—one way or another, you're going to run into her. Because I'm planning to see her again."

"What? What's that about?"

"If you two can't reconcile, that's your deal. I'm not angry with Emma or with you. And I want to see her again."

"You act like you have a thing for her or something," Riley said.

"I told you, she was my friend, too. I'm a little worried about her. It's important to me to make sure she's all right." He stood up.

"Do you have a thing for her, Adam?" she asked directly. Her brother, so handsome, such a wonderful man, was rarely in a relationship even though women sighed as he passed. She had even once said, *It's okay if you're gay, you know.* And he had replied, *And it's okay if you are.*

"You want to date her, is that it?" Riley asked.

"We had a glass of wine together," he said. "It was good to see her. We talked a little bit about Maddie, about her return home after that sideshow back east, the difficulties of finding work. She asked about Mom, about Grandma and Grandpa. Except for Lyle and the old widow she rents from, she's pretty much alone, but we had a nice hour or so together and I was really happy to see her again. While all that mess was going on in New York with her husband, then his suicide, I thought about her a lot. I checked in with Lyle now and then to make sure she was okay. Lyle was talking to her almost daily at the end—he was her sole emotional support. I should have called her. I think Lyle would've given me her number, but I didn't ask. I decided to wait awhile, see how things shook out, then there was the suicide and feds all over her possessions. I think what she endured must have been unimaginably painful, worse than most things I can envision. You know that Emma, like you and I, was left orphaned when her dad died, except we had Mom and who did she have? Rosemary, that coldhearted bitch. So yeah, it was nice to see her, talk to her, get reacquainted. I offered her a letter of recommendation. I gave her your business card. She probably won't ever call you or ask you for work, but I'm the one that gave her the card so don't be surprised. And if you don't mind me saying so—I think you owe her."

"Oh, God, don't lay that on me! I begged her forgiveness for Jock, which she did not give me, and I can't even repeat the horrible names she called me. She didn't leave here a broken woman, she—"

"Girl," Adam said. "She was just a girl." Then more quietly he added, "And so were you. You were girls."

"Don't do this, Adam. Don't get involved with her. I bear no grudge but after what happened, please don't bring her around. Please don't tell me I owe her. Not now. I know things turned out badly for her but try to remember that while I was scrubbing floors and trying to hold it together to raise a baby alone, she went from sorority princess to New York socialite, and never sent a word of forgiveness to me."

"Everything is past now," he said. "She's no longer a sorority princess or socialite and you're no longer scrubbing floors and struggling to take care of your baby."

She rubbed her temples with her fingertips and groaned. "It's over and I don't want it all coming back. Not now. Please, Adam."

"You can't erase the past any more than she can. But we can all live with it decently. If she calls you, you better do the right thing, Riley."

He was really deep down a kind person, and since he was just a boy had felt most comfortable when the whole family was together. He didn't like loose ends; he was a protector. He'd been like a father to Maddie since she was born. And there was no question, Riley would be lost without him.

"She will never call me," she said.

"Don't be too sure. It's really time to lay this thing between you to rest."

"I have no jobs but cleaning jobs. She'd have to get her hands dirty."

He laughed. "You don't think she got dirty in that New York life?" He was moving toward the door. "I'm just giving you warning."

When they were kids, people were used to seeing them together. They were known as Beauty and Brains. They were both smart and pretty, but very different. Emma was a tall, slender brunette with rosy lips and eyes more commonly seen on a doe—large and dark. Riley was blonde, four inches shorter with a tight little body and crystalline blue eyes. Both were incredibly popular. And while they seemed inseparable, they spent time with other friends, as well. Emma was a cheerleader and participated in gymnastics; Riley was in choir, was a pom-pom girl and the star in the school musical—*Grease*. Emma was the homecoming queen and Riley, the valedictorian.

There was another difference between them that Riley was extremely conscious of—she was the poor one. Emma protested that her family was not rich and privileged, just that her father, being a CPA, was extremely good with money. Plus, his business certainly paid better than cleaning houses.

When they were in grade school at St. Pascal's, Riley knew she looked shabby. By the time she was in eighth grade, thanks to a lot of babysitting and clever shopping, she was pulling herself together quite well. But Emma grew up in a five-bedroom house on a half-acre lot while Riley lived in a small, old three-bedroom, one-bath house that held five people. She and her mother shared a room. If Riley wanted Emma to spend the night, which was quite often, Adam would take the couch and say, "Only if Mom sleeps in my room because you would get into my stuff!" His *stuff*, as Riley recalled, wasn't all that interesting.

Even that hadn't driven a wedge between them. But Riley was only ten when she said, "My family isn't always going to be poor, you wait and see."

In all the years Riley and Emma were best friends, they had about three memorable fights. One was in seventh grade when Riley was invited to the first boy/girl party in their class and Emma was not. In fact, Emma was most deliberately excluded by some jealous girls. It was melodramatic and tragic and there were many tears. They were estranged for a long, painful month.

In their junior year Emma was asked to the prom by a senior and virtually abandoned Riley for the older crowd. She did her dress shopping with senior girls who were part of the new guy's clique. Riley was crushed and sat home on prom night playing Scrabble with her mother and brother. And Emma's prom night was a disaster—the guy got drunk and pressured her for sex, so she called her father for a ride home. At nine o'clock.

Both girls were miserable and sad. They sulked and avoided each other for a couple of weeks.

Then Emma's father was killed in a car accident—a drunk driver.

Of course Riley and her whole family went to Emma at once, embracing her, propping her up. The girls made up and swore they'd never let such differences divide them again. Emma was so sorry she put such stock in those prom friends, and Riley was devastated that she'd begrudged her best friend good times and was so sorry things went so badly. They bonded over Emma's grief. After all, Riley had lost her own father at an early age. She knew the pain of it too well.

Emma was left with that tight-ass evil grump, Rosemary, and her two nasty sisters whom she didn't feel were her sisters at all.

Then came college. Emma got a partial scholarship; her stepmother said she would be able to help a little. She bought new clothes and excitedly prepared for a whole new life. Riley and Emma parted tearfully and for the first two weeks called each other constantly, missing each other desperately. Then Emma settled in, became busy, got a part-time job. She had awesome roommates, was pledging a sorority, she was overwhelmed by her classes, loved the many social events and the surrounding rush. Also, Emma, being a vivacious young beauty, was getting hit on by the college guys. Even older college guys. She confessed to Riley that she was doing a little harmless hanging out with guys, a little innocent dating

that she didn't want Jock to know about. Of course her secret was safe with Riley.

Getting acclimated to community college wasn't nearly
as exciting. Riley found it to be very much like high school,
except they didn't take attendance. Big whoop. It didn't take
Riley long to begin to feel lonely.

As Emma settled into campus life, making new friends
and experimenting with her newfound freedom, she wasn't
in touch as much. She wasn't picking up when Riley or Jock
called; she wasn't answering texts or returning calls right away
and when she did, she didn't have much time. She was always
rushing off somewhere or it sounded like there was a party in
the background. All she wanted to talk about was herself and
all her cool new experiences. A week, then two, then three
went by with hardly any contact and what contact they had
was brief—just long enough for Emma to relate all the fun
things she was doing. By early October she'd already made
plans to spend Thanksgiving with one of her new classmates
and her family in Astoria, Oregon, rather than coming home
to Santa Rosa. "I saw pictures of her house, Riley," Emma
said excitedly. "I think they're incredibly rich!"

"We never talk at all anymore," Riley complained. "It's
like you're too busy to be bothered with me."

"No, of course not! Well, maybe we're growing apart a
little bit," Emma said. "On account of going to different colleges. But we'll always be best friends."

Riley, who used to talk to her best friend every day, several times a day, was lost. Jock, not one to go long without a
girl, was calling and hanging around Riley a lot. He said it
made perfect sense for them to be going out. "You can't tell
me she's not," he said to Riley. "I'm not sitting home until
Emma decides she has time for me."

Looking back, Riley remembered she'd felt deserted. Abandoned. Was it too much to expect her best friend to talk to her every couple of days? Twice a week? For more than three minutes? And maybe ask her about herself once in a while?

She and Jock were commiserating a lot. Jock was always around, calling her, taking her out for pizza, inviting her to join him for their high school's homecoming game and subsequent parties with old classmates. They were pals in their shared loneliness.

"Be careful of him," Adam had said to Riley. "He's been known to take advantage of girls."

"We're just friends," she said.

But Riley was growing very fond of Jock. She looked forward to every call, every casual date. They stopped commiserating so much and started laughing and having fun. They met friends at pizza parlors and on the beach. One crisp fall night they drove over to the coast and had a few beers by a beach fire, just the two of them. It was amazing how much they had to talk about—Emma's name never came up. Riley was astonished to find she was feeling far less abandoned.

She was falling for him.

"I think I might be way into you, too," he said. "Damn, I never saw this coming! I'm starting to think it probably should've been me and you from the start."

"We have to tell her, Jock. We have to tell Emma exactly how this happened. We couldn't get her on the phone for five minutes, we started hanging out, we got closer—at first because we were both missing her. But then because we have something. I don't know…chemistry?"

He laughed. "You think Emma cares? Go ahead—leave her a message. She'll get back to you in a week or two."

Then it went too far. Riley never meant for it to happen. At least not until she had thought it through much more carefully. Not until they came clean with Emma. She was telling herself it wasn't the worst thing in the world to spend so much time with Jock, to kiss and fondle and whisper in the dark of night, but then things got out of control and before she knew it, her shirt was pushed up, her jeans were around her knees and they'd gone all the way. Before they'd been honest with Emma.

"Oh, God, I wanted us to tell Emma before something like that happened."

"Baby, Emma could care less."

"But I think I'm falling in love with my best friend's boy-friend!"

"Whoa, whoa," he said. "Riley, let's just slow down here..."

"Aren't we in love?" she asked. "All those things you were saying, that you couldn't get through this without me and I'm the best thing that's happened to you and you probably should've hit on me first..."

"Hey, shoot me for being nice, huh? Of course I care about you—who said I didn't? That was totally up to you. You were totally into it. Just don't say anything, all right? You don't have to make an announcement, for God's sake. I won't tell her. I just don't know if I'd call it love. Yet."

"You have to break up with her. Tell her about us. You're the one who started things with me, not the other way around. Aren't you breaking up with her?" Riley asked.

"I don't think I'm going to have to," he said. "I think she broke up with me about three months ago. She's partying her ass off in Seattle."

"And there's no grass growing under your ass, now, is there?" she threw back at him.

Four weeks later, right before Emma came home for Christmas break, she told Jock she was pregnant. She'd taken the home test and it was positive.

"You sure it's mine?" he said. "I used a condom."

"I haven't been with anyone else," she informed him hotly.

"But I don't know that for sure, do I? Since I wasn't with you every minute. And like I said, I had protection."

"What am I supposed to do?"

"I don't know. I guess what anyone would do. You need a little money?"

She was so filled with shame, disappointment and rage she wanted to die, but she lifted her chin and said, "Go to hell, Jock."

But really, when it happened, she had thought she loved him. And she struggled with that feeling, on and off, for a few years after that.

Adam left Riley in her office and got in his car. He thought he'd drive by his mother's house and ask if there was anything she needed him to do, see what her plans were for the evening. He might tell her about Emma, but he hadn't decided yet. Those dozen or so times he had gotten in touch with Emma before she got married, when she was in college and then living in New York in the city, well, he never mentioned that to his family. Or to Lyle. And it seemed as though Emma hadn't talked about it, either. But maybe it hadn't left that much of an impression on her.

What's that about? Do you have a thing for her?

Oh, yeah. He had since she was about fifteen. That summer she'd gone from fourteen to fifteen—man, that was the pivotal summer in a young woman's life—and Emma had gone from the little sister to a woman of interest.

I see the way you're looking at Emma, his mother had said. *Do not touch that girl, do you hear me? She's like a daughter to me, like a sister to you and Riley and you're eighteen. She is off-limits. At least until you're both adults. This is non-negotiable. Her evil stepmother would love to throw you in jail!*

But not long after she passed her eighteenth birthday, she was gone to Seattle. Soon after that Riley was expecting Jock's baby. There was a significant part of Adam's heart that was very happy Jock was no longer Emma's guy, but he was smart enough to know that until Emma recovered from her broken heart, he'd better not step forward.

The next six years were a blur. Emma didn't return to Santa Rosa except for very brief visits and he didn't see her. He worked two jobs and went to school, his grandparents both died, he was helping his mother and Riley as much as he could. He grew very attached to Maddie, and Emma moved to New York. He always thought, one of these days…

While he was thinking that, she got married. And not to just anybody, but some internationally known millionaire.

All that had changed. And she was back.

chapter *five*

Emma didn't qualify for unemployment, as hers had been a part-time job. She did qualify for food stamps, which weren't called food stamps anymore. Although she had applied on-line, she had to invest four hours in the county welfare office, completed forms in hand. It was now a debit card that would come in the mail. Soon, they said—in about thirty days. If things went well. After her application was approved.

She judged herself against the great throng of people gathered in the county welfare office. She'd heard her husband rant about how many undeserving and entitled people took advantage of the welfare system, got all this free money without hardly trying. She felt like one of them and wondered if she deserved help. Probably not. She'd been married to him, after all. She also wondered where all that free money was and where those people who worked the system were. She'd always had visions of slick con men sauntering in and with the flick of a form, walking out with money or some other assistance. Most of the people in the office were women, more than half with small children hanging on their legs or sitting on their laps. At least half were Hispanic but as she'd read in the guidelines, they had to be documented to qualify. None looked like the type she expected. And no one looked at ease or comfortable about being there. As for Emma, she felt a little ill. Demoralized and ashamed, like further proof she'd done something wrong. But she looked better than anyone in the place. She still had some good clothes, expensive shoes and a couple of nice handbags, unlike everyone else there.

Her clothes didn't fit so well these days. It hadn't taken long for the extra pounds she'd gained from Burger Hell to fall off. Job searching, the stress of it and the sheer calisthenics of tromping all over hell and gone ate up a lot of calories. Not to mention the worry that she'd never be able to support herself again.

There seemed to be a lot of hair in her hairbrush these days. Was she losing her hair? She'd been grinding her teeth at night for a couple of years and she dreamed about losing her teeth. Awake, she worried about falling apart one batch of cells at a time.

She wondered what Rosemary, Anna and Lauren thought she was doing right now. How did they not have the slightest concern that she might be struggling? None of them reached out or asked her how she was getting by. When she'd been comfortable, before Richard's investigation began, they were always front and center, her *family*. They'd wrangled first class trips to New York on Richard's dime and just to save himself the annoyance of having them about, he'd put them up in a suite at the Plaza Athenee. It quickly became expected. Rosemary, the woman who couldn't even have been bothered to take her shopping when she was a girl, called and in her sweetest voice would say, "It's time for our annual trip to the city, dear. Will you book it for us?" And Emma had given them such generous, beautiful birthday and holiday gifts. They never even thanked her. They thought it was nothing to her. They probably thought one of her servants bought and shipped them.

The only jobs she seemed to qualify for were laborer's positions. Waitressing paid far less than minimum wage because of the tips, which waitstaff were obligated to report to the IRS. In the end she did better for herself by not mentioning her degree; she said she was educated through high school. Stealing a little bit from Riley, she said she'd cleaned houses for work and the only reference she had was Adam Kerrigan because she hadn't lived around here since high school.

So she took a job on the housekeeping staff of a hospital in Petaluma. After four days of training she began on the day shift, punching in at 7:00 a.m.

She made a decision, an easy one. She wasn't about to tell anyone her story. She'd like to at least pay her bills for a while. She kept it simple. She had been married to a man named Rick—no one had ever called Richard *Rick*—they didn't have children, he died of a brain injury. Hospital people took that to mean stroke or aneurysm, not a bullet. She never mentioned New York; she said they'd lived in Ohio. On the line that asked for her last address, she made up a completely fictitious address in Akron. She decided to come back to California where she grew up, where she had a few friends and some sparse family. It was a little dicey when people asked, in a friendly way, "Who are your friends? Who do you hang around with?" At which point Emma began to have secret, imaginary friends. "Oh, my girlfriend Mary Ann who I went to school with and a cousin, Jennifer, who's married with two kids. Then there's Ruth, my favorite aunt who's only four years older—I'm close to them."

The women on the housekeeping staff she worked with

were exceptionally friendly, reaching out to her, warning her about the supervisor who was a dragon lady named Glynnis Carlson. Glynnis was short, wore a forty-year-old hairstyle with one silver slash in front, came upon them like an unexpected storm and without even raising her voice threatened their very lives for having a cell phone out, for disposing of soiled linens wrong, for leaving streaks on the floor or porcelain, letting their carts get overladen or worse, understocked. And that was nothing compared to the way she berated people who weren't keeping up with their assigned area, which was very hard because nurses and aides were constantly summoning housekeeping. They didn't help with cleaning up beds or patients, of course, but anything that hit the floor was passed on to the housekeeping staff. There were a lot of messes that hospital staff didn't handle. The horrid ones.

"Be glad you're not in the ER or the operating room. Wear a mask and never work without gloves, just change them out," advised Barbara, one of the cleaning staff who had been around for years. "Wrap as much mess as possible in the linens, careful not to get any plastics or papers in them, get them down the chute fast as you can. Let it be laundry's problem. They transfer it all with big sticks and hooks."

There was a lot of that in a hospital. The doctors passed it off to the nurses, who passed it to the orderlies and aides, who passed it to housekeeping, who passed it to laundry.

It was hard, ugly work, but steady and among decent people. Emma had never been shy of hard work and she was growing confident and a little bit happy. She had work. She had just enough money and didn't require much to live on. Life in her tiny bungalow was compact and uncomplicated. Not only were her coworkers nice to her but the patients and their visitors were also pleasant, and under the direst of circumstances—illness. Cleaners weren't allowed to have traffic with patients—they weren't trained for that. But there was nothing preventing them from being cordial, going for an extra water jug for flowers, calling nurses when they saw a problem. "Just don't touch them," the dragon lady said. "Not even if one of them falls. Switch on the emergency light and stand by."

"Not even if they fall?" Emma asked, aghast.

"All you need is to help someone off the floor and break their neck or something. You'll lose your job and the hospital will get sued. You never move an accident victim. You let the professionals do that."

"Makes sense, when you put it that way," she said.

"Think of them all as accident victims," Glynnis said. "Just get their bathrooms clean."

But despite these terrifying warnings, Emma warmed to the patients, particularly the elderly. Little old people were so vulnerable when ill and she found she couldn't turn away. The old women loved her and the old men loved her more, and she just couldn't stop herself from offering the occasional sip of water to someone who was struggling with the tray table or a glass. It pleased her to hand a wet washcloth to someone who needed it. She even stayed late and read to an eighty-five-year-old blind woman, though she was careful to ask the dragon lady for permission first.

"I'm not allowed to help you to the lavatory," she told the woman. "I'm so sorry. But I'll get the nurse."

"I hate the nurse. I'd rather it be you."

"Oh, I'd be happy to, but the housekeeping staff has been threatened with dire consequences if we break the rules, even just slightly. I'm not trained in patient care. Let me get that nurse and I'll stay with you until she comes."

She started thinking about possibly training as a nurse's aide.

She had three very blissful weeks in her hospital job, though it was the hardest work she'd ever done. She didn't care; she went on break with coworkers, she ate lunch with her new friends, heard about their marriages, their kids, their aging parents, their car problems and vacation plans.

Emma began to have fantasies of a normal life. It wouldn't be a rich life for sure, but at this point a rich life only represented disaster and danger to her. She was looking for stability, nothing more. She had her food debit card, she handed out Halloween candy with Penny, the leaves finished turning, November came in wet and cold. She got together for wine with Lyle and Ethan, who was almost starting to believe she wasn't a bad person. She spoke to Adam on the phone a couple of times when he called to see how she was doing. She had a light dinner with Penny on TV trays, watching *Madam Secretary* with her, just like normal people. Penny invited her to join her with her girlfriends Susan, Marilyn and Dorothy for a potluck one evening and to her delighted surprise, these old girls liked martinis! Susan's son was the chauffeur for Susan, Marilyn and Dorothy. "I told him I was completely capable," Susan said. "But it's just as well he wants to drive us. That way we can have two!"

"William is such a nice boy," Penny said of Susan's son.

"That *boy* is fifty-nine years old," Susan said. "Before long I'll be chauffeuring him!"

At two weeks until Thanksgiving, Emma had more than one offer for the holiday feast. Lyle and Ethan were going to Ethan's sister's house and had graciously included her. She might've gone but for the fact that Penny and a couple of her widowed girlfriends who were sharing the feast also invited her—and they were to dine at Penny's little house. She dearly wanted to join them.

"Being one of the new kids at the hospital, I'm sure I'll have to work that day," Emma said.

"We took that into consideration," Penny told her. "We'll

be ready at about four—that should give you time to get home, shower, come over for some pre-turkey poo-poos and wine."

"Let me pick up the wine," she said.

"You're absolutely welcome to."

"And I'll visit Lyle's shop and see if he'll give me a break on a centerpiece," she added.

"Try your best, darling, but be warned—he's going to gouge you! I've been looking for a discount for years. I guess I can't complain," she said with a smile. "He gave me you."

Emma was having a life. She had friendly acquaintances at work, a paycheck large enough to cover her most immediate expenses, friends apart from the hospital, two invitations for a holiday dinner, a comfortable place to live. It didn't even bother her that her own family hadn't so much as called to check on her much less ask her to join them for Thanksgiving dinner. In fact, she was relieved.

Just as she was beginning to relax, something weird happened. One of the older nurse's aides was glowering at Emma for no apparent reason. Clarice seemed angry about something. Angry or on edge. Some others seemed to be following suit. It appeared to be an unhappy day on the ward. There was a static in the air and Emma knew something was wrong. There had been a couple of emergencies; maybe that was setting everyone on edge.

The static turned to an electric crackle. Emma tried not to notice but she was beginning to feel paranoid by the behavior around her.

It didn't last long. It was two in the afternoon, about an hour until shift change. A patient had been discharged and the room was ready for a terminal cleaning. Emma got her cart, mop, linens, gloves and went to the room. Standing there beside the now empty bed in a room with no other patients was Clarice.

"How much do you have stashed away?" she asked, her voice hard.

"What?"

"You heard me. How much do you have stashed away? Enough to take care of my elderly mother? Because Hugh and I can't afford her and she has to live with us now since her entire savings was stolen."

"What are you talking about?" Emma asked, fearing she knew.

"I know who you are, Mrs. Compton. We all know who you are. My mother's name is Roberta Sinclair and you took everything she had and I think you can find a way to get it back."

Oh, no! Even though she'd been over every possible scenario, now Emma didn't know what to say. She just shook her head. "There's nothing," she said. "I have nothing."

"You have assets in your name," Clarice insisted.

Emma shook her head again. "There's nothing in my name. Everything was in Richard's name and the few things that weren't, I surrendered. All our possessions were auctioned—I surrendered those, as well. Do you honestly think I'd be scrubbing floors in a hospital if I had anything?"

"For a while, yes," she said. "You'll lie low for a while, then when the talk has died off, you'll tap into your hidden money. I read the book!"

"The books are wrong! The internet is wrong! Everything is gone—my wedding ring, my wedding gown, wedding gifts—I gave it all back. I'm not lying low—I'm using my legal name. I haven't even colored my hair! I didn't know what was going on, Clarice. I had nothing to do with Richard's business."

"What about offshore money? One of the books says he was about to give the SEC account numbers when—"

"Gone. He was trying to negotiate a smaller sentence, but... There's nothing that I know of, nothing left to me, I swear."

"The book says you retained 1.4 million and a lot of valuable property..."

She was getting dizzy, shaking her head. "I kept a few thousand so I could drive back here and rent a small space. The US Marshals sold everything at auction. Everything. I kept some sheets and towels, a few dishes and pots. I gave most of my clothing to women's shelters. There's nothing. Do you think I want to be tied to that hideous crime? I was told that investors got roughly thirty-two cents on the dollar. I couldn't do anything more."

"You're lying," Clarice said. "You had lawyers! My mother didn't have a lawyer, she couldn't *afford* one! And she didn't get that much. She borrowed against her house to invest with Compton!"

That was not exactly how it worked, as Emma knew from the trial. Richard Compton worked with a number of financial managers and brokers who represented smaller investors, and it was they who invested in his company. Richard didn't talk anyone into mortgaging their house; he talked hedge fund managers into investing with him and he neither knew nor cared where they got their money. Large sums. Many collections of smaller investors. Richard was big-time. He had a minimum requirement, probably a hundred times the value of Mrs. Sinclair's mortgage.

"My lawyer was assigned by the court and he wanted me to keep enough to live on since finding work would be hard, but I didn't keep anything. I'm sorry," Emma said. "I'm so sorry. I would never have let something like that happen if there was anything I could do to prevent it."

"You're *lying!*"

Clarice picked up a bedpan that sat on the now vacant bed and hurled it at her. Emma blocked the missile with her forearms but that did little good. The damn thing was full. Since she knew the patient just discharged was ambulatory, Clarice must have looked high and low through the whole ward for just the right bedpan. Or more likely, she emptied catheter bags into one. The splatter threw Emma off balance. She stumbled backward, hit her tailbone on the pail on her way down and cracked her head on the metal door handle. She was covered in the filth.

When she tried to stand, the world was spinning and she ended up scooting across the floor, escaping out of the room into the hallway.

"Oh, my God," one of the other housekeepers said, running to her. "What happened? Are you hurt?"

Clarice walked out of the patient room and, lifting her chin in the air, walked past Emma. She went down the hall to the nursing station.

"Can you get up?" the other housekeeper asked.

"I don't know," she whispered. "Ugh. Oh, God, this is awful."

"How did this happen?"

"She threw a bedpan at me. Apparently she was swindled by… My late husband was guilty of… But I didn't know," she said, turning imploring eyes to her friend. "I swear I didn't. I would never. And he's dead now."

Two of the RNs on staff came running down the hall. One said, "Dear God." The other one said, "Clarice has lost her mind." They tried to get Emma on her feet but when she swayed and threatened to fall again, they went for a wheelchair and took her to the ER. She tried to briefly explain the problem, but it didn't come out well. She tried to tell them she'd been married to a bad man, a thief, but she didn't know it and it seems Clarice was one of his victims but Emma didn't know...

I should have done something, she thought. *I should have done something when I wondered why lawyers negotiated our prenup but Richard had hired both of them. I should have asked questions when this fabulously wealthy man wanted to marry me, but I didn't! I should have done something when the SEC started investigating him. I should have looked through his papers or found a way to hack his computer when I realized something was wrong, but I didn't know. I should have known. How could I not have known? I should have talked to the people who worked for him, the people who eventually testified against him. I should have found out how they were going to carry on—they got deals from the prosecutors. Everyone got deals— even his mistress!*

When everything was so murky, so mysterious, I should have looked into it! Maybe I should have hired a detective or something. Maybe I should have run!

"Clean her up and get a head CT," the ER doctor ordered. "Listen, you might have a concussion, Emma. Can you get a ride home today and a ride back for your car tomorrow?"

"I don't know," she said, thinking *I'm covered in urine! Who wants to drive me home?*

"Well, you can think about that. We're going to get you some clean scrubs, stand you in the shower and wash you off—Mandy will go with you and make sure you don't faint or fall in the shower. And while you're having your CT, think about who you can call. If there's no one, someone from the hospital can either take you home or put you in a cab. You can't drive for twelve hours, at least. And Mrs. Carlson is waiting to see you, but let's get you cleaned up first."

Glynnis! Glynnis was going to fire her!

She was taken to a shower, her smelly uniform was put in a plastic bag and a set of scrubs provided. "I think your shoes are fine," Mandy said from right outside the curtain.

"My shoes are fine because it hit me in the head and got in my hair," Emma said with a hiccup of emotion.

"Just to be safe, throw the shoes in the washer when you get home. Or spray clean them with some disinfectant cleaner."

"You can wash those?"

"I do it all the time—they're just running shoes. Canvas and that little bit of leather."

If I'd been doing my own laundry and cleaning instead of hiring people to do it, I'd probably know that, she thought.

Emma was given a comb and had a little lip gloss in her purse. By the time the doctor looked at her head CT, her hair was almost dry and completely mangy-looking. Without some product, a brush and a blow dryer, she looked a wreck. It was a relief to be clean, but she wasn't feeling much better about the whole thing. They gave her a list of symptoms to watch for and she had a very large bump on the back of her head, but that didn't hurt nearly as much as her tailbone where she'd hit the metal bucket on the way down. She was given some ibuprofen.

The doctor was insistent that she not drive herself. Emma thought about just ignoring the instructions. Then her wiser self intervened and reminded her that all she needed was to pass out while driving and kill a family of four. She couldn't bear the thought of calling Lyle and having Ethan snigger to learn that her past was kicking up trouble. She didn't want to call Penny; she didn't want her landlady having second thoughts about her decision to rent to her.

She texted Adam.

I fell and had a little accident at work and need a ride home from the hospital in Petaluma. Are you available? If not, I'll look around for someone who will give me a lift.

He responded immediately.

School's almost out so I'll come for you ASAP. It'll take about an hour to get there. Are you all right until then?

I'm okay. Text me from the parking lot and I'll come out. And thank you.

She went to Glynnis Carlson's office and sat outside her door, holding the plastic bag with her work clothes in it. It was a few minutes before the dragon lady opened her door and motioned Emma to come in. She indicated the chair in front of her desk. Then Glynnis folded her hands on top of her desk.

"Would you like to tell me what happened?"

"I'll try," Emma said. "My husband was Richard Compton. Do you know the name?"

Glynnis nodded. She explained that Clarice claimed her mother was a victim, but Emma had only met a few of Richard's clients socially; they were typically big investors or multimillionaires. She had seen a few in court and was surprised there was anyone from California, especially surprised to learn it was Clarice's mother, but the crime was Richard's. Not hers.

"You should have told me," Glynnis said.

"You wouldn't have hired me."

"I might've hired you and put you on the night shift. Well, spilled milk. Now, you have the prerogative of calling the police and filing assault charges. The nurse's aide who attacked you will be disciplined, possibly fired, but you can still—"

Emma shook her head. "It would be a mistake to draw attention to it. Plus, I do understand her anger, I really do. Thing is, I can't help her with this. I surrendered everything. I didn't want anything Richard had gotten by swindling people. There isn't anything."

"Why does she think there is?"

"There were a couple of books written about Richard's crime, lots of articles, news stories and internet posts speculating that I had some of his money hidden away. False, of course."

"Emma, you can't work with the public even though you've been exonerated of wrongdoing. Not for a long time. Do you understand that?"

"I'm trying to keep a low profile," she said.

"I'm applying for workers' compensation for you, Emma. I've taken you off the schedule. You should take two weeks and then my recommendation is that you resign and find something else. You'd do better in hotel housekeeping—less contact with the public."

"I'm not hurt that badly," she said. "I don't need two—"

"This isn't the place for you right now, Emma. You should take the time. You're entitled to it."

"But you're not going to fire me?" she asked.

"As far as I know you haven't done anything wrong. But I want you to think about whether this is the right job for you. I can put you on a different shift from the aide who beaned you with the bedpan, but I'm sure she has friends. Word will travel. Life could be difficult."

She almost laughed. "I might not have any choice…"

"While you're recovering, check out the hotels in the area. That's an option. You'd be working alone, not with a lot of other employees. You'd rarely come into contact with guests. Or…wait a second." She reached into her drawer and began to shuffle through business cards. "This woman has an excellent service—domestic, business, et cetera. But for God's sake, tell her the truth from the start. And if you need one, I'll write you a letter of recommendation. You've done a good job here in your brief employment."

Emma looked down at the card. Riley Kerrigan. Lord, she was everywhere. "Yes, ma'am," she said. The only advantage she could see was that she wouldn't have to explain her circumstances.

"Think things over. Call me with your decision, please."

"Yes, ma'am."

Emma went from Glynnis Carlson's office to the restroom. She took several deep breaths. Glynnis had been kind. Fair and kind. But Emma had to face facts; people would blame her. If they didn't blame her as a co-conspirator, they'd blame her for not taking action or for not testifying against Richard. They'd never believe she had nothing to say, nothing to add.

Keep your head, she told herself. *It's only been six months. This could go on awhile. You knew it wouldn't be easy, no matter where you went, no matter what you did.*

Then she put the bag holding her soiled work clothes in the trash can. She went to the locker room in the basement where they clocked in and grabbed her jacket. She wasn't going to wait around for Adam where other employees might pass her on their way to their cars. There was a nice little courtyard behind the emergency room. It was primarily there for those die-hard smokers left in the world, but no one was there at the moment. The sun was shining. It was a beautiful fall afternoon. She sat with her back to the door and talked to herself a little more.

It's only been six months. Some of his victims will be angry for the rest of their lives. Many will feel his death wasn't punishment enough. And there would always be those who believed she had some of that money, that she had a plan, that she was just waiting to emerge like a phoenix, rolling in dough, living the high life. *It's only been six months so don't cry.*

But silent tears streamed down her cheeks.

A few minutes had passed when she heard the door behind her open. She heard a little rustling, some footsteps, then a man walked past her. He was carrying a cellophane-wrapped bouquet, hanging down at his side. That was the rustling she'd heard—the cellophane. He walked all the way to the end of the courtyard then turned back toward her. He glanced at her briefly and sat on a bench several feet away and didn't meet her eyes. He was looking at his knees.

She gave her eyes a little wipe.

He looked up. "Bad day?" he asked.

She nodded. "You?"

"A little disappointing, but it'll all work out. What happened to you? You're a doctor?"

She shook her head. It was the scrubs, she realized.

"Ah. Nurse. I guess nurses can have all kinds of bad days."

She didn't respond because it wasn't required, except that she had this real problem with deception. No one would believe that, of course. She imagined almost everyone thought she was a liar.

Her cell phone chimed in her pocket. She took it out and saw Adam's text. "I have to go, my ride is here," she said. "I hope your day gets better."

He actually stood and she realized he was very handsome. Also tall and broad-shouldered. "I hope yours does, too. Here," he said, holding out the bouquet. "Take these. They'll go in the trash otherwise."

"Can't you take them home to your wife?"

"No wife."

"Your mother? Daughter? Sister?"

He smiled, improving his looks even more. "Nah. Here. Enjoy." She just stood there. "Come on, someone just did something nice for you. Take them."

She did. She said thank you. She went to Adam's SUV in the parking lot and climbed in the passenger seat.

He eyed the flowers. "Parting gifts?" he asked. And she burst into tears.

chapter *six*

Adam knew something was wrong. Something more than "I fell at work." He wasn't sure how he knew, but he knew. He stopped on the way to the hospital and picked up a couple of large mocha coffees with heavy cream. When he asked Emma what had happened, there was a lot of incoherent blubbering and he decided it was probably best to drive rather than sit in the parking lot while she emoted. And emoted.

He picked up a few things—someone had identified her, recognized her, threw a ripe bedpan at her head. There was a lot of whimpering about how she hadn't known, hadn't been complicit, everyone thought her a gold digger, a liar. She ended with some incoherent bawling about the disgusting state of her hair, comments that caused his eyes to widen in shock. What did this have to do with hair?

He found a nice park and pulled into the lot in the shade of a colorful tree. He handed her some tissues and after she'd made use of them, gave her the coffee. And the world slowed down and she began to just talk about it.

Adam had a feeling he was going to hell for this, but he wanted her to get this issue resolved, in her mind, at least emotionally, because he just couldn't pursue her the way he'd like to until that happened. She just wasn't ready. She wasn't moving on yet. Everything was so unsettled for her. And that had more to do with what Emma thought of *herself* than the people who might think badly of her.

"Thank God I ran into you at the burger joint," she said tearfully. "Just take me home, please, Adam. I didn't mean to unload on you."

"Nah, we're not going home yet. You're going to have some coffee, calm down and we'll just talk awhile."

"I'm sure you don't need all this chaos clogging up your mind…"

"My mind is fine," he said. "I'm a little worried about yours. It seems like maybe you're still feeling confused, out of control. Vulnerable. Victimized."

"Wouldn't you?" she returned defensively.

"Probably. But I want you to think about something, Emmie. Lack of power comes from lack of knowledge. Unless I'm totally off base here, you're still completely confused about what happened to you, how it happened, what to do about it now."

"I don't know what you're getting at," she said.

"Have you seen a counselor?" he asked.

"What kind of counselor?" she asked.

"Okay, I'm just guessing here, but I think you're still in shock. Maybe you have a little PTSD because you're not advancing beyond the shock."

He actually smiled slightly when he noticed she was looking at him with wide, startled eyes.

"PTSD isn't limited to war veterans, Emmie. Anyone who's been through a trauma qualifies. With a war veteran it might be a car backfiring that sends them into a series of PTSD symptoms—anger, sleeplessness, fear, panic, phobia, so on. For the victim of emotional abuse it might be facial expressions, certain comments, another's rage or threat. You should check this out, see a counselor."

"Listen," she said earnestly, scooting forward in her seat and turning in his direction. "I don't have the money for a counselor and I have health insurance for emergencies, but no one, I mean *no one*, is ever going to offer me discounted therapy because I suffered through kissing goodbye to millions of dollars after living like a queen for years."

"*Victim*," he said. "You are a victim. And you were probably a victim then, not a queen. You need some help. I'll check around. I might find someone, you never know. I know everyone—I've been teaching half their kids for fifteen years. But while I look, you might want to do some reading. From what you say, you still have so much mystery about what happened to you, you can't even figure out how you ended up in this mental-emotional minefield and there must be some kind of explanation. If there's not a clear explanation, there might be enough information out there to help you draw some conclusions. Hit the library. Read those books written by other people who think they've drawn conclusions. Find out who *they* think you are. And who they think your husband was."

She was shaking her head. "You have no idea what you're suggesting, how painful that is. Just the little excerpts are horrible."

"I know."

"You know? How do you know?"

"I read about it all," he said with a shrug. "Lots of theories about your late husband. About you. Varying theories."

"Why?" she asked softly. "Why would you read that trash?"

"Emmie, I'm a science teacher. We investigate. We look

shit up." Then he gave her a wan smile. "I'm just suggesting, since you can't escape it, maybe it makes sense to face it."

"I thought I'd been facing it for the last several years," she said. "I was in the apartment when Richard blew his brains out, after all. I had to hide from angry plaintiffs. I had to watch the house stripped of personal possessions. I—"

"You wanted it behind you, and who could blame you. Now that the whole fiasco is part of your identity and you have to live with it, would it help to understand it better? Like, what kind of man was he, really? Because you don't actually know, do you? You've said that had you known, you would have run for your life. So what do you know about sociopaths? Because that's my guess. He was a sociopath."

"What do *you* know about sociopaths?" she asked.

He shook his head. "Just a little bit, but I admit to being fascinated. I think when they were passing out consciences they missed a few people but they gave the surplus to me— my conscience seems to work overtime." He reached for her hand. "If you understood, at least as much as possible, could you be at peace?"

"I don't know."

"Find out," he suggested. "I'll help if I can. I love research. And I love talking to you. But first things first. You need a few days of rest and ice on your head."

"And my butt," she added.

"Did they x-ray that part?"

"No. They said if it remains painful to come back in, but it's already better from just a couple of Advil."

"Then let's keep moving forward. It's time to call Riley and see if you can get a job. It doesn't have to be a long-term job. But you have to have something..."

"Oh, Adam..."

"She'll protect you, Emmie. She knows how hard it is to start over, to rebuild your life after you've hit bottom."

"I can't believe she'd actually help me," she said.

"Sure she would. In fact, if she doesn't that would mean I don't know my sister at all. And that's not possible."

"Does she know we've been in touch lately?" Emma asked.

"She knows I ran into you at the burger joint. She knows we had a glass of wine and I gave you her business card. That's all she knows. In fact, I never mentioned we'd talked after you and Jock broke up, after Maddie was born…"

"It was more than a few times," Emma said. "And why didn't you tell her?"

He took a moment. "I didn't call you all those years ago for Riley and if I'd told her we talked, she would have asked a lot of questions about how you felt about her, how you felt about your situation, your feud, for lack of a better word. It would've been all about her and her relationship with you. That's not why I called you. You were around my house for years, all your growing-up years. I called you for *me*."

"Oh, Adam," she said softly.

"And same goes for you. Every time I called, it didn't take long to get around to Riley. Riley and Jock. Riley and you. Even after years had passed. I'll say one thing for you and Riley—you have some amazing stamina, keeping that tired old feud alive this long. It's still got some energy—you got tears in your eyes when I introduced you to Maddie."

"No," she said, shaking her head. "I mean, yes, that's true, I almost cried. Can you keep a confidence? What am I asking, of course you can. You haven't even told Riley how much we've talked since I've been back. It wasn't because Maddie should've been my child. Not at all, even though anything would have been preferable to where I landed in the end. Lord, what would I have done, pregnant with only Rosemary to lean on? No, it was because on top of everything else I went through with my husband, my marriage, it turns out I'm also infertile."

Well damn, Adam thought. It was his turn to be shocked speechless.

Three days later Emma was introduced to Lucinda Lopez, family, marriage and individual counselor. "It's the first time Adam has ever asked a favor of me," she said. "He was my first friend in teaching, a great teacher. I was not such a great teacher but I think I'm a good counselor."

"You didn't like teaching?" Emma asked.

"It paid the bills and I did an adequate job. I know I did all that was required of me. But there are some teachers, like Adam, who instinctively know how to inspire. He might've grown some real scientists. So—he tells me you're on a very limited income but in need of counseling. I haven't read your intake form yet—does that describe you?"

"I'm on workers' comp right now and looking for a new job because… Well, that job isn't going to work out. And the reason for that is the same as the reason I need counseling."

"All right, we'll get right to it. But before we take a lot of time on the story, tell me what you can afford. It's very important that you pay something for your counseling, that you make it in some way a priority. At any time you might decide it's not working for you, and that's entirely up to you, but please understand—if it's free, you won't value it. Make an effort, please, not for me—I'm not in need. For you. Your results will be better if you stretch yourself. If you commit."

"I don't know. I don't know how often I'll be seeing you. Can you help me with it?"

"The cost of the session? Sure. I provide a sliding scale based on income. Here's the graph," she said.

Emma looked at it. She was taken aback by the numbers there, which ranged from thirty-five dollars for a one-hour session to one hundred twenty-five. Presumably, she'd try to meet with the counselor at least twice a month. Even seventy dollars cut deeply into a budget as tight as hers.

"We better get right to it," Emma said.

"I'm ready whenever you are," she said.

Emma launched into her story, the condensed version. That took fifteen minutes, interrupted by a few questions from Lucinda, merely for clarification. It took only that long for Lucinda's face to begin to seem soft and accessible to Emma. She was a very pretty Mexican woman with just the slightest threading of silver in her pitch-black hair, the deepest black eyes, the softest smile. Her voice was likewise soft, but very confident and gracious.

When Emma had brought Lucinda up to the present, the counselor said she'd like to go back in time a bit, to before Emma met her husband.

"How far back?" Emma asked.

"I'm flexible," Lucinda said. "Take me back to a time that seemed pivotal in your life. A time of change, maybe? A time that required a great deal of you? A period of adjustment and a shift in your priorities. Does anything stand out?"

She thought for a moment. Then she said, "The year after high school. When I went away to college. A year after my father died."

"Good. Try, if you can, to tell me not just the events that you think caused a major change in your life, but how those significant events made you feel then and how remembering them makes you feel now."

"We may run out of time," Emma said.

"And try, if you can, not to worry about the time. We don't have to do it all today. In fact, a great deal is achieved in counseling when you leave me with things you'd like to think about. Because, Emma, I'm not going to solve your problems. You are. I'm just here to direct the traffic."

When Emma left, she hugged Lucinda. "Do you think I'm completely crazy?" she asked.

"I think you're remarkable. I'm so glad we met. Be sure to thank Adam for me."

Emma called several hotel chains to ask about job availability and each one invited her to fill out an application and possibly be called back for an interview. No one she talked to seemed interested in hiring. She looked in all the newspaper ads and online for employment opportunities, as she had been doing since the day she returned, and nothing promising turned up there, either.

She tried to bolster herself to call Riley and ask for help.

Sometimes words fade over time, sometimes they fester, blister, even swell. Burned into Emma's mind was when she screamed at Riley, "I don't ever want to speak to you or see you again in my life!"

"We can find a way to get beyond this! We said we'd never let a guy get between us!"

"Yeah, until he was *my* guy! Well, he's all yours now! I wouldn't take him back if he begged me. Not with your stink on him!"

"You'll be sorry you let this ruin us! You know you'll never have a friend like me again in your life!"

"I hope to God *not*!" Emma had hurled.

And now she was going to ask Riley for a job.

"I'm so sorry," the receptionist said. "We don't have any openings right now. But if you'd like to leave a name and number, I can call you as soon as something opens up."

"Sure," she said. "I'm Emma Shay and…"

"Oh, Ms. Shay, I reserved an appointment for you. Can you come into the office to meet with Ms. Kerrigan Thursday afternoon at two?"

"Um. Sure," she said. Was that a good sign? Adam had said Riley would help her, but what if he was wrong about that?

Sixteen years ago, right after screaming she hoped she'd never have a friend like Riley again, Riley had screamed at her, "Emmie, *please*! Please try to understand! I didn't mean for this to happen and I'm sorry. I can't lose your friendship!"

With a sneer, Emma shot back, "So get Jock to be your friend. Slut!"

Of course, Emma hadn't known Riley was pregnant but would knowing that have softened her words? Nah. It probably would have made her even more hateful. Emma didn't think she'd ever forgive Riley for what she'd done. But if she were Riley, she would never be able to forget those cruel words.

Why would Riley help her now?

She wore the same conservative but stylish skirt and sweater she'd been wearing to every interview. They were Chanel, brown wool with a little pleat in the front of the skirt right on her knee and a soft mauve sweater set. She wore hose and pumps, carried a matching Dooney & Bourke bag. Would she think Emma had obviously survived quite well, dressed so? The Riley she had known had never had such nice clothes.

Walking into Riley's office was one of the hardest things she'd ever done. She reminded herself that she'd walked down the steps of the Federal Court Building to the flashing of cameras; she'd walked from a grave site to her car through a clot of photographers. She opened the outer office door and the secretary looked up. She smiled at the young woman. "Hello. I'm Emma Shay and I have an appointment with Ms. Kerrigan."

"You can go on in," Jeanette said. "She's expecting you."

Emma gave a couple of courtesy taps and opened the door. Riley was concentrating on her computer screen. Without looking up she said, "Come in. Sit down. Give me a second."

Emma sat in one of the chairs facing the desk. She held her purse on her lap and crossed her legs at the ankle, her legs angled to her right. When Riley did look at her, her eyes rested for a long time on the purse.

Riley turned the screen away, folded her hands on the desk and focused on Emma. "Hello, Emma. How are you?" Riley asked.

"I'm all right, thanks. You?"

"Very well, thanks. Am I to understand you're looking for a job?"

"Yes."

"You do understand this is a cleaning company? House-keeping?"

"Yes. I can provide a letter of recommendation. My last supervisor offered. She's the head of housekeeping at the hospital in Petaluma—Mrs. Carlson."

Riley's eyes grew round. "That carries some weight around here. I've known Glynnis for years. Why are you leaving the hospital?"

Emma was surprised then realized she shouldn't have been. Adam was very tight-lipped. "I had a fall. Actually, an angry person who claimed to be a victim of Richard's fraud threw something at me and I fell. I'm not hurt. I was checked in the emergency room. But Mrs. Carlson took me off the schedule, put me on workers' comp and suggested I get another job."

Riley was frowning.

"If you don't want to take a chance on that happening while I work for you—"

"That won't happen in my company. I know which of my

customers know each other, so I know where gossip travels. We have a policy that our crews, while polite and helpful, do not become enmeshed with the client—that's how they get taken advantage of. Our crews take only first names into the jobs, and the majority of the time the client isn't home and if they are, they stay out of the way. There should be no reason for much conversation that isn't germane to the work. We have a pretty strict contract so that additional work is arranged with the company in advance and an hourly charge is made. But what's easy about this system is—everything goes through me or my director of operations, Nick. That way you're never put upon to argue with the homeowner or business owner. You're going to have to be trained. Can you make it till the Monday after Thanksgiving? Because I don't have training on my schedule until then."

"I can start anytime. I went through a rigorous training at the hospital."

"You'll be trained again," she said firmly. "The last time I skipped training because the housekeeper was qualified I ended up buying a new microwave because she took steel wool to it. Besides, the culture of the company is as important as the policies and I want you to understand."

"Maybe I should clean offices..." Emma suggested.

"I don't have any openings in offices. Those are night jobs and they're pretty precious—a lot of my staff prefer them. They pay a little more and many of them have two jobs and children to take care of. All I have is residential. It's very hard work."

"I know how to work hard," Emma said.

"I'm going to put you with Makenna Rice for training. She's young, tough, not particularly personable, has impeccable standards, can handle anything that comes along and will work you hard. But at the end of the day you will be proud of the job you did."

"Thank you."

"Fourteen dollars an hour to start. If you're still around after ninety days, you'll get a two-dollar raise. I provide training, uniforms, sometimes transportation—I have a few company cars and vans—and health insurance. Not the greatest health insurance, but competitive with most corporate plans. You won't need it but I have a deal for a discount with a day care provider—a lot of my workers have small children not yet in school. Any chance you speak Spanish?"

Emma shook her head. "Some very rusty French."

"A shame. A lot of my workers are Mexican, here with work visas. But don't worry—I have plenty of bilingual workers and my director of operations speaks Spanish." She looked at her squarely. "You won't get any special treatment. Are you sure you want to do this?"

"Yes, I'm sure. I'm very grateful."

"I'll give you a job," Riley said. "But that's all."

"I don't expect anything," Emma said. "I didn't even expect this much. Really."

"Jeanette will get you started on the paperwork. It should only take twenty minutes. Then I'll next see you the Monday after Thanksgiving, this office, seven a.m. Bring a tote or backpack that holds your lunch, water or energy drink, snacks. Jeanette will tell you where to go to get your uniform. I'll pay for one per year."

"Thank you," Emma said again.

Riley stood. "Come into the conference room to fill out your application and accompanying paperwork."

"Riley, I didn't do it," she suddenly said. She shook her head. "I had nothing to do with Richard's fraud. I was too stupid to know what he was up to, but I wasn't involved."

"Of course you weren't. Anyone with a brain knows he started building his Ponzi empire ten years before he met you. Come with me." She opened the door on the right wall of her office, exposing a shiny table and eight chairs. "Have a seat. I'll get Jeanette."

Emma sat down and waited. The interview wasn't exactly comfortable but it wasn't as bad as it could've been. It must have given Riley great pleasure to have Emma crawling back, begging for work. A lot of people who didn't even know her would feel the same way—the uppity young trophy wife, paying the piper every day. Every hour. Every minute.

Riley's clothes weren't baggy and worn anymore, she thought. In fact, she looked wonderful. She was obviously buying her clothes in San Francisco. That was a Marco de Vincenzo suit, a little young and short for Riley, but she wore it well. If Emma was a betting woman she'd think Riley pulled that one out of the plastic just for her.

She finished filling out her forms and went back into Riley's office, knocking before opening the door. Riley was on the phone but gestured her in, pointing to the chair. While she waited, Jeanette peeked in. She was wearing her coat and had her purse strap over her shoulder, obviously leaving. She gave Riley a wave and Riley waved back.

Now it was just the two of them.

Riley finished her phone call and focused on Emma. "Any questions?"

"Not that I can think of. Thank you again."

"Not at all," Riley said in a businesslike manner. "See you on your start date. On time."

"Absolutely." She rose to go.

Emma was almost out the door.

"Emma?"

She turned back.

"Now we're even," Riley said without looking at her. "I have no more debt to pay to you."

Emma was stunned and frozen, speechless for a moment. She finally found her voice. "Do you think I'm keeping score? You didn't have to do this. You didn't have to hire me just because of something... We were *children!*"

"We're not anymore," Riley said. "We're not going to be friends but this thing between us... I'm done with it. But stay away from my brother."

And she was completely refocused on her computer screen.

Emma slowly closed the door behind her. But then she opened it again. "Wait a minute," she said. "Are you angry with *me*? Because I said some awful things to you and I regret it, but I think you have to bear responsibility for what you did."

"It's over," Riley said.

"Obviously not!" Emma shot back, rather more hotly than she intended.

"It was all regrettable," Riley said. "And I'm sure there's plenty of blame to go around."

"It might be helpful if I knew exactly what blame I'm expected to carry," Emma said.

"I'd rather it be over," Riley said, standing to face Emma. "Let's call it done."

"Oh, no, you don't—you started this up again. Riley, I didn't sleep with your boyfriend behind your back! What is your grudge? Because of those terrible things I said to you out of anger? If that's it—"

"That's not it," she insisted loudly. "I guess you were entitled. I understood why you'd be furious."

"Then what?"

"You wouldn't forgive me!" she said. Riley's eyes glistened and she held her lips in a tight line.

Emma was struck silent. She said the only thing that came to mind. "I was too hurt. Too angry."

"Over Jock?" Riley demanded. She gave a short laugh. "You hadn't even returned our calls in weeks! It's so hard to believe your broken heart was serious enough to sustain such a grudge. We were best friends for ten years!"

She shook her head. "I got over Jock in a few months. I let it go so long ago," Emma said.

"And it never once occurred to you to send a note or even a text saying let bygones be bygones?"

"Riley, I… No, it never did. I figured we were best parting ways. That was one helluva fight."

"Yes," Riley said softly. "And I begged. I groveled. I sent a dozen notes, left messages. You wouldn't respond. You wouldn't even hear my side of the story. And you lifted your nose in the air and walked away to a better life, better friends."

Emma shook her head. "Not for long," she said. "Is that really what's up your butt? That I didn't say you're forgiven? Didn't listen to your story? Want to tell me now?"

"Hah! Now I don't even want to think about it, but it sure as hell had staying power!"

Emma laughed hollowly. "We should've both been furious with Jock, not each other!"

"I was. I still am some days, but he's Maddie's father and I'm stuck with him. You, I'm not stuck with."

"No, you're not. I don't need your charity. Well, I do, but I wouldn't take it if I were starving. But are you still giving me a job?" Emma asked.

"Yes, and by God you better not fuck up. I built this company and it means a lot to me. You mess up and I'll fire you in a New York minute."

"I'll do my job," she said, turning to go. She turned back.

"Really, I might not have said anything, I was a little busy, but I forgave you a long time ago."

"And until I saw you, I didn't think it still mattered. I thought I'd learned never to let down my guard."

"What's this about your brother? What did you mean by that?"

Riley took a breath. "I'm happy to give you a job as long as you pull your weight and earn your paycheck. But I don't think it makes any sense for us to try friendship again. Obviously irreparable damage was done. That being said, I don't need to run into you at family gatherings."

"I see. I guess it could be problematic."

"Just don't put me in an awkward position with my family."

"Of course," Emma said. "We didn't exactly kiss and make up, but can we lay this to rest now? Start over as employee and employer?"

"Absolutely. Starting a week from Monday. Seven a.m."

Emma exited, softly closing the door behind her. But glutton for punishment that she was, she opened the door again. "You should probably thank me," she said. "If you hadn't been so pissed off at me and scared to death, you probably never would have built such a successful company."

"Don't hang your hat on that idea," Riley said. "I had a good start on it before Jock messed up my plans."

And that actually made Emma smile at her. "You were so much better off without me. Who knows? If we'd remained friends, I might've convinced you to let Richard help you invest your money."

Then she closed the door and left.

Riley sat at her desk for a long time, just still and quiet. The phone rang twice, she glanced at the caller ID that appeared on her computer monitor and let it go to voice mail.

Well, that was dirty, she thought to herself. It took them about ten minutes to be thrown back in time and fight like a couple of junkyard dogs, just like they had when they were thirteen. Only when they were teenagers their fights would be high and hot and over in ten minutes. That wasn't going to happen this time.

Well, that had only been about ten minutes. And it felt remarkably over. In fact, she felt a little tired, like coming down off a good run. She folded her arms on her desk and put her head down. That was the hardest thing she'd ever done, and she'd done some hard things. It wasn't fighting with Emma or giving her a job that was so difficult. It was seeing her, talking to her, taking her in, reconnecting with her, all the while knowing it could end up hurting her again.

Their history was so convoluted, so complex. From treasured childhood friends to bitter enemies, through a maze of anger, guilt, envy, pity. For the longest time Riley only wanted Emma to forgive her or at least join her in blaming Jock. She went through periods of terrible emotional pain and sadness. Then periods of such anger—if Emma loved Jock so much, why hadn't she even returned his calls in weeks? And when she saw a picture of Emma in her designer wedding gown in a carriage in Central Park, as beautiful and regal as any duchess while Riley was getting by scrubbing floors and balancing the books late at night, she wondered how Emma could still be mad that things didn't work out with Jock. Emma seemed to always land on her feet.

Then she witnessed, from afar, Emma's monumental fall. And it ripped her to shreds. But she didn't reach out. No, she had too much pride for that. Emma hadn't reached out when Riley was struggling and feeling so alone.

I was hurt at least as much! Can't she see that? That it was all so hard?

They had always been there for each other, until that first semester of college. *You didn't have to be so mean*, she said to herself. But Riley wanted to be clear—this was her company, her business; it was a job, not an invitation to reconcile or renew the friendship. She would never beg again.

But at long last, she'd gotten it out. She said her piece. She saw Emma's surprise and remorse painted on her face. Emma said she was sorry and that she'd forgiven Riley long ago—it was done. It was really done. Neither of them would go back but maybe now they could really move forward.

Riley shut everything down, switched the phones to forward to her cell, grabbed her purse and headed for the parking lot.

chapter *seven*

Riley went to Starbucks, a place that saw her at least once a day.

She rarely sat around inside. She was usually in and out and on her way—always so much to do. There were those who camped in Starbucks for hours, doing their emails or writing something or studying. People who didn't have to be somewhere every minute. Not Riley. She never relaxed.

She bought a newspaper on her way inside. She had a lot to process, something she could do while hiding behind a newspaper, the great barrier.

It was such a cold November day—a hot coffee with heavy cream sounded good. And there was a nice little table by the window that looked out on the patio that Starbucks shared with the deli. She smiled at a couple of people she didn't know but saw in there a lot. Then she settled behind the paper.

Women, she thought. Difficult, complex, emotional creatures. She should know. Not only was she difficult and complex, she also had far more women employees than men. She had those teams of three or four females who found issues they couldn't get beyond just because of something that was said or a look they didn't like or maybe a little power struggle. She had to mediate all the time. Or Nick did. Nick was only good at getting results because he didn't get what was going on with the women so he just scared them. "Can you work this out? Or do I separate the whole unit and scatter you around on different crews? Because you might not like your new crewmates any better. If you can't get along, then do your job and don't talk to each other, but you'd damn well better communicate on job issues. Are we all clear?"

She smiled thinking about that. A typical father-to-little-girls approach. He might as well say, "Since I can't understand what you're all upset about, just stop it."

Nick took problems getting the job done properly a lot more seriously than he regarded bickering. But women, ah, they could dig in. Grudges between women could last centuries. And they were very personal—a woman who wasn't usually annoyed could be deeply offended by an offhand remark about the choices of her teenager. "If you'd tell that lazy kid of yours he's not getting free rent anymore, I bet he'd get off his ass and get a job or go to school." *Pow.* Instant feud.

Sexist as it was, this sort of thing happened less often with men. Oh, they had their fights and their feuds, no question about it, and were even less likely to have dialogue that worked it out. They might blow up but they were less prickly and it was rare for them to obsess.

Riley, tough and smart and successful, had obsessed about Emma for years. She felt wedged between two extremes— being furious with Emma and feeling guilty over what she'd done. She'd tried so hard to make up with Emma, to beg her forgiveness! And Emma turned her back. Now, when Emma was down and out, Riley was supposed to be the benevolent one? Looking at both of their lives, from that point till now, things had just been…awry. Off. Emma had hooked up with a bad man and Riley? No man. At. All.

"Excuse me," a male voice said. "Is this chair taken?"

What perfect timing, she thought. A man. She lowered her newspaper, trying to think how she would politely say she didn't want to share the table or have a conversation.

"Hey," he said, smiling handsomely. "It's you."

"I…ah…"

He put out a hand and didn't let her finish. "Logan. Logan Danner. We've never officially met, but we've run into each other at the grocery store at least five times, which means you either live or work around here."

Don't do it, she told herself. She took his hand. "Riley. I, ah…I work not too far from here and am addicted to coffee that costs seven dollars a cup. Bad habit."

He laughed and sat down. "I guess it could be worse. We could run into each other at a crack house… Now, that would be bad."

"Look…"

"Oh, I'm sorry," he said. "You weren't looking for company, my mistake. I'll just make this a to-go cup and catch you someday at the deli counter…"

"No, I'm sorry," she said with a heavy sigh. "I was just trying to shake off a problem I had at work. Go ahead. Take the chair. But I might not be very conversational."

He didn't hesitate. "I'm a good listener, if you feel like talking."

"No, thanks. Let's stick to the price of melons."

"I'm also a good talker, if you'd rather not. Or we can pass the time as if we're alone." He reached down and pulled a small laptop out of a canvas shoulder bag. He put it on the table and opened it up. He turned it on. He sipped his coffee. He peeked at her around the screen.

She laughed lightly. "You're being very obvious."

He gazed over the screen. "In what way?"

"Are you trying to get my attention? Interest me?"

"I am," he said. "How'm I doing?"

"You're actually terrible at it," she said, laughter in her voice. "You verge on annoying. More to the point, we keep running into each other. Are you stalking me?"

"That would be rude," he said. "Not to mention a felony. Well, it becomes a felony if it's threatening, but it's a misdemeanor when it's just rude."

"And you know these things how?"

"I'm a police detective."

She started to laugh. "Oh, man, the only pickup line that works better than that is being a Navy SEAL."

He shifted his weight around and pulled out his wallet. He flipped it open. Sure enough, badge and ID. "Hold on, there," she said. She reached into her purse and pulled out her phone, poising over the open wallet to snap a picture.

He put his hand over hers, redirecting the phone lens. "Does this mean you're going to find out if I'm real before you go out with me?"

She shrugged. "I might find out if you're real before I give you advice on melons again or warn you off the macaroni salad in the deli. A date has never occurred to me. Or interested me."

He let go of the phone, allowing her to take the picture. "You're brutal. Knock yourself out."

She snapped the picture. "What kind of detective are you?" she asked.

"Property crimes."

"And that is?"

"Be careful about making friendly conversation, Riley. You might be acting less like a meanie and more like a girl. Property crimes, burglary. Someone stole your computer and your diamond ring and I'm going to get them back for you. They did not rob you—robbery is when there's a weapon involved."

"A deadly weapon?" she asked, intrigued.

He raised one brow. "Any weapon could be deadly. A spoon could be deadly if you know how to use it. Property crimes is property stolen from private property—your house, your business, your car, your person, without the spoon, of course." He grinned stupidly.

"And why do I keep running into you?"

"This little shopping center is between work and my house. And I'm in the field a lot. But running into you all the time is one of the perks. So—what do you think? Dinner? Hike? Bike ride? Conventional date?"

"Coffee," she said. "We're having coffee. I don't date."

"I didn't see a ring..."

She shook her head. "Not married, just not dating."

"You have to have a reason," he informed her.

"No," she said. "I don't."

"Do you mind if I ask—what do you do?"

"I do mind, but I'll tell you, but only because I think you really are a policeman. I own a small business. Plus, I'm a single mother and have an elderly mother. So you see, very busy."

He closed the computer and leaned an elbow on it. "Look, I admit I've been hanging out at the grocery store a lot since you advised me on produce. Can't this be any easier? I'm overstocked in melons. What do you like to do besides work? Maybe we could go for a run? Play catch in the park? Meet for coffee a lot?"

"Why?" she asked.

He tilted his head. "I'm attracted to you?"

"Was that a question?" she asked.

"I haven't been out with a woman in a while. Well, haven't

had a date with a woman. My partner is a woman, married to a great big firefighter, three little kids. My sister and ex-wife are best friends and believe me, their attempts at fixing me up are miserable..."

"Oh, God, that must be interesting! Your sister and your ex-wife?"

"It's awful. But see, I'm interesting," he said, triumphant. He looked around. "Would you like something to eat? Doughnut?"

She laughed at him because he was so ridiculous. Also, undeniably cute. "So it's true—cops and doughnuts."

"I was thinking of you. I've had my quota today. Come on, Riley. Let's just plan something. It can be public, daylight, completely safe and platonic. I'll show you my gun," he said, lifting his eyebrows, Groucho Marx style.

She laughed again. "No," she said. She stood up. "See you in produce," she said, walking out.

It took him a moment to get his computer put away in his canvas bag and grab his coffee, following her. "Hang on," he yelled. He caught up with her and handed her a business card. "This will make your mission easier."

She looked at it. *Sgt. Logan Danner, Santa Rosa Police, Property Crimes.* Along with a phone number and extension.

"Would you like my cell number?" he asked.

"No."

"It's on the card anyway. Come on, Riley. I bet we'd have fun."

She turned before getting in her car. "No. And if you follow me, I'll call your boss. I'll tell on you."

"Hey, no worries. My boss likes me," he said.

Riley headed for home. But she smiled the whole way. He was handsome in a very hot way and adorably funny. He was tempting.

Whoa, Riley, she thought. *Really? Tempting? Now that's a first.* It wasn't as if she hadn't been flirted with or asked out on a date before. She'd actually been out a few times—nothing to write home about. Definitely no relationship stuff. It wasn't frequent since she hung out at work, at home, with Maddie and her mom, shopping for food and clothes, taking the occasional run…

Did he know about the running? Oh, if he'd been watching her, she was going to turn him in to his boss *and* tell Adam. Adam was *very* protective.

But for the first time in many, many years, she was feeling like maybe a casual friendship with a man might interest her. She wondered if seeing Emma and having that first confrontation behind her had anything to do with her change of mood.

But really, did he know about her running? Because if he did, she was going to deal harshly with him.

Still, she chuckled to herself. And I have his badge number.

She'd done the right thing with Emma. She'd had it out with her and given her a job. From now on she'd be nice; she'd be professional; she'd keep a safe space between them.

And maybe really get on with her life.

At last.

So Riley had drawn her line in the sand, Emma thought. It was clear—there were still some hard feelings, some resentment. Emma sulked for a minute, fighting melancholy. There was something about women and friendship that could run so deep, so personal, it was almost harder to say goodbye to a relationship like that than it was to break up with a man. She missed that friendship with Riley, so intimate and trusted. She grieved that it was forever gone.

But then she began to lighten up. She'd been beaned with a bedpan, for God's sake. Let Riley be a little superior—she'd survived better than Emma had. They weren't going to be friends. But Emma had a job. A decent job. And she had no doubt that tough little Riley wouldn't let anything happen to her. *That won't happen in my company!*

Once she settled that in her mind, she found herself almost breathless with excitement about her new job. There was no question in her mind, it would be physically demanding and dirty and she was ecstatic. She was sure it wouldn't be long—only days, perhaps—before this pink cloud would burst and the reality would settle in—she had signed on for hard work. But in the moment, it felt good on so many levels. She *wanted* hard work; it would help her scour from her past the stain of all that excess she had indulged in but never deserved. It would prove she could take on tough work and survive. In a way it felt like the hard labor she had earned. Her penance, though she was innocent. She was not innocent of loving wealth, however. And she had made trade-offs along the way. Not amoral or unethical trade-offs, but she had accepted her busy, sometimes indifferent husband, accepted loneliness, made excuses, ignored red flags, and all along she'd wondered, secretly and silently, what was wrong. And wondered, if he'd been penniless, would she have reconsidered? For that alone she should atone.

It would be dirty work for a clean paycheck, beholden only to her effort. And it would be safe.

To her astonishment, Riley made her feel safe. Riley's self-righteous stubbornness alone smoothly and effortlessly guaranteed a secure and protected work environment and... Dear God. And...Emma *trusted her.* After sixteen years of lamenting she could never really trust again, who did she put her faith in but the very person she feared could betray her. The very person who didn't want her for a friend.

"She gave me a job," she said into the phone to Adam. Her voice was quiet and breathy, astonished and secretive.

"Of course she did," he said.

"You didn't even tell her how often we'd been in touch," she said.

"I told you—I'm not interested in trying to reunite the two of you. How about a glass of wine to celebrate?"

"Can we meet at that wine bar?" she asked.

He chuckled. "I think instead I'll bring a bottle and some fruit and cheese over to your place, if you'll let me. I have to work in the morning. It can't be a late night."

"I should get the wine and cheese," she said. "After all you've done to help me…"

"You can do it next time. I'll stop on the way over. You'll have to tell me where you are."

Emma had had many boyfriends and one husband, but she'd never had a man she could talk to like she could Adam. He had evolved in exactly the way she would have expected him to. Looks aside, though his hard good looks must melt female bones all over Sonoma County, he was also smart, mature and engaging. So well-spoken, as one would expect a teacher to be; when he began to talk, he had her complete attention. He was also funny, making her laugh. And earnest—that was paramount. If he talked about his family, about Maddie, Riley or his mother, both the seriousness and sincerity of what he was saying rang through. *Mom hasn't changed since you knew her. Family is still everything to her and it's obvious she's nervous about idleness, having always worked hard. Now that she's finally been convinced not to work all the time, she volunteers. She does meals-on-wheels almost every day and sometimes she fosters rescue animals until they find a permanent home.* And, *Riley takes her achievements in stride but she takes her failures, however small, way too seriously. She's the overachiever in the family.* And, *If there's anyone in our family who understands pure joy, it's Maddie. She loves everyone, all of us, including Jock, and without any effort, with such simple authenticity, makes sure each one of us knows it.*

I live in a family of women, which can take its toll but keeps me sharp. I can't get away with anything. They lean on me, crowd me, are overprotective of me and demanding of me. They're in my business all the time. And I find I like it that way.

Emma wondered what it must be like to live with a man as strong and sensitive as Adam. She couldn't stop looking at his hands, scarred with hard work, so beautiful and strong. She learned he had worked in the vineyards, scarring his knuckles on the rough, hard vines. Also construction, where he learned enough building and carpentry to do all the fixing up and renovation to both his own house and his mother's—that work had also taken its toll on his hands. Those hands represented to Emma that he hadn't ever taken the easy way, but only traveled the path that demanded stamina and hard work. Honest work, something that had come to mean everything to her.

She was so grateful for him. Just knowing he was her friend, that he was in her camp, gave her a feeling of peace and comfort she hadn't felt in so long. She adored him. But at the end of the evening, when he was leaving, when he leaned toward her, she jumped away from him. She just couldn't let him muddy his relationships and his sturdiness by getting too close to someone like her. "No, no…" she said in a whisper.

"Sorry, Emmie. That was insensitive of me," he said. "You're recently widowed…"

"No, it's not that, it's…"

"Shhh," he said, putting a finger to her lips. "I'm with you. We don't want to complicate our friendship."

"Right," she said, because she was at a loss as to how to explain herself. If she'd ever wanted to be kissed, it was now.

THE LIFE SHE WANTS   123

And if she ever wanted a certain person to kiss her, it was him. But it wasn't friendship with him she feared complicating. It was hurting him just by being in his life. She couldn't bear the thought of being Adam's problem.

That's when he smiled, looked at his watch and said, "I've stayed way too late."

"No," she said, shaking her head. "Not at all. I hope we'll do this again very soon. Very soon."

"We will."

Then he was gone.

After having a conversation with Penny, Emma made some plans for her little bungalow. She was on a mission. She had very little time before starting her new job and she put it to good use. First of all, she bought a couple of cans of paint—a pale yellow, a pale blue and a nice supply of extra-light tan, a kind of heavy cream color. She wasn't exactly overconfident but she did feel she could spend a little on renewing her digs since she was absolutely determined she'd be able to keep her job indefinitely. As long as she stayed out of Riley's way.

She painted her bathroom to match the towels she'd brought with her. One wall in her tiny living room became yellow and the alternating walls the tan so light it was off-white. She was all over the small towns in Sonoma County on Saturday, haunting the garage sales, and found colorful throw pillows, a decorative blanket to cover the sofa back, small wicker shelves she could stack her bathroom towels on, a beautiful basket she could fill with fruit or gourds for the small table, a couple of bronze picture frames and a framed print for the bedroom wall. It was a Matisse and the frame was excellent. She found wood trays she loved and could use to serve wine and cheese because now she knew she'd have guests sometimes. She also found some beautiful wineglasses and dessert plates she didn't need but couldn't resist. And a distressed white denim jacket called out to her. "I gained weight," the lady who was selling it told her. "It's hardly been worn."

"Well, you look amazing and I lucked into a great jacket," Emma told her. So the woman threw in a navy blue scarf, a thin, soft knit that was almost pashmina quality.

The weather was perfect for walking the old-fashioned, tree-lined neighborhoods. Children still played in the street around here; there were a lot of front porches on old brick two-stories and people were out raking leaves, watching kids, chatting over fences. It was sunny, low sixties, and grocers put their late fruits and vegetables outside in large racks. She couldn't resist apples, zucchini, tomatoes, a couple of peppers, a fistful of green beans and a few onions. One of the things she had missed most in New York were the vegetable stands along the roads, owned and operated by the farmers who grew the stuff—it was as if you could taste the sunshine and hard work.

When she went home, she was pleased to see her little bungalow already had a newer, more cheerful look, more like the old Emma. She went back to the hardware store. She painted her little table bright yellow, one of the chairs bright blue and one Irish green.

It looked a bit like a summer house, she thought.

She invited Lyle to an antipasto and wine dinner so she could show off her new-old house, including the framed picture of Emma, Lyle and Riley, cutting up at a pep rally in high school.

"This is interesting," he said, picking it up. "Does this bode well?"

"I was saving this for our toast, but I can tell you now. Riley gave me a job in her company."

"Ah," Lyle said. "So at least one of you is open to reconciliation."

"Oh, don't get too excited. She was very cool, very professional and made it clear I wouldn't be getting any special treatment. We're not going to be friends. It's a job, that's all. But I'm very grateful. She'll be paying me almost twice per hour what I've earned since I've been back. Plus benefits."

Thanksgiving, possibly the last holiday she'd have off for a long time, was such a pleasure, such a breath of fresh air after the holidays she'd had the past several years, she wished it would never end. She not only bought wine for the meal at Penny's and had Lyle create a lovely centerpiece, she also spent the entire morning helping Penny clean the house, prepare the turkey and other food and appoint the table. It was so companionable, so stress-free.

"I wish I'd had a daughter," Penny said as they worked in the kitchen together.

"Do you have any children?" Emma asked.

"No," she said. "Bruce and I had a happy marriage, but we weren't blessed."

"When did he pass away?"

"Oh, it's been over twenty years now. It was awful hard at first, having no kids, you know…"

"I'm so sorry, Penny," she said. "You must miss him so much."

"Sometimes. But then I get ready for a celebration like this and I forget I was once married for thirty-five years and hardly did anything without him. We're all widows, in a way…"

"In a way?" Emma asked.

"Well, Susan is divorced from her second husband, a long while ago, but her first is now dying, hanging on by a thread, the old bastard. She never did get really free of him. Dorothy is divorced and her ex-husband finally kicked. Ew, he was a son of a bitch. Marilyn lost her darling husband a few years ago. They hadn't been married too long. Married late, had a good decade together. She's pulled it together pretty well. Not a one of us ever got a daughter. The injustice..."

Emma smiled. "I'll be your proxy daughter," she said. "I've been on the lookout for a quartet of hip mothers."

"We've been known to cause trouble," Penny said, grinning.

"Even better," Emma said.

chapter *eight*

Adam called Emma the Friday after Thanksgiving. He asked her if she'd like to drive up the road to Napa and have lunch at one of the vineyard bistros before she settled into her new job. "If you're free tomorrow," he said.

"That would be perfect," she said. "I'm anxious to hear about your Thanksgiving. And to tell you about mine!"

"Great. I'll pick you up around eleven-thirty."

He didn't linger on the phone. He was relieved by her cheerful mood, by her quick acceptance. He'd been worried that Emma might've been put off by his advances, concerned about what he wanted. He'd moved too fast, leaning toward her for a kiss. God, this was a whole new ball game! And so awkward. He was thirty-seven—he didn't think about things like this. First-date kisses were routine. Expected, even. A woman would think she didn't appeal to you if you didn't at least try… But Emma was different.

She wasn't even close to ready to entertain the notion of a man in her life and when she would be, there was no reason he should expect it to be him. He told himself that her husband hadn't been gone that long. He probably hadn't been a husband to her for at least three years, but her ordeal wasn't far behind her. She'd only been back in California for a few months.

He tried to remind himself: she'd come home, but she hadn't come home to him.

He intended to back off. She'd find her footing. He hoped she'd show signs of recovery pretty soon because he was dying to get his arms around her.

Amazing, how that feeling had come right back to him. The moment he saw her he was filled with it, like stepping back in time. When she'd finally come of age so many years ago, when it would finally be permissible to pursue her, there couldn't have been more complications if they were at war. She was in Seattle, he was struggling to keep up with work and school, then *bam!*—Riley was having Jock's baby. So he did what he had to do—he reeled the feelings back in.

But Emma never came home. She went from college in Seattle to New York. He'd just been working up his courage for a trip to New York to see her when she'd announced she was engaged. To the most wonderful man in the world.

He was hoping for a second chance, but Adam was realistic. This might be something he'd always wanted, but that didn't mean Emma did. Then he picked her up and she was absolutely alive with happiness to see him. She met him with a hug, her eyes glittering and her smile so beautiful. All the way to Napa, she chattered like a girl about what she'd been doing—painting, decorating, hitting all the garage sales she could find.

"I even bought this jacket," she said, laughing. "Used clothing from a garage sale! I hope Richard is spinning in his grave!"

"Emma!" he said, laughing at her.

"Is it too much to hope he's being eaten by worms by now?"

"What's gotten into you today?" he asked.

"It's hanging out with those merry widows, I think. You should hear the way they talk, especially about departed and ex-husbands who were not the best. They're incorrigible and I love them. Penny and I played host for Thanksgiving and we had a blast. It wouldn't have had to be much to outshine the holidays of the last several years, let me tell you, but it was fantastic!"

"I hadn't even thought of that," he said. "I'm sure your life the last few years didn't include festive holiday celebrations."

"It didn't before, either," she said. "Before the indictments came down, holidays were rich family showcases—parties, celebrations and open houses meant to outdo each other. I got into that, you know? I'm a designer by trade. It was once my goal to design and decorate big hotels, which included ostentatious holiday themes. There wasn't anyplace better than New York for that. But memorable family holidays that filled a person with comfort and joy?" She shook her head. "Richard didn't even invite his family to our home. He was very strategic. He gave them first-class tickets to the islands so they'd be conveniently out of town."

When they arrived at the restaurant she stopped talking while they were led to a pretty table for two in a small arbor. It was a little chilly in the shade, but there were a few space heaters around the patio. Even though it was a holiday week-end, there weren't many for lunch. The tasting rooms seemed to be overflowing and plenty of people were visiting the valley, but the patio of the small restaurant was quiet. Adam couldn't have planned it better if he'd called ahead and asked for a special table.

Emma was so animated, enjoying herself so much, you'd think it was her first lunch date. Maybe it almost was, he thought. Once they'd ordered she wanted to know all about Thanksgiving at his house, every detail, down to the kind of stuffing June made. So he told her everything, including the fact that Jock dropped by to see Maddie and stayed for dessert.

"I'm so glad to hear that," she said. "Does he try to be a good father?"

"He's a good dad, I think," Adam said. "His parenting has been complicated by the fact he lived in Sacramento for a few years for work. Then there was a brief marriage to a woman with children, and that didn't always go well. But on the upside, he's never missed a birthday or holiday and when she plays soccer and basketball, he makes almost every game, even when he had to come over from Sacramento."

"Tell me about you, Adam. How can you be single? You're such a catch! Surely there have been girlfriends."

"If you want to know if I dated, the answer is yes. I even had a couple of near misses, relationships that lasted a couple of years."

"And yet you didn't marry? You, such a family man? Why?"

"I don't know. It just didn't feel right. I wasn't in love enough, I guess."

"I wish I'd thought of that," she said.

"But you loved him, Emmie," he said. "From the way you described him, he walked on water."

"I loved him," she admitted, growing serious. She put down her fork. "I was twenty-four when I met him. He proposed almost immediately. I realized much later, I was hand-picked. He was looking for an idiot who could pull off the millionaire-wife image, from haute couture to decorating to entertaining to social grace under pressure. And of course I had to be able to take orders." She finished her glass of wine. "I'd like to tell you something." But then she stopped.

"Another glass of wine?" he prompted.

"I think I'd like a cup of tea. When the waitress comes back, I'll ask her. But I wanted to say something. I might've misled you. About investigating Richard so I'd know how I ended up in this place. I've already read everything, Adam. If there's anything new, I don't need to know about it. For over three years I was completely addicted to the news. I was glued to everything that floated across the internet. The books and biographical pieces started turning up long before he even went to trial. I read every court transcript, although I was usually there, in the courtroom. I had my own lawyers. For a long time they were the only people who talked to me.

"It didn't take long before all the things I suspected proved logical. Richard had strong sociopathic tendencies. As far as I know he didn't murder the neighborhood pets, but according to old classmates he lied and cheated his way through school. He used people. He enjoyed getting away with things. He liked deceit and winning by any means and he had no empathy. The state and the feds might've been able to prove his fraud and theft, but there was only conjecture about most of the other things, the things having to do with his ethics, his personality disorder. It all became so clear before his trial was over."

"Emmie," he said sympathetically, touching one of her hands.

"I didn't know, yet I did know, Adam. I lived under the same roof with the man, after all. Even though we weren't close, even though I can't say we had a loving marriage, I lived in his house. I traveled with him. The first time I suspected there was a mistress we'd only been married a year. He smiled indulgently, kissed my forehead and said, 'Why in the world would I have a mistress? I have you, the most beautiful woman in New York City.' I bought it, of course. He was so confident and convincing. But there came a time I just knew something was off. I overheard things—he had employees and they were well aware of what he was doing, feeding his business from the bottom, paying out dividends here and there when it would bring in more capital. He referred to it as seeding… Seed money… Satisfied clients brought in more clients. We never discussed it, but after we'd been married a few years, I heard things like that when he was talking to someone who worked for him or when he was on the phone with a client. I heard him moving money around to offshore accounts. He thought I was an idiot, at least about financial matters. I never really knew anything, but I strongly suspected that my slick and sleazy husband would stop at nothing to make big money.

"And I came to know about the mistress. Andrea Darius. I met her for the first time before we were married. Beautiful woman, so beautiful. Smart, classy, very high-society type. She looked kind of like Katherine Heigl—that stately, confident, above-it-all look. I'd suspected from the first time I met her. There was something in the way she looked at him, it was just there. She was an image consultant, a public relations expert who specialized in the financial sector. Lenders and investors are constantly scrutinized, especially private companies and hedge fund managers. But that was just a front. That was one of the first issues I faced when I looked the other way. I made excuses to make my existence more acceptable in my own eyes." She laughed hollowly. "While I'm a leper in Manhattan, Andrea is still a prominent figure in New York society. There's been speculation that she's a high-priced prostitute or even madam. Who knows? Who cares?"

The waitress came to their table, picked up some plates

and took their beverage orders. Adam really wanted another drink but he asked for a coffee.

"See, I didn't have any proof of any kind, but things he said and did made me wonder why I didn't understand him better. Then one day I realized I was married to a man I didn't know, a man who had no conscience. But by then it was too late."

"Why didn't you testify against him?" Adam asked.

She shook her head. When her tea came she added milk and sugar and stirred slowly.

"I really wanted the whole thing to just go away so I could make my escape, which I fully intended to do. I have no real defense, but it is true that any testimony I might have given wouldn't do any good for the defense or the prosecution. It was suspicion, hearsay, speculation. Nothing, really."

"You were trying to have a baby with him?"

She winced. It was unmistakable.

"It was madness. I don't know what I was thinking. We hadn't been married that long, a couple of years, and I was still so young, but I knew something wasn't quite right in our marriage. I thought I could fix it. I thought we could be a family and he would become more...*conscious* of me." She shook her head. "How stupid was I? Anyone knows that babies don't fix things! And God knows nothing was going to cure what he had! It's a blessing I couldn't get pregnant. I finally realized what a catastrophic mistake that would be.

"So you see, Adam—it's not necessary for me to gather up all the things written about Richard and the case against him. Or me. I'm up to speed on all that. I very rarely watch the news now. And those bios?" She shook her head. "I don't know if they're half true. But they sound suspiciously as if they could be."

"I'm so sorry, Emmie," he said.

"I haven't really talked about this. I can trust Lyle and I

dumped on him a little bit while I was going through it, but I didn't want to make his relationship with Ethan tense—Ethan thinks very little of me as it is."

"But Lyle…"

"The best," she said immediately. "So loyal, so wonderful and always there for me. And believe me, I put him through some drama." She sipped her tea. "I'm so grateful for Lucinda Lopez, who I've seen twice now. She's perfect. She makes telling it all so easy, and every once in a while she leads me to a perfect conclusion that explains everything, that makes me understand. Men like Richard Compton have a gift for finding the right sucker. He needed a girl who'd lost her parents, who had nowhere to go, who wanted someone who could make her think she was a fairy princess. Someone who wouldn't question his motives. And that was me to the core. Adam, I want you to know who you've gotten yourself mixed up with."

He frowned. "You think I didn't know most of that? I didn't know how you coped but I found out all that stuff—his scheme, his mistress, his lack of conscience, all the speculation from old acquaintances that he'd always been sociopathic. He was so narcissistic it's odd he killed himself."

"People think there's money hidden somewhere," she said. "I certainly don't know of any and I don't have any, but I think his suicide was part revenge and part *gotcha*. He didn't have much value for life, now did he? Not even his own."

"In the end, you were sure your conclusions about him were right?" Adam asked.

"Oh, yes," she said. "During our marriage, through the investigation, through all the depositions, he was one cool dude and we didn't discuss any of it. But in the end, when he'd been warned he was looking at anywhere from forty to seventy-five years in prison, he let the floodgates open and did some incredible lashing out. He proved to me and anyone within earshot that he was a beast with no remorse." She sighed. "There are things I just can't repeat, they're so vulgar."

They were quiet. She sipped her tea and he drank his coffee. The waitress silently refilled his cup and brought her more hot water, along with the check.

"It's okay, Emmie," he said.

"It's really not, Adam. You almost kissed me. You shouldn't do that. I'm damaged. I still can't believe what I allowed myself to be sucked into."

"You were twenty-four. And you were a great deal wiser by the time you were thirty. Give yourself a break."

"Rosemary always said, 'It's just as easy to fall in love with a rich man as a poor man.' She was full of sayings. After Richard's death, leaving me holding the mess of his crimes, leaving me the suspect, you know what my darling stepmother said? 'If you marry for money, you'll earn every cent.'"

"I never liked her," Adam said.

"She's got some great sayings, though."

"We're going to get through this, Emma," he said.

"I wanted you to kiss me," she said.

He had to work at keeping his heart from exploding.

"I wanted to be kissed and the only person in the world I wanted to kiss me was you," she said. "But, Adam, you shouldn't because I'm broken. I don't want to hurt anyone who gets close to me. We have to keep it friends. And Riley... Listen, she was totally professional, but she made it pretty clear... She wouldn't like the idea of us being close."

"You think I give a shit what Riley wants?" he asked.

"Well, I do. And you should. She's your family. I'm going to keep seeing the counselor for a little while. Maybe she's got a shortcut or two. I've got a few good years left and I'd like to live them happily."

He smiled. A few good years? She was all of thirty-four. She probably felt like she'd wasted a lifetime already. "We'll get through this, Em. You're starting a whole new life on Monday. Cleaning toilets and mopping floors. Wowser."

"I'm going to make Riley proud of me," she said. "Don't tell her I said that."

"I don't tell anyone anything."

Emma didn't necessarily feel better about laying all that on Adam, but she felt cleaner. More honest. He should know—she might not have been complicit in Richard's crimes but she was certainly a participant in ending up right where she was. She fell for every little trick he had. And before it was all over, he made sure she knew it. Snatches of their dialogue in the final weeks might echo forever, never leave her, might never give her peace.

Adam reached across the small table and held her hand. "One thing you're not going to do—you're not going to worry about taking care of me. I don't need you to protect me. All right?"

She knew he was strong. She knew he was smart. But was he wise to what association with a man like Richard had done to her? "I'm not innocent anymore, Adam."

"Not guilty, either. And you're a survivor. I know you are."

"Really?" she asked. "Is that so?"

He chuckled but not with humor. "Your father's death? Rosemary? God, a few years of her would damage anyone! You pulled yourself together after Jock. Picked up what you could carry and went to New York—one of the biggest, scariest cities in the country." He drank the last of his coffee. "I guess now I'll never see it."

"Why is that?"

"No way you're going back there," he said. "And I'm not

going back there without you." He briefly looked at their check.

"I'm afraid you're already getting in over your head."

He laughed and pulled out his wallet.

"Let's at least split the check," she said.

"Forget it. I'm not in over my head, Emmie. You don't scare me at all. And you've been through a lot, but I know people who have been through worse. Hell, I know people who have served in combat several times. They have issues, just like you, and they're working on them. It's very tough, too."

She was feeling a little desperate. He was clearly forging ahead, not taking seriously how bad she might be for him, and she wasn't going to be able to hold him back. She adored him for wanting her still. And she feared for him. "When I asked him why he'd kept a mistress, he said he needed someone to fuck that he could talk to!"

"It's hard to believe how pathetic he was," Adam said, peeling off bills to put with the check. "The dumb shit," he added, shaking his head.

"I accused him of being a common thief and he slapped me and told me there was nothing common about what he'd done!"

"He *hit* you?" he asked, his green eyes darkening dangerously.

"Just the once," she said more quietly.

"I kind of want to dig him up and beat the shit out of him, but dead is dead. I bet he didn't get away with anything this time. I may not go to church much anymore but I still believe there's a heaven and a hell." He put his wallet away. "About ready, Emma?"

"Yeah," she said. "Sure."

Walking to the car, his hand on the small of her back, she

gave it one more try. "Adam, you heard me, right? I'm coming out of a really dysfunctional situation. Beyond dysfunctional. Sick. Really sick. And it could follow me for quite a while. You don't want to be too close if—"

He stopped walking when they were almost to the car. He put his hands on her waist and looked into her eyes. "Emma, I've been waiting for you to come back for sixteen years. I'm not going to run scared now, just because some insane asshole did his best to leave you wounded. I told you—we can get through this." He leaned toward her and gave her lips a sweet kiss. "You don't have to warn me anymore. You didn't have to warn me in the first place. Now I'm going to take you home. And if there's a God, you're going to invite me in."

"I worry about the concept of us," she said. "I don't want you to be collateral damage when the detritus of Richard's crimes sprinkles down on me."

"I understand completely," he said. "Finished now?"

"Don't be a fool," she said.

"I won't."

All the way home from the restaurant, he talked to her softly of casual things, of the beauty of Napa, the way the cold drizzle of a Sonoma County winter had always made him crave soups and fires. She didn't have a fireplace of course, but he did. He was looking forward to showing off his house— it was over fifty years old in a quiet tree-lined neighborhood and he'd enjoyed renovating it. He'd done most of the work himself, tearing up old carpet and installing hardwood floors, texturing and painting walls. "I focused on the four most important rooms—living room, kitchen, master and bath. The new kitchen is so beautiful it almost makes me want to cook."

"Don't be hasty," she said.

He was seducing her with ordinary things, as if he knew

how starved she'd been for a reality she understood—soups and fires, rainy days in a home that hugged her, the love of a good man.

After their lunch they went to her house. He held her hand the entire drive and when she let him into her little bunga-low, he glanced around and said, "You've been busy."

"Just a little settling in," she said.

"Come here," he said, locking her door behind them and pulling her into his arms.

His lips came down on hers with an urgency and hunger she hadn't been prepared for. After one brief moment of sur-prise, she matched his passion with the surging need of her own. It wasn't just her need for intimacy because it had been so long but her need for it to be *him*.

Clothing was removed while they kissed. It seemed that it only took seconds for them to be in her bed, skin to skin, lips to lips. Emma hadn't felt the touch of loving hands in years. Adam's beautiful hands, his lips, his strong fingers, did the one thing she didn't think possible—took her away. Far away. She thought only of him, intoxicated by his scent, his taste, his body.

He was thoroughly beautiful. He had long, strong legs, muscled arms and shoulders, a smooth, hairless chest. With his thick brown hair, expressive brows, emerald-green eyes and strong jaw, he should probably be sculpted and put on display. For this moment in time he belonged only to her. And she to him.

She inhaled his breath, licked her way into his mouth, opened for him and welcomed him into her body. He was gentle and smooth, teasing her into a frenzy. He responded to her arousal with heat, finally taking her on a powerful ride that had her crying out his name as she came. And came. And came.

He joined her, softly whispering her name, his large frame shuddering, his mouth at her neck, his big hands in her hair. She trembled with the aftershock of orgasm and he chuckled, a deep rumble. He kissed her eyes, her ears, her chin, her lips. Her calm returned so slowly; he didn't leave her body, pushing into her softly, again and again. "Still worried about the concept of us?" he whispered in her ear.

"You drugged me," she accused.

He pushed into her again. "A little bit. Damn, woman, I knew we'd be great together, but I didn't have enough imagination to know how great."

They continued kissing, soft and deep and lovely. He moved inside her, filling her, rocking with her in a smooth, deep motion. It didn't take long before she was clutching at him, pushing against him, begging for more.

"I can't say no to you," he whispered. "I have a feeling I'll never be able to say no to you. God, why would I even want to?"

"I didn't say no, either, did I?"

"More it is," he whispered, pounding into her until they were both rising again, reaching for another mutual climax. The moment she started to clench and tremble around him, he went off like a rocket, a powerful blast that made her almost whimper in pleasure. And she finally collapsed under him.

Again he kissed her eyes, her cheeks, her lips, running his work-roughened hands all over her.

They were quiet for a while as their breathing evened and their bodies began to cool. He reached down to pull the duvet over them. Rolling onto his side, he brought her with him, gently holding her against him.

"Are you going to stay inside me forever?" she asked.

"Would that be inconvenient?" he asked. "Because it really feels like exactly where I should be."

"Funny," she said. "Feels that way to me, too."

"Friendship with you has perks," he said.

She was quiet for a moment. "Good," she finally said.

He laughed. "I don't want to be friends, Emmie."

"You don't?"

"Of course not. I don't share that with friends. There was nothing casual about that and you know it."

"Oh?"

"Wasn't a friendly fuck for you, either," he said. "That was some of the finest love I've ever made. Might be the absolute best ever."

"You think?"

"I know," he said.

She smiled. "I'm glad to hear that, even though it was probably not a good idea."

He raised up, looking down at her. "I think it was the best idea I ever had."

She couldn't keep from touching him, tenderly running her fingertips over the planes of his face. "I guess you're not going to come to your senses anytime soon..."

He shook his head. He gently brushed her hair back from her face. "You know how I feel. I think you've always known. Do you think you can talk me out of it?"

"Well, I thought I could..."

"You can't..."

She bit her lip and just looked into those fierce green eyes. She sighed. "Thank God," she said.

He smiled at her.

"Could be problematic that I just slept with my new boss's brother..."

"None of Riley's business who I sleep with. None of her business who you sleep with, for that matter."

"Do you think she'll agree with that?"

"Do you think I care?" he asked, raising a brow in question. "Come on," he said, pulling her closer so she was nuzzling into his chest. "Enjoy the moment. You'll have plenty of time to worry later."

She let herself be cuddled. "I do feel considerably more relaxed than I did a couple of hours ago."

"There you go," he said with a laugh. "God knows I do." After a few minutes of silence he asked, "You going to sleep?"

"No. I'm afraid I'll wake up and find out it was just a dream."

He kissed her forehead. "Nothing like that's going to happen. The bad dreams are over. The good dreams are just beginning."

The rest of the weekend was ideal, the kind of perfect Emma had given up on. After lying around in bed for a couple of hours, Emma showered and primped. When she came out of her bathroom, Adam was puttering comfortably around her little kitchen, making tea and checking out the refrigerator, taking inventory. He wore his jeans, his shirt hanging open over that gorgeous chest, socks on his shoeless feet. He looked so delicious like that she wanted to take a bite out of him.

"If you want to go out for dinner, I'll take you out," he said. "If I can talk you into staying in, I'll go get us something."

"You want to stay in?"

He grinned at her. "Oh, yeah."

Then his phone rang. He pulled it out of his pocket, looked at the ID and picked up. "Hi, Mom." He listened for a little while, nodding as though his mother might hear it. "You need me to fix that now?" A pause. "You did? I wish you wouldn't do that. I know it was irritating but what if you fell? All right, all right, I didn't mean to offend you, but re-

ally… Don't do it again, all right? Well, thanks, but I'm actually going out tonight so tomorrow I'll have errands and
have to get ready for school. Oh, nothing too exciting." He
winked at Emma. "Just having a glass of wine with a lady
friend. I don't think so, which is how I'd like to keep it for
now. Listen, if you need me to help with those Christmas
decorations… Jock is? Okay, I appreciate the pass and I'll get
the lights up after school one day this week, so no ladders.
Talk to you tomorrow? Great."

He put the phone back in his pocket. "Her smoke alarm
was beeping because the battery was dead and she climbed
up on a stepladder in the stairwell and changed the battery.
She's perfectly capable, but I hate thinking of her up on a
ladder. That's what I'm for." He made a face. "I change them
regularly to keep her off the ladder."

"You mentioned Jock?"

"He's pulling out the big boxes for Maddie and Mom.
Maddie must have asked him. Gives them a chance to hang
out for a while."

She shook her head. "She asked who you were going out
with…"

"She just asked, 'Do I know her?'" His smile was devilish.
"I'm going to get a shower before I go shopping."

"Adam, they can't know," she said. "I'm sorry, but Riley
can't know…"

"I wasn't planning to tell her," he said. "But I wasn't planning to keep it a secret, either." He frowned. "Is that your
plan?"

She bit her lower lip as she nodded. "Until she decides it's
okay I'm back, until I prove to her I'm an asset as an employee, please—let's keep it between us."

"You're afraid she'll be angry," he said.

"Of course. She isn't too sure of me yet. She was very

clear—giving me a job had nothing to do with making up or being friends. She isn't ready for me in her life. You are a huge part of her life."

"Do you want to stop this right now? Me and you? Because I can leave. I wouldn't like it, but if you need more time…"

"I can let you go but, heaven help me, I don't want to give you up. Not if you want to stay. Not even for Riley." She smiled a bit tremulously. "You should really think about this."

He smiled at her. "I'm going to take a shower, go to the store and stay as long as you'll let me. And if it's important to you that we keep it from Riley for a while, I can do that. I want you to feel safe."

"Thank you. I just need a little time to settle into my job. Not only do I need the job, I also want to prove to Riley that I don't expect any favors, that there's no debt to settle."

"If that's the way you feel."

"It is."

"Then that's how it will be," he said.

"Can I go shopping with you?"

He smiled at that. "So you're not hiding us from the world, just from Riley. Just for now."

"That's about right. Can you live with that?"

"It's okay, Emma. I know the ground still feels pretty shaky. But I think everything is going to be okay."

She hoped so. But she knew things would only become more difficult if Riley and Adam were pitted against each other because of her. And that would be terrible.

An hour later they were back at home with potato-cheese soup, mini ham sandwiches and antipasto from the deli, plus a nice bottle of wine. They ate on the couch in front of the TV then curled around each other for a while before going to bed. Adam didn't ask if he could stay; he just stayed as long as she didn't ask him to leave. She hung on to him all night long as if lost at sea, and rather than try to shed her clinging arms, he held her firmly to him.

In the morning they had bagels and cream cheese with their coffee and then went for a walk through the quiet town. Then back to Emma's place for more cuddling on the sofa.

"So this is normal, is it?" she asked, relaxed and blooming under his touch.

"You'll get used to it," he said.

chapter *nine*

After Thanksgiving dinner, Riley checked on a few of her cleaners, but only by phone. Of course they had clients who couldn't even wash their own dishes on a family holiday. Some people entertained on Thanksgiving, and while she found the fact that they hired help away from their own families on such an occasion somewhat tacky, it was also profitable. Riley made it profitable for her employees, too. And from what her people in the field said, all went smoothly.

It was a tradition for Riley and Maddie to help June decorate the house the day after Thanksgiving. Riley dropped Maddie off at June's then went out to run a few errands. By the time she got back to her mother's, Jock was in the garage, getting out boxes for Maddie and June.

"I didn't expect to run into you today," she said. "Isn't the store busy?"

"Worse than busy. I was there for a couple of hours this morning when they opened the doors to the crowd. And I'm going back later to work tonight. It'll be a zoo all weekend."

Black Friday was sale day and nothing sold like electronics. Computers, TVs, everything from headphones to cell phones. Jock was the manager now at least and had a little more control over his schedule, and though she hated to have to admit it, he put in some hard weeks.

She went into the house. She didn't like to look at him. He was still so good-looking that it kind of pissed her off. Couldn't he at least age badly? But he was still drawn to sports, worked out, played a little football, a little basketball, golf—and he was as fit as he'd been in high school. He still looked like the guy who'd stolen her heart and then broken it.

June was in the kitchen getting out all her Christmas cookie cutters. "I didn't expect to see him here," Riley said.

"I think Maddie asked him to come," June said.

"Why didn't she just ask Adam?"

June sighed in some aggravation. "Because Jock is her father, I suppose. And much as it galls you, they enjoy each other."

"It doesn't gall me," she lied. "What can I do?"

"Do you want to help go through the decoration boxes in the garage?" June asked with a sly smile.

"What can I do in here?"

"As soon as they find it, you can put the garland up on the bannister, string it with lights and hook up the extension cords."

"Fine," she said, heading for the coffeepot.

When Maddie was a baby, Jock spent time with her more often at June's house than anywhere. When he wanted to take her to his parents' house, he talked to June rather than Riley because June was more accommodating. When Maddie was in grade school, he pushed his presence more forcefully, but still cautiously. He insisted on being notified of school activities, from parent-teacher conferences to carnivals. He couldn't make them all, but he wanted to at least be told. "I'd rather not ask the teacher, Riley." Riley most often asked her mother to let Jock know.

Then there was that time when Maddie was ten that Jock suggested to Riley that they revisit the idea of joining forces. "I think we should get together, just you and me, maybe leading up to a date," he said. "Let's get to know each other again, see if we can remember what it was that brought us together in the first place."

"You've completely lost your mind, right?" she said.

"Not at all. I know you don't like it but I consider you and Maddie my family. Since there's no getting around it, we could explore it."

She was appalled. "I wouldn't even consider it," she said. "And why would you? You've dated a lot since Maddie was born. I don't consider you my family! Get someone else to take a chance on you."

"I hardly ever date," he said. "You really don't know anything about me."

"I think I probably know enough," she said. "Aren't you the guy who talked me out of my clothes and then dumped me?"

"You have a real blind spot when it comes to me, don't you, Riley? I apologized a hundred times for being a stupid eighteen-year-old when that happened but I really cared about you. I just got scared off. Mostly by you!"

"And what makes you think I'd be willing to take that kind of risk again?"

"Maybe because I'm not eighteen anymore and we have a daughter together?"

"Even more reason I should be cautious!"

And of course their conversation had deteriorated from there. They often did. She'd push his buttons, she'd get pissed off all over again and before they knew it they were sniping at each other.

So Jock married someone else, a young woman with two sons. The ink was barely dry on the marriage license when he was back on his own and the woman was back with her ex. And Riley felt vindicated—Jock was not capable of a committed relationship.

Starting in junior high, Jock began to communicate directly with Maddie and Riley would run into him at everything from car washes to softball games. And now she never knew when she'd run into him at her mother's house.

On Saturday Riley had worked for a couple of hours and Maddie had girlfriends over for the night, so she was trapped at home. On Sunday afternoon Maddie and June were going through the recipes and planning their Christmas baking. Riley was there by four o'clock to share a family dinner of Thanksgiving leftovers with them. All but Adam, who had begged off because he was busy. He'd told his mother he was running errands and getting his schoolwork done since he'd been out with a friend Saturday night. "Oh?" Riley had asked. "What friend?"

"He said I don't know her," June said.

It was hardly noteworthy. Adam was known to date, though circumspectly. As a rule, he didn't introduce a woman he was dating to the rest of the family until it had been weeks or months, proving they stood the test of time.

Riley met Monday with some excitement, some trepidation. Emma was starting work. She'd begin her training with Makenna Rice at 7:00 a.m. and Riley thought Makenna might scare the life out of Emma. Riley had made a secret pledge—no arguing or fighting. It was one thing to clear the air upon their first meeting—they had been alone in the office. But from now on they were only employer and employee and they'd be professional and courteous or Emma would have to go. "It's my company," Riley kept reminding herself.

Riley was at the office at six-thirty and, unsurprisingly, Makenna had beat her there. She already had her training manuals and supplies scattered around the boardroom.

"Well, good morning," Riley said. "Getting an early start, I see."

"I don't want us to be late for our first job. That would set a bad example."

Riley laughed. "Can I get you a coffee?"

"I'm all set, thanks. I didn't start the pot in the kitchen, knowing you'd be bringing your Starbucks. I guess I'd better put on the coffee, huh? Ms. Shay might need a cup."

"I'll do it while you set up here," Riley said.

Makenna was an interesting character, one of Riley's first employees. She was tiny but strong. She had spiked orange hair and dark brows, plenty of piercings on her ears and a couple of eyebrow piercings, a few colorful tattoos that had expanded over the years. The only one that showed while she wore her work uniform was a serpent that wiggled up the back of her neck. She reminded Riley of a biker chick but she was a straight arrow. She was a single mom like so many of Riley's employees—one fourteen-year-old son who towered above her already. And she was a strict mom. As far as Riley knew, Curtis didn't give her any trouble. Hell, Riley was afraid to give her trouble.

All the doors between the offices and conference room were standing open, the front door unlocked, the coffee brewing, and at six-fifty Emma arrived, ten minutes early. *Good.* She carried a tote that presumably had her drinks and lunch for the day, her uniform was new and pristine and she looked far too good to be cleaning houses. But that was the look

Riley wanted her employees to have because that was how her clients wanted the hired help to look.

"Good morning," Riley said.

"Good morning," Emma replied.

She blushed just slightly. It was almost imperceptible, but she glanced briefly away.

Was that about the words they'd exchanged when Emma was interviewed and hired, or something else? Did Adam really have errands? Errands my ass, Riley thought.

"How was your weekend?" Riley asked.

"Very nice, thanks. I had the best Thanksgiving. The lady I'm renting from and her girlfriends, all widows a bit beyond a certain age, had dinner and included me—it was fantastic."

"Good. What about Rosemary?"

"Didn't you know? Rosemary and her third husband, Vince, moved to Palm Springs years ago. I haven't heard a word from Lauren or Anna. I'm not even sure if they're still around here. With any luck, Rosemary and I are finished. I haven't heard from her since...since Richard's death."

Riley made a face. "With any luck," Riley muttered under her breath. She led Emma to the conference room. "Makenna is ready for you. Makenna, this is Emma Shay."

Emma put out her hand. "Pleased to meet you. And thank you. I'll try to be your star pupil."

"They all say that. Get yourself a cup of coffee if you like. We're going through the handbook first. Coffee's in the kitchen."

Emma reached into her bag. "I brought my coffee," she said, pulling out a large thermal cup.

"Save it for later. Get office coffee while you can. Meet me in here."

"Thanks," Emma said, heading for the kitchen.

Riley went to her desk. No, surely not, Riley thought.

Surely Adam wasn't spending more than a little time with Emma. He wouldn't get romantically involved with her, would he? Weren't they all conflicted enough without that?

I will fire her, Riley thought.

Emma eyed the handbook—a large spiral notebook two and a half inches thick.

"We're going to start with some important company rules and guidelines. I have a notebook like this for you to borrow. You can make copies, take notes, memorize, whatever works best for you, and you can have it for two weeks. There is always a book in the office. Nick Cabrini, director of operations, has this book on his computer and phone. I have one at all times and you can stop by here or call any of us with questions. Let me put that more clearly—if you have a question, please check the book to make sure you're acting within company policy before doing anything."

Emma frowned. "Like?"

"I'm going to tell you." Makenna flipped open the book. "Nick or Riley give the estimates and unless there are special conditions, the client contracts for our basic house or office cleaning services, which are very thorough. We'll go over the basic in a few minutes. Extra duties must be approved by Nick and he will make a charge, so please don't quote prices to the client. Extras include things like windows, refrigerator/freezer cleaning, garage cleaning, patio and outdoor furniture cleaning, cupboard clearing, laundry, special-event cleanup—like receptions, holiday entertaining, et cetera. We don't provide child care or care of the elderly or infirm. We're not plumbers—we don't unplug toilets. If they can't figure it out, we have subcontractors—plumbers, electricians, pool service, chimney sweeps, landscapers and gardeners and so on. There's a very long list, right here." She tapped a page in the book. "It's routine for our clients to ask for more without considering the time and expense, so we have a standard. We never use the client's cleaning supplies—only ours are approved. They've been known to come up with weird concoctions that stain, damage or create noxious fumes. They can damage their own possessions. Likewise, you will learn about materials and cleaning agents and will not take the homeowner's cleaning advice—for your own protection. When the lady of the house says, 'Just use a little bleach on this Oriental rug,' you will explain that doesn't match your instructions and offer the services of our in-house expert, Nick, who will be happy to consult before we have to buy her a new rug. And if you think clients haven't tried to dupe the poor, stupid cleaning lady into ruining something so it can be replaced for free, you're unbearably naive. For breakage, which is going to happen, we have insurance with a high deductible. The company will cover each team member for the first fifty dollars—that's the odd wineglass, ashtray, soap dish or plate.

"We use only the front powder room if the need for a bathroom arises and if there is no powder room, we'll designate an appropriate restroom in the home. We don't eat in the client's house but a drink of bottled water—our own—is appropriate. We don't accept new or used gifts or clothing. Under any circumstances. If they want to tip you in cash, it's acceptable. Individual cleaning teams cannot offer discounts or additional work without being approved. We don't develop personal relationships with our clients—be cheerful, helpful and courteous. If someone wants to discuss problems, if they're not cleaning problems, explain that you're not at liberty to offer advice or act as a confidante. We have a policy that individual employees not make arrangements with clients to work on the side. And there is a non-compete agreement that you will be asked to sign that states you will not work as an independent house cleaner or maid until you have been separated from Kerrigan's Services for six months.

"Our clients have an expectation of privacy and confidentiality. We understand that it is unrealistic to suggest cleaners never chat among themselves, but we do have an ironclad rule that no employee of this company discuss clients' personal matters outside of the company. It goes without saying—if you're accused of stealing, you will be investigated by the police. It has happened and I am proud to report, it has rarely been true. So if you have any legal issues, wants or warrants that will be complicated by a law enforcement intervention, best to say so now." She gave Emma a chance to say so. After a moment's silence Makenna cleared her throat and went on. "And if you run into burdensome issues you can't quite manage, please bring them to me, Nick or Riley. Believe me, we've seen it all."

Emma frowned. What kind of confidential things might she witness? "I'm almost afraid to ask…"

"Inside of two months, you won't have to ask, but I'll save you some time. Obviously, you're not going to be picking through drawers or closets, reading correspondence, diaries, or studying papers on desks. We don't look at personal papers or property, we dust it.

"But you're going to see things. Mrs. X, the cheapest client we have, one who has never tipped or given a holiday bonus, has a checkbook balance of one-point-five-million and a monthly credit card bill over twenty-five thousand dollars. She leaves these papers in plain sight, very hard to miss. Mr. and Mrs. Y carelessly leave out objects of intimate pleasure." To Emma's expression of consternation, Makenna said, "Sex toys, Emma."

"Ew," Emma said.

"Gloves," Makenna said. "And Mr. Z is knocking the shit out of Mrs. Z. She thinks no one knows."

"Oh, my God! And you don't do anything?"

Makenna glanced down at the pages of the employee manual. "Mrs. Z said someone made an anonymous call to the police department and they were visited by someone from the domestic violence unit, but I'm sure I wouldn't know anything about that."

"So—we don't get involved, even if someone's health and safety is at risk?"

"That would be one of those issues you're going to want to take to Nick and Riley. Very important that you do so, Emma. If a member of the household we service is at risk, we're at risk. If you have reason to believe someone is breaking the law, it's important you tell your supervisor. There are examples of difficult situations in this manual. The book was compiled by Riley over years. When a new situation arises it is not only added to the handbook, a confidential memo is also sent to team leaders so they can advise their crews." Makenna peered at Emma. "Are you going to be able to ignore the obvious? Look the other way?"

Emma almost laughed. "Oh, you have no idea," she said. "It's a skill of mine."

Makenna cleared her throat. "Now, let's go over some important issues—cleaning supplies, techniques, basic chemistry so you don't mix bleach and toilet bowl cleaner and end up a 911 call..."

The lecture was intense and fast-paced. Makenna put all of her supplies out on the table with corresponding color photos and explained how each cleaning implement was to be used and which cleaning chemicals were provided.

"I don't expect you to remember all of this, Emma. You're going to be trained on the job this week—I'll be watching you and helping you. To that end, I'm taking you to some of our more challenging homes. You'll have to learn to do it well, fast, not be distracted by your chatty home owner, cooperate with your team and employ all the smart moves—safety first. Don't lift anything over forty pounds, use your legs, not your back. We have knee pads in the van if you want them, as well as smocks and aprons, and do protect your uniform as much as possible. You're bound to get dirty, but avoid bleach marks or grease stains if you can." Then the little pixie smiled and said, "Ready?"

"Oh, God," Emma said.

"Good! Help me put this stuff away."

And with that they gathered up all of Makenna's training aides and headed out of the office, getting in the van. Two other team members—Shawna and Dellie, short for Delilah—were already there and ready to roll. Shawna held a clipboard.

"Okay, first house I have linens and dusting, Dellie has the kitchen and hardwood floors, the newbie Emma is passing the vacuum—do not forget the stairs! Do not slam the vacuum into walls or furniture! And it is with vengeful pleasure I give the bathrooms to Makenna."

"You don't scare me," Makenna said.

"You scare me," Emma said.

"Make nice tracks with that machine, Emma," Shawna said. "The clients like the tracks. The little things keep us popular."

"Is dusting the primo job?" Emma asked.

They all laughed. "It's the least difficult," Makenna said. "But there are blinds, high shelves, ceiling fans, plants, light fixtures, wooden furniture, books—it's endless. It's hard to be fast and keep breakage down. It takes practice. The vacuum is hard but safe."

"And the bathrooms are the worst job?"

"Sometimes, depending on the client," Shawna said. "Some of them aren't, how should we say it…?"

"Clean," Makenna supplied.

"Kitchens are hard. You never know what's happened in the kitchen this week. It could've been a big dinner out or a takeout week or there could have been a lot of cooking. Greasy, splattering, nasty cooking. People with regular cleaning service get a little lazy about a thorough cleaning after cooking. They never oil their cabinets or wash the floors. I hate cleaning kitchens," Shawna said.

Then it seemed like in minutes they were there.

"Let's do it," Makenna said. And they hit the ground running.

Emma was home in her little house at six. She walked in and collapsed on the sofa. It wasn't until she was in that position that she realized she still wore her knee pads—the last house of the day, she got the bathrooms. Six of them. Every one had been *thoroughly* used. If possible, the sinks were the worst she'd ever seen. The family must have been the hairiest family on the planet. They were obviously descended from the Yeti. The toilets… She couldn't think about them.

When she got some energy, she would call Adam. He had texted sometime after three that he couldn't wait to hear about her day. There hadn't been a moment yet. She went from the cleaning company's van directly to her car and straight home. Her carry pouch was empty of drinks and snacks, she was famished and she was sure there wasn't anything left in the house from her weekend with the bottomless pit, Adam. He'd bought plenty of food to sustain them during their "honeymoon" and he'd eaten all of it.

There was a knock at her door. It was unrealistic to expect it was a huge takeout order. Possibly it was Penny. She lifted her head. "Please be the pizza delivery boy," she called out weakly.

"How was your day, dear?" Adam. He stood over her, smiling.

"Oh. God." She struggled to sit up. He was holding bags. "Oh, you brought sustenance."

"Knee pads," he said, grinning like a fool. "Nice touch."

"What's in the bags?" she said, frowning at his attempt at humor.

"Food. Stuffed salmon, rice, Italian beans, bagels and muffins for morning, milk for your coffee, a couple of sandwiches for you to take to work tomorrow."

"Oh, you are a perfect man."

"You're hungry?"

"Starving. But these hands cannot go near food. My hands have been places…"

"Never mind," he said. He put his parcels on the table and went to sit on the chair facing her. "I've worked for Riley. A hundred and twenty teenagers every day is like a paid vacation." He touched the hair at her temple. "I also brought wine."

"Can you uncork it and just pour it straight down my throat?"

"Tougher than Burger Hell?"

"She was right, I was worked hard."

"She used to say, 'People have dirty lives and we clean them up.' I don't have to stay for dinner. I won't be offended."

"Oh, stay," she said. "Can I take a shower first?"

He nodded. "I'm not staying late tonight. I promise."

"What if I want you to stay late?" she asked.

"Just get your shower. I'll set up dinner."

"Nothing sexier than a man who brings dinner."

"If you had a real kitchen, I'd cook you dinner, but…"

"You provided. That's everything." She struggled off the couch but had trouble straightening. She groaned.

"Don't forget to take off the knee pads before you get in the shower," he said.

A few minutes later when she came out of the bathroom, the table had been set, the wine uncorked, the ibuprofen bottle sitting beside one plate.

"I hope this is a casual dinner," she said, indicating her pajamas.

He held a chair for her. "Madam?"

She took her seat and he poured her a small amount of wine. She sipped. "Well, your sister is amazing, Adam. Her business is impressive. Complex, well thought, practical, no detail omitted. It's brilliant what she's done. I have an employee manual I can barely lift, spent the day with a trainer..." She sipped again. "I had a personal trainer in New York. I was not worked nearly as hard by him."

Adam chuckled and served their food. "I know Makenna," he said. "She's a little demon, isn't she?"

"Depends on what you mean by *demon*. She's quite the handler. Five feet of brute strength and fearsome threats. I guess Riley hired her when there were no mob bosses or biker gang enforcers available. Where'd Riley find her?"

"I can't remember," he said. "She's been around forever. She's a fixture in the company. Riley keeps trying to move her into a management position and Makenna wants nothing to do with it. She likes her work and she's good at it. She agreed to work as a supervisor and trainer so it would be done right."

"I met Nick," she said. "He seems nice."

"Stay on his good side," Adam advised. "Some of the women make the mistake of thinking they can sweet-talk him. There are two people who can sweet-talk Nick and the first is his mother."

"And Riley?" she asked.

"You've been away from Riley too long. She doesn't sweet-talk anyone. The other, oddly enough, is Makenna. Though she rarely tries. Makenna eats nails for breakfast. And she don't need no *steenking* man."

"Hmm. This morning she had me instead of the nails," she said. She sampled the salmon. "Ohhh, Adam. I think I'm getting turned on."

He laughed at her.

When he was seated across from her on the green chair, she went after her dinner in earnest, trying not to gobble. "I didn't make a single mistake," she finally said. "I did everything right. Well, Makenna inspected my carpet tracks, my shining bathrooms, my oiled hardwood and made a few comments—nothing much. Clearly it was good enough. Better than good enough. Those women are workhorses."

"They're good," he agreed.

"Makenna indicated I was with an exceptionally good team this week but they weren't all this good. She also said sometimes there's a weak link, but she didn't say how she knew who that was. Do they tattle on each other?"

"Sometimes, but that's not how they do it. They measure client complaints and watch for similarities. Then Nick and Makenna get involved with the team. Often they'll split them up and move them around. Once they figure out who's not getting the job done, they try training, counseling, observing. They almost never have to fire someone for not working. It's other stuff."

"Like what other stuff?"

"Absenteeism, tardiness, breaking policy. The most irresistible is taking used clothing from clients. Obviously most of

Riley's employees aren't well-off and those high-end clothes are tempting."

"I never found out why that's not allowed," she said.

He chewed thoughtfully. "The risk that they'll be accused of stealing them is too high and there's no way to get to the bottom of it. The safe course is just forbid it."

She put down her fork. "Did Riley come to all these conclusions by trial and error or did she take some class or read some book about how to set up a business like this?"

"She read everything, took a few business courses and learned a lot through experience. It's really an amazing little company. The employees who work hard and honestly have excellent perks and benefits. Discounts at child care agencies was very hard to negotiate and worth a lot to a working mother. Not many companies help working mothers."

"Takes a working mother to know about that," she said.

She asked about Adam's day. He had a lab—that was always fun, especially if no one blew anything up. Test review for a couple of classes. He flipped a homeroom and study hall for a friend who wanted to go to the OB with his pregnant wife to see the sonogram of the baby. That had him finished at 2:30 so he went to his mother's and put up one row of Christmas lights across the front of the house for her. Then he cleaned up and stopped at the store on his way over to her house.

"Sounds like such a perfect, almost leisurely life," she said.

"I'll get out of your hair as soon as I help you clean up the dishes. I know you're tired," he said.

"If I'm not *that* tired?" she asked.

He left at 5:00 a.m.

chapter *ten*

Riley was very observant during Emma's first week on the job. The feedback was excellent. She was surprised, but shouldn't have been; Emma had always been a hard worker. Riley just couldn't get beyond the image of Emma riding through Central Park in a carriage on her wedding day, decked out in Vera Wang, no less. When Riley thought of Emma on her hands and knees scrubbing around the base of a toilet, she wondered what her budget for housekeeping had been in her Manhattan apartment.

She shouldn't have been surprised because when Emma wanted something, she had never been afraid to go after it. She was diligent. Determined. She wondered what Emma had done to land herself a millionaire. But in order to find out, she'd have to be on friendly terms with her and that just wasn't happening. Employer and employee—that was who they were.

Emma had always had to be enterprising. Her childhood had been tough. Her father's sudden death left her essentially alone, alone but for Riley and the Kerrigans. Somehow, Emma got through the worst of it with grace. She always managed to work hard, get by, put a good face on it. Like she was doing now, acting like it was her lucky goddamn day she got a job cleaning.

Really, she'd survived so much. Riley felt sorry for her. But she was also feeling something else. Trouble. Unease. Distrust. Maybe envy? Why would you envy someone who'd had so many bad knocks?

Because she was the beautiful, strong and tragic princess. No one would ever see Riley that way. Riley was the tough poor girl who made good. For that she'd get applause. But Emma? In her mind she saw that news clip of her on the courthouse steps, broken and crying, then rising stoically, lifting her regal chin and slowly descending as if she were on the red carpet, damaged shoe notwithstanding. Even in her most devastating moments, always chic. Always poised. In fact, Emma could wear devastation like a crown.

Friday night after work Riley dropped in on her mother. June was puttering around in her old kitchen. June was always cooking. She would never stop working even though Riley and Adam had convinced her to retire. So now she volunteered. At the church, in the neighborhood, at the animal shelter.

A mangy-looking dog wandered into the kitchen, walking slowly as if her feet hurt.

"And who is this?" Riley asked.

"This is Beatrice. Isn't she lovely?"

Riley gave a short laugh. "Actually…she's pretty ugly."

"Shhh. Be nice now—Beatrice has had a rough time of it. She's going to need a little time to regain her former beauty.

But she's a lovely lady and needs a place to relax until she has her forever home."

"If the whole world were as kind as you…"

"Where's Maddie tonight?"

"Hanging out at Kylie's house. Studying, she said."

"Ha," June laughed. "On Friday night? What do you suppose they're really doing?" Beatrice wandered over to the doggie bed in the corner of the kitchen and June told her she was a good girl.

"Eating junk, calling boys, practicing dance steps, plotting things… But Kylie's mother is home tonight so they can't get into too much trouble." She smiled as she looked at June, her *elderly* mother. June was sixty-three, kept her short hair a dark auburn color, still wore a size ten and her eyes sparkled with mischief. She'd worked hard all her life and it had kept her in excellent shape, except her feet gave her fits; she'd used them well, cleaning and waitressing, and sometimes they screamed in protest, but she was in excellent health and fitness otherwise. She looked her years, but beautifully so. She would be termed a handsome woman. "What are you building over there?" Riley asked from her place at the breakfast bar.

"I'm making a meat loaf," June said. "I'm so bloody sick of turkey. Aren't you?"

"God, yes. But you got a lot of mileage out of it," Riley said. "Why don't we have a glass of wine?"

"Perfect idea," June said.

"So… Adam's coming to dinner?"

"Not tonight. He stopped by after school yesterday to put the trash on the curb because apparently I'm too feeble to get it there." She laughed, washed her hands and wiped them on the towel.

"What are you going to do with that meat loaf, then?"

"Well, I'm going to eat some. With mashed potatoes. I

could share some with you, if you're interested. Then I suppose I'll freeze it, but I'm damn sure not eating another bite of turkey. At least until Christmas. But obviously I haven't had enough of mashed potatoes yet." She opened the refrigerator and pulled out a chilled bottle of white, already opened. "It's not as fancy as your preferred label but will this do?"

"Certainly," Riley said. June poured them each a glass and Riley took a sip. "Has Adam seemed to be awfully busy lately?" she asked June.

"I don't know," June said. "I talk to him almost every day. I haven't needed him for anything. Just the lights, which he finished this week. I hate doing the lights…"

"I've hardly talked to him," Riley said.

"Do you need him for something, Riley?"

"Well, no… But we usually talk longer than a minute. He hasn't been to dinner since Thanksgiving."

"He took some leftovers on Friday night, I think. He said that should do it for him."

"I think something is going on with him," Riley said. "And I should probably tell you—" She took another sip of her wine. "Emma's back in town."

"I know," June said. "She got back a few months ago, right?"

"I gave her a job," Riley said.

"Good for you! I hope to see her one of these days. I haven't gone looking for her—I'm sure she needs time to adjust to being back. I'm so glad she's free of that terrible mess. Does she seem well?"

"Oh, yes, beautiful as ever," Riley said, though the words did curl her lip. "Listen, I suspect Adam might be seeing her."

"Oh? And why do you suspect that?"

"He's seeing someone and he's mysteriously silent about it. And completely unavailable."

"Well, then…"

"Well, then?"

June put down her wineglass. "Riley, I want you to leave Adam alone."

"So he *is* seeing her!"

"Riley, you're not going to interfere. You're going to say nothing, do you hear me?"

"You can't tell me what to say!"

"I just did and I don't think you want to mess with me on this."

Riley slammed her fist on the breakfast bar. "Why are you in the middle of this? You seem to know what's going on well enough that you're telling me what to do! What to say!"

"I know about as much as you do. When Adam wants us to know more, he'll fill us in. Until then, you'll leave it alone."

"Did he tell you he was seeing her?"

June shook her head. "He told me she was back, that he ran into her and had a glass of wine with her one evening, gave her your business card and even though there's a good chance you'd work her to death, he hoped Emma would call you about a job. He had all faith you would do right by her. She'd be in a good work environment with fair pay. And I have absolutely no doubt that's what you did."

"I don't want her with Adam!"

"I think if you voice your opinion to Adam, you're going to get nothing but trouble. Telling him who he should or shouldn't date is overstepping your rights as a sister. You'll piss him off. You'll piss me off, for that matter."

"I don't entirely trust her," Riley said.

"Then you'll keep your distance. What the rest of us do is up to us, not you. Besides, what makes you think Emma is ready to be seeing any man? Hasn't she been through enough with a man?"

"Well, of course," Riley said. "But why are you acting like you know if you don't know?"

"I said he didn't tell me," June said. "Of course I know. I've always known."

"Known *what*?" Riley demanded, getting pissier by the second.

June took a breath. "Adam has been in love with Emma since she was fifteen. I threatened him with murder if he went near her before she was eighteen. You were too busy minding your own romances to even notice, which I considered a good thing. But Adam did all he could to steer clear of Emma. And we both remember what happened when Emma was eighteen—she went away to college. And never came home."

"And you think—"

"That my son hasn't found a woman who makes him completely happy in all that time? I've met a dozen perfectly nice women in the last fifteen years. A couple of them seemed to be around for a long time. That Natalie, remember her? She was looking at bridal magazines, but Adam was barely intrigued. No, Riley, in fifteen years, he hasn't said a word and I thought he was just going to live out his days as the bachelor uncle. Then he told me Emma was back and I saw a spark. He didn't say much after that and I didn't ask but I know my son. The woman he's wanted since he was a boy is back. And if you say one word, I'll make you sorry."

Riley was struck silent. "Well, jeez," she finally said. "Mama bear."

June narrowed her eyes. "He's entitled to take his time and have his privacy. We both owe Adam that much. He's been wonderful to us."

"Does he really need your protection?"

"He has it. And so would you."

"I can't remember a time you ever—"

Riley stopped talking. Of course there was a time. When she came home pregnant and needed the support of her family. Her mother didn't demand complicated explanations, didn't ask a lot of questions, didn't force her opinion. She asked Riley what she wanted to do and stood firmly beside her. Her grandparents' first reaction was that she'd better get married and take her lumps, but June protected her, kept her safe from the opinions of others, didn't judge her. June had done everything in the world to help her.

"Never mind," Riley said.

"Indeed," June replied.

"Am I supposed to be happy Adam has someone even if she's someone I can never have as a friend?"

"You should be very quiet in your speculation because you don't know and neither do I. I haven't seen Emma in many years. Who knows if she feels affection or just friendship? In fact, who knows if Emma is the one he's—"

"Oh, it's Emma," Riley said. But then she stopped herself from saying more. In her heart she knew that shy little blush was related to Adam. Because that's the kind of luck she had where that woman was involved. And also, she could still read Emma. And Emma could no doubt read her. Just like when they were young.

"I just hope I'll see her before too much longer," June said. "I can't tell you how often I've thought about that girl, worried about her. I practically raised her. For a while there I thought she'd lassoed the moon, but that didn't last long, did it? It nearly crushed the life out of her." She tsked, shook her head, took a sip of her wine. "I think your splitting up with Emma was as hard on all of us as it was on you."

I was a pregnant eighteen-year-old—nothing was as hard as that, she thought. "Always poor little Emma," Riley said meanly.

"Do you think… I mean, is it at all possible… Honestly, you think Adam has been *waiting* for her? All these years?"

June thought about that. She shook her head. "Not deliberately," she said. "And yet…"

They sipped their wine quietly. After a long spell, Riley broke the silence. "We're going to remodel this old kitchen. Get all new appliances."

"I like my appliances and I'm comfortable in this kitchen. It's like my skin."

"We're going to do it anyway. For resale value."

"When I'm dead," June said.

"I think that will be too late," Riley said.

"But not for me," June replied.

"I'm going to have to pass on the meat loaf. I have other plans."

"Oh?" June said.

"Since Maddie's going to be at Kylie's, I can grab a salad on the way home, get in my softest pajamas and read. I'm in the middle of a really good book."

"You haven't finished your wine," June said.

"I'm anxious to get out of these panty hose…"

"You want to ditch me so you can think about all this. Listen, don't think too much, Riley. Adam tends to act on instinct—just kind of feeling his way. You know things happen for a reason."

Not always, she thought. But yes, sometimes. Whether this was one of those times was still an unhappy mystery.

She stood. "I'm not going to think. I'm going to read and relax and enjoy a quiet evening. I hope I haven't disappointed you."

"I'm fine. I've become very happy about my own quiet time."

Riley kissed her mother's cheek. "I won't say a thing. I won't even make a face. I'll have to concentrate, however."

"It will go better that way, I promise."

Riley slipped into her coat, went to her car, drove to the nearest grocery parking lot and sat for a few moments. Thinking, of course. And letting her eyes well up with tears before she made herself stop. It was so crazy, thinking that Adam had, for all these years, thought of Emma, wanted Emma. Pined for her. To the point that the second she turned up, he was cooked. Done for.

Riley's hurt was deep. In all those sixteen years, Riley had felt such loneliness and guilt. And her family was now so happy, so relieved to have Emma back! Riley hadn't had the courage to trust a friend since Emma left.

She'd done everything she was determined to do in the last fifteen years. She'd focused on her business and her daughter, taking care of her mother, as well. Her best friends were the women she worked with and her family. In all that time, while other people had forged and ended relationships, sometimes moving on to loving unions that lasted, Riley had preferred not to be distracted or tempted. Even Jock, who she had once secretly wished would come to her and beg forgiveness and say he'd always loved her, had married and divorced. The only exception was her mother, and June claimed to be happy as she was; she had family and good friends and apparently no interest in romance. But Riley assumed that happened to old people.

Here was Riley, thirty-five and alone. No interested man. No partner. Sitting in a damn parking lot at night, crying because her friend had let her go sixteen years without forgiving her for that one little… Okay, that one major mistake.

She had a sudden vision of herself making meat loaf for charity, taking in old ugly dogs and watching movies alone for the rest of her life. Whimpering because Emma would never again be her friend. And it was her own fault.

She dug around in her purse until she found a business card. She flipped it over and found the cell number. She texted:

Are you completely out of melons already?

What came back was:

??

She texted:

I'm going to have some dinner at the Chinese Palace. Have you eaten? Riley.

When four minutes had passed, four of the longest minutes she'd ever endured, during which she could feel extreme embarrassment about texting him, she was ready to go into the grocery and get a salad. Then her phone pinged with a text.

On Wayside and Bayshore?

That's it.

Ten minutes or less.

I'll get a table.

Riley kept telling herself it was an experiment, just to see if she had any game left after all these years. She'd had the most uncomfortable feeling in her chest when she realized that not only had Adam managed to brave a relationship, but

Emma had somehow bounced back, too, after probably the most destructive relationship of all time. So who better to try this out on than a guy who intrigued her and was as safe as dating a member of the Royal Guard. He was a cop. If he gave her the least trouble, she'd call the police chief, whom she'd met on several occasions at community functions. The only thing that could make this better would be if one of her teams cleaned the chief's house.

While she waited for Logan Danner, she ordered wine and pot stickers. This might take more than one wine. Would he give her a breath test before she got in her car?

Her pot stickers had barely arrived when he came in the door. And she got instant nerves. He was attractive; he wore jeans, a beige sweater over a white shirt, a leather jacket. His light brown hair was just a bit too long. Not shaggy, but no buzz cut for this guy. And he had a bit of a beard growth. That sexy I-have-just-too-much-testosterone growth.

He slid into the booth across from her and grinned. "Date night!"

"Don't get frisky," she said. "This probably won't work out to be anything."

He shook his head. "What an attitude." The waiter came over and he asked, "Have you ordered dinner, Riley?"

"Just the pot stickers."

"Great. Bring me a Tsingtao," he said to the waiter.

Riley had a look of confusion on her face.

"Beer," he said, smiling. "In the end, you asked me out. How's that for a major upset?"

"This isn't really a date. It's two people sitting in the same booth, eating dinner."

"So you just couldn't stop thinking about me, is that it?" he asked.

"That is not it at all," she said.

He put his napkin on his lap. "So tell me about your day. That's how most dates start out. Which, by the way, is usually two people sitting in the same booth, eating dinner."

She leaned her head into her hand. "I knew I'd live to regret this…"

He laughed at her. "Okay, we'll start with my day. I was off today. I had stuff to do. I went to the gym, stopped by my mother's office—her car has a weird warning light so we swapped cars and I took hers to the shop. I did some laundry and ran the vacuum around the house, a couple of things I do every month like clockwork." He stopped talking to check her expression. "I was starting to think about dinner but I had something more lively in mind."

"Like a bar?"

"Yes. I have a foolproof system. When I'm flying solo I go to a noisy place where there will be people, some I know, some new to me. When I have a date, I pick a quiet place like this. Want to know what's different about tonight? I'll tell you—usually if I have a date and pick a quiet place like this, the woman talks my leg off and I don't have to work very hard to seem interesting and charming."

"Huh," she said. "I really don't date."

He sat back against the booth's padded seat. "I guess that makes me pretty special."

"I guess it does," she said. "It also makes you the only person I know who has any interest. Besides my brother, that is."

"I'll try to elevate my status," he said. His beer arrived and he took a drink. "Just out of curiosity, why isn't anyone interested? Or am I going to understand why in another ten minutes?"

"It's a long story, really…"

"Maybe you could give me the bullet points," he said.

"Okay, let's see. I'm a single mother. When my daughter

was little…very little…I was so focused on working, staying one step ahead of the bills. I absolutely did not consider a date. I probably wasn't very…"

"Nice?" he asked, lifting his brows.

"I was going for another word. Like *receptive*."

"So you were so not receptive that before you knew it, you gave off a vibe?" He cocked his head and waited.

"And this is your interesting, charming side?" she asked. She sighed. "Let's just order," she added, opening her menu.

"Vibe," he said under his breath.

She lifted her hand and the waiter was back at their booth.

"I'll have the chicken and broccoli with rice and egg drop soup and…" She looked at him. "Need a minute?" she asked.

He didn't even open the menu. "Shrimp lo mein, garlic chicken, another beer."

"You already knew what you wanted?" she asked.

"I've been here before. I live about two miles down Wayside. So—how old is your daughter?"

"Fifteen," she said, taking a sip of her wine, regretting more with every moment what she'd done and completely at a loss as to why she'd done it.

"And I'm your inaugural reentry into the world of men and women?"

She shrugged. "Time flies."

"So now we're going to have to try to unlearn a few things, right?"

"Like?"

"Like having dinner out with someone of the opposite sex can be fun. Getting to know someone new is like… Well, making a new friend who has had experiences you haven't had can be stimulating. I can tell you lots of things about police work if you're interested, and you can tell me lots of things about…about…" He indicated her with his hand.

"Cleaning house," she supplied.

"You clean houses?" he asked.

"Sometimes, but mostly I own a company that provides housekeeping services and other stuff. I bet you're fascinated."

He shook his head. "This is going to take longer than I thought," he muttered.

"What makes you such a know-it-all?" she asked. "Didn't you say you're divorced?"

"That wasn't my idea," he pointed out. "But we parted on very good terms, attesting to the fact that I'm an extremely amiable guy with lots of patience and am very nonjudgmental."

"Then why'd you get divorced?"

"Now, that's a long story," he said.

Elbow braced on the table, she leaned her chin in her palm. "The service here is slow. Give me the bullet points."

He sighed. "My wife wasn't cut out to be married... To a man..."

"Huh?"

He looked trapped. "She's playing on the other team, okay?"

"Are you serious?"

"As a heart attack," he said, making fast work of his beer.

Riley started to laugh. She covered her mouth, but then she just couldn't keep it in.

"I'm sure you're going to tell me what about that's funny..."

"Riley?"

She jumped at the sound of her mother's voice, tipping her wine over. She and Logan went after the spilled wine with their napkins. "Mom?" she said, looking up.

June had changed clothes. At least some of them. She wore a crisp white shirt with her jeans, covered by a blazer. She'd fluffed up her hair and put on lipstick.

"Mom?" Logan asked, sliding out of the booth.

"Hello," June said good-naturedly, smiling at him.

"Mom, what are you doing here?"

"I ordered some takeout," she said.

"But what about your meat loaf?"

"I lost interest so I put it in the freezer. My goodness, Riley, when you said you couldn't wait to get out of your panty hose, I had no idea—" She put out her hand to Logan. "I'm June Kerrigan."

"Pleasure to meet you. I'm Logan Danner. Would you like to join us?"

"Not on your life," she said with a laugh. "Have you two been seeing each other long?"

He gave a short laugh and looked at his watch. "About fifteen minutes now, as a matter of fact, though we've bumped into each other at the grocery store and Starbucks a dozen or so times."

"Isn't that nice," June said. "We'll visit more another time. I'm going to grab my dinner and head home. Have a nice time. Try to keep the drinks upright."

"Definitely," Logan said. He waited for her to pass their table before sliding back into their booth. "Your *elderly* mother, I presume?"

"She was a lot older last time I saw her," Riley said.

"This is going to be more fun than I thought," he said, his smile very wide. "You're going to need some training in dating..."

"You sure you're the one to do it?" she asked.

"Oh, yeah. I'm the guy."

chapter *eleven*

After Riley's mother departed and Logan got her another glass of wine, the whole mood of the date lightened and they laughed together like old friends. Riley told him all about her family, how she came to Santa Rosa to live with her grandparents after her father's death, her brother the schoolteacher, her mother—not elderly at all but very hip and cool and someone who'd helped her so much with her daughter, she couldn't have survived without her.

"What about Maddie's dad?" he asked.

"Oh, he's around. He came by on Thanksgiving to see her. It was my mother and grandparents who got me through the pregnancy and early years and I really hated Jock for his negligence, but we were eighteen, for God's sake. He was useless, his support was erratic and insufficient, but he was just a kid. Immature. He grew up over time." Then she laughed. "Not a lot, but he did grow up. He's good to Maddie. He loves her. He's very proud of her."

"Does he still love you?" Logan asked.

"He never really did," she said with a laugh. "I've been over him a long, long time."

"What does he do?"

"He's a manager in a big electronics chain. You know the guy—short-sleeved dress shirt, bad tie, khaki pants, sort of athletic-looking and he watches over the nerds who help you find just the right phone or laptop or speakers. He's very personable. Kind of perpetually happy. A little bit like a puppy. Now that I'm over being pissed off at what a lousy boyfriend he turned out to be, we get along all right. What about you and your ex?"

"I think I told you—she's my sister's best friend. My sister's married…" He paused and grinned. "To a man—they're not that kind of best friends. And my ex is a nice person, a real nice person. I admit, it threw me, but that was years ago. I'm over it. She's happy, she has a good life, she's successful…"

"But you took some heat?"

"I'm a cop, what do you think? There are some good women in the department but it's still mainly a guy's shop and yes, they didn't let up for a long time. They still give it to me from time to time. But they also like my ex. Because she's…" He shrugged. "Likable. But it's mostly over now."

"Mostly?"

"Well, there's that odd first date when you have to explain your wife left you because she's a lesbian…"

"I'm sorry, I was very rude. I shouldn't have found humor in it."

"You laughed your ass off," he pointed out.

"Well, just before that revelation, you'd been way too confident. So what does she do? Your ex?"

"Nurse practitioner. We dated a year, were married a year, been divorced eight years, still see each other all the time because she hangs out with Bernie, my sister."

"It sounds kind of nice. Family-like." She smiled at him. "Let's have coffee," she suggested.

Before Logan knew what was going on, over two hours had passed and he'd had one of the best first dates he'd had in a long, long time. He found Riley to be funny, cute, sexy and smart. He was intrigued by how she built her business. He loved hearing about the way she grew up, the family's struggles, the family's close relationship.

She never once mentioned Emma Shay and he grew hopeful that there was no strong connection between them.

"Why am I telling you so much?" she said, well into her second cup of coffee.

He shrugged. "I'm a detective. I know how to ask the right questions. I know when to ask them. But hey, I play fair— this is a date, not an interrogation. I'll tell you anything."

"Anything?"

"Pretty much. I can't talk about cases I'm working on but you'd find that boring anyway. Riley," he said seriously, "this turned out really nice. I think your mother catching you having a date broke the ice."

"I think you're right," she said. "And I'm never going to hear the end of it."

"Are you ever going to tell me why it was me?" he asked. "And why tonight was the night?"

She wore a mysterious smile. "Maybe next time," she said. "Or the time after that."

"That's what I wanted to hear."

Logan wasn't allowed a kiss that first night, but she did make plans with him for the next day. She agreed to meet him Saturday afternoon for a movie and early, casual dinner. He took her to see a disaster film—a violent earthquake took out the entire west coast—and if it had been a test, it was a very successful one; she loved the movie and it had her nearly sitting on his lap through the whole thing. And then during a dinner of pizza and beer he was more than happy to tell her his life story.

Logan's parents had divorced because his father cheated on his mother when Logan was at a very vulnerable age of thirteen. Although his father never remarried and his parents seemed to have made their peace with each other, Logan wasn't over it. "I'm thirty-eight, my dad has always stuck around, made amends as best he could, I get along with him as well as possible but the truth is, I'm still pissed."

"That's a powerful grudge," she said. "Remind me not to make you angry."

"Funny thing is, I don't think I'm that kind of person, not really. I didn't stay mad at my wife, did I? My sister's fine with him. But we just rub each other the wrong way. And the rest of the family gets chronically annoyed with both of us. Maybe we just don't like each other that much."

"Did you like him once?" she asked.

"I worshipped him," Logan said.

"And there's the problem," Riley said.

If that had been a second test, she passed with flying colors. She was good to talk to—perceptive and sensitive. Intelligent and compassionate.

"Might be time to let that little boy in you grow up," she said.

And she made him laugh. For Logan, a laugh was almost as good as a kiss.

Almost.

On Sunday they went to brunch in Bodega Bay then drove to a hilltop that overlooked the Pacific. Once there, Logan got his kiss and it was so excellent he helped himself to several more. He got the message Riley was just as pleased because in no time they were making out like teenagers. And it was good. She tasted good, felt good, responded to him in a lush and delicious way.

She stopped him. "Whew," she sighed. "I'm not ready for more than that."

He smiled and kissed her nose. "That's fine. You're probably the smart one here. But you have to admit—we have ourselves a very nice start."

"Meaning…?"

"Three dates in three days, good food, good talk, excellent making out…"

"Yes… And now the workweek starts and…"

"And?" he asked.

"I have long hours, family obligations… I don't usually have this much time to play around."

He hugged her close. "I'm not playing, Riley. And I understand about schedules, work, family. How about if I call you? How about we stay in touch? In close touch? Let's work out when we'll get together again."

"I guess…"

"You sound a little cautious," he said.

"It's been a long time," she said. "But yes, let's talk."

"When is too soon to call you?"

"Fifteen minutes after we say goodbye today," she said.

He laughed. "You read me, all right. I'll call tonight."

Then they kissed a little more.

Logan hadn't been looking. Well, he was always looking, but he hadn't been expecting to find anyone. This woman was a surprise—as pretty as any woman he might be physically attracted to, as smart as any he could be serious about, as sexy as anyone he could be completely into. It took him a little by surprise, but damn.

This one, he sincerely believed, had some outstanding staying power. A few things would have to be managed, however. Like the case he was working on. And the fact that Riley had only crossed his path because he'd been watching Emma Shay.

They talked late Sunday night, too late. That quiet, intense, getting-to-know-each-other, coming-on-to-each-other kind of talk. He had dreams. Fantastic dreams. He went to work early Monday morning tired with a love hangover.

"We got a break in the Compton surveillance," his partner Georgianna Severs said. "Her relationship with the Kerrigans flared—she took a job from Riley Kerrigan and it appears her casual friendship with Adam Kerrigan has been upgraded. I reviewed a week's worth of her phone log and she calls the brother at least three times a day. She took a job with Riley and she's boinking the brother, Adam. We've got her on tape referring to both Adam and Riley Kerrigan multiple times. I guess we know why she's back here."

Logan felt the shot to his gut. His suspect was involved with his new girl...

Logan slid down in his desk chair and said, "Fuck."

"What?" Georgianna asked him. "We knew they knew each other."

"Everyone knows everyone around here. She went to school with half the town but she hasn't been in touch with them. The word was they were estranged, hadn't talked in years. In four months we had one text to the brother's cell. One! They weren't in touch!"

"That we know of," Georgianna said. "Our warrant is limited to her phone and her banking. We don't have her under surveillance."

"We've been watching her," he said.

"Hit and miss, not surveillance. We're not sitting on her."

"I thought we'd be cutting this loose pretty soon..." He shook his head miserably.

They occupied a little cubicle, but it was early. Not too many people around. They wouldn't even have their morning briefing for another half hour.

"What did you do?" Georgianna asked.

"I'm hooked up with the friend. Riley Kerrigan."

Georgianna was silent. It took her a long time to speak. "Why?"

"Why? Why?" he asked incredulously. Then all the wind out of his sails, he put his head in his hands. "The flesh is weak," he muttered.

"Oh, my Jesus," she said tiredly. "What were you thinking?"

"What do you know?" he asked. "You were born married. You were seven the last time you were tempted. She's beautiful, all right? She's funny in a ridiculously arrogant sort of way—she thinks she knows everything, like all women, as you should understand. Besides, this just wasn't that much of a case. I thought she might accidentally give me some useful information and probably never even know it and *poof*—the warrants would expire, it would be over and—"

"And we agreed it certainly would be a major case if we caught her transferring money from a hidden account. In which case it would be a career maker. And there was probable cause for the warrant."

"Very thin probable cause that had nothing to do with Riley Kerrigan," he argued.

He got up from his desk and went for coffee.

A little over six months ago, shortly before the suicide of Richard Compton, Emma Shay Compton's cell phone had gone missing. So she claimed. It was not recovered, but in the interim the FBI monitored calls and there had been two placed from that number to Aruba where the Comptons had owned a beachside estate—their winter place. Based on the suspicion that Emma might have offshore funds in the islands, money set aside from her husband's estate for her to access, a judge had granted a warrant for surveillance of phone and banking records for six months. The six months would be up in February and if there wasn't any new probable cause, it would not be renewed.

It was a soft case now with Compton dead, everything either liquidated and auctioned or held by US Marshals for auction. The apartment in Manhattan and the estate in Aruba had been sold. Emma Shay had been thoroughly investigated and if no new incriminating evidence turned up before the expiration of the warrant, it was likely the case would be closed. The FBI was being assisted by local detectives Danner and Severs, but after the expiration of the warrant the local police would be off the case and it would be up to the FBI to sniff around Emma to see if she suddenly started living large or if she bought airfare to another country where she might access her nest egg without the interference of the US Government.

Law enforcement could investigate her forever if they chose to, but they couldn't access her property, phone records, banking records or other personal property and space without a warrant.

Logan and Georgianna had been watching, listening, and there had been nothing to indicate the former Mrs. Compton had access to illegally received money. And they had other cases to work. They were actually property crimes cops but both had had some previous experience in intel and fraud and it served a purpose to have them working in a division that didn't normally deal with white-collar crime. No one would suspect them of investigating Emma Shay.

Logan went back and sat at his desk. Their desks were pushed together, back to back so the partners faced each other. There were two computers, two phones, a couple of bulletin boards, a couple of shelves where spiral notebooks and loose papers were constantly stacked. George had pictures of her kids, parents and her framed awards on her side of the cubicle. Logan had a picture of his last dog, a German shepherd named Suzanne after an ex-girlfriend he hadn't had a great experience with. The accoutrements in the room were heavy on George's side.

"It's not going anywhere and we know it," he said.

"You have to tell Mike," she said.

Mike was the captain in charge of the fraud unit.

"When there's something to tell him, I'll tell him," Logan said.

"There's something to tell him now," she insisted.

"Are you going to get in my business here?"

"He's going to ask you to either drop and hand off your investigation or make yourself available to detectives for questioning. He's going to ask you, 'Do you want to work this case, which could be a career making case if you find something, or do you want to fall in love?' Because you can't have both. If you want to work it, then you're now undercover and everything you do with Riley Kerrigan is subject to examination, but you can't have both."

"I can if she's not in any way involved in a conspiracy to receive or help someone receive stolen money or property."

"But you won't know that unless you're undercover. I have no problem passing this to another team and..."

"And dropping it after months of work? What do we have—a surplus of bored detectives around here looking for extra work? By the time the warrant is expired we'll know what we're dealing with!"

"And you'll be in over your head," she pointed out. "You'll screw it up."

"No. I. Won't." He took a breath. "I know how to keep my work and my personal life separate. I've done it for fifteen years."

"Well..." she said.

"Okay, once or twice I might've blurred the line a little, but I'm not exactly famous for it."

She leaned on her hand, looking at him earnestly. George was beautiful. She was five-ten with shoulder-length bronze hair, big brown eyes, a knockout body and a drop-dead intelligence that she'd completely betrayed by marrying and reproducing with a big, burly firefighter. Cops had a love-hate relationship with firefighters. The smoke-eaters always got the girls and it just wasn't right. If Logan had seen George first, he might've married her, but unfortunately he'd been married to someone else back then. But he drew her as a partner and in that got one of the smartest detectives he'd ever known. He knew he should probably listen to her now, take her advice.

"I got it, George," he said.

"Why don't you go ahead and tell me how you justified this in your tiny little brain," she said.

"I was befriending her! I never would've gotten interested if I thought she could possibly be involved with our suspect! But then... I just found out, okay?"

"You've had five minutes, which is about all the time you give matters this important. Go ahead. Tell me."

"It's not going anyplace. So they know each other, so what? Everybody knows everybody—it's her hometown, that's why she's back. That doesn't spell conspiracy or fraud or anything. It's too soon anyway. If I'd been married to a multimillionaire who got all his money through fraud and if I had a little of that stashed somewhere I wouldn't tap it in six months. I'd wait a few years till there was no scent on the money. If she wanted some money, why didn't she take the settlement she was offered?"

Georgianna pulled a face. "Because she looks better this way and what she's got stashed is more."

"Then why didn't she take the settlement, move to the islands or something and have both? We talked about this. One of two reasons—either she's afraid she won't be able to travel because she'll end up extradited and prosecuted or maybe, just maybe, she's not guilty of anything."

"Danner, here's what you don't get—they were *married*. They lived together. They slept in the same bed. He probably talked in his sleep. They socialized with his employees and his clients. Do you really think he pulled off a Ponzi and she never thought something was weird? Really?"

"And here's what you don't get, George—not everyone is married like you are. Most of the cops in this shop don't tell their wives what happens at work and their wives don't ask. Not all married couples talk. Al's wife has these huge bills and he doesn't want to ask her what she's spending the money on and for that matter Al has a little issue with the slots, so he's not into sharing. Not all couples have that whole transparent thing going on like you and Mr. Universe."

Georgianna smiled. "He likes that you call him that."

"Great. Then I'm going to stop."

"So let me tell you another thing you don't get. If she didn't communicate with her husband, then if she has a secret of any kind she'll tell her girlfriend. Guaranteed."

"Shit," he said, knowing she was right.

"So what do you want, Danner? A new squeeze or a case?"

"Leave me alone. I can do this."

"I'm watching," she said.

★ ★ ★

Here's what was going to happen, Logan thought. He was going to work the case with George—they were considered a dream team because they were smart, instinctive and experienced. He'd listen to phone tapes and scrutinize bank records. He would gladly tell George anything he learned from Riley that had anything to do with a possible conspiracy and pointed a finger at Emma Shay. He would not share the personal and intimate details he hoped to achieve with Riley Kerrigan, and very soon. He would keep those two parts of his life separate.

If he learned from Riley that her girlfriend Emma was coming into money or had hidden money, then Logan would do the right thing—he'd tell George and they would hand over the case and report it to the FBI. Logan wouldn't break the law. Not even for his own mother.

But he was going to have something with Riley because he was irresistibly drawn to her. He thought he caught her scent several times through the day and night even though she wasn't anywhere nearby. He thought they could have one of those unique give and take relationships that was part fun, part intense, part sexual. He was into her, that's all. He might be an idiot about women, but he was into her and he was going for it until it worked or flopped.

He might've noticed Riley at first because he was checking out some of Emma's old friends, but that connection faded fast and he kept finding her because she appealed to him. And there was nothing illegal about that.

The second week in December was bitterly cold, with frost on the ground, dark clouds overhead, fires in every home with a hearth. But in Riley's heart there was a special warmth that she hadn't felt since her youth.

She laid her plans carefully. She left work early, went to the grocery store, picked Maddie up after cheer practice and took her home. Then she got busy in the kitchen. With her mom and Adam always ready and eager to plan family dinners, it wasn't necessary for Riley to cook very often. Of all of them, her hours were the longest. Adam was usually done at school by four at the latest, June was busy but liked to deliver her meals early in the afternoon—her elderly clients liked to eat early and looked forward to her visits. She was always finished before five in the afternoon. When they weren't eating at June's, Riley and Maddie often grabbed takeout, something for which her daughter was usually grateful.

Tonight she was making corn chowder, salad and biscuits. She set the table even though they usually ate in front of the TV. A fire blazed in the family room. She even refreshed her lipstick.

"I have some things to talk to you about," Riley said when her daughter joined her in the kitchen.

"Wow," Maddie said. "Must be deadly serious. Fancy spread."

"It's not. I mean, I think it's important but... Well, I just wanted to tell you—I met someone. A man."

Maddie grinned. "And you're finally going to tell me?" Maddie said, dipping a spoon in her soup and blowing on it.

"What does that mean? Did Grandma say something?"

"Well, she did, but only a couple of days ago. Really, Mom? You think I haven't heard you whispering into your phone late at night? And giggling? Or that I haven't noticed how nice you've been lately?"

Riley stiffened. "I'm not usually nice?"

"Sure you are. In a very businesslike way."

"Wow," Riley said. "I thought we were very close."

"We are. I know you love me. Now tell me about this

guy. We don't want to waste this cozy setting." Then she smiled prettily.

"Hmm," Riley said. "Well, I met him accidentally several times—grocery store, Starbucks—he lives around here. He's a police officer in Santa Rosa so I saw an opportunity to ask him to check on you and make sure you're not getting into any trouble and if you were, to tell me."

"You wouldn't dare!" Maddie said, outraged.

"Touché," Riley said, smiling. "He is a police officer, though. And I got a kick out of him—he's cute and kind of funny—and I thought, if I want to have a date again, maybe a cop would be safer than someone who had no ties to the community. Know what I mean?"

"You checked him out," Maddie said.

"Well, I'd have checked out any man before dating him…" Maddie laughed. "Oh, Mom."

"What? I don't meet them in school, you know!"

"I think it's great. Do I get to meet him one of these days?"

"Sure. Yes. Of course. There's something else I wanted to tell you. It's about an old friend of mine. Emma." She took a deep breath. "Emma Shay. We were best friends all through school and when she went away to college in Seattle, your dad was actually her boyfriend. But…" She shrugged and looked into her soup. "Emma kind of lost interest in him and, well, we started going out."

Riley looked up and Maddie was staring at her patiently. Waiting.

"I got pregnant. I suppose that's why things didn't quite work out with your father and me. He'd actually been Emma's guy. But…well…"

"I know all that. You and Daddy weren't really a couple but you got together and—bingo."

"You know all that?"

"Uh-huh. Daddy told me. A long time ago. At least a couple of years ago. Maybe more. He said it was all his fault and the biggest mistake he ever made."

"Well, that was delicate of him…"

"Not because of me! Because it screwed things up with you, Mom. He said the biggest mistake of his life was not begging you to marry him." She slurped a little soup. "I think he's still kind of in love with you."

Riley was momentarily stunned. "Well, that's news to me. He certainly has an odd way of showing it."

"He's kind of stupid that way," Maddie said. "But he's a very good guy."

"Well… So there's a reason I wanted to tell you about Emma. She's been through a really hard time. She married after college, had a miserable marriage, her husband committed suicide and Emma came home. She's had a struggle. So I gave her a job, of course. Grandma was also close to Emma when we were kids and can't wait to see her again, so I guess she'll be around. Also, I think Adam might be dating her, but I haven't asked, it's just that I have a good nose. So I wanted you to have all the information so you wouldn't be completely shocked if you actually meet her. There are lots of connections and complications there."

Maddie stabbed some of her salad. She pulled it off her fork with her teeth and chewed. "I know all that, too."

"Oh, really? And who explained all that?"

"Well, Uncle Adam wanted to give me a heads-up—he has a girlfriend and he hasn't brought her around yet because you're Emma's boss and she has history with the family, not all of it good. I figured out she's the one who used to be your friend and Daddy's girlfriend. And Adam suspects you might still be enemies."

"Huh," Riley said. "Is there any reason for me to be here

right now? Anything I can tell you that you don't already know?"

Maddie took another bite of salad, chewed and swallowed. "I seriously doubt it," she said.

Riley put down her spoon in exasperation. "What did Grandma tell you?"

"Hmm." She stalled. "Well. She said after all these many years you and Adam were starting to get your stuff together. She didn't say *stuff,* but you know Grandma can swear sometimes. And so do you, and yet I will be punished if I— Okay, so she said after all these years it appeared Adam might have a serious love interest and she caught you finally on an actual date. With a decent-looking guy who was nice and polite and kind of interesting..."

"She doesn't know anything about him!"

"You sure about that?" Maddie asked. "Who knows what she knows? This is really good soup." She slurped a little more. "I like these talks, Mom. When am I going to meet your friend Emma?"

"Aren't you more interested in the guy?" Riley asked.

"I want to know about you and Emma, like when you were kids. And when you were teenagers," Maddie said.

"What do you want to know?" Riley asked.

"Everything," she said. "Uncle Adam said if I wanted to know all that I had to ask you. I asked him was there secret stuff? Was that why I had to get it from you? And he said it wasn't because it was secret. It was because it was special. Really special."

Riley thought for a moment. "It was," she said. "She was the first friend I had here. We were nine..."

Riley told her daughter all the details, from nine to nineteen, and Maddie understood it all because she had best friends—the laughter, the fights, the trouble, the way they'd always helped each other through dark times. Although it was frightening, Riley also told about the end. She didn't quote Emma or herself, but she admitted there were hateful things said.

"Mom," Maddie said. "Mom, you're crying..."

Riley wiped at her cheeks. "I didn't realize," she said. "I didn't think it was still so real. It was such a hard thing... And then there was you, and you made it all worth it. Because I had you, my regrets were gone. I was sorry I hurt her, though. And I said so, I really did."

"Is she still mad?" Maddie asked.

Riley shrugged. "I don't think so. We haven't had that talk. We nibbled around the edges of it. She said she got over it a long time ago and I said that I'd begged her to forgive me and she never did. But then we left it without a real talk."

"Are you going to?"

"I'm her boss now so I don't know," Riley said.

"You better," Maddie said. "Know why? Because I don't think I've ever seen you cry before."

"Oh, Maddie, I've cried so much!"

"Not around me," she said. "And you know what? You're more real when you cry."

chapter *twelve*

Emma had to concentrate very hard just to keep up with the rest of her team so for the first two weeks in her new job she saw very little besides the dust and dirt she was waging war on. It wasn't just important that she be flawlessly thorough, but also fast. Clients had an expectation of not only a perfect job, but an on-time job, too. In most of the houses no one was home and it was usually planned that way; people didn't like being underfoot while the house was being cleaned.

Nick came by a couple of times as she was working to check on her. He was a happy and energetic guy in his early thirties, and two things were immediately clear—all the women liked him and he had eyes only for Makenna. He joked with her, complimented her, asked her a lot of questions, but she kept moving and gave him mostly short answers. Emma was amused by the way she tried to ignore him. Makenna was much friendlier with the women, though she was their superior. If Emma knew her better she might tease her, but she really didn't dare.

In fact, there wasn't much she dared. She very much wanted to prove she could clean as well as she could supervise a household staff. That first week, she didn't notice much, but there was one thing that drew her attention. The trash in the wastebasket of a fifteen-year-old girl. It appeared she'd thrown away some clothing. Emma didn't mean to inspect her trash, but she couldn't help but notice the price tags still on the clothes. She pulled them out—two pair of pants, three tops, a scarf, a blazer—all stuffed into the trash can. A wad of gum was stuck to a brand-new Free People long-sleeved knit top that sold for eighty-five dollars. There were designer labels on the other items. Prada. BCBG. Christian Lacroix.

She smoothed the clothes out on the girl's bed.

"What are you doing?" Makenna asked.

"She must have made a mistake," Emma said. "She threw away brand-new, very expensive clothing—these still have the tags on."

"It's not a mistake," Makenna said. "They're in the trash."

"But…"

"And please, don't talk to Dellie about the clothes in the trash. Dellie has three daughters, no spousal support and seeing this careless treatment would be hard on her heart."

Emma frowned. "But why?"

"Because her ex is an asshole, why else?"

"No—why are these things in the trash?"

"Some of that stuff we don't see, Emma. Her parents are never around, her mother's assistant buys the clothes, Bethany doesn't want them. In fact, she resents them and does it out of spite. But they can't end up on an employee's daughter. Who knows how much trouble that could create."

"Shouldn't her mother know?"

"Do you know her mother?" Makenna asked, lifting her dark brows.

"Well, no, but if I—"

"Don't project. Don't extrapolate. Telling her mother might only create bigger problems for us."

"How?"

"She'll fire us and hire a new service merely because we looked too closely and presumed to know more about her family than she does. Trust me. Or, to keep from getting in trouble with her mother, sweet little Bethany will claim we stole the clothes."

"Doesn't she care?" Emma asked Makenna.

"I don't know. And neither do you." And with that, Makenna stuffed the beautiful clothes back into the trash can and handed it to Emma.

Emma did as she was supposed to do and emptied that trash can into the big plastic bag she was carrying from room to room. She so hoped she'd see some of those expensive new things on a homeless person. "If she were mine…"

"I'm sure you'd care enough to take her shopping, listen to her likes and dislikes and be a perfect mother. Congratulations to you."

"I bet there are some homeless people who'd like to know where the best trash cans are," she muttered when she was out of Makenna's earshot.

She didn't say another word but she could begin to see how you could become hard, cynical. If the dirt the clients left behind wasn't enough to turn you, the private lives they thought no one could see might.

"We need to be invisible," Makenna reminded her. "We can't afford to be enmeshed with the client. It's not good for business."

Emma was surprised no exposé had been written by a member of her Manhattan household staff. Had she and Richard been more clever in concealing how obscene their private lives were? Looking back she thought she'd been a very decent mistress of the house but it was true; she didn't remember the names of all the people who served them. She knew the housekeeper, the driver, the cook, her part-time assistant. The cleaning people changed regularly, the florist's delivery people were always different, she'd had seven different personal shoppers in five years.

They had been invisible to her.

At the end of the second week on Friday afternoon, she went with Makenna back to the office to pick up her car.

"Here's your schedule for next week. Meet your team here. You can take a van to your appointments. And Riley asked me to tell you she'd like to see you if you have some time."

She was the boss. How could Emma not have time?

When she got up to the second floor, Jeanette was gone for the day and Riley's door was ajar. There was laughter coming from inside. Emma tapped lightly.

"Come in, come in," Riley called. "Well, you look pretty decent for a Friday night."

"I do?"

"You do," she laughed. "Emma, this is Brazil Johnson, our accountant and CFO. We go way back. Brazil, this is Emma Shay and we go back even further—we first met in fourth grade."

Brazil, a tall, lanky African American woman in jeans and crisp blouse with a scarf tied around her head, stood and put out a hand. "Emma," she said. "I like that. Emma. Is it short for anything?"

Emma shook her head. "No, and I wasn't named for anyone that I know of."

"I used to clean houses with Brazil," Riley said. "We were almost the original team."

"I'm happy to meet you," Emma said.

"Come in and sit," Riley invited. "Brazil isn't around the office too much and when she is I like to take advantage of her stories."

"My mother is an invalid now," Brazil explained. "I work from home as often as I can so I'm there for her. Most days she drives me out of my mind. But it's very good practice for me—might make me conscious of what it's like and keep me from burdening my daughter with the same." She shook her head. "Woo-eee, Denise wouldn't put up with a tenth of what Mama gives me!"

"Denise is an attorney," Riley said. "Also a single mother. So many of us."

"Do you have children?" Brazil asked Emma.

"No," she said, shaking her head. "It's just me."

"Well, your old friend Riley has created a company that welcomes single parents and makes it easy for them to work at a decent wage. She should get a medal."

"I'm thinking a statue in the town square," Riley said with a laugh. "How's work going? Any problems or revelations?"

Emma was a little uncertain. She bit her lip for a moment. "Work is fine. Is there a suggestion box around here?"

Riley's eyebrows were raised in question. "You have a suggestion? Already?"

"Just a thought," Emma said with some trepidation. "I understand why it's a bad idea to accept used clothing from clients…"

"It can be disastrous," Riley said.

"I was wondering, if it was managed and there was a receipt from the donor so there wouldn't be any misunderstanding…"

"I don't think it's a good idea to have our clients think we're needy, Emma."

"I understand, but the client doesn't have to know where

donated clothing goes. In fact, we could send out a notice to clients saying that if they choose to donate to a variety of worthwhile outlets from shelters to dress for success organizations that help to clothe people for job interviews…"

"The clothes you were forced to throw away wouldn't have made it into donation, Emma," Riley said. "That screwed up fifteen-year-old girl's clothes wouldn't have been donated. She was making a statement when she put them in the garbage."

"You know about that, huh?" Emma said.

"There's very little I don't hear about," Riley said. "I'm sorry, Emma. I think it's a bad idea."

"If someone came to you and said, 'Would you like to donate these nice clothes?' what would you think?" Brazil asked. "You'd think, 'Why's that cleaning woman picking through my trash?' that's what."

"Our clients want to think their cleaners don't need charity. They like thinking we don't see their castoffs, that we don't notice things like that."

"Tempting though, ain't it?" Brazil said.

"It is," Emma said.

"Look the other way, Emma," Riley said. "Anything else on your mind?"

She shook her head.

"I'm glad it's going well for you. Makenna tells me you're doing a very good job."

"Thank you," she said. "The team does a very good job. They're good girls. Women."

"That's all I have for you," Riley said. "I just wanted to check in with you. And here's your check," she added, handing Emma an envelope. "From now on Brazil will have your pay deposited in your account and Nick will give you the stub showing your deductions. Welcome aboard."

"Thanks," she said. And took her leave.

★ ★ ★

Emma had been in touch with Adam every day without fail. On those few nights they weren't together, they talked on the phone. Tonight Emma was going to Adam's house for dinner. When she was there, which had only been twice so far, she put her car in his garage so that if Riley drove by she wouldn't see it. When she arrived, he was busy in the kitchen, slicing and dicing, garlic being sautéed in the pan on the stove.

"It already smells wonderful."

"I have something to tell you," he said. "My mother asked me if I happened to have a phone number for you. She's planning to call you. I gave her the number. I hope you're okay with that."

"Will she tell Riley?" Emma asked.

"You can ask her not to, Emma. I don't think Riley finding out we're seeing each other will be as much of a problem as you think."

"It will be a problem for her, I guarantee it."

"I hope you're wrong, but we'll do things your way. My mother wants to see you. She knows Riley has your number and she didn't ask her."

"I don't know what's going to piss her off more—us being together or hiding it from her."

Every time Emma's phone rang, she jumped. She looked at the caller ID and it was either Adam or Lyle. Then on Wednesday while she was working, her phone vibrated in her pocket and she didn't dare answer it, even though the home owners were not home. When they took their break between houses, she listened to the message.

"Emma, it's June Kerrigan. Adam gave me your number and I've been looking for a time I could ask you to dinner when it would be just us so we could talk, catch up with no interference from eavesdroppers or others. Maddie is having a sleepover Friday night so her mother will have to stay home with them. How I got out of sleepover duty, I'll never know, but finally the house is my own. Can you come to dinner? At about six? When you were a little girl you loved my fried spaghetti—it was your favorite and your little feelings were hurt if we had it without you. If I make fried spaghetti, will you come? I think I've waited long enough!"

Tears came to her eyes and she sniffed loudly enough that Shawna turned from the front seat and asked, "You okay, girl?"

"Yes, sorry. I just got the sweetest message from an old friend…"

"It your birthday or something?" Shawna asked.

"No," she said, laughing. "She's going to make my favorite dish from when I was a little girl—fried spaghetti with pesto, black olives and pepperoni."

And both women oohed and ahhed.

On Friday afternoon, immediately after work, she went to the flower shop. She'd called Lyle and asked him if he'd make a Christmas centerpiece for her to give to someone special. When she got to the flower shop the guys were both there. With the holidays upon them, they were keeping the shop open a little later and Lyle hadn't gotten around to her centerpiece.

"Who's getting my masterpiece?" Lyle asked.

"You have to promise not to tell," she said. "June called me and invited me to dinner, just the two of us. Adam gave her my cell number."

"Adam?" Lyle and Ethan said in unison.

"Yes, Adam—and you have to keep him a secret, too. It started out that he was a very nice and helpful friend. You know, a little glass of wine, a cell number in case I needed a hand with anything, lunch at a vineyard bistro, then…"

They were leaning toward her. "Then…?"

"It got a little…you know…romantic."

"OMG, she's doing Adam, the love of my life," Ethan said, swooning into Lyle.

"Get a grip," Lyle said. "He's straighter than my hair."

"He actually is," Emma said. "Could you get on my page here? I'm reuniting with June tonight and I need a centerpiece. A lovely centerpiece. One that says I'm grateful for everything, for accepting me without questioning about Richard's crimes, for missing me, for welcoming me back, for still loving me."

"I've had a crush on Adam since the first day I met him," Ethan said.

She looked at Lyle. "What's going on here? Is Adam his hall pass?"

"It's completely meaningless," Lyle said. "Adam couldn't be less interested in Ethan. Come on back to the playroom, Emmie. You can supervise my creation."

"I'd love that," she said.

"And why are we keeping Adam and June secret?" Lyle asked.

"Riley is my boss and until Riley invites me to join her and the family, I'm staying back. She's keeping me at arm's length. Maybe someday, but not someday soon. But I so miss June."

"Understandable. Take your time. And tell me all about the job," he said.

"I told you," she said, finding a seat on a stool.

"Not really," he said, digging around for the tools of his profession—clippers, tape, scissors, foam, wire. "You did some groaning and whining about how exhausted you were but no details."

"We're not supposed to talk about details—the client, I am told, has an expectation of privacy."

"You aren't supposed to name them, Emmie, but you can tell tales to a person you can trust. That's me." He grinned. Then he stepped into the refrigerator and gathered up some stems, fern and baby's breath. "What's it like?"

"It's the hardest work I've ever done—and remember, I helped decorate a seventy-thousand square foot department store for holidays, on my feet, lifting and hauling and climbing for sixteen hours a day. I was a lot younger then, too. It's the hardest I've worked and I'm learning that to work for Riley is to get the best pay available for cleaners. Apparently clients cancel their contracts all the time and get cheaper cleaners but, because Riley and her two bulldogs, Makenna and Nick, keep everyone's standards really high, they end up returning and paying the money to get the good work. We do good work," she said, giving her head a shake. "Wow, do we do good work. And fast. I am appalled to note that there are so many jobs that pay better and have far less impact on the quality of life for a family. Families," she added. "You get a feeling for what family life is like in a house right away, which homes are run by the kids who have every possession imaginable and others don't even have family games. There are houses we clean where the wife hovers and inspects and says, 'My husband likes it this way or that way,' and houses I've cleaned four times and have yet to meet a home owner. You can pick out their nesting spot right away, the places that are used—a favorite chair, desk in the office, bathroom counter. We have one client who lies on the sofa watching TV until we get to that room, then she shifts to the bedroom. She eats all day and I've never seen her dressed in anything but lounge-wear. Some kids' rooms have awards and pennants and group pictures, some show no sign of any siblings or friendships or group activities. Some children's rooms are very, very sad."

"What makes a sad room?" he asked while he laid out a sheet of paper, placing baby's breath on it. The little ball inside the spray paint can bounced when Lyle shook it and with a quick, deft hand, he painted the baby's breath red.

"That's amazing, what you just did there," she said.

"Christmas colors. What's a sad room?"

"Well, there's a teenager's room that's so pristine it hurts. It's like a ghost room, but someone lives in it—there's evidence of living—trash in the bin, books moved, linens slept in, laundry in the hamper, towels in the bath have been used. When I moved the desk blotter to dust I saw something carved in the wood, something her mother would never see because her mother works long hours and doesn't clean or look at her daughter's things. She carved, *I miss her every day.* I assume she carved it. They're rich. They wouldn't have purchased a damaged piece of furniture."

"Wow," Lyle said, stopping his arranging. "Who do you think?"

"I don't know," Emma said. "Could be a sibling. There are no other children's rooms or family pictures anywhere. Maybe a friend? Grandmother? I have no idea. And you know what else, Lyle? I never realized this when I had help of my own but I realize it now. We're invisible. I always thought of myself as very tidy but now I wonder if I prepared for the cleaning staff—did I wipe the bathroom mirror? Clean the sink? Flush? Because now I see that some people don't."

"Ew," he said. "I certainly know I do those things."

"I think I did. I hope I did. But a hard truth for me is—I don't know the names of the ladies who cleaned our apartment. They changed regularly. But still…"

"My God, you're learning volumes about yourself. About people you don't know."

"It's humbling," she said.

"Are you humbled by who you are? Or who you were?"

"Both," she said.

She was so nervous. Anxious and nervous. She carried her centerpiece up the walk to June's front door and knocked. The door opened immediately and there she stood, looking only a little older.

"Emma! At last," June cried, embracing her at once.

Emma was left to balance the centerpiece in one hand and return the hug with the other.

"How I've missed you," June said. "I thought of you, prayed for you, hoped you'd come back to us. It's been so long."

Emma closed her eyes against tears. June's skin on her cheek was so soft, just as she remembered. She smelled faintly of Ivory soap, something so basic, clean and memorable. And she could smell clean sheets—June used to iron the pillow-cases, and the smell of hot linen that filled the room gave Emma such comfort. The arms that held her were the same, just strong enough but not overwhelming. June knew just how to cradle a person.

"June," she whispered.

June backed away a bit and looked at her. "You've held up so well," she said, wiping Emma's cheeks with her thumb. "Shall we stand here in the doorway and cry or will you come in?"

"I've been so excited and so nervous," Emma said.

"Now, stop that," June said with a little laugh. "From the very first day we knew each other we knew we'd be friends. Close friends."

"This is for you," Emma said.

"Ah, our Lyle hasn't lost his touch at all, has he? He's getting even better. Thank you, it's so beautiful. Come in, come in."

There was a small noise, a little whine, and Emma looked down to see the oddest-looking dog.

"Emma, this is Beatrice. She's staying with me for a while until she can recover from her last owner. She's a rescue and I'm afraid she was quite mistreated. I'm a foster mother for the animal shelter. Beatrice was once very beautiful and will be again after a little love and attention."

"She's so sweet," Emma said, reaching out.

But Beatrice just skittered away, going back to her bed in the kitchen.

"She usually needs a little time to get used to new faces, new smells." June carried the centerpiece into the kitchen where she had the table set with two places, candles and wineglasses. She put the flowers in the middle.

"Speaking of new smells... I haven't had fried spaghetti in so long. Since I was last at your house, I think."

"It's ready and in the warmer," June said. "We're going to light the candles, have a glass of wine and just talk for a while. Are you starving? I made us some crab rolls, just a little snack."

June busied herself getting the rolls, the wine, lighting the candles, then she sat down in the place next to Emma. She lifted her glass. "To your return, darling Emma."

Emma burst into tears.

It took her a moment and a couple of napkins to compose herself. June was the nearest thing to a mother she'd had and whether she'd admitted it to herself or not, she'd been afraid she'd never be reunited with her.

"Riley might not be okay with our private party," Emma finally said with a hiccup of emotion.

"Well, Riley's stubborn sometimes, but that's all right. Her pride and stubbornness probably got her through the tough times. She's a good woman. She's also logical and usually comes around eventually. And—I haven't mentioned this to her but not because I'm keeping secrets. Because she'd want to be here. And we need this time. I want you to tell me everything."

"Oh, June, you don't want to—"

"Yes, yes, I do. We always had the most important talks. About the hardest things, too. Tell me, Emma, did you love him?" she asked in a soft voice.

"I did," she said in a whisper. "I thought I was the luckiest girl in the world. In the universe. Richard was sophisticated and smart. He treated me as if I was some kind of precious gift. I loved him. I didn't think he was capable of doing anything terrible, of hurting people." She shook her head. "A couple of times I was selfish or demanding or complaining and he would just frown and say, 'Emma, Emma, this childish behavior doesn't suit your image at all. Don't you know how powerful you are? How many people watch you?' If I asked for something he would just say, 'Of course.' I thought he was kind. A few times I overheard him say things that were mean or harsh and if I questioned him he'd say he was sorry I had to hear that, that sometimes in business he had to be strong. Firm."

"Things like what, Emma?"

"Once I heard him on the phone, saying something like, 'That old bastard doesn't know what to do with his money anyway—he'll never miss it. Push on him a little bit harder and if you need me to, I'll call on him.' When I questioned him he said one of his clients was questioning his investment strategy, that he'd brought in more money in six months than the client's last broker had brought in over six years. And of course, he was sorry I'd seen him in such a negative light. June, he was so *nice*. Everyone loved Richard."

"You never knew what was happening," June said.

"But I did," she said in a secretive whisper. "I wouldn't let myself believe it. He had this PR person, Andrea. She'd worked with him for a long time before we got married. If he was having a relationship with her, why would he marry me? But they were together often. Sometimes she traveled with us. Sometimes with him—it was work. But I saw looks between them. Reckless, steamy looks. So I asked my husband—was he involved with Andrea? And he did what he did best—he calmed my worries, reassured me, said that was absurd. And later, much later, I learned Andrea was his mistress all along. Andrea was the one to tell him, 'It's time to marry for your image.' I wonder if he married me because I was too stupid to see what was in front of my face."

"No, no," June said. "He must have been that good at fooling people."

"But I let him fool me."

"What happened, Emma? What caused it to unravel?"

"The perfect storm. A couple of big clients didn't get good returns on their money and pulled out. There were flaws in the statements. Rich people have lots of CPAs running around, double-checking everything, and Richard made a few mistakes. Not mistakes—irregularities. There was a banking and investment corporation crisis and people were pulling their money out everywhere—no one wanted to be the last one holding the bag. Richard's funds were not insured or guaranteed. People were losing money everywhere else but not with Richard. Investments across the board were crashing like crazy, but not Richard's. A reporter from the

Washington Post started sniffing around, angry and paranoid investors complained to the SEC, an investigation began..." She shrugged helplessly. "And I began to see a whole new Richard."

"Oh, Emma, was it terrible?"

"It was terrible," she said. "Want to know why I stayed? Why I went to court? Because it was the only way I was going to find out the truth. He wasn't going to tell me. I was making assumptions, I was guessing, I was reading the papers, financial journals, watching the news—and they got so many facts about me wrong, I couldn't be sure they were getting facts about him right. But at the trial there was evidence. I wanted to know who he was and what he'd done. I probably should have left. But I wanted to know."

June straightened. "That's what I would have done."

"You would?"

"Absolutely. Ignorance isn't really a happy place, it just seems like it for a while. I would have wanted to know."

"He thought he was a god, June," she whispered. "He thought he could do anything to anyone, that he was the most important person alive. He used people, lied to people, laughed at them."

"Emma, what was it like to be rich?" she asked.

"It was isolating," Emma said. "Most of the time I felt like I was just visiting my own life. Then I'd remember, I was hired to play a part—the part of the great Richard Compton's wife. I'd always wonder how many others were pretending to be who they were. When you have a big pile of money, it should mean security. Safety. It didn't. All our friends were rich and they worried about having the most, spending the most, trying to figure out how it could make them the best. They trusted no one. You know that silly saying, he who dies with the most toys wins? I think for a lot of people it's actually true."

"For a little while were you happy? Did you think you'd been crowned?"

"Looking back, not for very long. Two days into our honeymoon, Richard got a phone call that sent him hurrying off to Dubai and he couldn't take me—it was business. He worked long days, had business dinners, business trips. I was like a happy little girl whose daddy had finally come home when he spent an evening at home. He took employees along on vacations. He never rested. June, I loved him because I didn't know him. I didn't know him at all. By the time he was convicted I wondered how I'd been so easily duped. How I managed to stay blind—that's the part I don't get. How can I ever trust myself again?"

chapter *thirteen*

Emma and June talked for hours, talked over dinner and then a cup of coffee. It reminded Emma of those times when she was a girl and she had issues or heartaches and she and Riley would sit on June's bed and talk it all out. When her father died and her stepmother and sisters weren't very comforting, June was there. Then it was worse when Rosemary remarried less than a year later, bringing home a man they didn't even know. A creepy man who made Emma so uncomfortable just by the way he looked at her. She was always at Riley's house and Rosemary didn't miss her at all. And June was constant, always there for her, no matter how tired she might've been. Even when Emma and Riley fell out, June wrote Emma a lovely letter saying she hoped one day they could make amends, but no matter, June would always love her like a daughter. "You are the daughter of my heart, Emma, and no matter what happens, I will always embrace you. If you need me, just call me."

It was ten o'clock when June nearly pushed her out the

door. "I'm afraid to leave," Emma said. "I don't know when we'll ever have another chance to do this, to talk like this."

"There will be many chances, Emma. I promise. Maybe you'll invite me to your little house."

The second the cold night air hit her face, Emma realized she was emotionally exhausted. Wrung out. She was glad Adam's house wasn't too far away; she was so happy he invited her back tonight. She hadn't packed a bag or anything but she was going to impose on him, steal one of his T-shirts and curl up next to his big warm body and sleep forever, maybe till Sunday.

"Emma?"

She nearly jumped out of her skin at the sound of a man's voice. She shrieked and crossed her arms over her chest.

"Oh, Jesus, sorry. I didn't mean to scare you."

"What are you *doing* here?" she asked, panting a little out of fear as who should come out of the shadows but Jock.

"I was waiting for you. I thought maybe we could talk. Just for a few minutes?"

"About what? And why are you waiting around here in the dark? How did you know where I'd be? Are you *following* me, Jock?"

"Oh, hell no, Emma. Maddie told me you'd be visiting June tonight. In fact, I think Maddie helped plan it."

"Huh? What are you talking about?"

"Maddie and her grandmother," Jock said. "You gotta watch those two. They're co-conspirators." He rubbed his hands together and stomped his feet, freezing.

"Why didn't you just call me?" she asked.

"Because Maddie didn't have your number. And I wasn't going to ask Adam or Riley." He snorted with laughter. "Oh, that would be interesting, like either one of them need another reason to be pissed off at me." He blew on his hands.

"Hey, could we just sit in the car for a few minutes? I won't take too much of your time."

"Why didn't you just tell Lyle you wanted to talk to me?"

"Because he might not have given you the message and even if he had, you might not have wanted to talk to me. Come on, Emma—it took me forever to get up my nerve. And I'm freezing!"

"Have you been waiting outside all this time?"

"I didn't think you'd be in there so long. And I didn't want to miss you. Look, I only want to apologize. Explain and apologize."

She shifted her weight to the right foot. "I don't know if that's wise, getting into the car with you, late at night, isolated like—"

He laughed. "Seriously? You think I'd hurt you? When did I ever hurt anyone, huh, Emma? My little girl told me where you'd be tonight. You think I'd do that to my little girl? For the love of—"

"All right, all right... But hurry up. I'm so tired I could lie down in the street right here and fall asleep!"

He put his hand on her elbow to steer her toward his SUV. "I know I'm a fuck-up, but I thought this was the right thing," he said, handing her into the car. He went around to the driver's side and got in. He started the car for heat and rubbed his hands together. "So, Emma, this isn't going to come as news to you—I cheated on you."

Emma couldn't help herself, a short burst of laughter escaped her. Then another laugh and another, until she had to put a hand over her mouth.

"I didn't think it was that funny," Jock said.

"I might be feeling a little emotional," she said, wiping tears of laughter off her cheeks. "I know, Jock. You were slightly unfaithful. Your daughter is now fifteen."

"Well, I pretty much screwed up everything. I'm sorry I hurt you."

"What about Riley?"

"I'm sorry I hurt her, too. But what I'm really sorry about is that I didn't get my shit together in time to be a real father to Maddie. I mean, I'm a real father, don't get me wrong. I'm crazy proud of that girl. She really did get the best of me and Riley—she's beautiful and smart as her mother, she's fun and athletic. She's going to set the world on fire. I don't know what she's going to do—I bet a doctor or scientist or something. If I'd done the right thing fast enough, we'd be together, but hell, I was a stupid kid. I didn't know what I was doing. I didn't know how I felt. Plus, even if I did know, I couldn't put it into words. Or actions."

"No, Jock," Emma said, shaking her head. "We wouldn't be together. It didn't take me very long to come to that conclusion. We were falling apart right away. We were too young to hold together a long distance—"

"Not you and me, Emma. Me and Riley and Maddie. It's my fault, I get that. I didn't step up like I should have. To tell the truth, it scared me to death. I had a part-time job at a gym, for God's sake. I mostly picked up towels, wiped down equipment, showed people how to use the weights, checked IDs and got to work out for free. And that was right before I got a part-time job at the store—in shipping. I was in school, showing everyone how stupid I was, mostly. When Riley said we should tell you, I couldn't face it, couldn't face you. Couldn't face her family—you know how tight they are. Sheesh. So I was too late. When I did go back to her and suggest we get married, she told me to go to hell." He shrugged. "Can't say I blame her, but I never got another chance."

Emma was a little stunned. "You cared about her?"

"Of course I did, what do you think? Okay, I was an idiot

and I thought maybe me and Riley would be friends with benefits for a while till I was ready, you know. But I was eighteen. And let me tell you about those Kerrigans…" He whistled. "You don't have five minutes to think with them, know what I'm saying? Riley's grandpa went straight to my dad and threatened to lock me up, for what, I don't know—we were over eighteen. Adam coldcocked me and told me to never set foot near his sister again or he'd kill me. Riley—Riley said I'd ruined her life, caused her to lose her best friend and I'd be lucky if she ever even let me *see* my child. And you never came back. I was so screwed. I couldn't win."

Emma was frowning. "You really cared about her?"

"I was a little slow, okay? I admit it—I didn't speak up fast enough."

"And Maddie told you where to find me tonight? What does Maddie know about it?"

"Everything," Jock said. His expression was composed and confident.

She tilted her head to look at him. He hadn't changed too much, actually. His hair was still a little shaggy but he had that handsome square jaw, pretty blue eyes and brows a little thick and bushy. And the lashes. Whew, girls would sell their mothers for some of those lashes.

"Everything?" Emma asked.

"I'm real close with Maddie. 'Course Maddie's real close with everyone. She's got a kind of gift. She knows how to make people feel okay about themselves. I told Maddie the truth a long time ago. I told her her mama was embarrassed about it all, maybe still upset about it. And I told her it was my fault because it was. But I wanted her to know—I really cared about her mom."

"But, Jock—you didn't even go to the hospital when she was born!"

"Yes, I did. I just waited for the Kerrigan clan to clear out. No point in getting my blood all over the maternity ward! But I went. I went a lot. The nurses knew the family was pissed—they let me in after hours. And I snuck over to her house when Adam and Riley weren't around. Took me a year to get Maddie to my house so my mom could fuss over her. In the end, Riley's fair. Plus, there was June. June put a stop to all the fighting and stuff, for Maddie's sake."

"Well," Emma said. "You didn't carry a torch long, did you? You got married, didn't you?"

"Yeah, I'm so brilliant—that was me showing just how smart I am. Maddie was around ten or so and I figured Riley had no reason to hold off on us getting together. I thought it all through—I'd been helping with Maddie, keeping her sometimes, giving Riley whatever I could for support—I know it wasn't much but I didn't have much of a job back then. So I worked it all out in my head and ran it by Riley— we could be a family. Something about the way I did it really pissed her off. I mean *really* pissed her off. She said, 'In your dreams, Jock.' So I did the most rational thing I could think of—I married this woman I worked with. She had two kids, she was crazy about me. I wanted to have a home. It didn't take me long after Riley shut me down to realize once I grew up a little bit, I wanted to be a family man. Turns out she wasn't crazy about me for long. But you know me, Emma—I'm such an idiot, I think there was a part of me that was gonna show Riley— See, someone wants me. I actually thought Riley might be a little jealous. So trust me, I learned my lesson."

"My God, you have to tell her all this, Jock! You should tell Riley you screwed up when you were eighteen but you really care about her."

"Nah, that ship has sailed," he said. "I'm not good enough

for her anyway. You know how smart she is? I'm just lucky we don't fight anymore. We get along okay. Maddie's happy. Maddie—she's incredible. You know Maddie's even proud of me? *Me?* I don't do much to brag about but I play some mean softball and Maddie comes to my games. All my friends and their families know her." He laughed. "Riley even came to a game once. She left like her pants were on fire, but hell— she did come."

"You used to play some serious football, as I recall," Emma said, her voice soft.

"Only for fun after high school," he said. "I've been with Mackie's Electronics for a long time and I do all right now. To tell the truth, I do better than all right—I have the management of a store. I have a mortgage. A house and a mortgage. Riley won't take support money anymore so she said just put some aside for Maddie for college. I'm sure Riley thinks I just ignored her, but I didn't. I think Maddie can pick any college by now. Not that she's going to need tuition—she's the smartest kid in school. Like her mom was. Riley was valedictorian."

Emma laughed. "Yeah. I was there."

"So I'm sorry, Emma. Sorry I cheated on you. I should've broken it off with you when we stopped talking, when I started hanging out with Riley. If I'd done that one thing…"

"Well, it's all behind us now. You were forgiven a long time ago."

"You okay, Emma? I heard about how bad things got for you. Anything I can do?"

"Nah. I have a job. I'm back in a town I know. I have a few friends."

"Maybe you could count me as a friend," he said. "No ulterior motives," he said, holding up his hands. "But if you need anything…"

"That's very nice, thanks. Right now I have to go. I

worked all day and seeing both you and June... By the way, Riley doesn't know I had dinner with June."

"I know. Maddie said we're not exactly keeping secrets, but we're not talking about it."

Emma laughed. That was what keeping secrets was. She made a decision—she was going to tell Riley about dinner with June. If it made her angry, she'd have to get over it. Emma was relatively sure Riley wouldn't fire her. In fact, she might have to tell about Adam, too. Now for that, Riley might fire her.

Jock was right. Those Kerrigans could really close ranks. But what should you expect from a family that had to stick together to survive?

She shook hands with Jock, wished him luck, thanked him for making amends. By the time she got to Adam's house it was almost eleven. The front door was unlocked. He had a fire going and was nursing a drink.

"I had almost given you up for lost," he said.

"For a little while there I thought I was lost. My night started with your mom and Beatrice..."

"I know Beatrice," he said with a chuckle.

"And ended with Jock waiting for me so he could apologize for cheating on me—sixteen years ago."

Adam was tempted to beg for every moment of time Emma would spare him, to keep her close, to possess her. Hold her. But he knew she had to untangle her life. And he was part of it. She said, very clearly, she needed to try to build her life as a woman before she thought of herself as part of a couple.

Last night in the glow of the fire she'd asked him, "Were you too hard on Jock? Did you scare him too much? Discourage him too much? Because it turns out he always cared for Riley. I mean, I think he loved her. And he adores Maddie."

"He was an irresponsible idiot," Adam said. "*Then*. Back then, I mean. I know he's gotten better over time. And don't kid yourself, he's not afraid of me!"

"He did a lot of stupid things," she said.

"That's an understatement."

"So did I," she said. "So did Riley. You appear to be the only perfect one."

But he'd lost his temper with Jock. He'd hated Jock. He didn't hate him anymore but he wasn't crazy about him.

Emma went home to help Penny rake up some dead leaves in her garden, to shop for her lunch supplies for the week, to launder her uniform. But she did invite him to share a pizza and a movie later. He knew that meant he'd somehow manage to spend the night. So he planned to spend some of his Saturday checking on his mother and buying another big box of condoms.

He'd had plenty of sex in his adult life. Great sex, as a matter of fact. But he'd never had a woman who wanted him like Emma wanted him. She unfolded like a rose in full bloom when he touched her. She said his name with a kind of breathy awareness that turned him on so much, he was completely helpless. He'd always thought of himself as a man with great control, but he lost that with her. He teased her until she became a little wild and then he was done for—he went crazy with her and they blew up together. He thought he knew why it was that way with them. He was in love with her.

After the weekend, Emma found herself actually looking forward to work on Monday morning, even though it was getting particularly difficult cleaning with Christmas approaching and all the decorations littering the houses. She'd never seen her own Christmas decorations looking shabby or dusty! She now realized she must have had an excellent cleaning crew.

Makenna had no trainees this week so in addition to working with Emma, Dellie and Shawna, she was visiting other teams at either Riley or Nick's request. Makenna was part of quality control. "The fabulous four rides on," Shawna said of their team. "I'm glad they haven't moved you to another team, Emma. I like working with you."

"Why?" she asked before she could think.

"You're a hard worker and stay in a good mood," Shawna said.

"She's still happy she got work," Dellie said. "She'll turn into one of us before you know it."

"If I have to push someone along all day..." Shawna made a face. "It just puts me in a temper." Then she launched into a litany of shortcomings about team members who didn't meet her expectations, everything from laziness to lying.

In ten minutes they pulled up to their first house, the Christensens'. They cleaned here twice a week but it hardly needed once. Mrs. Christensen, Makenna had informed them, knew if they missed a piece of lint or a hair on the bathroom countertop. They were here every Monday and Thursday. Emma hoped she wouldn't get the vacuum cleaner—those tracks had to be perfect. The house was huge.

This was where Bethany, the fifteen-year-old with the carved-up desk lived.

"How long have you been cleaning the Christensens' house?" Emma asked.

"I don't know," Shawna said. "I've been on it a year, I think. Dellie, how long?"

Before Dellie could answer, Makenna jumped in. "The company's been in that house four years now, but we've changed teams a few times. A couple of times Mrs. Christensen found the cleaning unsatisfactory and the other times it was just time for a schedule change. New people on the job usually freshens things up."

As luck would have it, Emma was assigned the dusting, vacuuming and linens upstairs. This time she meant to take a closer look in the bedrooms. Maybe there was a mystery to unravel. Maybe she'd spy some evidence of a visiting grand-mother or another child. She'd like to at least see a picture of Bethany, the girl who threw away the expensive new clothes.

The bathrooms and kitchen in this five thousand square foot custom home were usually fast work—Mr. and Mrs. Christensen had very demanding jobs and long hours. They didn't seem to do much cooking, and the only even slightly challenging bathroom was the master bath. There wasn't even much kitchen trash. Since they weren't contracted to clean the refrigerator, it was against the rules to look in it but Emma had an aching desire to know what kind of food was there.

She went to vacuum and dust Bethany's room first, fiercely curious. As she started ripping off the linens she found that the lump in the bed was Bethany. The girl shrieked and Emma jumped back, crying out.

"Oh, my God, I'm sorry! I didn't know you were in bed!"

Bethany grabbed for her covers. "I stayed home today."

"Oh, honey, are you sick?"

"Sort of," she said, burrowing back into her bed. "Sick of school."

"Oh. Can I get you anything? Call someone to look after you?"

"I'm fifteen! I look after myself!"

"Right," Emma said. "Would you like me to skip your room?"

"Yes. Just go. And look…" She talked from under the covers. "Just…don't say anything."

She's frail, Emma thought. Thin and pale and completely miserable. Who does she miss every day?

She moved on to the parents' room. Why did they have a cleaning service at all? They were immaculate. She stripped the bed, applied new linens, began dusting the furniture and heard Dellie in the bathroom, cleaning. She leaned against the door frame. "Skip the girl's bathroom," Emma said softly. "She's home, sick in bed, asked me to leave her room."

"All rightie," Dellie said. "I bet she's cutting school."

"No, she's sick," Emma said. Then she wondered why she was protecting the girl. She went back to dusting the bureau. A drawer was ajar an inch and impulsively, irrationally, she pulled it open a bit. Then a bit more. And there it was—the thing that was the root of all the pain and forced order in this house—a family portrait in a frame, hidden from sight, lying atop folded clothes. Mom, Dad and Bethany. A plumper, slightly younger Bethany who smiled as if the very sun was inside her. They were a beautiful, happy family a few years ago. Bethany was robust, rosy, healthy. That Bethany was gone now and in her wake, terrible pain.

She closed the drawer and felt her face catch fire. Her hands shook a little while she tried to concentrate on her dusting. If anyone knew, she would be fired. She would *have* to be fired.

What had happened to this family? Why was the only picture in evidence hidden in a drawer?

Then, later, as she pushed the vacuum around the room, she realized something significant—it was the father's drawer. How strange that seemed. She could envision the father demanding all the pictures be removed and the mother clinging to one. But it was the father holding on...and the mother's assistant was buying Bethany clothes.

Emma knew without even thinking about it that the next time they cleaned, the next time she had vacuuming and dusting, she would look in the mother's drawer. Look for a picture.

Then she thought of her stepmother. Rosemary dispensed with Emma's father's personal effects quickly, and the pictures soon followed because less than a year after his death Rosemary remarried. Emma kept pictures, however. So had her little sister, Lauren.

The next house was a filthy mess. It took too much of their time but it removed all that conjecture about Bethany and her family from Emma's mind for a while.

Makenna left them for a while to go with Nick and check a few crews. The next house wasn't bad, but messier than usual. The lady of the house was at home because her arm was in a sling. "Fell and dislocated my shoulder and might've injured my rotator cuff, but I had X-rays and it will be fine," she explained. "I'm just resting it and the doctor said to keep in immobilized for a few days." Then she laughed and said, "I could have gone to work, I just can't fix my hair with one arm!"

Then she stayed out of the way. When they were finished and back in the van, they took a break to eat a little lunch. "Fell my fine ass," Shawna said. "That's about her fifth fall this year!"

Emma almost choked on her drink. So—that was one of the households they knew too much about.

"It's possible she's clumsy," Emma said. "Isn't it?"

"Humph," was the answer. "She's being kicked around. Know how I know? Because I see it in her eyes and I've seen it before. When I looked in the mirror."

"Oh, dear God, Shawna," Emma said.

"Don't waste pity on me—I found the way out, even if you never get all the way out. If he isn't still out there posing a threat then he's in here," she said, tapping her head.

"Don't you worry none about Shawna," Dellie said. "Her boys are as big as he is and they take good care of their mama."

"They do. Now we're gonna get over to Ms. Fletcher's... She's the clumsy one."

"I think I might know what makes her so clumsy," Dellie said. Then the two of them cackled madly.

"What?" Emma asked.

"She's a wino," Shawna said. And they giggled some more.

It had taken her a while, but now Emma figured it out— she was hearing all this gossip because Makenna wasn't with them. Makenna was part of the executive trio with Riley and Nick, the holders of the holy grail, the policy manual. Violation of the policies got you fired.

"What's up with the Christensen house?" Emma bravely asked.

Shawna shrugged. "Career couple."

"Someone's got a little OCD going on there. I vote for her."

"Could be him," Dellie said. "We wouldn't know, they're never home. It's an easy house."

"Not a speck of dust anywhere."

"You gotta wonder why they hired a cleaning crew," Shawna said.

"For the carpet tracks," Dellie said.

"You gotta wonder why they had a kid," Emma ventured.

"Yeah, poor kid. Typical."

"Typical?"

"All they think about is work and money. Everything has to be perfect," Dellie said.

"I like it that way better than the Brewsters—those boys have every toy and gadget ever invented, they're sloppy, with no manners or respect and—" Shawna said.

"And I bet they already got accepted to Harvard even though the oldest one is twelve."

"That is a hard house," Emma agreed. Dirty, messy, cluttered with stuff. If she'd had a child, she would have taught him to put away his things, even if they had household help. When she dumped the trash in the master bath it was full of the lady's outrageous price tags. She smiled to herself. Those numbers hadn't always seemed outrageous to her.

How many of her cleaning staff saw her price tags? Well, hardly any of her things *had* price tags as they were designed specifically for her. But there was the odd outrageously expensive purse purchased at Neiman's...

She had an urge to unburden herself to her new friends, new friends who would never understand. She'd like to tell them what she knew—that those people with all their possessions could wake up one day to discover they'd been living a lie, that the identity they thought they had was gone and they would have to figure out all over again who they were.

Of course she couldn't. This was why she'd come back. There were a few people here who knew her before and after, who knew who she had been growing up and who she was again.

Only Emma was having a hard time getting a fix on her identity.

Emma had a message on her cell phone from Aaron Justice so she called him back before leaving the parking lot after work.

"I just wanted to wish you a pleasant holiday," he said. "And to tell you—we're working on an accounting of your father's estate according to his will. It should be ready after the holidays. I don't want you to get your hopes up but I anticipate a late Christmas present for you."

"Thank you, Aaron. And don't worry about my hopes. Just seeing you again has been an enormous treat. I wish you a lovely holiday."

"I'll be with my sons and grandsons. One of them is talking about making me a great-grandfather!"

"What a fantastic Christmas present for you! Thank you, Aaron, for trying to help me. Your friendship is so valuable to me!"

"Your father would be proud of you, Emma."

Proud? She wasn't sure about that. She'd made some pretty bad choices in the last decade. But she hoped she was making better choices now.

"I hope so," she told Aaron.

chapter *fourteen*

Riley was very much out of practice with the whole dating thing, but one thing she knew she wanted to do—she wanted to introduce Logan to her daughter. Their relationship had always been honest and up-front with those few little exceptions Riley had held back, like that whole Riley/Jock/Emma thing, which was now mostly out there. So she nervously asked Maddie if she'd like to meet Logan and have dinner with him.

"Dinner? Wow, we're going all out, I guess. Will Gramma and Adam be coming, too?"

"I thought we could just be the three of us. You know, we've got Christmas in a couple of weeks—Logan has a family, I have my family, we'll all be busy. We might see each other but I'm not planning on merging families over an important holiday like Christmas. So I thought I'd cook something simple, invite him over, let you get to know him a little…"

"What about Dad?" she asked.

"No, I definitely won't be inviting your dad," Riley said. "Maddie, I'm dating Logan. Sort of."

"Sort of? You're dating him for real, Mom. You giggle on the phone. Even I haven't had a boyfriend like that yet!"

"What about that Brian Breske?" she asked. "Wasn't he a boyfriend? You invested a lot of time in him."

"That was seventh grade. Kid's stuff."

"Oh," Riley said. "Well, I haven't quite elevated Logan to boyfriend status yet."

"So you're not sleeping with him yet?" Maddie asked.

"Oh, my Jesus, you did not really ask me that!"

"Of course I did." She grinned. "Is there anything we should talk about before you get in over your head?"

"I thought I'd cook," Riley said.

"Ew, you don't want to scare him away, do you?"

"It's cold. I could make chili and corn bread muffins."

"Are you going to actually make it?" Maddie asked.

"Possibly."

Maddie laughed herself stupid.

"Listen, I want you to be nice to Logan," Riley said. "I've met men for a drink or coffee over the years but I think I've been out to dinner twice since you were born. Really, the men out there are dismal. Logan is kind of fun. He's interesting— he has cop stories. His partner is a woman. He says she's the smartest cop he's ever known. There probably won't be time for more than one dinner like this until after the holidays so let's pretend we're very excited to have him over. Very happy to meet him. Hmm?"

"I can do that," she said. "Will he bring his gun?"

"Lord, I hope not!"

"Well, what fun is that?"

Riley was used to Maddie's humor, her teasing. But she

sincerely hoped Maddie could put a good image forth and impress Logan a little bit.

On the day they had chosen, just over a week before Christmas, the house was decorated a little bit. No point in going crazy with decorations when they'd spend most of the holiday celebrating at June's house where the decorations were over the top, complete with outside lighting. Riley did have a tree, however. You can't be a single mom and ignore the tree!

She told June what she'd be doing and June deftly pulled a big bucket of her best chili out of the freezer and handed it to Riley, telling her to just dump it in the Crock-Pot. June whipped up some corn bread muffins—it took her under thirty minutes. "Are you going to be able to throw together a green salad?" June asked Riley.

"Of course!" she said indignantly.

Riley stopped at the grocery store on the way home and worked her way around the salad bar in the deli section, looking over her shoulder the whole time, hoping not to get caught.

Then she saw him. There he was, standing in the check-out line with a bunch of flowers and a bottle of wine. She just shook her head and chuckled to herself. She went and stood behind him.

He jumped in surprise and attempted to hold the flowers behind his back. But when he saw her holding the salad, he relaxed and returned her smile with his own.

"So this is how working people date," she said.

"Do you like these?" he asked, holding out the cellophane-wrapped bouquet. "If you want to pick something you like better..."

"I like them very much," she said. "Want to follow me home?"

"I've wanted to for weeks now."

★ ★ ★

The chili and muffins were exceptional—June liked her chili with a little kick to it, something she didn't share with the elderly on her meal route. But Logan thoroughly enjoyed it. Since they'd run into each other at the store, Riley told him the truth, that it was her mother's chili, and it was a good thing she did because Maddie wasted no time in selling her out.

Riley and Logan started off with a glass of wine and she arranged the flowers. The table was set, the chili was in the Crock-Pot, she put the muffins in a basket to warm in the microwave. The house was, as usual, immaculate.

"How was your day, dear?" Logan said.

"Perfectly ordinary. Yours?"

"It was a day full of reports, meetings, paperwork and no fun stuff."

"What's the fun stuff, I'm afraid to ask?"

"Chasing bad guys. Haven't done hardly any of that lately. George and I have been on this task force with feds and we've been sorting through a lot of paper. Feds love their paper."

"What kind of task force?"

"I'm not allowed to talk about it yet, but give it a few more weeks and when it's behind me and closed, I'll tell you all about it. It will help you sleep. It's boring."

That's when Maddie came into the kitchen, was introduced to Logan and poured herself a Diet Coke.

"Wow," she said, eyeing the table. "Fancy. Watch out, Logan—when she sets a fancy table it usually means something serious is coming down."

"Is that right?"

"That's affirmative," she said, mocking police lingo. "My Gramma made the chili because my mother really doesn't cook much."

"I'm a pretty good cook. I just don't have a lot of time and Gramma loves to cook so we eat over there a lot," Riley said. She put the flowers on the table and they all sat down.

"Will Gramma be making Christmas dinner?" Logan asked.

"Oh, most definitely," Maddie said before Riley could open her mouth. "She'd be brokenhearted if we changed tradition. And so would my dad!"

"Your dad?" Riley asked.

"We always spend quality time together around the holidays and he usually comes over to my Gramma's at least for dessert. He was there on Thanksgiving. We're kind of a close family."

"We are?" Riley asked.

"My parents might not be married but they get along very well. What do you do on holidays?" she asked Logan.

"Go to my mother's," he said. "I have a sister, brother-in-law, niece and nephew."

"And are you divorced?"

"Maddie!"

"What? It's a getting-to-know-you dinner, right?"

"That's okay, Riley. I am divorced. Eight years and yes, we're still friendly. No kids."

"Do you wish you'd had kids?"

Logan leaned toward her. "I have an unmarked police car. Want to go outside and press the button for the lights and siren?"

"Gee, tempting as that is, I'll pass. Mom, want me to help you dish up?"

"I thought we'd visit a little first and then I'll serve, Maddie," she said slowly, measuring each word. What was this? Riley wondered. Asking about his divorce?

"So tell me all about the family, Logan," Maddie said.

"Mom, Dad, sister, et cetera." She leaned her head on her hand, waiting.

And so it began. Maddie interviewed Logan. Logan did great at avoiding and evading and punctuating with his own questions because he was, after all, a detective. But Riley was soon horrified. Maddie managed to insert lots of information about Jock, making her dad look like he was extremely desirable and quite accomplished.

My dad is in electronics. He has a business degree. He works for Mackie's. It's a national chain and he's the manager of one of their biggest stores. Oh, my mom and dad still spend a lot of time together— they go to all my games and meets together and they chaperoned the homecoming dance together. My dad was all-conference in high school and he's still as athletic as ever—are you interested in sports, Logan?

"Yes," Logan said to that last question, beginning to look annoyed. "I'm very athletic. I frequently throw very large men over the hood of my unmarked car and cuff them. And I often chase bad young men *and* women who have committed crimes and I always catch them."

"I'm going to put on the coffee," Riley said. "And I have cheesecake. Store-bought."

"May I be excused?" Maddie asked.

"Absolutely," Riley said.

"Thanks," she said. "Really great to meet you, Logan."

"Likewise," he said. "Please tell your gramma the chili was outstanding."

There was no sound in the kitchen but the dripping and bubbling of the coffeepot and then, the closing of Maddie's door. Riley and Logan let out their collective breath.

"Logan, I'm sorry about that. That was the last thing I expected."

"Don't worry about it. I think I can get her a job if she's interested in grilling hardcore criminals."

"You handled it great, but I have no idea what she's talking about—that I spend a lot of time with her dad. I don't. At least, I sure don't feel like I do. We try to coordinate plans so I know where Maddie's going to be on a given—"

"I don't think that had anything to do with her dad," Logan said. "But I think we got a close view of her preference."

"It makes no sense," Riley said. "She was excited to know I was finally dating someone."

"Then come here," he said, pulling her chair closer, putting his hands on her waist. "Date me a little." He leaned toward her for a kiss and she obliged. "She's not quite ready," he said very quietly. "She's going to need a little more time. And apparently I'm going to have to prove myself in athletics, electronics and a few other things."

"I've never felt a stronger urge to spank my daughter."

"I think you better talk to her instead. See what's going on. But for now, kiss me better."

"Are you wounded?"

"Nah, not too bad. I'm having a talk with myself right now. Families are complicated and I'm going to be patient. You know why? I want us to work, that's why. I think it's going to be okay but it's Christmas, and Christmas has a way of stirring things up, so I'm taking my lead from you. I want to be together as much as you want to be—you're going to have to drive this train. Can you do that, Riley?"

"Are you kidding? It's one of my most serious flaws—I like being in charge." She wiggled away from him and poured two cups of coffee and dished up two slices of cheesecake. Then she sat back down, closer to him than necessary. She put a little cheesecake on her fork and fed it to him. "The only part of this dinner I made was the coffee."

"Modern women turn me on," he said. "I have a feeling

this first Christmas of ours isn't going to include our families, but that's okay. We're still new, there's lots of time." He fed her a bite from his plate. "So my busy season is here," Logan said. "And not because I'll be partying. More burglaries, domestics, drunk driving—it all adds up to overtime. But maybe we can sneak in our own little Christmas. I want you to think about it, tell me when you have time, help me decide what kind of day or evening you'd like."

"I'm sorry about Maddie. She's really not like that. She's one of the most accepting, generous, warmhearted people I know. And I don't think she got it from me."

"Who'd she get it from, then?" he asked.

"My mom I think. My mom is like that."

"Can I help with the cleanup?" he asked, feeding her another bite.

"No, no. Cleanup is my specialty. My profession."

They finished dessert and coffee, then Riley treated Logan to a very nice, deep, meaningful kiss and some heartfelt caressing by the front door. Riley was starting to ask herself why she'd avoided this kind of contact for so long. No one had interested her, true. But why had no one interested her? Was it because after Jock she fasted?

She cleaned up the kitchen very slowly and quietly. She had a dishwasher but sometimes she liked washing and drying the dishes by hand. When she was finished and the kitchen was perfect and shining, she went to Maddie's room. She knocked before going in.

Maddie was in her pajamas—ballerina and heart pajamas, perfect for a five-year-old girl, but her girl had long blond hair, blue eyes and was five foot eight.

"You want to tell me what that was about?" Riley asked.

"What?"

"Don't pretend you don't know, Maddie. I've never seen

you act like that. Didn't you like him?" She came into her daughter's room and sat on the bed.

"Yeah, I liked him. He seemed nice. He's even kind of hot. What kind of cop is he?"

"That's kind of up in the air, I think. His business card says property crimes but he says he's doing some special project at the moment. Now, why were you going on and on about your dad? That's not really true, all that stuff you said."

"Sure it is. I talk to him every day, he's never missed a game or meet, he always comes by on special occasions even if we're at Gramma's, he takes me to my other gramma's, though not as much, and he's around you a lot because of me. He's nice and he's handsome, too."

"But, Maddie, your dad and I couldn't work things out—I explained all that."

"Not really. He did a better job of explaining than you ever did. And when I told him you were dating some guy, it made him so sad." She shrugged. "I think he's lonely. And he still loves you."

"Maddie, I don't think he ever loved me. And Lord knows he wasn't ready to be a father."

"Well, no kidding! That would be like me being a mother! But he's older now."

"Maddie, you have to be realistic. Your dad has been married. He loves you very much but he doesn't have any feelings for me."

"I know. He's pretty embarrassed about that marriage. He didn't know what he was thinking. He said he should've known better. But he said he's always loved you and always will."

"Because I'm your mother," Riley said. "That's all it is."

"No, Mama, that's not all. But it's okay. Logan is nice. And he's nice to you. That's what matters, right?"

"Right. Are you going to be nicer the next time he's around?"

She nodded, but bit her lower lip. "You know, you never went out on a date. I thought maybe you and Daddy still might have a thing for each other."

"Listen, I had a couple of dates. A few, actually. I never said anything."

"You probably said you had meetings…"

"Probably. But I was asked out. I met a couple of guys for coffee, went to a couple of happy hours, went out to dinner a couple of times, but it just wasn't the right time, I guess. I was bored. I figured if it was right I'd get a little excited."

"Does Logan get you excited?" she asked.

"I don't know. But he makes me laugh. I'm comfortable with him. I feel good about myself when we're together and it seems like we have a lot to talk about. But, Maddie, it's not serious. It's friendly. It could get serious, but I've only known him a few weeks. Relationships take time. And I'm in no rush. Now, is there anything else you need to know?"

"One thing. I hope you'll tell me the truth…"

"Maddie, I always tell you the truth!"

"Okay. Did you ever love Daddy? I mean, really?"

It was the oddest thing—Riley felt tears in her eyes. She blinked a little wildly, willing them away. She cleared her throat. She wiped her palms on her slacks. "Yes," she finally said, her voice soft. "Yes, I did."

"Really?" she asked.

"Painfully so," Riley said.

Emma steadfastly refused to announce to Adam's family that they were officially seeing each other, though everyone but Riley knew. "Let's not push our luck," she said. She didn't want any trouble or friction from Riley and mostly she didn't want a brother and sister at odds over her during Christmas. "Riley has to be the one to invite me back into her life, even as just an acquaintance. We'll never be good friends, I get that, but I don't want to push my way into your family before she's ready."

"You know I don't give a damn what Riley thinks about this," Adam said.

"That's exactly what worries me."

"Why are you so intent on having it the hard way?"

"Is that what you think? Oh, you're wrong. I want it the peaceful way. Especially now—my first Christmas home, with a nice place to live, a decent job, a great fella. I'm going to invite your mom over to see my little place and host her for a couple of hours. I'm going to spend some time with Lyle and Ethan, bring them a nice bottle of wine and some Brie and caviar, wriggle my way into Ethan's good graces. I'm spending an evening with Penny and her girlfriends—they have a little Christmas party every year and I'm now officially part of the club."

"And me?" he asked.

"I'm sure we'll have lots of quality time together."

"How about Christmas Eve?" he asked.

"I'll wait up," she said.

She wanted to enjoy the days leading up to Christmas. She didn't have much to spend on her few friends and she enjoyed it more that way. She found a lovely pashmina shawl for Penny, a couple of small but pretty tree decorations for the other ladies, and for Lyle and Ethan, a Christmas serving platter. For June, a decorative Christmas table runner that was lovely and on sale. For Adam, a soft, cuddly navy blue sweater with a white button-down shirt, a pair of delicious slippers because she had noticed he didn't have any and a book, a Nelson DeMille novel. She had studied his bookcase—he loved that particular author and although he had an e-reader, he liked to read paper.

She bought herself a few modest decorations for her little house. Adam still came to her place, though she knew he really liked his house and was so happy when she was there with him. "It's going to be a long time, Adam, before I'm good for more than this, than what we have right now. I'm working through everything but it's slow. Everything that came before us is weighty."

"Is Lucinda helping?" he asked.

"I think so, but I'm not seeing her again until the New Year. I'm feeling almost secure," she said. "I'm afraid to blink."

"I'm not going anywhere," he said.

The holiday decorations in the homes they cleaned were a beautiful pain in the ass—difficult to clean and tidy around. Still, Emma enjoyed them as never before. It was entertaining to see what each family had done—the Douglases with the three spoiled boys had enough presents under the tree to take care of all the children in an orphanage. The Nesbitts had grown children and grandchildren, and they kept the number of gifts reasonable, yet decorated lavishly, many of the things meant to be fun for the children—advent calendar, talking Rudolph, nutcracker soldier. The Parkers had no presents under the tree—they'd be spending Christmas in Maui.

She was looking forward to seeing what the Christensen family had done. The last time she was there nothing had been done to decorate and she feared nothing would be done. But voilà! Just in time for Christmas the decorations had appeared and they blew her mind—it was a decorator's dream. She knew the cost of many of the ornaments and tabletop decorations. A nativity painted in gold and draped in Swarovski from Bergdorf's, crystal reindeer from Tiffany's, a stunning wreath—surely those weren't real diamonds, but it was copied from the real one created by Pasi Jokinen-Carter. Their tree and staircase garland were decorated by a professional, she could tell. The few packages under the tree were wrapped in expensive paper that matched some of the glass balls; fancy ribbon was coordinated with the home furnishing colors. There were silver candelabra with red candles, fresh Christmas flowers in the dining room and foyer, an expensive tapestry hung on the staircase landing and a garland to end all garlands, fresh and adorned with balls and ribbons that matched the tree.

Dellie and Shawna gasped when they saw the house.

"Stay away from the tree and garland," Emma told the girls. "Most of those ornaments came from jewelers, not Target."

Both of them backed up fearfully. "How do you know that?" Shawna asked in a whisper.

"This isn't my first rodeo," was all Emma said. "In fact..." She got out her cell phone. She called Makenna. "We're at the Christensen house and you might want to check this out. The Christmas decorations are worth more than the van. No one wants to dust them. We'll wait for you."

They started upstairs. As usual, nothing was disturbed except for a damp towel in the hamper, which Emma scooped up and put in the laundry bag for pickup. The laundry and dry cleaning was picked up and delivered twice a week, expertly timed for the moment the Kerrigan cleaners were finished cleaning.

Bethany had left her diary open on the table next to her bed, the bed she meticulously fixed in the morning even though it was cleaning day, clean sheet day. There was only one sentence written on the page and Emma couldn't stop herself. After all those years of not noticing things, now she was a damn runaway train!

I just wish there was someone to talk to.

It clutched at Emma's heart and before she could reason with herself, she picked up the pen and wrote a note. *Talk to me.* She wrote her cell number. Then her cheeks flamed so red she thought she might pass out. This house, this family was going to kill her and she was going to end up getting fired over it. She quickly passed the vacuum, leaving perfect tracks. *I am totally fired,* she thought.

She wasn't even done with the vacuum when Makenna was at the house and with her, Nick. They took one look at the decorations and called Emma down.

"Good call," Makenna said. "How'd you know?"

Makenna didn't know about her past? Riley hadn't told her closest coworkers their complicated history, Emma's spectacular and horrifying past? She was stunned. "I...ah...this isn't my first fancy house. Believe me, you don't want to break anything at Christmastime around here."

"Doesn't it just give you that warm, fuzzy holiday feeling?" Makenna said. "Stay away from all the ornamentation. I'll take care of this."

Emma wondered if there was any way to sneak upstairs to Bethany's room and remove her note from the diary. But of course it was written in pen. The only option was to tear out that page, and she couldn't bring herself to do it.

Makenna and Nick seemed to be outside conferring, talking on their phones for a long time. They sat in the company car for a while, talking. And then without saying another word, they were gone. Before leaving the house, Emma called Makenna. "What's the verdict on this house and the ornaments?"

"Riley will be discussing it with Mrs. Christensen. Clean around them the best you can. Riley agrees we'll need a release of liability on the care and cleaning of apparently priceless knickknacks. Leave everything."

"Who *are* these people?" Emma asked.

Makenna sighed. "Olaf Christensen owns an import-export business and his wife is the CFO. They're very successful, very driven, both perfectionists."

"Import-export," Emma said. "Well, that explains some of these precious decorations. They're in the buying-and-selling business. We already dusted around," Emma said. Then to her partners she said, "We're on the road again, girls."

The next house was messy and dirty, which put them a bit behind schedule, but this was the way things went during the holidays, what with all the partying and clutter. The last house of the day was the Andrewses and they were a bit late. Mrs. Andrews had had her arm in a sling last week but this week no one answered the door.

"Going to fight the damn cat hair," Shawna said. "I hate cat hair."

There was a sudden but definite commotion inside, the sound of a man shouting and a woman's voice. Emma rang the doorbell again and a third time.

"This ain't no good, trust me," Shawna said. "Time to go make another call to Makenna."

"Wait," Emma said. She leaned her ear up to the door. She couldn't hear what he was saying but he was barking, yelling, and she was wheedling, maybe whimpering. "I'm worried about her," Emma said. "I can't leave her in there with him."

"We call Nick now," Dellie said.

"Open it," Emma commanded.

"Now, that's something we don't wanna do," Dellie said.

Emma leaned her ear against the door again and suddenly it popped open and she fell inside, right onto a skinny, smelly, worked-up man. He growled and pushed her off him with surprising strength and stood up. He muttered something then walked briskly to the car that sat in the drive.

Dellie and Shawna lifted Emma to her feet.

"See what I'm talking about?" Dellie said. "We don't need any part of that!"

Emma was still frowning after the man. He was balding, short and ugly. His ears were big, he had a beak for a nose and she was sure she saw a sizeable wart on it. He cast a mean look over his shoulder; the three of them stood on the front walk with their supplies—dusters on extenders, a big plastic carrier with all their chemicals, vacuum, bag of rags, knee pads and gloves.

He spit on the ground, got in his Mercedes and drove away.

"We're not cleaning this one today," Shawna said. "She'll pay her bill, don't worry about that."

But Emma walked into the house. She found Mrs. Andrews on the floor in a crumpled heap, crying. She still had her sling, all askew, and she held her arm as if it hurt. There was a fresh slap mark on her cheek and her neck was very red, like he'd been choking her.

Dellie and Shawna followed Emma slowly. Cautiously. Working together, they lifted Mrs. Andrews to the couch. "Someone get Mrs. Andrews some ice. I'll just be a minute," Emma said.

"What are you going to do?" Shawna asked.

"Today I'm working on getting fired, it seems," she said. She walked to the front door and standing just outside she called the police.

chapter *fifteen*

Riley's heart was heavy. Every time she thought about her conversation with Maddie she felt both confusion and regret. Confusion because she couldn't exactly remember her explanations about herself and Jock the way Maddie remembered and wondered if she'd fed her daughter a series of excuses. And regret because now that she looked back on it, she had probably glossed over things so it wouldn't sound like what it was. After about sixteen years even she didn't remember it as accurately as she should because she'd been trying to blot out some truths—that she'd fallen for her best friend's boyfriend, that she'd loved him, slept with him, expected him to stand by her from that moment, but instead she lost them both.

Sex for girls is a defining moment; sex for guys is sex.

She shook her head as if to clear the memories. After Jock had said no, he wasn't in love with her, after she had groveled and begged Emma to forgive her, after finding herself completely alone except for her mom, there was just no going back. She was completely damaged, felt like a fool, was not about to be hurt like that again.

No one could ever know how much it tore a woman apart, to trust your heart and be completely wrong. For Riley, nothing was quite as hard as being stupid.

The one thing she hadn't counted on all these years of ignoring Jock, just putting up with his attempts to be a family man, was that all that time he was talking to Maddie. Apparently honestly. From the heart. Expressing his own regrets. Who knew Jock was even capable of that! Maddie seemed to think he still wanted them to be a family.

As usual, Jock's timing couldn't be worse. Riley had only just met someone she actually liked. A smart guy with a career.

Jeanette had left the office early to do a little last-minute Christmas shopping and Riley turned back to her computer. She'd write Jock a letter. She'd never send it, of course, but she could get her thoughts and questions all lined up in her head by writing a letter. This was something she did with regularity—she often wrote letters to demanding and obnoxious clients, then hit delete.

Dear Jock,

I've been talking to Maddie and it comes to me that my perception of our history is very different from yours and I need to know— did I miss something? Was I sleepwalking through that whole time, not catching the innuendo? I'm sure I was conscious when you panicked because I said I loved you. I believe I was paying attention to detail when you said, "No—wait a minute—we can't call that love! That was consensual sex, not love." And I was pretty pregnant when you said, All right then, let's get married. I apologize if that didn't sweep me off my feet, but there you have it. I wasn't convinced it would be a marriage worth having. When you married and divorced so quickly... Ah, well, you must understand why I wasn't

*convinced of your good judgment. But to tell Maddie this silly thing,
that you always loved me, that you wanted to get married but I was
too angry, that you probably wouldn't be worth a damn to another
woman, that you'd resigned yourself that this was all you were going
to get... Now, how does all that make me look? You lamebrain, you
dipshit, you mental midget, you—*

That was typical of her write-but-don't-send cathartics.
She was reduced to name-calling. Sometimes that helped,
too. *Jock, you stupid idiot, I loved you! You cast me off. I'd betrayed
my best friend for you and you left me high and dry. The next years
were so unbearably hard...*

"Riley?"

"Eeek," she squeaked and jumped about a mile. She grabbed
her chest. She wasn't talking out loud, was she? "Logan! Dear
God—"

He chuckled. "Whatever you're writing, you were really
in the zone there, I guess. Your door was open."

She cleared the screen and actually blushed. "I was... I
mean... A proposal... An itemized..."

"I didn't mean to scare you," he said.

"Come in, come in. What are you doing here?"

He walked into the room and sat in one of the chairs facing her desk. "I was in the area and hadn't seen you in a few
days..."

"We talked," she said, feeling a little defensive.

"Not quite as much fun. Listen, I have a crazy week coming up and you probably do, too. Can I take you to dinner
tonight? Might be the only chance we get for a while."

"Oh, gee, that would be..." She folded her hands on top of
her desk. "We didn't really talk about this, about Christmas.
I'd love to have you come over to my mom's either Christmas Eve or Day, but I figured you have to see your family.

And I don't know if you want to meet everyone in my family for the first time on a holiday."

He just grinned at her.

"But if you'd like to—"

"It's okay, Riley. My debut with Maddie didn't go all that well."

"I'm sorry, that was so unexpected. I guess that's what I get for never dating. But I don't think it would be that awkward at my mom's house."

"I think I'll just take care of my own family for the holidays. I can spell my partner so she can have time with her husband and kids. And God knows, I want to be available for my ex-wife—I'm sure she'll be at least stopping by. And my father." He rolled his eyes. "But dinner tonight would be excellent. Or tomorrow night. How about it?"

"That sounds like a great idea. Where would you like to go?"

"How about Riviera Restorante?"

"I love that place!" She glanced down at herself. She was wearing pants and a blazer today. "Am I dressed all right? So I don't have to go home?"

"You look perfect." He looked around. "I wondered about the office. This is really nice, Riley. Very—"

The outside office door opened and a moment later there was a light tapping on Riley's door. Emma peeked in the door.

"Oh. Sorry. When you're finished..." she said, beginning to pull out.

"Come in, Emma. This is a friend of mine, Logan Danner. We were just making plans for dinner. Logan, can you give me five minutes with Emma?"

"Of course," he said, standing.

"Oh," Emma said. "It's you! From the hospital."

He frowned slightly. "The hospital?"

"I was waiting for a ride. I was a little upset. You gave me your flowers," she said.

"That was you?" he asked, peering at her. "Huh, that *was* you! You said you were having a bad day."

"That was the last day I worked at that job. I was in hospital housekeeping. I came here immediately after that. That was nice of you—the flowers."

"I was visiting a coworker who had checked out. I wasn't going to take the flowers to her house. I saw that as problematic." Then he grinned.

"You two know each other?" Riley asked.

"We never met, actually," Emma said. "We both happened to be waiting outside of the ER and I looked like I felt—at the end of the line."

"I told her to take the flowers or they were going in the trash," Logan said. "Just a spontaneous gesture. I could have left them with the nurses but..." He shrugged.

Emma looked at Riley. "It's all right with me if he stays. It's going to take about one minute." Emma took a breath. "I did something today that was against policy. In our last house, the man was beating his wife and I know I'm supposed to call you or Nick or Makenna with issues, but I called the police."

"Oh, my Jesus," Riley said. "Sit down, Emma."

"I'm sorry, I know our policy is not to see the client's personal stuff but I just couldn't look the other way."

"Emma, that wasn't personal, that was assault. Against the law! That's not the stuff you're supposed to pretend not to see. That Reverend Douglas likes to wear his wife's lingerie is what we don't see, not crimes."

"Reverend Douglas wears his wife's lingerie?" Emma and Logan said at the same time.

"I didn't say that," Riley said. "I wish you had called me, but not because I'd ignore something like that. Because I'd file the complaint, drive out to the scene and wait with you for the police and hopefully Mr. and Mrs. Andrews would blame me and not you. Hopefully they'd forget you had anything to do with it."

"That wasn't going to happen," Emma said. "I was listening at the door to see if I could hear her crying for help and he opened the door suddenly. I fell on him. *Splat!* The mean little squirt." She huffed a little. "I wish he'd taken a hand to me!"

"Was she badly hurt?" Riley asked.

"I don't know how badly but they took her to the hospital in an ambulance, and that took some convincing. I have a feeling they've been there before. He might've broken her arm. And he tried to strangle her."

"Oh, my God!" Riley said. "Okay, listen, Emma—this isn't the first time we've faced an abusive situation. When we enter their homes and clean their personal space, we enter their lives in ways even they don't comprehend. If you ever suspect abuse or unlawful behavior, please don't hesitate to say something to me. Or if you're not able to reach me, call Makenna or Nick. We've been doing this longer than you have."

"I just couldn't wait," she said. "I'm sorry."

"No need to apologize," Riley said. "I would have done the same thing. You did fine. I just like to take my employees out of the equation when possible, if possible. They'll discontinue our service, there's no question—we saw too much. Good riddance." Riley smiled. "And I heard about your call on the Christensen home—smart move."

"I was afraid to breathe," Emma said.

"I can't wait to hear what that's about," Logan said.

"Go ahead. Tell him," Riley said.

She looked confused for a moment. Tell him what? "Well, in a previous life I had some experience working with decorators and I recognized the Christmas ornaments and decorations in one of the homes were very expensive. And very fragile. Even the most careful housecleaner can upset an ornament—these were balls from Wedgwood, from jewelers, crystal from high-end stores like Tiffany's and Waterford."

"What's expensive?" he asked.

"One Waterford ball—couple of hundred. A couple of Tiffany reindeer statuettes, fifteen hundred. A Swarovski wreath. Everything was high-end."

"Wow," he said. "You must have had a lot of experience handling that stuff."

"A little," she said. "I didn't want me or my team getting stuck with a big bill just for dusting."

"Mrs. Christensen has decided to have her decorator come in and make sure all her priceless decorations are shiny clean. We're going to leave that stuff alone," Riley said. "Thanks for stopping by to explain, Emma. I'll follow through."

"Thank you," Emma said, noting the meeting was over. She stood. And so did Logan.

Logan reached in his pocket and fished out a card. "If you ever have a problem or need some advice on police matters, don't hesitate. Use the cell—I'm in the field a lot. I'm only in the office a few hours a day."

"You're a police officer?" she asked.

"Yep. And if I don't know the answer to your question, I can get it. I worked some battery domestic and assault as a patrol officer and I have friends in those specialized units. We're not a huge department."

"Well, thank you, Mr. Danner..."

"Just Logan, Emma."

"I appreciate that," she said. She looked at Riley. "Hopefully the rest of the week is a little less exciting."

"Things always get a little wacky during holidays. Have a good week."

"Thanks," Emma said.

She's very pretty, Riley thought. *Even at the end of a difficult day.* Wouldn't it be tidy if Logan took to her? He seemed to light up a little bit when he saw her.

And why would you think that? she asked herself.

Emma's mind was really working as she drove. The domestic battery was so disturbing, so in-your-face horrid. The first thing she told herself was that her situation had never been as bad as that! She'd never been abused like that. Never.

But then how many of her New York household had noticed that her husband didn't hold her, that the troop of worker bees who often traveled with them were not all for work, that he had such a developed sense of entitlement he had a mistress right under her nose and bilked his clients for a hundred million dollars. No, she'd never been abused, nuh-uh. Her life had been ruined by the very man who vowed to love and protect her.

Mrs. Andrews must ask herself those same questions every day. How did I marry that man? How did I trust him with my life, my future? And now she was undoubtedly asking herself how she could get away from him.

Emma didn't have to go to Riley's office. She could have just called Makenna and Nick and chances were one of the other girls had after it was all over. But Emma wanted to look Riley in the eye as if to say, *Here's your chance. I blew it. I didn't follow the rules—fire me.*

But Riley stood up for her. Supported her. Wanted to protect her. Emma didn't kid herself that it was because she was Emma, it was because she was an employee. Adam had been so right about his sister—she ran a good company, provided a safe work environment, took good care of her people, was steadfast. Riley could ignore the fact that she really didn't want to be around Emma and see the situation professionally and fairly.

She sighed. Ah, what did it matter? She didn't want a new best friend. She just wanted to work, live, enjoy a simple peace that helped her heal. That was all.

Her cell phone rang and it picked up in her car. She didn't recognize the number. "Hello," she yelled into the speaker.

"I know who you are," said a very timid, female voice.

Emma was right in front of a side street and made an abrupt turn, no signal involved, earning her a blast from a car behind her. She pulled over.

"Hello?" she said again. She pulled her cell phone out of her purse and turned off the car. "Let me get you on my cell. Okay. Here I am."

"I know who you are," she said again. "The cleaner."

"Oh. Uh. I'm sorry I read your page. I'm not supposed to."

"I know. I left it where you would see it."

"Oh," Emma said. "You want to talk?"

"I go to the counselor twice a week to talk and that hasn't done any good."

"Oh, I'm glad, you have someone. Why isn't it any good?" Emma asked.

She was met with silence and she thought, *I'm an idiot. I should have apologized, asked her not to tell, confessed to Riley again and—*

"Because they don't want to talk to me, they have to. They're paid to."

"Ah," Emma said. "I understand."

"Now I think you're doing it. You some kind of spy?"

"No," Emma said, laughing a little in spite of herself. "I'm a cleaner who's going to get in big trouble for touching your personal property. I apologize."

"Why'd you do it, then?"

"Well… Well, there have been times I had no one to talk to. Really, no one. And I had a lot on my mind. A lot of worries and no one to listen and I know how that feels."

"Like when?"

"Well…when I was sixteen, my dad died in an accident. I didn't have a mom. I felt kind of alone then." It was a lie. She had the Kerrigans, though she was still shot through with pain and grief. Emma was trying to understand what this girl might be up against.

"Did you have a sister?" she asked.

"Ah…I had a stepsister. And a stepmother. It was a dark period." She cleared her throat. "Do you have a sister?"

"No. They figured out after me that there couldn't be more kids," she said. "My mother is dead. And I have a stepmother. I hear she's wonderful."

"Oh? You don't sound like you believe it."

"I guess," she said. "My stepmother says this family is getting back in the groove." She laughed. "How'm I doing getting back in the groove so far?"

Emma bit her lower lip. She knew nothing about this sort of thing. She'd never even been to a counselor before Lucinda. June and Riley were the nearest things to counselors she'd ever had.

But she'd had a stepmother. "Do you like your stepmother?" she asked.

"I want to. She's a good person. But I try and I can't."

"Why?"

"Really? Really, why?"

"Only if you want to say," Emma said. "You can talk about something else if you—"

"She wears my mother's clothes."

Emma felt her stomach cramp and her throat closed. She couldn't speak. No one was that insensitive. No one. Not the stupidest person. Even Rosemary had been more subtle than that.

"She asked if she could," Bethany said. "We said yes. My dad and me. But my mother's dead and she's wearing her clothes."

"What did that counselor say?" Emma asked.

"The counselor asked me if I thought she was trying to replace my mother and that's why I was upset."

"But you told the counselor why you were upset, right?" Emma asked.

"I was upset because she was wearing my mother's clothes!" she said, her voice suddenly strong. "They'll be worn out pretty soon and she'll have to get new ones. I hope, but I don't think so."

"Did you tell your dad it bothers you?" Emma asked.

"My dad is...you know...he's not the same. I can tell even if he smiles all the time and acts like we all just got tickets to the Ice Capades, it's all fake. Inside he's just so sad. He can't do anything."

Emma's cheeks were wet with tears. "You should tell him, though. You shouldn't just hurt inside without anyone to talk to. Your dad wouldn't want you to do that."

"I have you," she said.

"But—"

"Except I don't know your name or anything."

I should call Adam tonight and we should have a good dinner and maybe two bottles of wine and a long night in each other's arms because I'm going to be looking for work very, very soon.

"I'm Emma," she said. "And I've been alone and sad, too. But I'm not right now so I can talk to you. Except I'm not

allowed to use my phone during work—during the day. I'm off at five. And on weekends."

"This weekend is Christmas," she said sadly. "It's a little harder at Christmas."

"I know, honey."

"I need to go," she said. "I'll call you sometime."

"Okay. And you can leave a message if I'm working. Or in the shower or something."

"Or text?" Bethany asked.

"Sure. But hey. Let's talk. Okay? It's what you want to do."

"Yeah. I think. Don't tell them, okay?"

"I'm not telling them." *I hope. I might have to, but let's see.*

"This Emma seems like an interesting character," Logan said.

Riley smiled. They were at the restaurant, chatting about nothing at all. "You made it all the way to the antipasto," she said.

"What? Did I say something wrong?"

"Not at all. I've been expecting you to say something. You kind of came to life when Emma showed up."

"Did I? I think I came to life when she recognized me but I didn't really remember her. Could the world get any smaller?"

"This is a small place. And Emma is very pretty," Riley said. "Unforgettable."

"She did the right thing, you know," he added.

"When there's trouble of some kind, I like it if they go through me. Or Nick. Nick is brilliant with situations like that. He's not a big guy—he's a short, stocky Italian—but he manages to seem six foot six if he has to. To the women who work for us he's a sweetheart until they push him too far, try to take advantage of him, then he's great at getting serious and making his point firmly. Not meanly, but firmly. With the men, he's one of the guys until they try to take advantage

and then he's clearly the boss. No one wants to mess with Nick. He's got a look. A scrappy look. Often a potential client will get an estimate from Nick and then come to me, looking to sweet-talk the lady boss into a better, cheaper deal." She laughed and shook her head. "It hasn't worked even once.

"I'd have liked it if Nick had been there when the police came," she went on. "I'd have liked it if Nick and I were both there when the police confronted Mr. Andrews, but that's asking for a miracle."

"I'm sure they found him," Logan said. "He'll turn up at work or a bar or come to the hospital to try to offer up some lame excuse for beating the shit outta his wife."

"What will happen to him?" she asked.

"He'll go to jail," Logan said, spearing an artichoke heart with his fork.

"His wife might think to make peace by denying—"

"There was a witness and evidence of a beating. You think the police don't know what she's up against? They know what she'll say, what she'll do and they've heard it all before. By now she's as messed up as he is. There are two lawbreakers who can't make bail—battery domestic violators and drunk drivers. They get to spend the night. In the first case so their victim has time to get away if he or she will do so and in the second case, to sober up."

Riley thought about that. "That's very clever of the police," she finally said. "Here I thought abusers and drunks could get away with stuff all the time."

"They do, even with all the stops in place. But we're awful smart. We know how they think and act."

"You are smart," she agreed with a laugh.

"So tell me about Emma," he said.

"Why do you want to know?" she asked.

"Because you're friends," he said.

Riley scooped some more greens from the salad on her plate, focusing on the antipasto and not him. "We're not friends, actually. I've known her for a long time but she has only recently come back to Santa Rosa after being away for years. She needed a job. That's pretty much it."

"Oh, no, it's not," he said, laughing. "You two have some kind of important relationship that goes beyond work."

"Is that so? And how would you know that?"

He shrugged. "Experience. Body language. Tone of voice. Eye contact. The way you two respond to each other. There was a lot of chemistry in your office for a little while."

"Sassy," she said, lifting her eyebrows. "You're a smarty-pants, aren't you? We were friends, in younger years."

"I thought so."

"We went to school together. But Emma went away to college, moved away after college, got married and just recently returned. After the death of her husband."

"Aw," he said, chewing. "She's young. That's sad."

"I gather it was a bad marriage."

"Abusive?"

"Why would you ask that?" Riley wanted to know.

"It would explain her sensitivity to that woman being abused."

"Huh," she said. "And I thought I was intuitive. But I don't know if the marriage involved that kind of abuse. Her husband was not a good man, I hear. And he killed himself. As soon as she buried him and sorted out her affairs, she came back here. I suppose she feels comfortable here where she still has a few friends."

Logan whistled. "Suicide. That's ugly."

"I suppose that would be hard to deal with even if you hated the guy."

"Yeah. I hope he left her something…"

"I doubt it. If he'd left her anything, would she be cleaning houses?"

"Were you and Emma close friends in younger years? Because even though you're the boss and she's the employee, I detected something—like an element of familiarity. Intimacy."

"Intimacy?" she asked, aghast.

"Not sexual intimacy. Or maybe it was trust."

"From her?" Riley asked, a bit incredulously.

"Well, from both of you. If you looked anything alike, I'd make you out to be sisters. There was that familial give and take, like sibling love/hate. You know what I'm talking about, we all have it. I can call my sister a bitch but no one else can. There was... You know each other very well."

She smiled at him. "We were good friends as kids. But that was a long time ago. We haven't even been in touch in over fifteen years. Don't you love the Riviera antipasto? Isn't it the best there is? We should have gotten the bruschetta, which is also the best there is."

He put his elbows on the table, leaned forward and smiled at her. "If there's something you'd rather not talk about, you can just say so."

"When I'm on a date, which I so rarely am, I'd rather not talk about another woman," Riley said. "Besides, if your secret motive is that you'd like to date her, I believe she's taken. And I'm not one bit happy about it, either."

His eyebrows shot up and his eyes were as round as saucers. One look at him and she knew he wasn't going to let that one go.

"Do not be a tease," he said.

Riley sighed in defeat. "I suspect she's seeing my brother. Adam said he ran into her, that it was really great to see her again after so many years. They went out for a glass of wine and he passed on one of my business cards. I said she'd never call me for a job, never work for someone she'd felt kind of competitive with when we were kids. Not nasty competitive, not rivals, nothing like that, but still… Adam's been curiously busy and stupidly happy lately…"

That made Logan smile. "Why Riley, you little witch."

"Well, she works for me! Do you think I want to see her at every family function? That would be a little complicated, don't you think?"

The waiter was just passing by and tried to snatch the antipasto platter and Logan stopped him. "We're still working on this, but I'll have another beer and I think the lady will be ready for more wine in a few minutes. Thanks." Then to Riley he said, "I think there's more to it than that, but I don't want to screw up the rest of our date. I like the way our dates end—slowly with lots of personal contact. So… How about those Lakers?"

"I didn't want to give her a job *and* my brother," she said.

He reached for her hand. "I thought she was a good-looking woman and have absolutely no interest in dating anyone but you. You're a showstopper, Riley. And I want to make out with you like mad."

"I might be falling out of the mood," she said.

"Drink more wine," he urged. "We're going to be on hiatus over Christmas and by the time we get to— Hey, should we make plans for New Year's Eve?"

"Maybe," she said. "Can I check with my daughter first? I want to be sure she's not on the loose while I'm partying with you."

"Fair enough," he said. "Here comes dinner. And save a little room for the tiramisu. Damn, does that look good or what?" He gave her hand another squeeze. "Come on, baby. Let's get in the same canoe here. Tonight's about us. I want to impress you with my manners, good taste, brilliance and sexual allure."

She laughed at him. "I don't want to hear another word about your sexual allure. Especially in front of the waitstaff."

"Killjoy. Some women find the spectacle of a man willing to make a fool of himself in public very titillating."

"Do they, now?"

"You know they do, Riley." And he winked.

Logan had learned something tonight, like what an idiot he could be. First of all, a detective with a working brain would have waited for her to bring up Emma before homing in on her and their friendship. And second, whatever was in their past was enough to take Riley to another place and nearly ruin the evening. Maybe he wasn't smart enough to balance a budding relationship and a case because he was hot for Riley. He liked her in a way he hadn't liked a woman in a long time.

By the time the conversation got around to Emma possibly dating Riley's brother, she was shutting down, moving away. Riley didn't seem to mind talking about the fact that Emma was pretty, that she'd had a bad marriage, but she didn't want to talk about Emma and her relationships with men.

After dinner he managed to persuade her to do a little kissing beside her car. He even talked her into getting in the car for a little more. But when he asked her to come to his place for an hour or so, she was too smart for him. "I'm afraid not, Logan," she had said. "I'm not ready for that next step." And he said he was ready whenever she was and she replied, "I know. I can tell. I'm so smart that way."

So now they were driving home to their own houses in their separate cars and he had the feeling something had changed. Instead of going forward, they were moving back.

And this had something to do with Emma even though Riley had no idea of his interest in Emma.

His cell rang and the number popped up on the dash screen in the car. Georgianna. He pressed the connection for the hands-free. "What?" he said.

"Hello, dear," she said. "You're late for dinner again."

"What do you want? What if she'd been in my car?"

"Didn't you say you'd be meeting for dinner? Why would she be in your car?"

"Because she drank too much wine and I had to drive her to my house, which I very much tried to do. But she left most of her second glass and declined my invitation. And I'm a little unhappy so why don't you just leave me alone."

"Did you learn anything?"

"No. Not anything useful."

"Why don't you go ahead and tell me, huh? I'm much more objective than you are."

He took a breath. She was right. "There's some significant history between the girls but it's obviously complicated. When I started to ask about their history, using all of my brilliant detective skills, she mentally moved away from me. That's when I lost her. She was fine talking about Emma coming back here, needing a job, getting over a bad marriage—generic on the bad, no details—but when I asked what their relationship was like when they were young, she shut down. Oh—and she thinks Emma might be seeing her brother."

"She doesn't know?" George asked.

"Not for sure, I guess. How firm is that?"

"Every night."

"How do you know?" he asked.

"The only conversations they have are about what's for dinner and when will you be here."

Logan thought Adam Kerrigan was getting a lot luckier than he was. "I don't get it," he said. "They're one nice big happy family. I saw Riley and Emma today, working through a tense situation, supportive of each other, friendly. The brother and the mother obviously like her. But Riley's smart. She's scary smart. You think she knows something and doesn't want her family mixed up in it?"

"Possible," George said. "If you don't have anything interesting to tell me, I'm going to kiss the kids and hit the sack. Bruno's on shift."

Bruno was not his real name. Mr. Universe's real name was John.

"Good. Don't call me anymore."

"You know it's probably a good thing you didn't get laid…"

"Shows what you know. That's almost never a good thing."

"Oh, I can think of a ton of circumstances when getting laid would be a really bad—"

He hung up on her.

chapter *sixteen*

Emma received her second phone call from Bethany two days after the first, again while she was driving home from work. She learned that Bethany's mother had died from a freakishly terrible case of the flu almost two years ago. She got sick, then got sicker, was admitted to the hospital then to the ICU. It was the kind of thing that usually happened to the extremely frail, chronically ill or elderly, but it got Danielle Christensen, taking her life in a week. The family was, understandably, wrecked by it.

Then Olaf Christensen brought home a woman he had worked with for a long time, a CPA in his import-export company. There were many such businesses in the port city, the Bay Area, and the Christensens' was successful. Danielle had only been gone a couple of months, but it seemed to help him a great deal to be seeing this woman. Liz was forty and had never married, had no children and before six months had passed, they were married. Everyone loved her—she was good at her job, active in her church, popular at work, laughed a lot and showered attention on Bethany's father. But she never laughed with Bethany, only with Bethany's father and other adults.

Before they even married, Bethany's stepmother was taking over the house. She fired the cleaning lady who'd been with them for years and hired Riley's company. She made every meal or ordered something she could pick up on the way home or booked reservations. The once comfortably lived-in house became spotless and sterile. Danielle's clothes were moved to a guest room closet and chest of drawers, then little by little they moved back to the master bedroom. The family pictures were removed. Liz said, "They're certainly not helping our situation, these constant reminders." Bethany was told to clean her room to Liz's specifications and if she didn't, Liz went in her room, put things away and tidied up. In order to keep Liz out of her room, Bethany followed the instructions. When Bethany just wouldn't stop acting depressed, Liz found her a therapist.

"I heard her saying I should be put in a hospital or boarding school but my dad didn't agree. Maybe I should. I would be away from them."

Bethany told Emma she took a bunch of drugs from Liz's medicine chest and had to have her stomach pumped last Christmas.

Emma gasped. "Oh, sweetheart, how terrifying! Please tell me you'll never do that again!"

"No, I won't. It was horrid. It turns out Liz doesn't have any good drugs," Bethany said.

"Well, I guess that's a point in her favor," Emma said. "I know Christmas is hard, Bethany, but if you start to feel terrible will you please tell a school counselor? Or teacher? Or someone?"

"I could try, but I think I'm just going to ask my dad and

Liz if I can be a foreign exchange student. My dad wants everything to be all right. But I think Liz would be happy to see me go."

"Do you have pictures of your mother?" Emma asked. "Pictures you can look at to give you comfort?"

"I have some in my drawer."

"Bethany, what about your grandparents?"

"My grandma is in assisted living. She was so good but when my mom died… She just got so old, so fast."

"And what about your friends from school?"

"I have friends at school, but they don't want to hang out anymore. I think I make them sad or something. And Liz makes them nervous. She's too much."

Emma was almost surprised to hear the sound of her own laughter. "Okay, I wasn't going to tell you this but I have a stepmother. And she's too much, too."

"No way," Bethany said.

"Rosemary. I remember when my adviser in high school told me I was so lucky to have a mother like Rosemary who was strict and made sure my homework was done and had a strong set of values. She said I'd appreciate it someday. Rosemary was kind of scary. Her smile was fake, if you know what I mean."

"I know what you mean," Bethany said. "My stepmother doesn't like me. She pretends in front of my dad, but it's not real. Sometimes I can hear her complaining and crying to him, saying I don't appreciate her. Maybe it's just because she's not anything like my mother, I don't know. It's like we don't live in the same house anymore."

"Tell me about your mother," Emma said.

"She was so sweet. Not that she couldn't get mad—she chased me with a mop once, yelling her head off. But she couldn't catch me and then she laughed her head off. She was kind of messy. She left her clothes on the closet floor all the time and our cleaning lady, Mary, she used to grumble and mutter and complain and my mother would laugh and say, "Come on, Mary! I'm such great job security!" But my mother could cook and bake! The house always smelled great. And she loved to go to my school things. She worked at my dad's company, too, but she'd take off to help at school, to go on field trips, to watch my concerts and programs and stuff. And she used to…" Bethany's voice slowed and stopped. Emma could tell she was crying. "We used to get in bed together and talk and rub each other's backs and heads and laugh and fall asleep in a pile."

Emma struggled to find her own voice. "I love your mother," she finally said.

"Thank you for saying that because I believe you, and you don't even know her. I wish I could be with her."

"She's with you in your heart and I believe she's watching over you. You're going to be like her, you know. Maybe not tomorrow or next week, but you're going to have a great life and make your house smell like great things are baking and laugh with your children and fall asleep in a pile. You will, Bethany. I grew up and moved away from my stepmother and you'll move away from yours."

"Did you move away and have a great life?"

Emma bit her lip. It wasn't really a lie if she thought about where she was now. "Yes, I have a lovely life. A happy life."

"Cleaning houses?"

"Yes. And meeting wonderful people."

When they hung up, Emma drove the rest of the way home, crying all the way. Was she helping by taking these calls from this poor, grief-stricken, lonely girl?

She remembered when her life was at a point like that,

when she'd lost her father, when she was just sixteen. But she had Riley. And Riley hadn't been afraid to hang out.

The twenty-third of December fell on Friday and that was the day Penny and her girlfriends chose for their little Christmas party. The girls had decided that everyone would bring substantial hors d'oeuvres and Marilyn agreed to make two desserts. They were going to have a cocktail party and ornament exchange.

Earlier in the week Emma had helped Penny bring in her tree and put her decorations up. She brought another centerpiece and wine; her wrapped presents were under Penny's tree. She'd been looking forward to this holiday for weeks, her first Christmas as a free woman. And especially her evening with the girls, Penny, Susan, Dorothy and Marilyn. But all the while, it was hard for her to shake off Bethany's call.

Their wine was poured, their cocktail plates were loaded, they were comfy in Penny's little living room and someone toasted, "Another year gone to hell." They all said *Here! Here!* with laughter.

"You're not quite as perky as usual, Emma," Marilyn pointed out. "You haven't had another pan of pee tossed at your head, have you?"

Emma shot wide eyes to Penny. "You *told*?"

"Way to keep it to yourself, Marilyn," Penny scolded.

"Well, I don't have to keep it from Emma, do I? You haven't had a falling out with that lovely Adam, have you?"

"No, he remains lovely. Really, Penelope, I can't believe you told about that! I'll see Adam late tomorrow night after he has his dinner and celebration with his family. I have the littlest work problem, that's all."

"Do tell!" three of them said at once.

"I shouldn't. I don't believe you're entirely trustworthy," Emma said.

Dorothy laughed. "Don't worry about that, angel. No one listens to us anyway. What happened at work?"

She sighed. Truthfully, she was dying to talk to someone and these old biddies were good listeners. As long as she didn't name names. "I've gone and done the dumbest thing."

"What? Tell us at once!"

"But it's not a happy story," she apologized. "I don't want to cast a pall on our party—I've been looking forward to it."

"Pah, we love trouble and misery. We can take it!"

"Indeed," Emma said with a frown. "It's quite sad, really."

They had no trouble talking her into it; she was more than ready to unload. She started with the new clothes in the trash, the scarred desktop, then the diary and her bold move in leaving her number.

"Oh, bless you, little darling!" Susan said. "You're all mush, aren't you?"

Then Emma explained Riley's rules and Bethany's two calls.

"Oh, my dear, you did absolutely the right thing!" Penny said. "Someone has to talk to that child!"

"But what can I do to help?"

"I'm sure listening helps, love," Dorothy said. "Where is that girl's grandmother?"

"I asked, as a matter of fact—apparently she went downhill fast after her daughter died and is now in assisted living. I don't know the details, but I gather she can't be of much help in her condition."

"Some of us are frail," Marilyn said. "Not *us*, mind you. *We* turned into leather. Tough old broads who have outlasted way too many friends. You can give her our numbers, Emma.

There's no group of grannies who know more about the pain of loss and the way to move on than we do."

"I bet you would be good for her," Emma said.

"What about that woman, the new wife. Wearing the dead woman's clothes! That should be against the law. I'm calling my lawyer after Christmas. I'm going to give him a list of names of those approved to be seen in my clothing after I'm gone," Marilyn said.

"Save your dime," Penny said. "No one wants your old-lady clothes."

"It is awful, though, isn't it?" Emma asked. "She made a point of saying she asked them, but what's a young, grief-stricken girl going to say?"

"Sounds like she can't help herself," Susan said. "She's probably a well-meaning idiot. Trying to make her new husband happy, keeping the house immaculate to impress anyone who's watching that she's a caring mother, getting expensive clothes for the girl, rather than giving time and understanding..."

"They put her in counseling," Emma said.

"So what? I have an ex-sister-in-law who was a counselor!" Susan exclaimed. "Worst fucked-up piece of work I've ever seen."

"Nice language," Dorothy said. "You know what you should do, Emma? You should talk to that nice Adam about this. You said he's lovely with teenagers."

"With his niece, I've seen a little of that. But I'm working for his sister. I broke the rules. I wonder if he'd feel obligated to tell her. Because it wouldn't be the first time I've broken the rules. Not long ago I called the police on one of our clients..."

They all leaned toward her as one. Their eyes were wide and hungry. "I don't believe you mentioned that, darling," Penny said.

"I'm going to need another glass of wine," Marilyn said. "Don't tell about it until I've gotten reloaded here."

"A man was assaulting his wife. Beating her," Emma said, going through the story, explaining she was supposed to call her directors or Riley but she just called the police.

"Good for you!" everyone said.

"I thought strong women had died off, but look at you go!" Dorothy added.

"I might've chased him with a tire iron, the bastard!" Penny said.

"Exactly why I carry," Susan finally said.

"I just wish I could've seen them arrest him," Emma said. "Say…" She looked around the room. "Penny, just how much have you told them about me?"

"Well, there was that story about the bedpan. Slowed down the bridge table a bit, that one. And of course that little bit about the Ponzi…"

"You told them all that, did you?" Emma asked.

"You wouldn't want them to be caught off guard," Penny said.

"I say good riddance," Marilyn said. "Thank goodness he had that Saturday night special in his office!"

"It was a Glock, you dolt," Susan said. "At least keep your weapons straight."

Emma was shaking her head.

"What's the matter, darling?" Penny asked.

"You're incorrigible," she said. "There is no logical reason why I should want to be exactly like you. Yet…"

They all giggled and lifted their glasses. "To women with balls," someone said.

If Riley was asked by a client to provide holiday house-keeping service, she charged double and offered the jobs to her senior housekeepers. There were always at least a few eager for the extra money and they would arrange their holiday celebrating accordingly. She was careful which jobs she accepted and who she sent because Nick and Makenna shouldn't be asked to supervise. And Riley wanted to be called only in an emergency, which shouldn't happen with a skilled crew.

Christmas was a holiday she'd dearly loved since Maddie was born. They did most of their celebrating at June's house and Maddie wouldn't have it any other way. Jock had joined them for dinner a few times, usually showed up early Christmas morning to watch Maddie open gifts, even stole Maddie away for a few hours to spend time with his family. He was always very cordial and respected Riley's wishes, not pushing too much. He still spent most of his major holidays with his mom, dad, brother and sister. Once he'd asked if Maddie could stay over so they could have Christmas at his mom's. Riley had known that wasn't asking too much. But she'd said no, and he had come to June's instead.

Riley loved helping her mother with the meals, Adam was always there Christmas Eve and Christmas Day, and over the years there had been the occasional extra guests—a girlfriend of Adam's or friends or coworkers who would otherwise be alone. Now that Maddie was a teenager, Christmas morning wasn't such a big deal and they'd do their gift opening later in the morning while the turkey roasted. June cooked all day, talking, laughing and singing carols when the spirit moved her. Riley spent the whole day with her mother and daughter. Adam was in and out because he liked delivering gifts and good tidings to his friends at their homes, just as friends and neighbors stopped by June's house, knowing there would be eggnog, coffee and cookies. It was always warm, cozy, low-key, and made Riley feel secure. After all, she'd drawn the blueprint for this life.

She had a feeling everything was about to change. She could smell it in the wind.

Maddie was getting older, more mature. She was asking the questions Adam had predicted, and then some. She wanted to know how she came to be. Did her parents love each other? If they did, why did they stop? Riley could no longer live in denial—Jock was a pretty good dad and Maddie loved him.

And Adam, he would never leave them, but he wasn't going to belong to them anymore. It was the elephant in the room—Emma had come back and Adam was different. Emma had come back and Riley had lost fifteen years, feeling thrown back in time. She wanted to ask where Emma was today but she wouldn't. Surely Lyle would look after her. Or her landlady would.

Riley tried to savor the two days, to fill up on them, as if they'd have to hold her for a long time. The presents were a success and dinner was slowly being prepared. She stood at the stove and sink with her mother, got out the Christmas dishes and set the table. Maddie came into the dining room, her cell phone to her ear. "Put an extra plate on. Daddy is coming to dinner."

"Does he know it's at four?" Riley asked.

"He knows. He's glad. He'll have to go to work early tomorrow."

Because Mackie's would be a madhouse, Riley thought. People would be returning and exchanging all their gifts. He'd worked for Mackie's full-time since getting his degree. Which took him over five years to accomplish, she reminded herself.

But he'd been there for fifteen years—part-time at first while he went to school, steadily working his way up. It wasn't a big job but it was solid.

He wasn't the senior partner of a law firm or chief of neurosurgery, but he worked hard, long hours in a tough, competitive business and his employees loved him. *So when are you going to give him a break, huh?* she asked herself.

He arrived, wearing the ugly Christmas sweater Maddie had gotten him, thrilling her and forcing a laugh out of everyone, even Adam. And too soon it was coming to a close and Riley had a sinking feeling the Christmas holidays she'd known since Maddie was born would never be the same. Maddie was growing up. She was so smart they were already looking at colleges. Riley, though still young, was staring in the face of a different life. June would age, Adam would leave her, Maddie would build a life of her own.

Riley's phone rang and she fished it out of her purse.

"I just wanted to call to wish you a merry Christmas," Logan said.

"And merry Christmas to you!" she replied cheerily. "We're just sitting down. Can I give you a call after we eat?"

"Perfect," he said. "I am blessedly finished with my family. I'm home."

"I'll call in a little while," she said.

Jock and Adam both left while Riley and June were cleaning up the leftovers and washing the dishes. Maddie was on the phone planning a big shopping day with Gramma and two of her girlfriends for tomorrow bright and early. Riley would go to the office. The Monday after Christmas was always a busy day for her crews.

That left only tonight. Maddie was staying overnight with Gramma, and Riley was alone. She felt a little guilty that seeing Logan hadn't even come to mind. It was only seven and Christmas was over.

It was a dark, cloudy night and she drove to Jock's house. He'd lived in this house for three years now. It was small and one of the newer houses in Santa Rosa, a new construction.

He was proud of it. Riley had never been inside but she knew where it was because she'd dropped Maddie off there to visit many times. Maddie hadn't spent the night very often; her life was still mostly with her mom and gramma and girlfriends. Jock didn't push any kind of custody arrangement. He didn't dare. Riley scared him, she knew that.

She sat in her car out front for a while, just thinking. She wasn't sure what she was going to do, but here she was. She was driven by some sentimental force she didn't understand. After ten minutes or so, she walked up to the front door and rang the bell.

Jock threw open the door and looked at her in shock. "Riley?" he said. "You need Maddie to stay over?" he asked, looking over her shoulder.

He had gotten rid of the sweater and wore an old sweatshirt—Seahawks. His jeans were old, torn here and there and looked like a beloved garment and in absolutely poor taste. He was in his stocking feet and held the TV remote in his hand. The TV was muted but there were football players paused like statues on the screen.

"You shouldn't just open the door like that," she said. "I could've been a home invader or something."

"In Santa Rosa?"

"We have crime here, you know."

"Would you like to come in?" he asked.

"I don't want to interrupt. I just had something on my mind and... Maddie's growing up so fast."

He stepped back and held the door open. "I'm having a cup of coffee. Would you like one?"

She absently rubbed her tummy. "I've had too much of everything today. But I wondered if we could have a little talk."

"Something wrong?" he asked, walking back into his living room.

"No, I—" She stopped talking and looked around. He had a tan velour sectional, a tall dining table surrounded by stools—looked like a poker table. There was a wall unit and a big-screen, but it looked like someone had actually helped him decorate. There were female touches—throw pillows, a marble bowl on the table, a couple of framed prints on the wall, shelved books, a shadow box with pictures of Maddie from childhood. "This is very nice, Jock."

"Would you like to see Maddie's room?" he asked.

"Sure," she said.

He led the way and she was stunned to see an actual girl's bedroom. The furniture matched, the bulletin board was covered with pictures, there was pretty bedding, a couple of her trophies were on the bureau, there was a desk and chair, and her pom-poms from seventh grade were hanging up on the wall. On her bedside table was a professionally done portrait of Jock and Maddie. It was beautiful. She walked over to it and picked it up.

"When did you have this taken?"

"Last year. We'd have given you one but I was pretty sure that wouldn't work. My mom has one."

"Why didn't Maddie tell me?" she asked.

"I suppose because she thinks you don't like it that I'm her father," he said.

"Oh, nonsense," she said defensively, with the slightest blush. "I'm surprised by all this. Maddie doesn't stay over here very often."

"She has, though. Did you think I put her on the couch? She knows she has a room here whenever she wants it or needs it. I bet she has a room at Adam's..."

"No," Riley said. "No, of course not. But if Mom and I were both going somewhere and needed a babysitter, he wouldn't mind coming over to my house. Or Mom's house. But this is so nice. Thanks."

"She doesn't use it that much," he said. "Come on, Riley. What do you want to talk about? You never want to talk."

She turned and went back to the living room. "We talk," she said as she went. She sat at the end of the sectional, as far from where his coffee cup sat as she could get. She put her purse down on the floor beside her but didn't even open her coat. "We talk," she said again.

"Not really," he said, sitting down. "You're very business-like."

"Well, I suppose that goes with the territory. I run a business and I'm used to being that way."

"And tonight?" he asked.

She sighed deeply. "I don't know why, but it just struck me—things will be changing again. Maddie's growing up. She's a woman now."

"I wouldn't go that far," he said. "She's still a young lady to me."

"Jock... I did a good job, didn't I?"

"Huh?" he said, obviously completely confused.

"A single mother, barely holding it together, living with her mother and brother... Maddie seems to be remarkably well-adjusted. Don't you think?"

"She's fine, Riley. She's amazing."

"She's been asking me difficult questions lately."

"Really? Like what? She hasn't had anything new for me," he said.

"She said you two have talked a lot about back when... When we were so briefly together."

"I wouldn't say a lot," he said. "I think she was about twelve when she asked me why we weren't married. I figured that'd be coming. So I told her."

"But what did you tell her?"

"I told her that getting pregnant was an accident, that we weren't careful about preventing it, about birth control. Mostly my fault. And I issued a warning—teenage boys and young men are idiots, do not trust them. So—we were pregnant and we talked about marriage but didn't think it would work for us. We were too young, for one thing. But we both wanted her—I made sure to tell her that. My mom always said that kids want to know two things—that you love them and wanted them."

"You offered to give me money for an abortion," Riley reminded him.

He shook his head sadly. "Look, I did what I thought men did, what I thought they were expected to do. I didn't think it through. Thank God you didn't want that. Thank you for that, Riley. You've always been the smart one."

"You didn't tell her about that, did you?"

"Of course not," he said. "That wouldn't do one single positive thing for Maddie and I'm so damn grateful for her, you will just never know. I did tell her that as far as stupid eighteen-year-olds go, I was the dumbest. I told her I had a lot of regrets but none had anything to do with her. She made me the luckiest dimwit alive."

"She wants to know things, like did we love each other," Riley said. "I told her I loved you."

"That was good, to say that. She should think that her mom and dad loved each other when she was made."

"Jock, I *did* love you. I told you I loved you and you said, 'Whoa, wait a minute...'"

He rested his elbows on his knees and briefly hung his head. Then he looked at her. "Riley, there's no way I'm ever going to be able to go back in time and fix mistakes like that. I never should have done that. I never should have talked that way. I'm telling you, I was a stupid boy and I was scared to death. I didn't know how I felt. I just didn't know what to do."

"You wouldn't tell Emma…"

"Yeah, the list just gets longer and longer. Riley, I'll be the first person to admit it took me way too long to grow up, to know my mind, to figure out that life was handing me a gift and there was no way I was ever going to deserve it. But I admit I'm a damn lucky man and really, I'm so grateful. And I made my peace with Emma. I finally got to see her and tell her I was sorry that I did that to her, that I cheated on her."

"Huh," Riley huffed.

"I should have called her and told her we were together. Things might be a lot different if I'd just done that."

"You saw her?" Riley asked.

"Well, yeah." He laughed ruefully and shook his head. "That daughter of yours, Riley. She's fifteen going on fifty, you know that? After I told her I was someone else's boyfriend when I fell for you, she started asking me if I ever said I was sorry to Emma. Of course I hadn't. I'm too clumsy for that. It would've meant finding her number in New York and we both know she was in a bad place—she didn't need to hear from me. Then Maddie told me she was back. She'd met her. I guess she was with Adam and they ran into her. Maddie isn't sure but she thinks Adam likes her. And Maddie told me Emma would be having dinner with your mother so I hung around and waited for her to leave so I could…"

"Wait! What?"

"What what?" he asked, looking confused.

"Emma had dinner with my mother?"

"Yeah. A week or two ago, I think. You didn't know?"

"No," she said, feeling her blood pressure rising. "And Adam is seeing her."

"I don't know. She didn't mention…"

"He is," Riley said, angry. "I can tell. And my mother is having dinner with her behind my back and not telling me. And you're seeing her, too. Making up with her?"

"Sort of making up. I just wanted to say I was sorry about all that, sorry that it hurt her, not sorry it happened because we're very lucky to have Maddie and—"

"So everyone has personal private stuff going on with Emma and no one finds it necessary to mention any of this to me!"

"Holy Jesus, maybe if you weren't so mad all the time!" he fumed. "Don't you ever get tired of people walking on eggshells around you?"

"Why aren't people at least honest with me?" she demanded.

"I don't know, Riley! Could it be because you get so freaking *angry*?"

She stood up. "So you said you were sorry you cheated on her. Did you ask her for another chance?"

Jock stood, as well. "Oh, for the love of God, of course not! I don't want another chance! Why are you so upset?"

"Oh, I don't know, Jock. Could it be because everyone is keeping stuff from me? My daughter, my brother, my mother, you! But who gave her the job? Me! Why am I always the one picking up the pieces?"

Jock just stared at her in shock. "Is that what you think? That you pick up the pieces? Not June or me or even Adam? Aren't we the A-Team? I know no one counts on me much but you all can. I do everything any of you asks. You weren't left alone, goddamn it! You had all of us! All of us doing it the way you wanted it done! And here you are, your girl is almost grown and you found someone, she tells me. You finally found someone who deserves you. Well, good for you.

And I said I was sorry every way I could so you can get over it now and move on. I never stood a chance with you anyway."

"You didn't want a chance with me!"

"I asked you to marry me! More than once!"

"To be with Maddie! To be with your daughter!"

"No! To put our family together the way it should be! To be with you! But you never got over blaming me for all your problems. Me and Emma. So let me clear that up right now—we all make our own messes and as messes go we got real damn lucky. We got ourselves a beautiful fifteen-year-old mess who's going to do great things with her life in spite of us."

"You didn't want me," she said. "You were married six months later!"

"Yeah, another brilliant move of mine. I was so hungry for someone to love me, to want me, I married the first woman who convinced me I was trusted, that I was desirable. It lasted less than a year but it was over in a day."

"Bullshit. Women have always wanted you!"

"Just not the right one! Don't you get it, Riley? I did my best. My best has never been good enough."

"Now you're just feeling sorry for yourself. Maddie's proud of you."

"Kids will do that."

"She nearly ruined the first dinner we had with Logan. All she did was brag about you. It was very uncomfortable."

Jock smiled. "I'll have to thank her. She run him off?"

Riley raised her chin. "No. He doesn't scare easily, I guess. I'm going to go," she said, feeling exhausted.

"The next time you want to talk, give me about forty-eight hours advance warning, okay?"

chapter *seventeen*

After leaving Jock's, Riley had herself a hard cry, something she hadn't done in quite a while. It felt as though everyone was showering love on Emma and just not acknowledging how this might affect her, how she might feel like the bad girl, being punished all over again. Left out and unloved. Damn Emma! Had she come back and taken over Riley's support group?

She felt like a thirteen-year-old girl. A baby. An ogre who tried to prevent Adam and her mother from embracing their old friend. Tried and failed and now they knew how selfish and mean Riley could be.

At midnight she heard her phone chime with an incoming text. It was Logan.

Just wondering if everything is okay?

Crap! She'd never called him. Although she was in bed and had a stuffy nose, she called him.

"I'm so sorry," she said. "I'm fine. I got caught up in a difficult family discussion. You know how those things can sneak up at holidays."

"Oh, yeah," he said with a laugh. "My dad and I usually entertain the family by acting like assholes. We did pretty well this year. We stayed on opposite sides of the room and there wasn't too much friction.

"It's funny, here we are, twenty-five years later and I'm still a pissed-off little boy. Everyone else has forgiven him and let him back in the family. My mom and dad are as close to being a couple without being one as you can get. They're not remarried or anything, but he's at every family thing. I think he should be shunned."

"Gee, only twenty-five years?"

"You're probably not going to believe this, but I'm actually a pretty easygoing guy. I think. I wouldn't have a problem in the world if my mother just hated him."

"Sadly, I understand completely. Let's talk tomorrow," she said. "I've had such a long day."

"Sure," he said. "And, Riley? We have a new year ahead of us. Let's make it a good one, okay?"

"Absolutely, Logan."

What a nice guy, she thought. She snuggled back into the covers. But she didn't think about Logan. She wanted to. A smart woman would make something positive out of that relationship.

Why do people do these things on the holidays? she asked herself. Why couldn't Jock have saved his outburst for another time, another day?

Jock's outburst? her conscience mocked her. *You started it! You always start it!*

Maybe she should start to admit it if only to herself. She was so scared and hurt, felt so alone even though she had

Adam, her mother and her grandparents for a little while after Maddie was born. When she wasn't crying she was bitching. In the beginning, when she was pregnant, Jock didn't come around much. When Maddie was born he only came around when he felt safe, when Adam wasn't around. He often visited Maddie when June was watching her because June might've been unhappy with Jock but she was never mean. Though he didn't come to see the baby on a schedule or often, he did come regularly. And he called. He called Riley until he could just call Maddie.

It seemed like forever that every time she saw him her heart ached and her throat burned with tears she wouldn't shed. But she got over it. As she grew older and met more and more women who were raising children on their own, she learned how to bear it.

But it left her hardened and somewhat bitter. She didn't want to be that way. Here she was, the mother of a beautiful and brilliant daughter with everything in the world to be grateful for and she could behave in the most ungrateful manner sometimes.

It had had the opposite effect on Jock. Having Maddie had sweetened him. Mellowed him and made him more mature.

I made one mistake, she thought wearily. *And it was the best thing that ever happened to me. Yet I've managed to suffer for it for years. How do I stop it? How has Jock moved on with grace?*

How has Emma?

Just before falling asleep she remembered, *I fell for you*, he had said. *I was never good enough for you*, he had said. Was that what he'd said? She must've misunderstood.

Emma wasn't at all unhappy with the quiet way she spent the holiday weekend. On Christmas Eve she went with Lyle and Ethan to Ethan's sister's house for dinner. Given that Lyle and Ethan had their own flower shop, a centerpiece wouldn't do, so she borrowed Penny's kitchen and recipes and made crab croquettes and a cheese ball. It was a rather hectic and noisy evening; Ethan's sister was pregnant and his niece was two. Emma enjoyed the two-year-old for about an hour and then started to wonder how young mothers did it—the toddler was tired, cranky, hungry, restless and generally bad. One of her first rebellious acts was to pitch the cheese ball at their Labrador retriever.

"Yeah, this is about ninety percent of the time these days," Ethan said.

"I don't think I was prepared for how fast a two-year-old can move," Emma said.

"Watch your valuables," Lyle said. "She swallowed Mommy's diamond engagement ring about six months ago."

"It's okay, I got it back," Ethan's sister yelled from the kitchen.

"Ewww," Emma and the two men said together.

When she got home at nine that night, Adam was waiting for her. She regaled him with stories of dinner and the fate of her cheese ball. She insisted he open his gifts; she wanted him to try on his new slippers. He liked the book and sweater and had a gift for her, a very big box. Inside was a black waterproof trench coat, a very stylish maxi length with a belt. She told him to wait right where he was. She took it to her little bedroom to try it on and when she came back he admired the sleek design with her pumps. Then she untied the belt, opened the coat and flashed him with her nakedness. Although they roared with laughter, it only took a minute for it to be replaced with the sound of kissing and panting, the new coat on the floor on one side of the bed, Adam's clothes on the other.

On Christmas morning she woke up to see Adam raised

up on an arm, watching her. "I've made a decision," he said. "I've decided to wake up like this every Christmas morning."

"Ah. Will Santa approve?"

"I'm very nice," he said. "And you're a little naughty. Sounds perfect to me."

While Adam did his family thing, Emma relaxed, gathering her strength in the quiet of the day. She'd been warned that the week following Christmas was sheer hell at work. Some of their clients had been out of town over the holidays but many more had extra people in, company from out of town, lots of refuse from the gift exchanging, greasy and splattered kitchens from the constant cooking and baking. School was still on break until after New Year's, which meant general messiness everywhere and a tougher time cleaning while stepping over people.

And there were a few things she was eager to find out. First, was Bethany okay? She hadn't called since before Christmas, but the Christensen house was one of the first on her schedule for Monday. When they arrived, she ran right up the stairs, tapped quietly on Bethany's bedroom door and when the girl told her to come in, she stuck her head in. "Okay?" she asked quietly.

Bethany gave her a sheepish smile. "Okay," she answered.

"Was it a nice Christmas?"

She nodded. "And I saw my grandparents. I'm just so glad it's over. I feel so much more in control now."

"Life will be easier now, I think," Emma said. "Holidays are always a bit tough when you've had losses. You have my number."

"I do. I'll call you."

When Emma was pulling the door closed she turned and came face-to-face with Shawna, who was frowning. "You're gonna make trouble for yourself," she predicted.

"It'll be all right," Emma said, because that's what she'd been telling herself.

The Christensen home reminded her a little bit of her own New York apartment—spacious, pristine, the furnishings rich and carefully chosen, and while it was filled with warm colors and dark wood, you could almost feel the emptiness. It was too quiet. Homes were made to be filled with conversation and laughter and even arguing from time to time. It was too clean, too orderly. It felt so lonely here.

Emma, Shawna and Dellie got busy and as predicted, there was more cleaning than usual. Mr. and Mrs. Andrews had not canceled the cleaning service. Nick caught up with them on Tuesday to tell them he was sending a different crew and he would be watching closely to be sure there wasn't any trouble. He wouldn't allow Emma's crew to return to that volatile house. "For two cents, I'd cancel them," Nick said. "For now I'll be keeping a very close eye on that house."

At the end of the week when they were nearly finished with the last house, Riley texted Shawna and asked that the three of them stop by the office when they returned to turn in the van. They found a full staff gathered—Nick, Makenna, Riley and her young assistant, Jeanette.

"Come in, please," Riley said. "Something terrible has happened and I wanted to tell you. You'll hear about it tonight if you watch the news. Mr. Andrews is dead. It appears Mrs. Andrews shot him. The police have taken her into custody." Riley cleared her throat. "Our crew let themselves in and found them."

Emma actually swooned against Shawna. "Dear God," she whispered.

"Here, sit down," Nick said.

"That man probably got what he had coming," Shawna said. "He was beating that woman."

"Has anything like this ever happened before?" Emma asked.

"We've had a delicate situation or two over the years. One of our clients was found unconscious—he had a stroke and went to the hospital and from there into a special care home. Nothing like this. People don't just have dust and dirt," Riley said. "They have complex personal lives. Some of them have serious problems. And we're in their private space. We have to be vigilant and blind—it's a very difficult balance. I'm sorry this happened."

"The other crew," Emma said. "Are they okay?"

"Not at all," Nick said. "It was Cora, Maria and Connie—and they're shook up. They're going to take Monday and Tuesday off and if they need to see someone, like a counselor, we'll find someone."

"Was it horrid?" Dellie asked.

"One bullet in the back of his head," Nick said. "He still had the TV remote in his hand. Looked like it might've happened much earlier or even the night before."

"Ew, that ain't gonna play good for her," Shawna said.

"Had he been beating her again?" Emma asked.

Everyone shrugged.

"I'm sure we'll get more information as time passes. I just wanted to be sure to tell you personally since you know the couple and had some dealings with them and the police. Everyone okay?"

"Sure," Dellie said. "They have kids, you know. Grown kids in their twenties."

"I know. Emma?"

"Yes. Fine." She shuddered, remembering Richard. Remembering the cruelty of his suicide. The horrific sight. The smell of blood and gun powder. His open eyes and gallons of blood. The smell of death and all its atrocities. "Fine," she said again, standing.

"Then I think we're finished here. Nick, you'll let me see that memo before you send it out to our crews."

"Definitely."

"Thanks, everyone."

Emma lingered as people slowly left, talking among themselves. When Riley was alone behind her desk, gathering up her purse and briefcase, she approached. "Um, excuse me. When would be a good time to talk? There's something I should tell you."

"Is it going to upset me?" Riley asked.

"Probably."

Riley hesitated. "Sit down. Let's get it over with."

Emma told Riley about Bethany's house, Bethany so frail and pale, Emma leaving her phone number and Bethany calling it. "You have got to be kidding me," Riley said.

Emma shook her head. "And I don't regret it. She sounds better since the holiday is past, but I have no idea how to help her. The family situation sounds so sad—her stepmother wearing her dead mother's clothes? My God, I don't know what to say or do. I just know that it won't help her if I cut her off, if I don't take her calls. Mostly I just listen. Are you going to fire me?"

"You've put me in a terrible position here," she said. "You know perfectly well I can't fire you. My family will only come down hard on me if I do that. My mother, who I have learned you've been seeing, my brother, who is your current champion…"

"Adam has been a good friend. He's the one who suggested your company, which, by the way, I happen to like." She laughed and shook her head. "I actually look forward to work. The girls I work with are fantastic. The clients range from difficult to weird to sweet. Some of them I would actually miss."

"Employees with a high school education and citizenship usually stay with this company for an average of nine months. And I am stuck with you."

"I should think it would give you great satisfaction," Emma said. "But tell me truly, Riley. Just for a second put aside whatever differences we've had and tell me—if you'd been in my position and saw that note, would you have done something? Anything? You have a fifteen-year-old daughter—what if she were that lonely? And had no one? Would you wish someone had answered her call, even if it was a lowly cleaning lady?"

"First of all, cleaning ladies are not lowly. Haven't you learned yet? We know more about our clients than they know about each other! Second, I don't know that I'd have done *that*!"

"Oh, you would, too," Emma said. "Just as you'd have called the police on Mr. Andrews."

"I wouldn't have left my number," Riley asserted. Then her own phone chimed. She looked at it and pressed a button, sending it to voice mail. "I admit I would have watched. Waited. Tried to think of a solution. A counselor…"

"She has a counselor," Emma said. "A counselor who asks her if she's jealous of the new stepmother."

"Dear God, what an imbecile! I knew of Mr. Christensen's marriage. When he filled out his contract, we always ask them to list the family members and pets in the household and I knew he had a teenager and was engaged to be married. But I didn't know he'd been widowed."

Riley's phone rang again. Again she looked at it. "She really wants me. I'm sorry," she said before clicking on. "Yes, Maddie?"

"Mom! We were in an accident! Someone hit us. We're taking Daddy to the hospital. Mom, he's hurt! He's hurt!"

"Slow down, Maddie," Riley said. She completely forgot about Emma as she put the cell phone on speaker so she could gather her purse, keys, coat. "Are you hurt?"

"No. Not really. But they couldn't get Daddy out right away and they wouldn't let me go in his ambulance because they needed the room to work on him. Oh, Mom, what if he dies?"

"He's not going to die," Riley said. "What hospital are you going to?"

Maddie asked someone. "Petaluma."

"Are you sure you're all right?"

"A couple of bumps, that's all."

"All right, I'm coming. I'm on my way."

Riley ran around her desk, past Emma and out the door. Two seconds later she ran back in and said, "Jock and Maddie were in an accident."

Emma grabbed her tote and ran out with Riley. "I'll come. Lock the door, I'll be right behind you. You might need me."

For just a moment Riley was thinking, *Why would I need you?* But she didn't say anything, she just locked the door without bothering to check the office, turn off the lights or anything. She bolted for her car and without looking back at Emma, she jumped in and flew out of the parking lot and down the road.

She still had Maddie on the line. "Okay, I'm driving. Tell me how you are," she nearly shouted into the phone.

"We're here! I'm going in with Daddy! No more phones!"

Riley growled as they were disconnected.

It took thirty minutes to get to the hospital and Riley ran from the parking lot into the ER. She asked for Jock Curry or Maddie Kerrigan and was directed to the waiting area. "But are they all right?" she asked in a booming voice.

"Mom?" a voice called. "Mom?"

Ignoring all protocol, Riley pushed people aside to go into a treatment area where a series of beds were enclosed by curtains. "Maddie?" she called.

"Here!" Maddie said.

Riley found her sitting on a bed, holding an ice pack to her forehead, tears running down her cheeks. She embraced her and squeezed her too tight.

"Mom, Daddy is hurt. They took him upstairs to see if he needs surgery. I had to call Gramma and Grandpa because I'm not old enough to make decisions for him."

"Maddie, is he conscious?"

"He was talking a little. He has pain in his shoulder and stomach and he got a cut on the head that bled everywhere and he said he was bruised all over. He says he's fine. But the doctor says he's not fine and needs X-rays and stuff and to be checked for internal injuries and a head injury, so he's gone upstairs."

"Have you been checked over?"

She nodded. She took away the ice pack to reveal a contusion. "I might've hit his head. Someone just ran into us—*kabam!* She hit Daddy's side of the car and they could hardly get him out!" Then she burst into tears. "Mom, what if he isn't okay?"

"Shh, Maddie. He was talking and conscious—that's a good sign. They'll take good care of him."

Adam jogged into the front entrance of the hospital and Emma was there, waiting for him. "How are they?" he asked.

"Maddie is fine and they've taken Jock to surgery, but they're not sure they're going to operate on him. He has some kind of spleen injury that they might be able to manage with medication, but they'll have to watch him, keep him.

His parents came right away. Maddie and Riley won't leave until he's completely out of the woods. And I knew you'd want to see them."

"Where are they?"

"They're all in the third floor waiting area outside of surgery. Quite the group."

"Okay," he said, grabbing her hand.

"Ah… I'm going to go. Will you call me if you need me? If there's any change?"

"You don't have to go, Emma."

"I think I should. I'm not family and I'm not family of family. I just wanted to be here until everyone arrived, just in case…well, in case Riley needed me."

"I'm going up there," he said. He leaned toward her and kissed her on the forehead. "Thank you. I'll call you the second I know something."

"I'll be around. Go take care of your girls."

Emma was glad to be leaving, though she was worried about Jock. She had a soft spot in her heart for the guy after his amends. If they kept him in the hospital for the weekend, she'd swing by and pay him a visit.

Her phone chimed with a text and she saw it was from Lyle.

Can you call or come by the shop before we close?

She got in her car and turned it on for a little heat, but she sat in the parking lot while she called Lyle. "What's up?"

"You might want to hear this in person. Are you far away?"

"Half hour, I suppose. Just tell me. It's been a crazy day."

"Well it's about to get crazier. Lauren Shay stopped by the shop today."

"My sister?"

"She wanted me to get a message to you. Rosemary wants to see you."

"Well, that's going to be pretty difficult as I can't go to Palm Springs," Emma said.

"She's back. She's ill, Lauren says. She's back in the family home with Lauren and Anna and..." He took a breath. "She's in hospice care."

"Wow. What about her husband?"

"I didn't ask. I have no idea what this is about, just that she's back and she's apparently dying and she wants to see you. I have Lauren's number if you need it."

"I don't know," she said. "You know I'm afraid of Rosemary. She's mean. Do you suppose she's thought of one last mean thing to do to me before she dies?"

"I'll go with you," Lyle said. "You might want to call Lauren and get more information before you walk into the lion's den."

"Are you almost ready to close the shop?" she asked. "Can we grab a glass of wine? I have a bottle in the refrigerator at home."

"Won't you be with Adam?" he asked.

"Not for a while. See, Jock and Maddie were in a car accident and Adam's at the hospital. Maddie's all right but Jock isn't—they might have to remove his spleen. The call came while I was in Riley's office. We were having a little meeting because one of our clients murdered her husband and a cleaning crew found them."

"And you want a glass of wine?" Lyle asked. "If I'd had that kind of day I'd just hook up a nipple to the bottle and go to town."

"Want to come over and watch me unwind? I'd like to talk out this situation with Rosemary."

"I'll be there in about thirty minutes. Don't start without me."

★ ★ ★

Adam found Riley alone in the waiting room and she jumped up when he came in.

"How did you know to come?" she asked. "I was going to call you and Mom in a little while, but I didn't want to scare you. Maddie is okay."

"Emma called me. Where's Maddie?"

"She's in Jock's room. She won't leave him. She's fine, but it really scared her to see her dad all banged up and medical people rushing around him."

"What happened?"

"A young woman ran a light and T-boned him on the driver's side. Her airbag deployed so she escaped injury. But both cars are likely totaled."

"Maddie wasn't driving?"

Riley shook her head. "Thank God."

"Emma said his parents are here."

"They went down to the cafeteria to get coffee. Mrs. Curry is a little shaken. I think they're going to call Jock's brother and sister. There could be a crowd soon and he's in a holding room being monitored so they can take him into surgery if they have to. Apparently he has some internal injuries. He said he feels like he's been thrown down a flight of stairs. He's in a lot of pain and they have him medicated. The bruises on his face are starting to show up." She winced. "He looks awful."

"Are you trying to get Maddie to leave? Go home?"

"No, we're going to stay. I might run home and get her a change of clothes—she has blood on her clothes from Jock's head. Not much of a cut but it sure bled a lot."

"And Maddie? Anything at all?"

"Goose egg." She touched her own forehead in the spot. Then her eyes filled with tears. "I had words with Jock Christmas night."

Adam frowned. "I thought the two of you did fine," he said.

"Not at Mom's. I drove to his house. I wanted to talk to him about... Oh shit, about nothing, really. Just that Maddie's growing up so fast and she'll go off to college and get married and have children and... How are we going to balance all that?"

"Divorced couples do it all the time," Adam said with a shrug.

"I'd never been in his house," she said quietly. "He has a nice house. He has a room for Maddie."

"What's the matter, Riley?"

"I was mean to him. I kind of picked a fight with him. And he said he did his best but it was never good enough. You know I'd never even been in his house?"

"You said that already," Adam pointed out. "It's okay. The only relationship you had with Jock was the parenting of Maddie and you both do that pretty well."

"He implied I never gave him a chance," she said.

"Riley, what the hell is this?"

"I don't know, I don't know," she said. She went for the purse she'd left sitting on the chair and dug around for a tissue. She dabbed her eyes and blew her nose. "I think I've made so many mistakes."

Maddie came into the waiting room with a doctor; the doctor had a bolstering hand on Maddie's shoulder. "We're going to take Mr. Curry into surgery. I think he's going to have to part with that spleen, after all, and while I'm in there I can look around for any other problems."

"Can I talk to him?" Riley said, looking suddenly panicked.

"He's being prepped," the doctor said. "He'll be in surgery about an hour then in recovery." He turned to look down at Maddie. "When he wakes up in recovery you can see him, but then you should go home for the night. He's going to be groggy and it would be best for him to sleep."

"I'll be quiet," Maddie said. "I'll sit with him and be quiet."

"If I thought he needed someone to sit with him, believe me, I'd put an RN at his bedside. But he's going to be monitored, checked regularly and we're going to take good care of him. If there's any change in his condition, I'll call you personally."

"But I'll see him after surgery?" she asked.

"Absolutely. I've got this."

"Okay," she said meekly.

Adam waited around for the two and a half hours it took for Jock to have surgery, regain consciousness in recovery and see Maddie. During that time more of Jock's family showed up, all wanting to see him. Adam had called June and she came. He stepped outside a couple of times to text Emma and was relieved to know she was home and having a glass of wine with Lyle. When the doctor was finally ready to kick the whole lot of them out, June left with Jock's parents, holding Jock's mother's hand and reassuring her.

Maddie seemed to be exhausted. Adam walked them out to Riley's car. "Would you like me to follow you home? Feel like talking about it?"

"What is there to say?"

"Well, I think maybe you have something heavy on your mind. Mistakes, Riley? I've always felt like you do everything right."

She looked at him with a weak and rueful smile. "Shows what you know."

"I'm coming over," he said. "You can put Maddie to bed and we'll talk a little bit."

"No offense, Adam, but I don't feel like talking right now." She stopped walking and looked in her purse, patted her pockets and said, "Nuts. No cell phone. It must be in the waiting room. Adam, take Maddie home please? I'll be right behind you."

"Sure. I'm parked right over here, Maddie. Let's get you home so you can get out of those bloody clothes and get a shower."

"Yeah. I guess," she said, leaning on Adam.

He put his arm around her and opened the passenger door for her, settled her into his car.

"Thanks, Uncle Adam, for coming to the hospital."

"Everyone came. It was like a party." He reached across the console and patted Maddie's knee. "You feeling a little better now that he's out of surgery?"

"I guess so. It's just that I know so many people who lost a father when they were still young, and just the thought... Two friends at school, and even you, Uncle Adam." She sniffed back tears. "I want Daddy to have a chance to be happy, that's all."

"Your dad seems pretty happy to me," Adam said.

"He says he's fine, that he's happy, that he's proud of me. But one time when we were talking he said his one biggest regret was that he couldn't get Mom to marry him so we could be a real family. But he doesn't blame her. He said he made mistakes."

"Mistakes," Adam muttered. "Lots of talk about mistakes these days. You know what I think? I think I'm tired of hearing about mistakes. It would be a lot more productive to leave the mistakes behind and just think about the future."

"Don't you have any regrets, Uncle Adam?"

"Everyone does, Maddie. But I think my life has turned out exactly the way I meant for it to. And it's a good life. Our family might be a little different, a little chopped up here and there, but last time I checked, we were all feeling pretty lucky with what we have."

"Maybe till tonight," she said. "I'll feel a lot better when I know Daddy's all right."

"See what I mean," Adam said. "He's a lucky man."

Riley got off the elevator on the third floor. She pulled her cell phone out of her coat pocket and glanced at it. Four missed calls from Logan. She had texted him about the accident, told him everyone was fine but she was tied up and would call him later. Then she'd turned her phone off.

And she knew where her cell phone was all along.

She was relieved to see that none of Jock's family remained in the waiting room. She went into the recovery area where she'd seen Jock not ten minutes ago and there he was, sleeping off his anesthesia and pain meds, mouth open slightly. She felt tears threaten again. She walked over to his bed and gently touched his forehead. "Oh, Jock," she whispered. "I'm the screwup. Not you."

All those years of being angry, of being awash in pride and determined to keep Jock from ever hurting her again, she held him back, held herself back. She put her head down and worked like a maniac, single-minded in aiming to succeed in business and show them all—*I am not a bad person, am not a disloyal, betraying friend.* "All I wanted to do was keep myself safe," she whispered to him. "To keep Maddie safe. To prove to the world I could make it without trusting anyone."

He opened one eye and she sniffed.

"You're right about me, Jock. I was always angry. And scared. I never gave you a chance."

He lifted his hand to where hers rested on the bed rail. "It's okay, Riley," he rasped out. "It's going to be okay."

"What if you'd been killed in that accident? What if I never got to say I'm sorry?"

"Shhh," he said. "It's okay."

"It's not really," she said with a hiccup of emotion. "But maybe when you get better... If you think you can give me another chance, I'd like us to be friends."

He smiled sleepily. "Okay," he said, letting his eyes drift closed. "Boy, you really make a guy work for it, don't you?"

A huff of laughter escaped her. "It wasn't my intention."

"What about the other guy? The new guy?" he asked, not opening his eyes.

"Not much going on there, Jock. But listen, let's not say anything to Maddie. I don't want her having fantasies about us."

"Okay," he said. He gave her hand a little squeeze and she bent over and put a soft kiss on his forehead.

Suddenly there was an orderly and a nurse at the bedside, interrupting them. "We're going to take Mr. Curry to his room now. You can follow us if you like, Mrs. Curry. But then you should let him sleep and come back in the morning."

"I'm not... Okay," she said. "I'll follow you so I know where to find him in the morning."

chapter *eighteen*

Adam and Emma stayed in for New Year's Eve. Emma parked her car in his garage in case Riley or June drove by. "I think the point of this discretion is just about moot," Adam said as he was taking her coat. "My mother has guessed, I think Riley has guessed and Maddie wouldn't care."

"Still, until Riley assures me there are no longer any hard feelings between us, we will be discreet. One of the last things she said to me just before her phone chimed with Maddie's call was that she was stuck with me because of her family. She's not ready. By the way, where is Riley spending New Year's Eve?"

"She and Maddie took some snacks and a couple of board games to the hospital to spend it with Jock. I'm pretty sure they won't be allowed to stay until midnight but they're keeping him company tonight."

"Aw, that must make him very happy. He'd probably risk another car accident to get this much attention from Riley."

"Now, why would you say that?" Adam asked.

"I think he cares for her very much. I think he might love her. The way he talked about Riley and Maddie, about how he screwed up with Riley... It just sounded like he has deeper feelings than he lets on in front of you." She put her arms around Adam's waist and looked up at him. "Do you ever think about ways things could've been different?"

"Like how?" he asked, really wanting her perspective.

"Well, Jock could've started dating Riley in the first place. Then I think we would all have remained friends. But Riley might not have built her business—I get the impression she did it out of survival. Or I could have come back here after college and fallen in love with you ten years ago."

He stroked her cheek with the back of his knuckles. "Are you in love with me now?"

She nodded. "Pretty much. It all hangs on what you feed me tonight."

"If I'd known that I would have tried harder. I have a big assortment of finger foods—your favorite crab balls, stuffed mushrooms, a cheese ball and no dog present, spinach/artichoke dip and a veggie tray."

She put her arms around his neck. "My absolute favorites. You're a shoo-in. But, Adam, when do you think you'll fall in love right back?"

"Emma, I've been in love with you since I was eighteen. I'm just waiting for you to get your life back so you can share it with me."

"Well, I didn't expect this, you know. I thought I'd be spending my Saturday nights with my gay boyfriend and his jealous partner, looking for work all the time and trying to forget the debacle that was my marriage."

"I don't know if you'll ever forget it," he said. "We can move on in spite of it. Are you finally over the idea that being with you will hurt me?"

"I'm still worried that it might, but I'm now convinced I couldn't change your mind if I tried. There has been yet one more complication, one more piece of unfinished business I have to deal with. I'm going to see Rosemary tomorrow. She asked Lauren to get in touch with me. It seems Rosemary can't die in peace without seeing me and she's come back to Santa Rosa to die. She's in the house that had belonged to my father."

"And you're going to do it?" he asked.

"I am. Maybe I'm crazy but I'm hoping that since she asked for me, staring death in the face has made her kinder. But honestly? I'm scared to death. Our last words weren't very nice."

"Let me go with you," he said.

"You are my champion," she said. "That's what Riley called you, 'my champion.' Lyle also offered, but I told him no. You I might take along. I always feel a little braver with you around."

The house Emma grew up in was now about forty years old and because it was a custom home built on a large lot, it had held up handsomely. It was, she remembered, one of the best homes in the area, at least in the parish where her Catholic school was located. Compared to some of the homes Emma had cleaned lately, it seemed ordinary, but it wasn't. It was a large five-bedroom, three-bath home decorated in Country French style. With its huge kitchen, spacious master bedroom and bath, and twelve-foot ceilings, it had been considered very much upscale forty years ago. The curb appeal was still there; the house was very attractive with its well-maintained lawn, shrubbery and a couple of formidable trees, sitting on a wide street with well-spaced homes.

Of course Emma didn't have many good memories of the

place. She was not Rosemary's child. Rosemary introduced Anna and Lauren as her daughters, Emma as her stepdaughter.

"I've never been in the house," Adam said.

"Never? How is that possible?"

"If I came to fetch Riley and walk her home, I waited on the stoop."

"I never noticed. But that doesn't surprise me. Let's get this over with."

At first Emma wasn't sure which of her sisters opened the door as they looked very much alike and she hadn't seen them in a few years. It took her a moment to realize it was Lauren for not only did she look tired and ashen but she'd gained about a hundred pounds. And then right behind her was Anna, thirty-seven now and morbidly obese. They both looked entirely miserable, but how should they look, knowing their mother was dying?

The house was cluttered and held a strange smell. Dust, chemical cleaners, perhaps death.

"Happy holidays," Emma said, presenting Lauren with a gift basket filled with salami, cheeses, olives, wine and other goodies, like chocolate.

Lauren didn't thank her but took the basket and left it on the table in the foyer. "Come with me," she said, turning so they could follow.

They went in the direction of the master bedroom where Rosemary lay in a hospital bed rather than the bed that had been in there. Rosemary had always been heavyset but now she was shockingly thin, her color a bit jaundiced and her hair extremely sparse. All that sudden weight loss left her face sagging. There were bottles and vials on the dresser, an IV hooked up to her arm, and the room was messy with medical supplies. Her bible lay on the bed beside her. Rosemary's eyes were closed.

"Rosemary?" Emma said, merely breathing her name.

She opened her eyes. "Oh. It's you."

"Lauren said you wanted to see me."

"Yes. Who is that? Another man so soon?" Rosemary asked weakly.

"It's Adam Kerrigan. You remember him. Riley's brother." She looked around the room. "Rosemary, where is Vince?"

"Vince isn't here. He didn't sign on for this."

Emma actually grimaced. She hadn't liked Vince at all but hadn't they been married quite a long time for him to bail out on her like that?

"So, you turned your lawyer on me," Rosemary said.

"No," Emma said, shaking her head. "Mr. Justice was my father's lawyer and helped him with his will. He offered to—"

"I am the trustee of my late husband's estate and I want you to know what to expect. Your father left some money in a trust. It was left up to me to distribute with discretion. I have my own lawyer. He'll tell your lawyer if there's anything to distribute, but I highly doubt it. Then we have no further business. And I forgive you."

Emma's mouth hung open. "You forgive me for *what*?"

"For being an ungrateful brat. For bringing shame on our family with your scandal. For never appreciating your good fortune. I'm going to die in peace, knowing I did everything I could and more than necessary."

Emma had to bite her lip to keep it from trembling. So, Rosemary had seized one last moment to be cruel. "And the house?"

"It belongs to my daughters now."

"My father's house," Emma said weakly. It was not a mansion by any means but California real estate was valuable. Just guessing, she would think a custom home this size on such a generous piece of property would go for a great deal of money.

"It became my house," Rosemary said.

"You've never mentioned money before," Emma said. "You said there wasn't any."

"It was a modest amount. There was no reason to discuss it," she said. Then she winced as if in pain. "I was given discretion to use it for the children responsibly, and I did."

"You didn't use any on me," Emma pointed out.

"You were married to a millionaire!" Rosemary screeched, which sent her into a coughing fit. Lauren came rushing to her side. She held her mother up until she recovered. Then she gently lowered her again.

"I was sixteen when my father died," Emma said. "I paid for college with scholarships, part-time work and loans. You remarried..."

"You don't need it now," Lauren said bitterly.

"My father built this house," Emma said.

"He left it to me and it has been transferred into my daughters' names. I want you to tell your lawyer this business is finished, that we have nothing more to discuss. I want to be at peace with this. Please tell your lawyer that you're satisfied everything is settled and stop pursuing this idiocy. Leave my poor girls what little I left them and go away. Don't be picking my bones like a selfish brat."

"Stop," Adam said. "Stop it right now. I'm sorry for your ill health, Rosemary, but I think you've abused this woman enough. It's over." Adam turned Emma around. "We should leave. There's nothing more to discuss here."

"I just want to leave peacefully knowing you won't visit your vengeance on my daughters," Rosemary said.

Emma just shook her head. "Why would I?"

"Knowing you, you think you deserve everything. You've always been haughty, miss homecoming queen. Don't steal what I left for my daughters."

Adam just shook his head. "Let's go, Emma. You wouldn't want this house. The meanness has seeped into the walls by now." He looked at Rosemary with a frown.

Adam took Emma's hand and pulled her away. "Don't listen to her anymore, Emma. These people are poisoned with envy. Come on."

She let him pull her to the car and help her inside.

She sat still, saying nothing, stricken. He started the car and began to drive away and still she was silent. A good five minutes passed before she spoke. "I thought I was beyond being surprised by them. I thought I was beyond being hurt. She must hate me so much. Why does she hate me so much?"

"I think Rosemary might hate a lot of people. At the least, I think very few people are cherished by her. Emma, you can walk away from them knowing you were very kind. More kind than I would've been. I think that woman stole from a grief-stricken child. I wouldn't want to be where she's going."

"She might meet Richard where she's going—his values were similar, I think."

The following week Emma finally met with Lucinda Lopez again.

"It's been over two weeks," Lucinda said. "Your first Christmas in your hometown in at least ten years."

"More than that," Emma said. "More like a dozen. It didn't take me too many years after my father's death to see that my stepmother and sisters didn't really want me to interrupt their celebration. But it's a whole new life now—a simpler, quieter life. There was a little excitement here and there." Emma told Lucinda first about Bethany and how she seemed much brighter and stronger now that the holiday was past.

"That's very kind of you to take the time to listen to this troubled girl," Lucinda said. "Would you do something for me? If you think she trusts you, will you please promote the idea of her talking to her counselor? And if her counselor isn't helping her, suggest she ask for a new one or talk to someone at school. Kids that age who have suffered loss are feeling isolated and fragile. And they're very unpredictable. I don't want you to find yourself up against a situation you can't handle. The loser could be the girl."

"Yes," she said. "Yes, of course. Can I suggest you?"

"You can suggest me, sure. In fact, you're welcome to tell her you're seeing a counselor. Sometimes that has a positive effect. I just worry when someone who has been depressed suddenly becomes cheerful."

Emma then told her about her visit with Rosemary and her plea that Emma leave her daughters and their inheritance alone. "My father's been gone for eighteen years and while we were comfortable, he wasn't a rich man. I can't imagine there's much, if anything. And I'm not going to stir up the curious press by going after money. In fact, I don't want to hear the word *money* associated with my name in any way."

"You'll do whatever makes you comfortable, Emma. I would like you to think about one thing. What your father had in his will was his ardent wish. If he willed something to you, he meant for you to have it."

"I understand that. But it was meant for college. He told me when I was just a little girl that he was saving for college. Well, college was paid for a long time ago."

"And you just had a very simple, very quiet holiday. Much different from what you've experienced the past decade, I suppose."

"I spent Christmas Eve and Christmas morning with Adam, who is more wonderful than you can imagine. He had dinner with his family at his mother's house then came back to my little bungalow, bringing the best leftovers. I had to work the next morning but he's off—Christmas break. He gave me a beautiful trench coat and I gave him a sweater and slippers. Lucinda, it was perfection. So peaceful. All the stress of the world was somewhere else for a change. No flashy baubles, no fancy parties."

"None of that filthy lucre," Lucinda joked. "After some of the Christmases you've experienced in past years, how did it compare?"

"I've never felt richer," Emma said.

Jock was released from the hospital after a few days but would not be cleared for work until after his next visit with the doctor ten days post-surgery. His mother wanted him to come home with her but he flatly refused. His mother said she would stay with him at his house and he said, "Oh, just shoot me." Riley witnessed all of this as she and Maddie were at the hospital visiting at the time.

"Don't worry, Mrs. Curry," Riley said. "We're close. We'll check on him frequently. And we're just a phone call away if Jock needs anything."

After his mother left to pull her car to the front of the hospital, Jock said, "Thanks, Riley. But there's nothing to worry about. I'm finally going to have time to watch all those golf tournaments I recorded. I'm not going to need help with anything. I'm not going to be moving furniture."

"You're just going to camp on the couch, right?"

"That's my plan."

"Maddie's back in school so we'll swing by after school tomorrow and we won't stay long."

"Stay as long as you like. Or you can just drop Maddie off if you feel like it."

But she didn't feel like it. She wanted to take stock of his refrigerator, make sure his house was tidy because he couldn't do it; she even put fresh sheets on his bed because there was no telling how long it had been.

She left Maddie with Jock and went to her mother's house. She asked for some of her plentiful stock of frozen meals she had prepared for her volunteer meal service. For Jock, she explained.

"This is interesting—you going to such trouble for Jock," June said.

"Did you see how frightened and upset Maddie was when he got hurt? Had surgery? I knew Maddie was close to Jock but for some reason I thought it was no closer than she is to Adam. But I was wrong—she's very close to Jock. I'm going to have to try harder to get along with him."

June gave her a dubious look and said, "Of course."

She didn't take the meals to Jock's house. She took them home and put them in her freezer before going to collect Maddie. Then the next day at around noon she retrieved them and dropped in on him.

He answered her knock looking a little rumpled, scruffy and slightly stooped because his incision was still sore.

"Riley?" He looked over her shoulder, looking for Maddie.

"It's just me. I brought some of Mother's meals for your freezer. And I also have some milk, orange juice, eggs, bread, lunch meat and veggie salad from the deli."

"You didn't have to do all that," he said, but he let her in. "Aren't you working today?"

"Uh-huh," she said, loading things into the refrigerator and freezer. "I took a long lunch. These meals are all frozen, thaw in just a few hours and they're labeled. You have meat loaf and mashed potatoes, mac and cheese, lasagna, that meatball concoction she makes..." She raised her head and listened. There wasn't even a TV on. "Were you napping?" she asked.

He indicated the kitchen table where his laptop was set up next to a cup of coffee. "Paying bills," he said.

"Oh, Jock, are you going to have financial issues because of the accident?"

"Not serious ones," he said, shaking his head. "I won't get what I need on that car, but I guess the lady—a girl, really—was charged with running the light so maybe her insurance company will step up." He chuckled. "At least she has insurance. The last guy who rear-ended me didn't."

Riley frowned. "Did someone rear-end you?"

"Ten years ago. Maddie wasn't in the car. She was still in a car seat back then, wasn't she? She wasn't in my car very often."

Because Riley had avoided that as much as possible. Not because Jock wasn't a safe driver. Because she liked having control. Especially over him. She shook her head a bit mournfully. Maddie obviously adored him. And Riley had tried to give Jock as little time with her as possible.

"Have you had lunch?"

"Not yet. I'll graze around in there when you're done. And thank you. That was nice of you."

"I'll make you a sandwich and some salad. Go ahead and finish with your bills. Do you have more coffee?"

"Right there," he said, nodding toward the counter.

She was a little uncomfortable and she could tell Jock was both confused and suspicious. But she had to start somewhere. So he went back to his computer and she got out what she needed—knife, fork, plate, bread, mayo. She was impressed to see he was very tidy. His refrigerator was clean as a whistle—that was a good sign. "Nice," she said. The refrigerator was always one of the last things to get scrubbed. He had lettuce and tomatoes, so she added that to the sandwich.

She bravely dished up a little salad for herself as well as

him then delivered the plate to him. She made herself a cup of coffee and joined him at the table.

He looked at her for a long moment. "You're joining me for lunch?"

"Just a bite of this salad," she said. "If that's okay."

"It's okay. So you meant it. You want to be my friend?"

"Listen, if you'd rather I leave…"

"You want to just tell me what this is about?"

She put her hands in her lap, her salad and coffee untouched. "Right," she said. "First of all, I felt bad about Christmas night, about the argument we had, and I couldn't stop thinking about it. You nailed it, Jock—I've been angry. It's true, and I thought I had every right to be angry. But then when you got hurt and I saw how terrified Maddie was, it hit me hard that you'd always tried with me, even if it didn't go very well most of the time, and I didn't really try with you. And our daughter loves us both."

"Yes, she does."

"And you've had a very close relationship with her, one that I was barely aware of. It seemed you didn't see her that often."

He shrugged. "You weren't easy about that and there was no reason to make life tough for Maddie by pushing you too hard. So I got her a phone and—"

"She was much too young for that phone!"

Jock waited patiently for her to get over that little outburst and she did. There she was again, jumping to conclusions, controlling things. She twisted her lips a little. "Ach," she said, chagrined.

"I got her a phone and a laptop so we could communicate and we stayed in close touch. I went to all her school things, when I could. My hours weren't always good—I had the store a lot of nights. But we were able to talk. She's so smart, Riley. Like you."

Riley felt her cheeks grow a little hot, flushing. "You're smart," she said. "She definitely got your legs."

He laughed. "Yeah, you've been looking up at her since she was thirteen. She's a beauty."

"I didn't know you'd told her about Emma. I didn't know a lot of the things you talked about."

"I told Maddie it wasn't a good idea for her to carry stories about me to you and about you to me. I told her that would cause more friction between us. And she didn't want that."

"I don't know where we start," Riley said. "We've been kind of at each other's throats for a long time."

"Not really. Not always," he said. "I really pissed you off a few times but around Maddie we were always nice to each other. At least tolerant, thanks to June. But there is one thing that kind of grates on me. I don't know if I dare talk about it."

"Maybe you better," she said. "Let's get it all on the table."

"You have to promise not to scream or throw things. I'm recovering from major surgery."

"I have never…" She stopped herself because her voice had become shrill. "I've never thrown anything."

He smiled. "You seemed angriest with me when I tried to tell you I cared about you. I wanted us to have a chance. I thought I could be a decent husband and I liked being a father. I knew I'd screwed it up completely in the beginning, I knew I wasn't really good enough for you, but I—"

"We didn't get off to a good start…" she said.

"My fault," he said. "I don't have any excuses. I take that back—I have nothing but excuses. I was young and dumb, terrified, confused, not to mention I felt completely incompetent. I wanted to do the right thing and I was pretty sure I wasn't capable of it. I had no education, no money, just a shitty little part-time job—"

"It wasn't all your fault," she said. "Look, there's no way you can understand this, but I had a lot to overcome. I was a poor kid. A poor fatherless kid. I'd cheated on my best friend with her boyfriend and she hated me, which she was bound to. I was ashamed and angry and pretty desperate. It gave me a little satisfaction to blame you for all my problems. Then I started my company and I was afraid to look up for at least twelve years. When you asked for another chance, I couldn't hear you."

"I asked a few times…"

"You married Laurie…"

"I thought it might fix what was hurting. I shouldn't have done that to her."

"But she dumped you!"

"We knew right away it wasn't working, but I'll be honest with you—I was going to stay. I wasn't going to fail twice. But if you think our relationship is complicated? Jesus, Laurie's life was a train wreck. She's back with her ex. They probably never should've divorced in the first place. And they fight twenty-four-seven."

"Is it even possible for us to pick up the pieces after all this time and be friends?" she asked. "Do our grudges just run too deep?"

"I don't have any grudges, Riley. I've made peace with my screwups. I have a great family, a beautiful daughter, a good job, a few friends and a decent life. If we can be friends, I'll be a happy man."

"Did we bicker too much in front of Maddie?" she asked.

He laughed a little bit. "No more than your average married couple," he said. "You take one look at Maddie and know—she's pretty normal for a daughter of mine. You're a wonderful mother. And you're not the poor kid anymore, that's for sure."

She sighed. "You can't imagine the kind of desperate ambition that took. I've craved a nap for fifteen years." She gave him a long look. "Don't you ever get…lonely?"

He shook his head. "Hardly ever. Sometimes I go too long without seeing Maddie, but I can always talk to her. But lonely? Not so much. Do you?"

She nodded. "Even though I have good people in my life, too. Sometimes it feels like there's something missing."

"Now, *that* I understand. So—is the new guy going to be okay if you're friendly with your daughter's daddy?"

"New guy?" she asked. Then she remembered. "Oh! Logan, the police officer. Um, I'm not sure that's going anywhere. He's a great guy. But..." She bit her lip.

"Riley, he's the first guy you've dated since we split," he pointed out.

"Nah, I went out a few times," she said. "Nothing ever clicked."

He just smiled. "So here we sit. Two people who had a child together, raised a little girl together, bickered like cranky old married people and could never find anyone else to fill the gap. Doesn't that make you a little curious?"

"Let's be very careful here, Jock. If we screw up again, we might end up hating each other."

"If I screw up again, you might end up hating me, but I'll never hate you. I never have. I've gotten a little pissed here and there, but I've always loved you. I just didn't know how to behave. I was a boy."

He's not a boy anymore, she thought. "Go slow," she said.

They ate their lunch, talked about Maddie, then Riley cleaned up the kitchen and said she had to go back to work. He walked her to the door. Then he turned her toward him and put a gentle kiss on her forehead. "Be very careful, Riley," he said. "I love you. I always have. But I'm not going back and forth. If being with me doesn't work for you, that's it. I don't want to experiment," he said. "You're not the only one with feelings."

"I know. I know."

chapter *nineteen*

All the way to Aaron Justice's house Emma was anxious. She was looking forward to seeing him again but a little worried about how to pay him for the work he'd done when it turned out there was no money left in that estate. She should have called him and told him to stop whatever he was doing—he'd already invested valuable time. She'd find a way to pay him eventually. And she'd made up her mind—she wouldn't try to take that house away from her sisters. Really, it wouldn't make her happy anyway.

Aaron now kept a small office in his house, the home he'd shared with his late wife. It was a lovely house that Emma had never been to before.

"Emma, how good it is to see you. Come in, I've made us tea."

He invited her to sit down. "I'm not sure how many details you recall from our visit when we went over your father's will immediately after his death. You were so young and in a state of grief. I encouraged you to call me, but you never did."

Emma shrugged. "I didn't see the need," she said. "I remember that you said there should be a little money to help with school, should I go to college. And Rosemary did send me spending money sometimes."

He frowned. "Let's go over the conditions of the will just to refresh your memory."

The assets John Shay had accrued were to be split in two—half to Rosemary, his wife, and half to be divided by the children. Rosemary was the executor of the will. She was also the trustee, which meant the inheritance held in trust for the children couldn't be spent on some young boyfriend. Emma almost laughed out loud—*as if!* The will included all three children, even though Anna was not John's biological child. And his plan had been to distribute the proceeds over time—half of their portion when each child reached the age of thirty, the second half at the age of thirty-five. Those assets, however, were available for certain reasonable expenses—welfare—as in the cost of housing and such, education, down payment on a home, extraneous medical expenses not covered by health insurance, etc.

"I paid for my own college," Emma said.

"I know," Aaron said. "As I told you, Rosemary got herself another lawyer soon after your father died. A few years after that she changed lawyers again. She asked her new lawyer to write her a new will, which she was entitled to do. But the money your father set aside for you and your sisters was part of an irrevocable trust, meaning that if she withdrew any of it on your behalf for things like college, she had to have records. And she was to inherit the house, as well—it was not held in trust. Emma, did you receive anything from your father's estate?"

Emma shook her head. "Rosemary said that just maintaining the house and raising three girls to the age of independence had been all she could afford. I counted myself lucky to get an allowance while I was in school. Small, but it helped."

"She had receipts for tuition and housing…"

"She asked me for receipts. For records, she said."

"When you were thirty, you were due some money."

"Wow," Emma said. "I didn't know that. Or maybe I just didn't remember. My father was a pretty simple guy. I knew there might only be enough to get Rosemary through the difficult period of getting three daughters into adulthood."

"Rosemary's attorney has provided an accounting of the trust. I have a balance due you that might be grossly inadequate, given the house, the funding that was misdirected, small details, and I recommend a good forensic accountant. You should challenge the trustee."

Emma let out a huff of rueful laughter. "Aaron, the trustee is dying. I saw her. She has very little time left and she wasn't pleasant. She asked me to leave her daughters alone—said that she's leaving the house and whatever money there is to them. I'm not going to challenge them. I'm not ever going back to court."

"Unfortunately for Rosemary, she can't redirect the terms of the trust. The sum left to you is grossly inadequate. You're entitled to more. I'm afraid she was irresponsible."

She shook her head. "I'll take whatever it is and I'll pay you, but I'm not going to pursue this—she can take the burden to eternity with her. Those mean girls who got the house and the bulk of my father's life savings and insurance can choke on it. I've learned a few things about money, Mr. Justice. It can turn sour in your mouth."

"You should think about your future, nonetheless…"

"And challenge a will? Oh, wouldn't the newspeople love that. No, if there's a thousand bucks left, I'll pay you. Otherwise, the idea of going after my father's money just holds no appeal at all. I know, you'd think I'd be more pragmatic, but I watched what that whole thirst for money can do to a person. I'm cleaning toilets for a living, Mr. Justice. I have a boyfriend who's a schoolteacher, a wonderful schoolteacher. I feel richer now than I did when I was married to Richard. I don't need anything more. I'm good."

He was speechless for a moment. His hands were folded primly on his desk and he looked at her earnestly. "Emma," he said. "It's more than a thousand dollars."

"Well, how lucky for me," she said with a laugh. "And here I thought Christmas was over. How much then?"

"This would be half—what you were due at age thirty, with another payment due quite soon, when you're thirty-five. Before even doing an audit to see if there's more buried in there, it's $463,072."

Emma's mouth hung open and she stared at him in shock. Then her eyes rolled back in her head and she fainted, falling off the chair and hitting the floor with a thud.

Sitting at his desk Logan felt frustrated by his failed attempts to get Riley alone at all over the holidays. First came family, he understood that. And she had explained that people didn't cancel housekeeping services, unless of course they were out of town and the office cleaning arm of the business stayed steady.

And then there was her ex's car accident. They might never have married but there was no disputing he was the ex. And although Riley insisted it was for Maddie's peace of mind and not hers, she was spending an awful lot of time with the guy.

But now the holidays were past, Maddie was back in school and the ex was cleared to go back to work. Everyone could get on a normal schedule and by the end of next month he and George would be closing out the surveillance on Emma Shay. Six months of watching and listening, no one had talked about money, the banking was tight as a drum, Emma was still cleaning houses and all seemed right with the world. It was possible the federal judge could extend the warrant, but it wouldn't be based on anything George and Logan had discovered. No calls to Aruba, no suspicious dialogue, no funny money.

"Good news," Georgianna said. "We caught a break. She's moving money."

"Huh?" he asked, dumbfounded.

"Large sums, too. We got a wire transfer for almost a half million."

"No shit?" he said, stunned. "We know where it came from yet?"

"We'll know soon. We just have to exercise the warrant. And I think we notify the feds and offer to open an investigation."

"We can notify the feds and let *them* open an investigation," he suggested.

"It's our investigation," she reminded him.

"It doesn't have to be."

"Is this you making the easy choice?" she asked. "You skipping out so you don't mess things up with the girl? Should we pull you out of this investigation for conflict of interest?"

"There's nothing to indicate Riley had anything to do with Emma Shay's financial situation."

George sighed, took a deep breath. "Emma's tied into the Kerrigan family in a big way. A bigger way than I think you realize. She works for Riley Kerrigan, she's sleeping with Adam Kerrigan, she's socializing with June Kerrigan, and the other guy? Your girl's ex? That was her boyfriend in high school and they've rekindled their friendship. She's referred to him in conversations with Adam. And there's another twist that makes me uncomfortable and suspicious. Emma Shay is having serious dialogue with a teenage girl she calls Bethany and I'm asking myself if that could be Maddie Kerrigan with an alias or a close friend of Maddie's. Emma and the girl are close. They seem bonded over something and I'm not sure what. The girl complains about her stepmother sometimes and Emma commiserates. Is it possible that it's Emma's child, given up for adoption? Could that be her motive for hiding money? A child?"

"*What?*"

"Just a thought. A guess, really. Quite a coincidence that Maddie Kerrigan is fifteen and this Bethany, whoever she might be, is fifteen and troubled. That aside, just with the money transfer we have enough probable cause. We'll get the okay, we'll get a little more traction on this then bring her in for questioning."

He winced.

"There's a reason we don't get involved with our suspects."

"Riley isn't a suspect!"

"She's a person of interest with a close relationship to our suspect."

Logan knew this was not going to bode well for their relationship. Riley was not dumb. She was going to have no trouble connecting the dots. He didn't simply come upon her in the deli section, innocent of agenda or intention. He knew Emma had some connection to the Kerrigans and stumbled across Riley and then damn! She was just the kind of woman he wanted. Somehow, he thought he could get the skinny on Emma without damaging his budding relationship with Riley.

"This is why we don't shit where we eat," George told him.

He knew why. He just didn't want it to be true this time.

It was the second week in January by the time Riley finally got around to having lunch with Logan. She invited him. They met at a small, quiet restaurant on a Sunday. Riley was already having a glass of wine when he arrived. He smiled a little sadly as he sat down at her table. "This is a little obvious," he said.

"What do you mean?"

"I'm in a barely populated restaurant at a somewhat isolated table on a Sunday so you can give me some bad news."

She sighed heavily. "Come on," she said. "Let's have a glass of wine. Let's talk. Let's have lunch."

"I'll join you for the wine but I reserve judgment on the lunch." The waiter was there immediately, taking his order. "You don't have to wait for the wine. Go ahead. Lay it on me."

"What exactly do you think is going to happen here?" she asked.

"I think you're going to break up with me."

"First of all, I hadn't considered us steadies," Riley said. "And second, I know I've been hard to reach the past couple of weeks—since Maddie's accident—but that's exactly the sort of thing I hate about dating. Just because we have a few nice dates and fun conversations you have this expectation of some priority when I have a daughter, a business—"

"And an elderly mother?" he asked. "Don't spoil it, Riley. Men are clumsy assholes who just don't call when it doesn't work out the way they wanted. Women are completely different. They feel the need to be honest, to explain, to iron out all the details and make sure everything is smooth. Fixed." His wine was delivered and he took a sip. Then he tapped her glass. "Do it. Do what you came here to do."

"Wow, you make it seem horrible. I think from now on I'm going with the not-calling route."

"Nah, this is classier. I'm ready to hear it. I think I know but I'm ready to hear."

"What do you think you know?"

He shook his head. "No way. It's your show."

"I'm sorry. I'm going to put our dating adventure on hold. Maybe for a while, maybe forever, time will tell. It seems I have some old issues to sort through. Some baggage. I'm as surprised as you are."

"The ex," he said.

"You shouldn't really call him that. He's Maddie's father."

"And the accident made you realize how much you care about him," Logan said. It was not a question.

"Not exactly, but close. We all spent Christmas dinner at my mother's, which is pretty typical unless Jock could convince me to let him take Maddie to his mother's house. And afterward I dropped by his house to talk about Maddie. Nothing urgent, just the fact that we're moving into a new phase in this co-parenting. She's growing up and we'll be visiting colleges next year! I realized I had never seen the inside of his house. I didn't know Maddie had a perfectly lovely room there that she hardly ever uses. I was a little shocked to realize how difficult and distant I'd been where Maddie and Jock are concerned and... Well, the next thing you know, there's an accident and he's seriously injured."

"And you realized you nearly lost your chance?"

She shook her head. "No, it was Maddie. She verged on hysterical. She was so shaken and terrified—her father means a lot more to her than I realized. How could I have been so dumb? So I'm trying to help out a little—visiting him in the hospital, with Maddie of course, taking him some meals while he's recovering and most of all just talking to him."

Logan looked down.

"My daughter is almost sixteen years old, Logan. And I've spent the last sixteen years being mad at Jock for being the idiot to screw up everything. More than once! And he's the first to admit he made some incredibly immature mistakes. I've been very pigheaded. I thought maybe it's time to know the guy now that he's grown up. I don't have any expectations—you'd think if we were meant to be a couple it would've happened long before now. But I want to explore the idea of us being friends, if you can understand that. One day we'll be grandparents to the same grandchildren."

"And we can't date while you're working on getting along with your ex for the sake of the grandchildren?" he asked. "You're not fooling me, Riley. You want to be open to something more than friendship. Deny it, go ahead. Because I already know you don't lie."

"Then you also know I don't move very fast," she said. "And you're moving a little fast."

"I don't have fifteen years."

"I certainly wouldn't suggest you wait that long for someone like me," she said. "Will you still have lunch with me?"

"Why? Is there more?" he asked.

"Please, Logan. I like you. I like you very much. I think our timing is a bit off and I'm being completely honest when I say that I'm not sure where this thing with Jock is headed. Is it possible you and I can remain friends?"

"Let's order lunch," he said, opening his menu.

"Yes, let's," she said, opening her menu. They made their choices, ordered and she said, "Thank you."

"Don't thank me yet," he said. "We're going to have lunch. And then I'm going to tell you—I don't really want to be friends. I was falling in love with you and I think you know it. And I also think maybe you're afraid of that. I was willing to wait, to put up with being third or fourth on your list. I was willing to take chances for you. So we're going to have lunch, talk a little then say goodbye. And if you're ever ready to pick this up where we left it, which was pretty close to the next level in the man–woman equation, you have my number. But I'm not waiting around while you check out your ex."

"I don't think you understand at all," she said.

"Oh, yeah," he said. "I understand. You might intend to just get to know him so you can be grandparents together but I guarantee you, that's not how he's going to see it."

"How do you know that?"

"I'm a guy, Riley. That's how I know."

It turned out that John Shay was the millionaire next door. An unpretentious, hardworking man of sensible but excellent taste. He and his first wife built themselves a solid house in a good neighborhood and he saved and invested all his life. Emma didn't come along until he was thirty-five and he lost his wife to diabetes-related kidney failure a year later. He had accrued a nice little nest egg by the time he died, and insurance paid off the house, which was valued at a million and a quarter.

John bought good cars and drove them until they died of old age, did all his own yard work and could have indulged in European vacations or maybe had a summer home, but instead he saved and invested. His second wife had worked, his children were always well dressed and he insisted on a good mattress. They never scrimped on food; they ate good, healthy meals. Emma would have expected her father to have left a reasonable sum that was meant to cover his retirement but she was completely unprepared for the estate to be worth several million dollars.

It was obvious that Rosemary did what she always had done where Emma was concerned—she took what was Emma's and gave it to Anna and Lauren, two young women who had inherited their mother's anger and bitterness. For a little while Emma was sad that those two had her father's house but then she thought about the two of them living there to-gether in old age and her sadness turned to pity. She had no idea if either of them had a significant relationship or love in their lives but they seemed far too unhappy for that. But then Rosemary was a stiff and negative woman and she'd been married three times.

Emma gave Aaron her banking information and he ar-ranged to have the money she was entitled to transferred into her bank account—she wasn't sure what she was going to do with it yet. After her experience with Richard she wasn't eager to turn it over to a broker or money manager so she thought maybe she'd study a little about investments her-self, do something that felt safe. She was her father's daugh-ter, after all.

Rosemary died and Emma paid her respects. Adam was her escort. She went only to the visitation and had a very large floral arrangement delivered. There weren't many peo-ple present, mostly friends of Anna and Lauren's, and Emma didn't stay long.

She told no one about the money, not even Adam. When he noticed she was a little melancholy she made the excuse that the final goodbye to Rosemary and probably her sisters had left her feeling a little let down. But it was the money. It bothered her. Worried her. She decided she had to get that off her back and planned to explain to Adam that she'd been blown away by an uncomfortably large sum.

She asked if she could cook dinner for him at his house on a Friday night. It was the end of January and he was thrilled by the offer. She wasn't much of a cook—so little practice over the years—so she made an extra-large pot of spaghetti and meatballs, bought prepared garlic bread that only needed a few minutes in the oven and threw together a simple salad.

"Perfect," Adam said.

"I made a big batch so we can have fried spaghetti tomorrow night. If I'm invited back."

"I want to be with you every night you'll have me," he said.

"Adam, I have something to tell you. I've been keeping something from you. Just for a couple of weeks, but I have to tell someone and you're the only one that really matters."

"I thought something was wrong," he said. "I've been worried."

She explained about the will. She didn't tell him how much she'd received but she said it was substantial.

"Emma, that's fantastic! But how in the world did Rosemary think she'd hide it from you?"

"I'm not sure, except that she managed the trust. The lawyer, who was my father's friend, said there was more, especially a third of the value of the house, if I wanted to fight for it. Adam, I put the money in the bank and I hope I don't regret it, but I asked Aaron not to pursue this any further. There's another check due when I'm thirty-five and I'll put that in the bank. My sisters…my lonely, angry, heartbroken sisters might be very rich but I won't challenge the management of the trust. I'm done. Just having more than ten thousand dollars in the bank makes me uncomfortable."

He laughed. "Something for you to talk to Lucinda about," he said. "But you have a little savings, Emma. The sky isn't falling anymore."

"Why does having anything make me feel bad? Guilty?"

"And why does that surprise you after what Richard did? Listen, if you can't beat the guilt even with therapy, you can always give it all to charity."

"Would you?"

"Oh, hell no," he said with a grin. "I've been working my whole life for a savings account. I'm thirty-seven, have an IRA, a little money socked away, a schoolteacher's pension and my mortgage will be paid off in ten years because I always throw a little extra at the principal. Mom is taken care of, Riley is very successful, Maddie's college tuition is in the bank... We're in great shape. If someone dumped a bunch of money in my lap, I wouldn't feel guilt unless it was stolen."

"But I bet you'd use it to help people," she said.

"Emma, I help people every day. My mom helps people and animals. Riley thinks she's just working herself to death but look at what she's built and how it caters to the single mothers she employs. For most people helping people is either a way of life, or it's not."

And she thought, *he is so right. I will just be still and quiet for a little while and I'll know exactly how to make my father's legacy help people.*

"One of the best ways to help the world is to never be a burden to it. Give money, give time, give love, and make sure you give yourself a little to spare so you're not the one in need."

"You are so wise," she said.

"Poor boys work harder to be wise," he said. "I'm very grateful not to be a poor boy anymore. And I'm really grateful for this spaghetti. And to know you have no real reason to be sad."

They talked late into the night. They kicked back and forth many ideas of what it meant to really live well, to live in the moment, to be present and aware and to be grateful. What was plenty, really? Emma had been up and down the financial spectrum so many times—she should know. She'd been one of the well-off girls in school, struggled in college and almost didn't have enough money to join a sorority. Her first years in New York were awfully tight, but also filled with like creatures and great fun. Then there were the years with Richard during which she often felt like a visitor in her own life. And here she was in the arms of a good, honest man and everything seemed so real to her. So rich.

In the morning she began to stir when she heard him moving around. He got up, started the coffee, got in the shower. When she heard the shower shut off she went to the kitchen for coffee and the second her feet hit the floor she felt strange. Her stomach was upset. Her knees were a little weak.

She got to the kitchen and was overtaken by instant and powerful nausea and she dashed for the sink to be sick. She retched and choked, not that there was much there. She felt Adam come up behind her, take hold of her hair and gently rub her back. She ran the water, rinsed her mouth, reached for a paper towel and slowly, shakily, turned to face him.

He lifted one brow. "That spaghetti worked fine for me," he said.

"I have no idea what's wrong," she said. She sniffed. "I feel completely fine now. That coffee even smells good."

"Emma," he asked. "When did you last have a period?"

"Oh, shit," she said.

It was next to impossible to get an immediate appointment with an OB, especially if you were a woman about four weeks pregnant. What they routinely did was give you vitamins and see you for the first time at a couple of months, maybe three months. But Adam taught with a man whose wife was an OB and called in a favor because Emma was worried. She was afraid she'd gotten a positive pregnancy test because something was terribly wrong. After all, she'd been through a little over a year of infertility tests and treatments.

"I can't see that anything is wrong," Dr. Winnet said. "And you are definitely pregnant. Due in the fall."

"But I was told my only hope was in vitro!"

"I'll request the records from your specialist and do a little blood work, but if you were infertile, you're not anymore. And you appear to be in excellent health."

Her records were electronic and therefore transferred from Dr. Grimaldi in New York within a couple of days. Dr. Winnet called her. "I'm a little confused. You say he did a fertility workup? Because all I find in your chart is regular exams, birth control medication, one cyst removal."

"No, no, not birth control pills. I was taking hormones to stimulate ovulation. I was x-rayed for blocked fallopian tubes. We were getting ready to harvest eggs for in vitro when..." She stopped. *When Richard said, "I don't have time to deal with this while I'm consumed with the investigation. They're demanding records constantly. Just let me get through this and we'll give it a go."*

"Maybe I can find better records at the hospital or surgical center where the procedures were performed."

Emma took a deep breath and tried to think clearly. It couldn't be that it had all been a lie. "Dr. Grimaldi had his own surgi-center." And she had gone with Richard after-hours because of Richard's impossible schedule.

"I'll call them, ask if they have records for your procedures."

But there were none.

"Could the records have been lost?" Emma asked.

"Possible, but unlikely," Dr. Winnet said. "It has happened, though it's rare. But all that aside, your blood work is good, your physical was excellent and you have no reason to worry."

Emma would never know for sure, but she strongly suspected she'd been pulled into the web of Richard's many lies yet again. When she first suggested a baby, he didn't like the idea because of his age. When she pestered him, he made an appointment with Dr. Grimaldi—early evening when there was only one nurse present and no other patients. Emma had felt, as she often did, that she was given special treatment because of Richard. She was flattered to be seen by such an important doctor after the office was closed. Dr. Grimaldi had seemed thrilled to help Richard with this little problem. And now she thought Dr. Grimaldi had probably been very well paid for his fraud.

"I'd bet my life on it," Emma told Adam. "He pulled off things I never could have dreamed of."

"Well, the only thing I want to pull off with you is a child. I didn't think I'd ever be a father."

"You don't have much choice now, do you?" she said.

"You're going to have to come clean with Riley," he said. "We can do it together, you can do it your own way, you can enlist June to help, but it has to be done. Like it or not, we're all family now."

"I'm sorry for the surprise, for the shock," Emma said.

"I'm not," he said. "I wasn't sure how I'd ever convince you to give me a chance. I couldn't be happier about it. And all I want to do is make you happy. Think you can live with that?"

She smiled and touched his sweet face. "I'm sure I can."

chapter *twenty*

Maddie had a date for the Valentine's dance. It was her first official date, the kind where a boy formally asks a girl for a special occasion, when a perfect dress has to be found. But, there
were three sophomore couples going together, not a sixteen-
year-old among them, thank God. So they were chauffeured
by parents. And Jock came over to Riley's house to see Maddie all dressed up and picked up by her date.

He didn't act like one of those caricature dads who growled
and threatened the skinny young man, and Riley was so proud
of him for that. He was completely comfortable, complimenting Maddie, grinning at the kids, taking a few pictures and
texting them to his side of the family. And when they were
gone, off to the dance, Riley opened a bottle of wine and
poured them each a glass.

She clinked his glass in a toast. "That's going to be hard
to get used to—watching her go off with a man like that."

"That wasn't a man," he said. He pulled her down on the

couch beside him. "She's going to figure us out real soon, you know."

"I think she has no idea it's you I've been talking to at night."

"It's probably none of my business, but what happened to the other guy?"

"We parted on friendly terms," Riley said. "I invited him to lunch, told him that many circumstances combined to make me realize I wanted to get to know my daughter's father better. He was pretty civil about it."

"*Pretty* civil?" Jock asked.

"He's a very nice guy and I suggested we stay in touch, remain friends, and he said no, thank you."

"Smart man," Jock said.

"What are we going to do if we don't work out?" Riley asked.

"You mean if it doesn't work for you? It's working pretty well for me."

"I don't want Maddie traumatized," Riley said. "You know she'll be thrilled to think of her parents romantically involved. What if we hit a wall, fight, split apart again? What if that happens?"

He smiled and just shook his head. "Couples argue sometimes. People disagree." He put his arm around her and pulled her closer. "It's okay if that happens. But those things that kept us apart as teenagers—we don't have those things to wrestle with anymore. At least I don't. I'm not scared and immature anymore. And you and Maddie are my family. You think I won't do anything under the sun to protect that?"

"How long have you been like this?" she asked him.

"I don't know. Look, I'm not the smart one. But my mother says I have good common sense."

"There hasn't been anyone for me," she said. "No one."

He chuckled. "I wish I could say the same, but I made a few women completely miserable, looking for someone to love."

"It is positively ridiculous that we've loved each other for all these years and couldn't get together on anything."

"I think Emma has something to do with it."

"Emma?"

"Riley, you've been hung up about Emma for sixteen years. Feeling guilty, angry, lonely. You blamed yourself for so much. You blamed her when you couldn't blame yourself anymore. Then she came back, wounded after all she went through, and you saw that she was just a hurt little girl willing to do whatever she had to do to get her life back. Just like you had been. The two people who had failed you in the worst time you'd ever faced—me and Emma—are back, hoping for another chance to be there for you."

"I get that you are, but Emma?"

"Emma. Working for your company, following your rules, staying away so she doesn't crowd you, visiting your mother in secret so she doesn't anger you. Just coming back, she reminded you that all our mistakes were so, so long ago. And some of them turned out to be real gifts. She wants to be your friend again, Riley. And I want to be your man."

"After all this time," she said.

"I couldn't get close to you before now," he said. "It wasn't your fault. I don't blame you. I was such an asshole. But we have what it takes now."

"Ever since you lost your spleen, I've been very satisfied."

"Nice to be a little older, isn't it? The backseat of a car or a sandy beach sure can be a challenge. Maddie can't come home early without calling one of us for a ride. Let's go to bed and take our time, huh?"

It amazed Riley that her old passionate feelings for Jock when she was so young could feel just as fresh and new now.

But vastly improved. Now she couldn't help but be aware that his every touch was meant simply to please her. They had only renewed this part of their relationship about a week before and already they were like seasoned lovers, like old pros. He worked her body like he'd been doing it for years. The Jock she'd been so angry with had been replaced by a tender and unselfish man. The Jock she always thought of as an idiot was actually a very funny, intuitive man. And the man who had been such a giving father to their daughter proved he could be trusted.

She curled up to him and whispered, "I think you are a wonderful lover."

"Or you are and it makes me look good," he said, kissing her.

Pressed up against his warm body, she drifted back in time for a while. They didn't have the tools to make it when they were kids. Nor the wisdom and patience. But they had those things now.

It seemed that only seconds had passed when the sound of the front door opening woke them. Riley looked over Jock's shoulder at the clock. It was midnight. "Oh, God, what are we going to do?"

"Mom?" Maddie yelled.

"I think we're coming out of the closet," Jock said. "Unless you have a better idea."

"Mom? You went to bed? I thought you'd wait up to hear about the—" She stood in the doorway. Her mouth hung open; her eyes were big and round. "Dad?" she asked, confused. "What are you *doing*?"

"Hmm. Well, we couldn't find the Scrabble game..."

Late Sunday morning, Riley went to Emma's little bungalow. She knew the address from her employment records and she wasn't going to do what she had to do at work. She immediately thought it was so cute, sitting on a street with a lot of little houses, big trees and old people—not a child in sight. She parked on the street and recognized her brother's SUV in front of the house. Hmm. That should make things easy. Sort of.

She tapped on the door and Emma opened it wearing jeans and a sweatshirt, her hair pulled back in a ponytail. She jumped in surprise when she saw Riley.

"Sorry for the shock," Riley said. "Sorry I didn't call ahead. I didn't want you worrying about what I wanted. I didn't want you to waste a lot of energy trying to prepare yourself. Can we talk?"

"Adam's here," Emma said almost shyly.

"I saw his car."

Then there he was, right behind Emma, his hand on Emma's shoulder. And he was frowning. "Riley?"

"I just wanted to talk to Emma for a moment. And you, also. Okay?"

"Sure," Emma said. "Of course. I just fixed a cup of tea. Would you like one?"

"That would be nice. If you're sure it's all right..."

"Come inside, Riley," she said, holding the door open.

"I'll get that tea," Adam said.

Riley looked around the pleasant little room and smiled. It was very understated, comfortable and homey. "You must really like it here," she said to Emma. "But what a difference for you."

"A very positive difference. Riley, I wasn't intentionally keeping my relationship with Adam a secret. It felt as if... Well, as if you really didn't want to know."

"One of the many things I probably should work on—that control thing. Emma, we've worked well together..."

"Despite the fact that I can't seem to follow the rules…"

"I'm not here about that. A long, long time ago I did you wrong and I'm sorry. I wasn't just being a terrible girlfriend, an untrustworthy friend. There was a bit more to it—I fell for Jock. I don't blame you at all for being furious, for ending our friendship. It's what I would have done."

"It was a long time ago," Emma said. "My feelings were hurt and I was angry, but if I'm honest I have to admit, I'd already moved on from Jock. I think I kept up the grudge for so long because I'd lost you."

Adam handed Riley a cup of tea, but she put it on the small sofa table in front of her. "I think we were all collateral damage. Jock and Adam and Mom, too. A couple of girlfriends, friends for life, fell out over a guy and there were dead bodies everywhere. I'm here to tell you again, I'm sorry for what I did to you. And I'd like another chance."

"Of course," Emma said. "Why now?"

"Because Jock and I are back together. After sixteen difficult years."

Emma actually stood up from her chair. "Really?" Then she slowly sat. "Really?"

"Jock's always been a good father to Maddie, when I'd let him. And when he was in the accident and I saw how terrified Maddie was I decided I'd waited way too long to have a closer look, to make an effort with Jock. He loves Maddie so much. He's not the same kid who messed up our friendship, Emma. He's a good man. And I find I still care about him."

"Oh, that's so sweet," Emma said. "What could be better? Yes, of course we should give ourselves another chance. But don't worry—I will remember you're my employer when we're at work."

"I'm not worried about that. I have a feeling you won't work for me much longer. You have too much talent…"

Riley took a breath. "So? You two are official?" she asked of Emma and Adam.

"More than official," Adam said. "We're pregnant."

"Are you kidding me?" Riley said. "Does Mom know?"

"We have to take care of that," Adam said. "Easier now that you know."

"And you're getting married?" Riley asked.

"We're still kind of in shock, but probably."

Riley got a little teary. She felt the emotion welling up inside her. "We should've worked on this a long time ago, let go of the baggage and grudges—"

There was suddenly a hard knocking at the door and they all froze. There was something about it that signaled it was not an ordinary visitor. Certainly not Penny. Adam opened the door and was met with two badges. "We're looking for Emma Shay."

Riley stood. "Logan?"

"Riley," he said with a nod. "Ms. Shay, we've met. I'm Logan Danner. This is my partner, Georgianna Severs. We have some questions for you and would appreciate your cooperation."

"What kind of questions?" Adam demanded.

"Yeah, what kind of questions?" Riley chimed in. "What are you doing here?"

"Just some questions, Ms. Shay. We'd like you to come to the station to be interviewed."

"About...?" Emma said.

"About the disposition of your late husband's estate."

"My late husband didn't have an estate," she said. "Am I under arrest?"

"At this point it's just an investigation."

"She's not going anywhere with you," Adam said.

"Wait a minute here," Riley said. "Is this a coincidence? You wanting to question Emma?"

"Ms. Kerrigan, we don't have any reason to detain or question you," Georgianna said. "Ms. Shay?"

"No, wait," Riley said. "Have you been investigating Emma?"

"Ask me whatever you like," Emma said. "Just make it quick."

"We'd like you to come to the office so that we can record and have a record of our interview."

"I wonder if my lawyer would approve of that idea..."

"We're not filing any charges at this point. We're not going to be reading you your rights. If you'd just answer those questions you can, we'd very much appreciate it. No one wants to arrest you."

"And this is in regards to...?" Emma persisted.

"Large sums of money appearing in your accounts, ma'am," Georgianna said.

"Ah," she said. "So you've had a warrant, the only way you could legally watch my account. I see. I'll drive myself to your office and I'll answer your questions—with my lawyer present."

"No, Emma," Adam said, taking her elbow in a soft grip. "I don't want you to do this. There's no reason."

"Yes, let's get this over with," she said. She looked at Logan. "Is the warrant for banking records?" He nodded. "And what else? Have you been in my house?"

Logan shook his head.

"What else is your warrant for?" she asked.

"Banking and phone. Let's do this, Ms. Shay. You're eventually going to have to answer our questions. We don't want to ask for an arrest warrant."

"And I don't want you to," she said. "I'll call my lawyer

and drive myself over. I'm not going to take off." She grabbed her purse and jacket. "This must be exciting for you," she said. "It's Sunday morning."

"And you knew exactly where to find her," Riley said.

"They've always known, Riley," Emma said. "They've been watching me. They want to know if I have some secret hidden money from my husband. They're going to watch me forever. And they're not going to find anything because there isn't anything." She looked at Logan and Georgianna. "Let's get this over with."

"I'm going with you," Adam said, grabbing his jacket.

"I'm going, too," Riley said.

Three hours later Emma and Aaron emerged from the interview room to find Adam and Riley waiting. By quick consensus, they decided to go to a nearby Mexican restaurant to talk and order something to eat and drink. Aaron excused himself from the group. Riley beat them inside and secured a booth. The waitress was beside them right away.

"I think we're going to need three wines. Any preference?" Riley asked.

"I'm having tea," Emma said. "Just any hot tea, please. Milk and sugar."

"I'll have hers. Chardonnay," Riley said.

"I'll have a beer, whatever's on tap. And how about some nachos?" Adam asked.

When they were alone again, Riley was the first to speak up. "I think that bastard dated me because he was watching you."

"They were very nice," Emma said. "Tiresome, but polite enough. I was warned this might happen. When we settled up in New York the lawyers told me there would be victims and law enforcement who would find it preposterous that I'd surrender everything, right down to my engagement ring. I didn't want anything that had come from Richard. But I did recently come into some money. My father's estate, which Rosemary always claimed was hardly worth talking about, actually had something in it. Rosemary, God rest her soul, failed to let me know. She clearly meant for her daughters to have it. But my father's lawyer followed through and some money came my way. He showed them a copy of the will along with all the financial information. It's all completely legitimate."

"Is this going to keep happening?" Riley wanted to know.

Emma shrugged. "Until there's nothing to notice, I suppose."

"But you were already investigated and cleared," Riley said.

"And I remain a curiosity to some. The best way to handle it is to be cooperative, show them the quickest route to the information they want or need."

"Emma, how have you stood this kind of treatment?"

"I've found that if I just put myself in their shoes, I get it. And it's best to just be honest and forthcoming. I learned right away, refusing to answer just intensifies the whole process. According to Logan, they'll make their report to the FBI Fraud division and it will probably be over. Not to say it can't start up again in the future." Her tea was delivered along with the drinks for Riley and Adam. "I've made peace with that. I understand why they want to be sure I'm not a part of his crimes."

"You are a brave soul," Riley said, lifting her glass to Emma. "I still want to punch Logan. The bastard."

"Go easy, Riley. He has a job to do. And I'm just guessing but I don't think he had to date you to do it." Then she smiled. "Even so, the best news I've had lately is that after all this time you and Jock will find a way."

"Jock," Adam scoffed. "What the hell kind of name is that, anyway?"

"You know he was named for his grandfather. Are you going to start being nice to him now?"

He took a drink from his beer. "I guess I'll have to."

"Emma, do you need a day off to recover from Dragnet?" Riley asked.

"Nah, I'll be fine. Let me catch my breath and then I think we should tell June she's going to be a grandmother again."

Despite the stressful police questioning, Emma was feeling euphoric. Her world was coming into focus and she had so much to look forward to. She had Adam's perfect love, something she never for one second anticipated when she was making her way home to Sonoma. Riley had finally come around and it looked as though they all might not just be friends but family, as well. June was so happy about the baby she cried. Even Maddie and Jock were excited.

She was anxious to tell Shawna and Dellie, but there were a few details to work out before she went public. A date to get married and merge households would help.

Adam, as protective as when they were kids, asked her to quit work, at least working that hard. His income was modest, but he'd been a teacher for a long time and he could support a family. She said no. She wanted to work.

She spent more time with Riley, a little while after work most days. They had so much to catch up on. "Will you be my maid of honor?" Emma asked her.

"Yes, absolutely! And will you wear a mask while you clean so you don't inhale bleach? I don't want my nephew to have two heads."

So Emma carried a mask in her pocket and discreetly slipped it on when she was using bleach in the bathrooms. But Riley's concern gave her deep happiness.

And then a text came from Bethany.

I'm sorry, Emma, but it's just too much. There's no laughter. There's just no love here and I've had enough.

Emma was cleaning another house but because it was Bethany, she read the text and responded immediately.

What's too much?

The girl had been mostly cheerful since Christmas. Emma had hoped her feelings of sadness and helplessness were starting to wane.

No reply. If that had been Adam or Riley, she'd have waited until she was between houses, but she smelled an ill wind.

Bethany, where are you?

No reply.

She tried calling, but it went directly to voice mail.

She went to Dellie; Dellie had daughters and there was something about teenage girls, even those not in crisis, that was so terrifying, so filled with drama. "Dellie, Bethany texted me this," she said, showing her the phone. "I can't reach her."

"She's just wanting some attention, probably."

"What if she's not? She took a bunch of her stepmother's pills a year ago or so and it just knocked her out for a while, but that's something to think about. What if this means she's given up? What if she's suicidal?"

"You don't even know where she is," Dellie said. "She might be on top of the Golden Gate Bridge."

"I think I have to go to her house," Emma said.

"We're not done here!"

"I'll call Riley. I'll go check and come right back. I'll even stay late and help if we get behind."

"You're getting sucked right into this girl's drama," Dellie said.

"I guess so. But if anything is wrong and I don't check on her, I'll never forgive myself."

"Oh, Lord, you're gonna be the death of me. Shawna!" she yelled. "We gotta go check something and come right back!"

"You don't have to," Emma said.

"Better we all stay together. That house ain't so far from here. Don't pack up. We'll be back here in half an hour."

"Thank you," Emma said.

While Shawna drove, grumbling about how this day was gonna get long, Emma called Riley. She had to leave a message. She called Makenna and Makenna said, "Do not do this! I'll call her parents but you just stay out of it!"

When Emma disconnected, Dellie wanted to know what Makenna said. "She said go ahead and good luck." Then Emma swallowed hard.

When they got to the house, Emma looked up and down the street. All the houses were separated by trees and shrubs, sitting back on huge lots. Running to the neighbors would take too much time. She took the keys and went to open the front door, but it wouldn't open. There was a security lock that could be used at night, locked from the inside. So she banged on the door and rang the bell. She pulled out her small notebook, looked at the key code for the garage and punched in the numbers. The garage door slowly rose and she ran inside, trying the door to the house. It was bolted, as well.

She was frozen. What if Bethany wasn't even in there? She called Makenna. "Did you reach her parents?"

"No," Makenna said with a sigh. "I said it was important but I haven't gotten a call back."

"Listen, I'm sorry, but I'm scared," Emma said. "She's fragile. She's been talking to me and she's… She has good days and bad days but her mother died, her stepmother moved right in and… She's fragile…"

"Oh, crap, you're involved…"

"She needed someone…"

"Emma, you are *at least* on probation!"

So Emma called the police. Once they established that there was no missing person, no cry for help, no family member seeking a welfare check, they said they'd send a patrol by when they could.

She dialed another number.

"Logan Danner," he said in answer to her call.

"Logan, it's Emma. Listen, I have a situation. I've been talking to a fifteen-year-old girl from one of the houses I clean. She's troubled. She's maybe suicidal. I might be suicidal in her situation. It's complicated, it's—"

"Bethany Christensen?" he asked.

"How did you know?" she asked.

"I listened to your telephone conversations," he said. "We were a little confused about that one but it didn't seem to have anything to do with the transfer of funds."

"I'm at her house. She left me a suspicious text—it's all too much, she said. She said she's had enough. And the doors are bolted from the inside."

"Did you call the police?"

"They weren't impressed. I'm calling to tell you to get out your handcuffs because I've decided to break in. I really want to be wrong…but I'm going to break in…"

"Can you wait for me? I'm not far away."

"I can't wait for you. I'm sorry, but I can't let anything terrible happen. Her parents aren't returning calls, no one cares about this girl. No one." She hung up the phone.

I am clearly insane, Emma thought. *I don't know that much about her but I'm completely involved, totally sympathetic, terribly scared for her.*

There was a workbench in the garage that, like the rest of the Christensen home, was far too clean and tidy. She eyed a hammer, a big screwdriver, a crowbar. She took the crowbar and wedged it into the tight space right where the doorknob was and started prying with all her might. She was at it for a good five minutes when she heard a car pull into the drive. She looked over her shoulder. Shawna and Dellie were standing in the driveway behind her, staring in wonder. Logan strode toward her.

"Give me that," he said. "If we're going to do it, let's do it."

"Thank you," she said, rubbing her upper arm.

It took him three powerful tugs with the crowbar, some splintering wood and a great big kick and the door opened. Logan was inside first. "Bethany!" he shouted.

"Look through the downstairs," Emma said. "I'll check the upstairs bedrooms."

Their feet pounded through the house, each of them shouting the girl's name. Emma went immediately to Bethany's bedroom and found the room undisturbed, the bed made as usual. She checked her bathroom—it was spotless. She called out, checked the master bedroom—again, everything in order. The master bath was clean as a whistle and she thought, I've made a terrible mistake...again!

She heard a soft moan and opened the door to the large, walk-in closet and there, in a little pile on the floor was Bethany, covered in blood. "Logan!" she screamed. "Up here! Help me!"

She rolled Bethany to the side and it seemed the blood was coming from her thin, pale wrists. "Oh, God, Bethany! No!" She put her fingers to Bethany's neck and felt a faint pulse. "In here!" she shouted again.

"Is she alive?" he asked.

"Yes, but unconscious and her pulse is weak."

Before Emma even finished talking, Logan had grabbed a white shirt from a hanger, bit a tear in the hem and ripped it into a couple of strips. He tossed one to Emma. "Pressure," he said, ripping the shirt again and again. "Nice and tight."

When that was done he got on his cell and called for paramedics.

Over the next fifteen minutes, the master bedroom began to fill with people. Emma and Logan stayed beside Bethany, Emma holding her gently, rocking her, telling her she must be all right, *must*. First Dellie and Shawna were there, watching. Then Makenna, followed quickly by Riley. Both of them were stunned and angry that this poor girl could have suffered so much and there seemed to be no one to help her. Finally paramedics arrived and by that time Bethany was moaning and whimpering weakly. After an IV was started and the gurney stood ready to take her to the ambulance, Olaf and Liz Christensen appeared. Liz gasped and covered her mouth while Olaf rushed to his daughter.

As the paramedics transferred Bethany, Olaf Christensen faced Emma. "Who are you? And how did you know my daughter was in trouble?"

"I clean your house, Mr. Christensen. And she reached out to me. I wanted her to reach out to you, but she didn't think you could handle it. She's been in a lot of pain since her mother passed away."

"But I got her a counselor!" Liz Christensen said.

"Yes, and you also cleared out all the family pictures and started wearing her dead mother's clothes. How you thought that was going to be okay, I'll never know."

"I asked," she said defensively, looking a bit confused. "I asked permission! From Bethany! And the pictures… I didn't think that was helping us become a family!"

Emma took out her phone and revealed the text. "Bethany lost her family. She told me when her mother was alive they laughed a lot, they hugged and laughed and fell asleep together. She told me your assistant bought her birthday and Christmas presents. She was so, so lonely."

Olaf Christensen read the text. "God," he said. "I just wasn't looking, was I? I don't know how to thank you for finding her. I don't know how you knew she would need you."

"Well, I've looked the other way at times in my life when I shouldn't have. I won't ever do it again."

epilogue

June Kerrigan threw a nice party for her family and friends two days before Christmas. It was a buffet featuring her favorite dishes. Her house was decorated to such an extent it made her shudder to think about the taking down and putting away. She may have gone a little overboard, but this was a very special holiday to her.

Emma Shay Kerrigan no longer cleaned houses for Riley. Now she was a full-time student and mother. John Shay Kerrigan was born in October, a little early but a good size, while Emma was supposed to be in a lecture at UC Davis where she was studying toward a masters in counseling. Now at his first Christmas, John was being passed around to every person present.

Adam was married and a new father, something June had nearly lost hope for. Riley and Jock were married, too. Riley had just announced that Maddie would be getting a little brother or sister in the spring.

Penny Pennington had been invited and had spent a lot of

time in the kitchen with June and was busily monitoring the buffet table to make sure fresh hors d'oeuvres were always available. Ethan and Lyle were literally waiting in line for their shot at John. Aaron Justice had come, bringing a huge wreath with him. Beatrice, the particularly ugly rescue dog, had found her forever home with June, though she had not gotten very much prettier. And Bethany, Liz and Olaf Christensen were there, together, laughing at all the old Kerrigan family stories.

But the nicest thing—June saw Riley and Emma lifting their glasses in a secret toast. Smiling. Emma had her favorite wine and Riley had sparkling cider. They were friends again.

They'd been each other's maid and matron of honor and would be raising their children together. After all.

★ ★ ★ ★ ★

acknowledgments

Many thanks to my readers for the continuous outpouring of support and encouragement. You make my pursuit of creating good fiction such a joy.

Special thanks to Kurt A. Johnson, Esq., for showing me the path through the complex world of wills, trusts, and miscellaneous estate details and laws.

To my favorite financial wizard, Kayla Koeber. Thank you for helping me understand the many mysteries of the world of finance. You are so patient and wise.

Any errors or alterations in the technical aspects of the story are not the fault of my adviser but mine, most often license to create a strong story, and I appreciate the reader's indulgence.

Thank you to a very hardworking PR machine: Michelle Renaud of Harlequin, Nancy Berland of Nancy Berland Public Relations and Sarah Burningham of Little Bird Publicity. I would be so lost without you!

My deepest gratitude to Craig Swinwood, Loriana Sacilotto, Margaret Marbury and Nicole Brebner, my Harlequin Dream Team. Every day of working with you all is a privilege.

To Dianne Moggy, thank you for that special day eighteen years ago when you said yes to a submission from me, changing my career path and my life. I am so grateful for the opportunities that started right there.

To my agent, Liza Dawson, thank you for your dedication and loyalty through the years. It's been quite a wonderful trip and an honor to call you my friend.